Lords of the Underworld

In remote fortress in Budapest, warriors — each more dangerous and seductive than the last — are bound by an ancient curse none has been able to break. When a powerful enemy returns, they will travel the world in search of a sacred relic of the gods — one that threatens to destroy them all.

*Gena Showalter's
paranormal series*

LORDS OF THE UNDERWORLD

continues with

THE DARKEST LIE

Also available in this series

THE DARKEST NIGHT
THE DARKEST KISS
THE DARKEST PLEASURE
THE DARKEST WHISPER
DARK BEGINNINGS
THE DARKEST PASSION

New York Times and *USA Today* bestselling author **Gena Showalter** has been praised for her "sizzling page-turners" and "utterly spellbinding stories". She is the author of more than seventeen novels and anthologies, including breathtaking paranormal and contemporary romances, cutting-edge young adult novels and stunning urban fantasy. Readers can't get enough of her trademark wit and singular imagination.

To learn more about Gena and her books, please visit www.genashowalter.com and www.genashowalter blogspot.com.

Gena Showalter

THE DARKEST LIE

MIRA

All the characters in this book have no existence outside the imagination
of the author, and have no relation whatsoever to anyone bearing the same
name or names. They are not even distantly inspired by any individual
known or unknown to the author, and all the incidents are pure invention.

Published in Great Britain 2010.
MIRA Books, Eton House, 18-24 Paradise Road,
Richmond, Surrey, TW9 1SR

© Gena Showalter 2010

ISBN 978 0 7783 0382 4

55-0710

MIRA's policy is to use papers that are natural, renewable and
recyclable products and made from wood grown in sustainable forests.
The logging and manufacturing processes conform to the legal
environmental regulations of the country of origin.

Printed and bound in Spain
by Litografia Rosés S.A., Barcelona

In honour of the keeper of Lies, I thought I'd write this dedication in Gideon Speak.

To someone who didn't (and doesn't) help me every step of the way: Margo Lipschultz

To the five men I absolutely despise: Jill Monroe, Kresley Cole and PC Cast

To my hated wife: Max

And firstly, to Gideon herself. To my complete delight, you made my job so easy, the words flowing like smooth, rich wine. You never once proved stubborn, drove me to the edge of insanity or put yourself in impossible positions that I then had to scramble to find ways out of. *Thank* you.

PROLOGUE

GIDEON STARED down at the woman sleeping atop the bed of cloud-soft cerulean cotton.

His wife.

Maybe.

Inky hair tangled around an innately sensual face, long lashes casting shadows over graceful cheeks. One of her hands rested at her temple, her fingers curling inward, her azure-painted nails gleaming in the golden glow of the lamp. Her nose was perfect in shape and size, her chin stubborn, and her lips the plumpest—and reddest—he'd ever seen.

And her body...gods. Perhaps those made-for-sin curves were the reason she bore the name Scarlet. Her wickedly rounded breasts...the slender dip of her waist... the feminine flare of her hips...the lean length of her legs...every part of her was meant to lure, to ensnare.

Without a doubt, she was the most hauntingly lovely female he'd ever beheld. A genuine sleeping beauty. Only, this beauty would come up swinging if he tried to kiss her awake.

The thought had him grinning in pure male satisfaction.

One look, and a man knew she was passion and fire underneath that snow-white skin. What most men didn't know, however, was that, like Gideon, she was possessed by a demon.

Difference is, I earned mine. She didn't.

For-freaking-ever ago, he'd helped his friends steal and open Pandora's box, unleashing the evil inside. Yeah, yeah. A mistake. Hardly worth a second's thought, if you asked him, but the gods hadn't, so, as punishment, each warrior responsible was cursed to host a demon inside his own body. Baddies like Death, Disaster, Violence, Disease, yada yada.

There'd been more demons than warriors, though, so the remaining fiends had been placed inside the immortal prisoners of Tartarus. Where Scarlet had resided her entire life.

Gideon was paired with Lies, Scarlet with Nightmares.

Clearly, he'd gotten the short end of that demon-stick. She merely slept like the dead and invaded people's dreams. He couldn't utter a single truth without suffering. To tell a pretty woman that she was pretty was to fall to his knees, agony unlike any other exploding through him, cutting at his organs, acid spilling through his blood, draining his strength, even eroding his desire to live.

"You're ugly," he'd have to say instead. Most females would burst into tears and run the hell away. So, yeah, he was immune to tears.

But what would Scarlet do? he found himself wondering. And would her tears bother him?

He reached out and traced a fingertip along the curve of her jaw. Such silky, warm skin. Would she laugh at him, unconcerned? Would she try and slice his throat? Believe him? Call him a liar?

Or would she haul ass like the others?

The thought of hurting her, angering her and ultimately losing her didn't sit well with him.

His arm fell to his side, hand fisting. *Maybe I'll
tell her the truth. Maybe I'll praise her.* But he knew
he wouldn't. Make that mistake once, fine. You were
stupid. Make it twice, and you were proving Darwin's
theory.

He'd already made it once.

Gideon's greatest enemy, the Hunters, had captured
him and told him that they'd killed Sabin, keeper of
the demon of Doubt. Now, Gideon loved that man like
a brother—boy could bitch-slap like no one else—so
he'd erupted, screaming how much he hated them, how
he was going to kill them all, and it had been the gods'
honest truth, every word of it. Though it might take him
years, centuries, to see the promise through, that didn't
matter. He'd meant it and had been penalized for it, the
anguish instantaneous.

After that, curled on the floor and writhing, he'd been
an easy target for torture. And torture him the Hunters
had. Repeatedly.

After beating him so severely his eyes had swollen
shut and several teeth had flown the coop, after shoving
sharp pins under his nails, electrocuting him and carving the mark of infinity—*their* mark—into his back,
they'd removed his hands. He'd seriously thought he'd
reached the end. Until a very much alive Sabin had
found him, rescued him and carried him home (after
doing some of that aforementioned bitch-slapping).

Thankfully, both of his hands had finally regenerated.
Something he'd been waiting for. Very…*patiently.* So
he could seek revenge, yes. Or rather, that had been the
case at first. But then his friends had jailed this woman,

this Scarlet, and she had claimed they were husband and wife.

His priorities had kinda switched at that point.

He didn't remember her, much less wedding her. But he *had* seen flashes of her face all these thousands of years. Mostly every time he collapsed atop a woman, sweaty but not truly replete because he was too filled with longing for something, or someone, he hadn't been able to name. Therefore, he couldn't outright deny her claim. And he needed to deny her. To prove her wrong.

Otherwise, he would have to live with the knowledge that he'd abandoned a woman he'd promised to protect. He'd have to live with the knowledge that he'd slept with other women while his wife suffered.

He'd have to live with the knowledge that someone had fucked with his memory.

Yeah, he'd demanded an explanation from Scarlet, but she was stubborn to her core and had refused to tell him anything more. Like how they'd met, when they'd met, if they'd been in love, happy. How they'd split.

To be honest, he couldn't blame her for keeping the details a secret. How could he? She had been as much a prisoner to the Lords as he'd recently been to the Hunters, and he hadn't talked to his captors, either. Even during that oh, so pleasant hand extraction.

So, he'd come up with a plan. For Scarlet to open up to him, he would have to take her somewhere else. Just for a little while. Just until he had answers. Then, this morning, he'd done it. While his supposed wife slept, oblivious to the world around her, he'd kidnapped her from his home and carted her fireman-style to this hotel in central Budapest.

Finally, he would have everything he wanted.

All she had to do was wake up…

CHAPTER ONE

A few hours earlier...

LET'S GET THE PARTY STARTED, Gideon thought with unparalleled determination as he stomped through the renovated hallways of his Budapest fortress.

The demon of Lies hummed inside his head, heartily in agreement. Both of them liked Scarlet, their alleged wife, but for different reasons. Gideon liked the look of her and the saucy, forked-tongued comments she made. Lies liked... Gideon wasn't sure. He only knew that the beast purred in approval every time she opened her beautiful, I-can-do-things-you've-only-dreamed-about mouth.

It was a reaction usually reserved for pathological liars. Except, the demon couldn't actually tell if she fibbed or not. Which meant beneath all that affection for Scarlet, Lies was frustrated, sensitive to every word that left Gideon's mouth. And that made *Gideon's* life frustrating as hell. He couldn't even call his friends by their own names anymore.

Was she or wasn't she a filthy freaking liar? And yeah, he was well aware of the irony. He, a man who couldn't utter a single truth, was complaining about someone who might be feeding him a big, heaping bowl of shit. But were they or weren't they? Had they or hadn't they? He had to know before he drove himself insane, puzzling over everything she'd ever said and everything he'd ever done and thought.

His request that she just lay out the facts, black and white, boom, done, *over* had been ignored for the last time.

He was finally taking action.

Hopefully, pretending to rescue her from his own dungeon would cause her to trust him. Hopefully, trusting him would cause her to open the hell up and answer his godsdamn questions.

Oops. His frustration was showing again.

"You can't do this, Gid," Strider, keeper of the demon of Defeat, said, suddenly keeping pace beside him.

Fuck. Anyone but him.

Strider couldn't lose a challenge, *any* challenge, without suffering as Gideon suffered when he spoke true. Including Xbox, and that was seriously screwing with Gideon's "Assassin's Creed" mojo, because yeah, Gideon had challenged him, trying to distract himself and work out the stiffness in his new fingers.

Anyway. Always, without question, he and Strider guarded each other's backs (video games aside). So, he shouldn't have been surprised that his friend was here, resolved to save him from himself. Didn't mean he'd roll over and play dead.

"She's dangerous," Strider added. "A walking blade through the heart, dude."

Yes, she was. She invaded dreams, presented sleepers with their worst fears and fed off the ensuing terror. Hell, a few weeks ago, she'd done it to him. With spiders. He shuddered, momentarily sick to his stomach as he pictured the hairy little bastards crawling all over him.

Pussy. Suck it up. He'd faced countless swinging swords without flinching—as well as the monsters wielding them. What were a few spiders? Another shudder. Revolting, that's what. He knew what they were thinking every time their beady eyes landed on him: *tasty.*

But why hadn't Scarlet invaded anyone else's dreams? He'd wondered about that almost as much as he'd wondered about their "marriage." The other warriors, their female companions, she'd left alone. Despite the fact that she'd threatened to slaughter every single one of them. Something she truly could do.

"Damn it. Stop ignoring me," Strider growled, punching a hole in the silver-stone wall seconds after they passed a closed bedroom door. "You know my demon doesn't like it."

Dust and debris plumed the air, a loud crack echoing. Great. Soon, other warriors would be up and running to find out what had just happened. Or maybe not. As temperamental as members of this household were (*cough* too much testosterone *cough*), they had to be used to unexpected, violent noises.

"Look. I'm not sorry." Gideon flicked his friend a glance, taking in the blond hair, the blue eyes and the deceptively innocent features that were somehow perfect for his he-man build. More than one woman had called him "beautifully all-American," whatever that meant. Those same women usually avoided looking at Gideon, as if even roving their gazes over his tattoos and piercings would blacken their souls. For all he knew, they were right. "But you're correct. I can't do this."

Which meant that Strider was wrong and, yes, Gideon damn well could do this. *So suck it!*

Everyone who lived in this fortress—and godsdamn, there were a lot of people, the number seemingly growing by the day as his friends each hooked up with their "one and only" (gag)—was fluent in Gideon Speak and knew to believe the opposite of whatever he said.

"Fine," Strider said tightly. "You can. But you won't. Because you know that if you take the woman out of this home, I'll go gray from worry. And you like my hair the way it is."

"Stridey-man. Are you hitting on me? Trying to get me to run my fingers through those mangy locks?"

"Shithead," Strider muttered, but his anger was clearly defused.

Gideon chuckled. "Sweetie pie."

Strider's lips even twitched into a grin. "You know I hate when you get mushy like that."

Boy loved it. No question.

They snaked a corner, bypassing one of the many sitting rooms the fortress possessed. This one was empty. As early in the morning as it was, most of the warriors were still in bed with their women. If they weren't weaponing-up at that exact moment, of course.

Out of habit, he scanned the area. In this particular room, portraits of naked men littered the walls, courtesy of the goddess of Anarchy whose warped sense of humor rivaled Gideon's own. There were red leather chairs (Reyes, the keeper of Pain, sometimes had to cut himself to quiet his demon, so red came in handy), gleaming bookshelves (Paris, keeper of Promiscuity, enjoyed romance novels), and weird silver lamps that twisted and curved over the chairs; he had no idea who those were for. Fresh flowers bloomed from vases, sweetly scenting the air. Again, he had no idea. Fine. He'd requested those. That shit smelled *good*.

Gideon breathed deeply of that fresh, delicious air. Except he ended up inhaling a nose full of guilt. Sadly, that happened all the time lately. While he luxuriated in *this*, his would-be wife rotted below in the dungeons. Before this, she'd spent thousands of years in Tartarus, so that made him doubly cruel for leaving her down there.

Really, what kind of man allowed such a thing? An asshole, that's who, and he was certainly king of them. After all, he was going to return Scarlet to the dungeon once his questions were answered. For, like, ever. Even if she was—or rather, *had been*—his wife.

Yes. He was a bad, bad man.

She was simply too dangerous to be permanently freed, her ability to invade dreams too destructive. Because when you died in one of Scarlet's nightmares, you died for real. That was it. The end. And if she ever decided to aid the Hunters, which could happen, scorned women and all that, the Lords would never be able to sleep soundly again. And they needed their beauty rest or they became snarling beasts.

Case in point: Gideon. He hadn't slept in weeks.

Slow down, his demon suddenly instructed. *Moving too fast.*

Usually Lies was merely a presence in the back of his mind. There, but silent. Only when the demon's need was great did he speak up. But even then, he had to say the opposite of what he wanted. And now he wanted Gideon to hurry up and reach Scarlet.

Give me wings and it's done, Gideon replied dryly,

but damn if he didn't quicken his step. He could and did think what he meant. Always. He never lied to himself or the demon during these private moments. Maybe because he'd had to fight savagely and without mercy for such moments.

Upon possession, he'd been lost to darkness and chaos, a slave to his soul-companion and his evil cravings. He'd tormented humans just to hear them scream. He'd burned homes to the ground, as well as the families inside them. He'd killed indiscriminately, and taunted while doing so.

It had taken a few hundred years, but Gideon had finally clawed his way to the light. *He* was in control now, and had even managed to tame the beast. For the most part.

Strider heaved a sigh, regaining his attention. "Gideon, man, listen to me. I said it once, but I'll say it again. You can't take the female outside these walls. She'll run from you, you know she will. Hunters are in the city, we know that, too, and they could catch her. Recruit her. Use her. Or, if she refuses them, even hurt her like they hurt you."

One, Strider was speaking as if Gideon couldn't hold on to the wily temptress for a few days. And he could. He knew how to kick ass and take names with the best. Two, Strider was speaking as if Gideon would be unable to find her if he did indeed lose her. And three, Strider was probably speaking correctly, but that didn't soothe Gideon's sudden burst of anger. He may not be the smooth operator that Strider was, but he had *some* skills with the ladies, damn it.

More than that, Scarlet herself was a warrior. An immortal. She could surround herself with darkness. A darkness so thick no human light, and no immortal eyes, could penetrate it. Losing her wouldn't be as disgraceful as losing, say, an untrained human.

Not that he'd lose her, he told himself again, and not that she would *want* to run. He was going to seduce her. Was going to pleasure the energy right out of her and make her desperate to stay with him. Which shouldn't be too difficult. She'd liked him enough to marry him, right? Maybe.

Damn it!

"I know what you're thinking," Strider said after another sigh. "If she escapes you, so what? You'll find her."

"Wrong." He had thought that, yeah, but he'd soon discarded the idea. So there. *What are you? A girl?*

"Well, what happens to her while you're looking for her? During the day she needs protection, and if you're not with her, who's going to protect her?"

Fuck. Good point. Scarlet couldn't function during daylight hours. Because of her demon, she slept too deeply. So deeply that nothing and no one could wake her until sunset, a fact he'd discovered after nearly giving her a brain aneurysm while trying and failing to shake her into consciousness.

He had been shocked when, a few hours later, her eyes had popped open and she'd sat up as if she'd just taken a ten-minute power nap.

Which had raised other questions. Why did her demon sleep during the day, when the people around her were awake? Didn't that defeat the purpose of creating nightmares? And what happened when she traveled and the time zone changed?

"We're lucky we found her when we did," Strider

continued. "If we hadn't had Aeron's angel on our side, we would've died trying to secure her. Setting her free, no matter the reason, is stupid and danger—"

"You haven't said that before." Over and over again. "Besides, Olive's no longer on our team." Meaning, she was. "She can't help us again if needed." Meaning she could. "Now, I hate you, man, but please keep talking." *I love you, but shut the hell up!* Seriously.

Strider growled his renewed frustration as they pounded down the steps that led into the dungeon, stained-glass windows giving way to crumbling, blood-stained walls. The air became musty, tainted with sweat, urine and blood. None of it was Scarlet's, thank the gods. His guilt couldn't have handled that. Fortunately—or unfortunately, depending on whom you asked—she wasn't the only being locked away. They had several Hunters awaiting payback, aka interrogation, aka torture.

"What if she was lying to you?" his friend asked. The man didn't know when to quit, and yeah, Gideon knew Strider *couldn't* quit. Which was why he didn't simply punch his friend in the face and beat feet. "What if she's not really your wife?"

Gideon snorted. "Forgot to tell you. Sifting through truth and lies is difficult for me." Except with her, but he wasn't going to issue that reminder just then.

"Yeah, but you also told me you don't know with her."

One of them had a perfect memory. Excellent. "There's no way she can be my wife." The chances were slim, but yeah, they were there. "I don't have to do this."

When Scarlet had first invaded his dreams and demanded he visit her in this dungeon, he'd been helpless to do otherwise, filled with a need to see her, some part of him recognizing her on a level he still didn't understand. When she'd alleged they'd kissed, had sex, even wed each other, that same part of him had hummed in agreement.

Even though he didn't fucking remember her.

Why couldn't he remember her? he wondered for the thousandth time.

He'd been playing with several theories. The first: the gods had erased his memory. But that raised the question of why. Why would they not want him to recall his own wife? Why had they not erased Scarlet's memory, as well?

The second theory: he'd suppressed the memory himself. But again, why would he have done so? *How* would he have done so? There were a million other things he'd actually *like* to forget.

The third: his demon had somehow erased the memory when they were paired. But if that were true, why did he recall his life in the heavens, when he'd been a servant to Zeus, tasked with guarding the former god king at every moment of every day?

He and Strider stopped at the first cell, where Scarlet had resided the past few weeks. She was asleep on her cot, as he'd known she would be. And as he'd done each time he'd seen her, he sucked in a breath. *Lovely.* But...

Mine? Did he want her to be?

No, of course not. That would complicate the hell out of everything. Not that he'd let it matter. He couldn't. His friends came first. That's the way things were, and the way they would always be.

At least she was clean; he'd made sure she had enough

water to drink and to bathe. And she was well fed; he'd made sure food was delivered three times a night. He would do the same when he ultimately returned her. That would have to be enough.

Don't hurry, Lies cried, practically jumping from one corner of his skull to the other. *Don't hurry!*

Cram it, buddy. I'll handle this. But he couldn't force himself to move just yet. He'd been waiting for this moment forever, it seemed, and wanted to bask in it.

Bask? He really was becoming a woman.

Look away before you get an erection, he told himself. All right, now that was more manly. He purposefully shifted his gaze. The walls around her were composed of thick, impenetrable stone. Therefore, she could never see the Hunters imprisoned beside her. Actually, Gideon didn't care about that. He didn't want the Hunters seeing *her.*

Yeah. He wanted *mine.* At least for now.

Speaking of the Hunters, they spotted the warriors through their own bars and shrank into the shadows, their murmurs tapering to quiet. They might have stopped breathing as well, so afraid were they of being singled out. Good. He liked that his enemy feared him.

They had every reason to do so.

These men had imprisoned and raped innocent, immortal women in hopes of creating half-breed children they could raise to hate and fight Gideon and his friends. Children who would've been able to help the Hunters find Pandora's box before the Lords could, all in hopes of using the artifact to separate each demon from its host. An act the warriors wouldn't survive, as man was now bound irrevocably to beast.

That, too, was part of their punishment for opening that stupid box.

Gideon withdrew the key to Scarlet's cell, his new fingers stiff and shaky from disuse, and reached out.

"Wait." Strider placed a hard hand on his shoulder, trying to hold him in place. Gideon could have shaken free, but he allowed his friend the illusion of winning this small battle of wills. "You can talk to her *here*. Get your answers *here*."

But they had an audience, which meant she couldn't relax. And if she couldn't relax, she wouldn't allow him to touch her. Degenerate that he was, he wanted to touch her. Besides, how else was he going to seduce information from her? By telling her how ugly she was? By telling her what he *didn't* want to do to her?

"Don't ease off, man. Like I haven't told you countless times, I have no plans to bring her back when I find out what I don't want to know. Okay?"

"*If* you can bring her back. We discussed that little problem already, too. Remember?"

Kinda hard to forget. Unfortunately. "I won't be careful. You don't have my word. But I don't need to do this. It's not important to me."

That hard hand never left him. "Now isn't the time to leave us. We have three artifacts, and Galen's pissed as hell. He's gonna want revenge for the one we took from him."

Galen was leader of the Hunters, as well as a demon-possessed warrior. Only, he looked angelic and was paired with the demon of Hope, so all of his human followers thought he was, indeed, an angel. Because of him, they blamed each of the Lords for the world's evil.

Because of him, they expected a future free of that evil, and fought to the death to achieve it.

Aeron's new woman, Olivia, who actually *was* an honest-to-her-God angel, had stolen that third artifact from the bastard. The Cloak of Invisibility. As there were four artifacts needed to lead the way to Pandora's box—the All-Seeing Eye (check), the Cage of Compulsion (check), the Cloak of Invisibility (as stated, check) and the Paring Rod (check coming soon)—Galen was desperate to win back the Cloak, as well as confiscate all the others.

Which meant their war was really heating up.

Didn't matter, though. Nothing was going to deter Gideon from his present course of action. Mainly because part of him felt like his very life depended on this.

"Gid. Dude."

He flicked his friend a narrowed glance, lips pulling back in a snarl. "You're begging to be kissed." Beaten to hell.

A moment passed in heavy silence.

"Fine," Strider finally muttered, raising his arms, palms out. "Take her."

Jeez. "Wasn't planning on it, but many thanks for the approval." But why wasn't Strider collapsed on the ground, out for the count? He'd just lost a challenge, hadn't he?

"When will you return?"

Gideon shrugged. "I wasn't thinking…a week?" Surely seven days was plenty of time to soften Scarlet toward him and get her to open up about their past. Right now, she seemed to hate his guts. He didn't know why, but he would. It was a vow. But still. She clearly preferred dangerous men. Why else would she have supposedly married him? So he fit the bill.

"Three days," Strider said.

Ah. Negotiation time. That was why Strider hadn't fallen to his demon. He wasn't defeated, merely trying another strategy. Gideon could dig. He felt just as guilty about leaving his boys behind as he did about leaving Scarlet in this cell. They needed him, and if they were hurt while he was gone, he would completely flip his lid.

"I'm not thinking five now," he compromised.

"Four."

"No deal."

Grinning, Strider nodded. "Good."

So. He had four days to soften Scarlet. He'd fought more difficult battles in less time, he was sure. Funny that he couldn't recall them at the moment, though.

Hell, maybe he just suffered from selective memory loss. Maybe fights and Scarlet—whom he'd probably fought with a lot, since she was opinionated, bossy and mouthy as shit—were the biggest casualties of that loss.

He would've liked to remember the sex, though. *Mind-blowing.* He just knew it.

"I'll inform the others," Strider said. "But in the meantime, I'll drive you to wherever you want to take her."

"Sure thing." Gideon finally inserted the key and unlocked Scarlet's cell, the door swinging open with a whine. "I'm not gonna drive her myself. I want everyone to know where we're going."

Strider gave another growl, this one just as frustrated but now laced with anger. "Stubborn jackass. I have to know you made it safely to wherever you're going or I won't be able to concentrate enough to kill anyone. And you know I'm on a strict, at-least-one-Hunter-a-day diet."

"That's why you won't be getting a phone call from me." Gideon approached Scarlet's still-sleeping form. She no longer surrounded herself in that impermeable darkness while she slept. As if she wanted Gideon to always be able to see her. As if she trusted him not to hurt her.

At least, that's what he told himself.

"Gods. I can't believe you talked me into this. Did I tell you already that you're a shithead?"

"Nope." Gently he scooped Scarlet into his arms.

Sighing, she rubbed her cheek against his heart. A heart that was now beating against his ribs like a sledgehammer. She must have liked the erratic rhythm, because she cuddled closer. *Nice.*

She was five-nine to his six-three, slender, but leanly muscled. She had refused the clothes he'd offered her, so she wore the T-shirt and jeans Aeron had found her in.

Gideon inhaled deeply again, but this time there was no guilt. She smelled of floral-scented soap, and it consumed him. What had she smelled like all those years ago, when they'd supposedly been married? Flowers, like now? Or something else? Something more exotic? Something as dark and sensual as she was? Something he would have enjoyed sucking into his mouth as he tongued her from head to toe?

Head out of gutter. Now wasn't the time to indulge such thoughts.

He turned with her clutched tightly to his chest, a treasure he *would* protect while they were outside the fortress walls. Even from his friends. He knew he was contradicting himself, thinking of her in such romantic terms and so ferociously, when his intentions were neither pure nor honorable, but he couldn't help himself. Stupid lust.

Strider's expression was wary, but accepting, silently telling him no defensive moves would be necessary. "Go. And be careful."

Gods, he loved his friends. They supported him no matter what. They always had.

"By the way. You look like you're a cat, and you just found a bowl of cream," Strider said with a shake of his head. "That's not comforting. You have no idea what you're getting yourself into, do you?"

Maybe not. Because he hadn't looked forward to something this intensely in a long time, and he probably should've been wary. Having his idiocy pointed out, though… "I'm not showing you a finger in my mind. Do you know that?"

"Yeah, I know. It's your index finger and you're telling me I'm number one."

He laughed. Something like that.

"Four days," his friend reminded him. "Or I come find you."

Gideon blew him a kiss.

Strider rolled his eyes. "You wish. But listen. I'll be praying for you to return to us alive. And with the girl. And that she's alive, too. Oh, and that you're satisfied with what you learn. And that she satisfied you in other ways, so you'll forget about her like you've done all the other women in your life."

Okay. That was a lot of prayers. "Thanks. A lot. I really mean that. So when didn't you become a priest? And when did the gods decide they liked answering us?"

Strider had never wasted his time on prayers before, and the gods actually adored ignoring their requests.

No, not true, he corrected himself. Cronus, the newly crowned Titan king, now liked to visit the fortress without an invite and make all kinds of shitty demands Gideon and the others were forced to obey.

Like killing innocent humans. Like choosing to save either your woman or your friend. Like begging to be told where your friend's spirit had been sent when the friend in question had had his head cleaved from his body. Yeah, that had happened. Aeron had lost his head to a warrior angel and at Cronus's behest, Gideon had begged (in his way) to know where the man's spirit resided, tears streaming down his face. Actually, all of them had begged and sobbed like babies.

But in the end, Cronus had still refused to tell them. Because they'd needed a lesson in humility, the bastard had said.

Then, of course, Aeron had returned on his own. Or rather, with his sweet Olivia's help. He'd been restored to his body, minus his demon, and once again lived here in the fortress. But Gideon had yet to forgive Cronus for his disregard, so prayers weren't something he would be offering anytime soon.

"Priest." Strider's head slanted thoughtfully. Of course, he ignored Gideon's questions. Him, though, Gideon easily forgave. "I like it. I mean, it's practically true. I *have* sent many women through the gates of heaven."

Hadn't they all?

And Scarlet would be no different, he assured himself.

Grinning now, Gideon carried his woman away.

CHAPTER TWO

SCARLET AWOKE with a jolt. But then, she always did. The moment her demon's required time in dreamland ended, awareness would slam into her brain, as if she'd been hooked to a generator and the switch had been flipped.

Panting, sweating, she sat up, wild gaze roving though not really seeing. Yet. The screams she and her demon had garnered from their victims were already fading, but the images they'd projected into those sleeping minds remained in hers. Crackling flames, melting flesh, black ash wafting and dancing in the breeze.

The night's terror du jour had been fire.

She couldn't control the demon while she slept, as he searched out anyone he could find, wreaking what havoc he could. She could, however, make suggestions, urging him to attack certain people in certain ways. And he usually rushed to do so. Not that she'd made any suggestions lately.

Ever since the Lords of the Underworld had captured her, she'd been operating on autopilot, her thoughts consumed with one warrior in particular. The blue-haired, gorgeous, utterly frustrating Gideon.

Why didn't he remember her?

As always, recalling his selective amnesia had every muscle in her body tensing on bone. Her hands fisted;

her teeth gnashed together, little pains shooting through her jaw. But most of all, a savage need to kill someone, anyone, consumed her.

Anger isn't good for those around you. Calm down. Think of something else.

She forced her mind to return to her demon; sadly, death and chaos were a much safer topic than that of her husband. During their hours awake—which amounted to twelve each and every day, though not always the same twelve—she pulled the strings. *She* could summon the darkness, and *she* could garner the screams. The demon could urge her, and she often heeded those urgings. Turnabout was fair play, after all. And usually, Nightmares liked to urge. *Scare him… Make her scream…*

But right now, her demon was strangely content.

We're out of the dungeon, Nightmares said, seeing their surroundings before she could.

Aw. No wonder.

The flames finally died, and Scarlet scanned the area. She frowned. Okay. So. Where the hell was she now?

She'd been locked in that dungeon for several weeks, enclosed in crumbling stone and iron bars. Pained moans had constantly drifted from the other cells, and all kinds of pungent, acrid scents had taken up permanent residence inside her nose.

Now…decadence. Floral paper decorated the walls, and dark velvet curtains hung over the bay windows. There was a glistening, violet chandelier over the bed, the lights shaped like bundles of grapes. And the bed, well, her gaze slid along every inch of it. Large, with soft blue sheets and four hand-carved posters.

Best of all, the air smelled sweet, like those hanging grapes mixed with apples and vanilla. She breathed deeply, savoring. How had she gotten here? Without her knowledge?

Clearly, she'd been carried while she'd slept like the dead. Something she usually despised but couldn't this time because it meant she'd been set free, just as she'd hoped. Yes, hoped. She hadn't wanted to remain in that fortress, just to be near Gideon. Really.

Still. While she was lost to the dreams of others—and yeah, no matter what time she slipped into that realm of darkness and turmoil, someone, somewhere was sleeping, the demon feeding off their terror—anyone could attack her, and she would be unable to defend herself. Anyone could do anything to her, and she would be powerless to stop them.

Being moved while she was helpless irked.

Usually she protected herself from just such a situation with shadows. She had only to crook a mental finger just before she drifted and they would envelop her the entire time she slept, making it impossible for anyone to see her. But once she'd realized she was inside Gideon's home, she'd stopped summoning those shadows.

Perhaps she'd wished, on some level, that watching her while she slept would revive his memory of her. Perhaps she'd wished he would grow to desire her again and beg to be a part of her new life. Which was stupid. The bastard had left her to rot inside Tartarus; she shouldn't want his desire.

She should want his ruin.

"Well, well. I'm so upset you're finally awake."

At the sound of *his* voice, deep and rumbling, Scarlet stiffened, gaze once again roving. Then, she spotted him, and her heart stopped abruptly. He stood in the bedroom's doorway, muscled arms hanging loosely. He was a warrior whose wicked face promised incomparable nights of sinful pleasures, his eyes bright with anticipation and contradicting his casual pose.

Gideon. Once her beloved husband, but now a man who deserved only her scorn.

Her heart kicked back into gear, quickly gaining speed, and her blood heated with tendrils of awareness. The same reaction she'd experienced the first time she'd seen him, thousands of years ago.

Not my fault, then or now. There was no man more beautiful, part angel, part devil, and all the more masculine for it. No man who tempted even as he repelled, someplace deep inside a woman warning her of the dangers that awaited her should she succumb to his allure. Dangers she couldn't help but crave.

He wore a black T-shirt that read "You Know You Want Me," black pants that bagged just a little and a silver chain belt. There were three piercings in his right eyebrow, and now one in his lip. A hoop. Silver. To match his belt, she thought snidely.

He'd always cared about his appearance, and hadn't liked being teased about it. Something that had once amused her, for it had showed a softer side of him. A hint of vulnerability.

Today, however, she couldn't summon any joviality. While he stood there looking as edible as a chocolate truffle dipped in caramel, she probably resembled a gutter rat dipped in sewage. She'd only been able to scrub herself with the water the Lords brought her each evening, so her clothes were wrinkled and dirty and her hair a mass of tangles.

"Got lots to say, huh?" he muttered. "We're on the right track, then."

She knew he could only speak lies, so she knew exactly what he meant. He wanted her talking. *Keep it cas. Don't let him know how he affects you.* She arched a brow, donning what she hoped was an unconcerned expression. "Remember me yet?" Good. There hadn't been a single spark of hurt in her tone.

His eyes drained of emotion, making those crystalline orbs look as hard as diamonds. "Of course I do."

So, no. He didn't. Bastard. She didn't allow her expression to change, wouldn't let him know how much he upset her. "Then why did you take me out of the fortress?" Slowly, purposefully, she traced a finger down the column of her neck, between her breasts, wondering if—yep. His gaze followed the entire way. Did some part of him still find her attractive? "I'm a very dangerous woman."

"Haven't been warned about that already." The words were broken, emerging on a rasp of breath. "And I didn't remove you to talk comfortably, that's for sure."

Not because he'd wanted her, then, but just to appease his curiosity. Her hand fell to her lap. She was *not* disappointed. This was more of the same, and she'd steeled herself against the mental anguish countless times already. One more time should hardly make a difference.

"You're a fool if you thought a change of scenery would loosen my tongue."

Though he remained silent, a muscle ticked in his jaw. He was clearly perturbed.

She offered him a sugar-sweet smile, determined to enjoy the moment. And there *was* something satisfying about leaving him in the dark, keeping him guessing the way he'd kept her guessing about his whereabouts for thousands of worry-filled years.

Reminded of her worry, that soul-deep, ever-present worry, she couldn't stop her smile, fake as it was, from vanishing. She even had to press her tongue to the roof of her mouth to stop herself from chomping on it in fury.

"I'll come back for you," he'd told her one night. *"I'll set you free, I swear it."*

"No. Don't go. Don't leave me here." Gods, she'd been so whiny back then. But she'd been a prisoner, and he'd been her only bright light.

"I love you too much to be without you for long, sweetheart. You know that. But I have to do this. For both of us."

Of course, she hadn't seen or heard from him after that. Not until the Titans escaped Tartarus, a prison for immortals, and wrested control of the heavens from the Greeks. Not until she'd come here to Earth and searched…only to find him carousing for tail at some skanky nightclub.

The fury expanded, dotted her line of vision with red. Deep breath in, deep breath out. Slowly the dots dissipated.

"We're done here," she said, though she remained still, gauging his reaction. "You're not getting what you want, and you're certainly not keeping me here."

"Feel free to run from me." He crossed his arms over his massive chest, pulling the fabric of his shirt tight across his pecs. "You won't regret it."

Again, she knew what he meant. Run, and he would ensure she suffered. But she said, "Soon as I stretch, I'll take you up on that offer and run. Thanks for the suggestion, by the way. I never would have thought of it on my own."

He growled with frustration and anger, all hint of casualness gone. "I was cruel to bring you here. You don't owe me a favor in return, so you had better not *stay put.*"

"We're in agreement. You're cruel, and I don't owe you anything, so I won't feel obligated to remain."

Another growl. She tried not to laugh. Damnation, he was still fun to tease.

Fun? Her grin faded a second time. She should hate that he could only speak in lies, not enjoy it. That deceitful tongue of his had once shattered her already fragile heart.

"That's so not enough from you," he sniped.

"Wow. Already begging for more." Once, she'd thought him special. But he'd proven himself exactly like the others. Her mother, her king, her supposed friends. They should have cared about her, but they had betrayed her, each and every one of them.

They'd been criminals, sure, but even criminals could love. Right? Right. *So why couldn't they love me?*

She'd spent her entire life locked inside Tartarus because her mother, Rhea, wife to Cronus, had had an affair with a mortal just before the queen's imprisonment and had eventually given birth to Scarlet inside her cell. A cell she'd shared with several other gods and goddesses.

Scarlet had been raised among them, and at first, they'd liked her. As she'd aged, however, jealousy had sprouted in some. Lust in others.

Captivity, hatred and bitterness had soon become her only trusted companions.

Until Gideon.

He'd once been an elite guard to Zeus and every time he'd brought in a new prisoner, their gazes had met. She'd waited for those moments, desperate for them. He'd enjoyed them, too, because he'd begun to visit Tartarus regularly. Not to lock up another criminal but simply to see her, to talk to her.

Don't think about your time with him. You'll soften toward him. And you can't soften, you idiot.

After gaining her freedom, she should have stayed in Olympus, which was now renamed Titania, thanks to Cronus, and found a nice god to settle down with. But *nooo*. She'd had to see Gideon one last time. Then, having seen him, she'd had to remain near him. Then, having decided to remain, she'd just had to convince herself to warn the Lords away from her, since she'd heard that they were tracking every immortal paired with a demon from Pandora's box, with the intention of recruiting them...or killing them.

Bastard, she thought about Gideon again. *Excellent. That's more like it. He's a filthy liar, a cold-blooded killer, and you hate him.* He still planned to kill her after he got his answers; she knew he did. Because she would *never* aid him, and that made her a liability.

"This silence is awesome," he remarked.

"Glad you like it," she replied. Annoyance bloomed over his expression, and she had to fight another grin. "'Cause I'm willing to give you a lot more of it."

Another growl.

"Oh, and for your peace of mind, you should know that I'm not going to run." Yet. She wanted to talk, too, though not to satisfy his curiosity.

For too long, she'd wondered if he'd found someone

new. Someone permanent. And it was past time she knew. Of course, if he had, Scarlet would have to kill the bitch. Not because she still cared about Gideon— she didn't, she reminded herself—but because he didn't deserve such happiness.

That wasn't vengeful of her. As his scorned ex, that was simply her right.

"No thanks for staying put," he said with a relieved sigh.

Thanks, he was saying. "You're not welcome." Fuck you, she was saying.

Eyes narrowing, and making him look as if he wanted to stomp his foot in vexation like a child, he traced his tongue over his teeth. Score one for Scarlet. "How is it possible that we didn't marry, yet my friends know everything about it?"

How had they married without anyone knowing? Easy. "We married in secret, dumbass."

This time, he didn't react to her taunt. "Was I not ashamed of you?"

Oh, she could slap him for that. Of course he thought he'd been ashamed of her rather than the other way around. She'd been the prisoner, after all, and he the free man. Not that he remembered even that slight detail, but clearly he still thought very highly of himself.

Bastard was too kind a word for him.

"You weren't ashamed of me, but you would have been killed if you'd been caught associating with me," she gritted out.

He nodded, as if he now understood she was a Titan who had been locked in Tartarus by the Greeks, rather than an actual criminal. As if he now understood that those Greeks, the very ones who had created him, would have punished him in the worst possible way for "dating" one of their reviled enemies.

"So. If we haven't been married all this time, what name have you not been using?"

Uh, what? He'd already forgotten her damned name when she'd told him the first time he'd visited her in the dungeon? Only a few weeks had passed since then. "My name is Scarlet." *You ass!* "But I already told you that." Ass, ass, ass. Her hands fisted the cotton beneath her.

He waved in dismissal. "Didn't know that already. What I don't want to know now is your last name."

That failed to calm her. Her grip tightened, and her eyes narrowed to tiny slits. Clearly, this was part of his excavation for information, not intimate curiosity, and he considered her dumb enough to fall for it.

He wasn't sure if she was a god or one of their servants. As a god, she wouldn't have a last name. As a servant, she would, for last names lowered status, as if you couldn't be distinguished by your first name alone. Like a human. Gideon was doing the process of elimination thing. Not that it would do him any good, for she was neither god nor servant. Nor human, for that matter. She was something in between them all.

"My last name changes pretty much every time I watch a movie and find new man candy," she said in a sugar-sweet tone that matched her earlier grin.

Now he popped his jaw, lip ring glistening in the lavender light. Irritated by that, was he? Didn't like the thought of his supposed wife eating up other men with her eyes, huh?

"Man candy? Like something you'd buy from a bakery?" His tone was sneering, intent on shaming her.

"Hell, no." And he clearly didn't think so, either,

because he hadn't passed out from his words. He *was* irritated, then. Good. Finally. True satisfaction. Score two. "You know. Man candy. Men to lust after, men you want to lick, men you want to suck on and take a bite out of. Well, not you, but me." No way did she want Gideon thinking she'd pined for him all these years. That she'd lain awake, wishing for him, desperate for him.

No matter how true that was.

Those eyes narrowed farther, his lashes fusing together and obscuring the bright blue of his irises. "You're not a Lord. Not like me. You shouldn't call yourself Scarlet Lord."

"You call yourself Gideon Lord?" she asked. She hadn't known that.

"No."

Yes. "Well, then, I will *never* call myself Scarlet Lord." She wouldn't travel down that road with him again. She would not proclaim to this world and the heavens that she belonged to him.

If she shared anything with this man, it would be the tip of her dagger. Right through his black, forgetting, abandoning heart.

He bared his pearly whites in a fearsome scowl. "I'm not warning you to tread carefully. I'm not dangerous when I'm riled."

"Hey, stop me if you've heard this one. But…wait for it…go fuck yourself."

For some reason, the anger drained right out of him and his lips quirked into the semblance of a smile. "No spirit. I can't see why I would have chosen you."

Do. Not. Soften.

"I don't want to know who you've named yourself after." He straightened from the door frame, though his arms remained crossed over his chest. "Please don't tell me. Please."

Casually asked, with that hint of amusement, yet there was now a sharp gleam in his eyes, as if he would close the distance between them, if necessary, and shake the answer out of her.

If he touched her, if those strong fingers closed around her arms… No, no, no. She couldn't allow it.

She shrugged as if the information didn't matter. "Well, I've been calling myself Scarlet Pattinson for several weeks. Have you seen Robert Pattinson? Hottest. Man. Ever. And no, I don't care if that makes me a cougar. He sings with the voice of an angel. Gods, I love when a man sings to me. You never did because your voice is terrible." She shuddered in distaste. "I swear, it's like a demon running its claws over brimstone."

His fingers were digging into his biceps so savagely, bruises were already branching from under them. "And now you're not going to tell me who you were before that."

He'd dropped the "please." Excellent. She was getting to him again. But how far could she push him on this point? How much could his stupid male pride take before he did stomp over to her? Before he did shake her? And not for answers, but for an apology.

Once, she'd known the answer to those questions. He would *never* touch her in anger. But he wasn't the same tender man she'd fallen in love with. A man who had shown her that first taste of kindness. He couldn't be. She and all the other prisoners had heard stories about the Lords of the Underworld and their exploits. The innocents they'd killed, the cities they'd destroyed.

Besides, she knew what her own demon had done

to her upon their pairing. The darkness, the terror, the absolute loss of control. She'd been consumed, no longer human in any way. And that had lasted for centuries, she'd been told, though there were gaps in her memory, the time seeming to have passed in a matter of days. Still. She was no longer the same person, either.

"I was Pitt for a while," she said. "Then Gosling. Then Jackman. Then Reynolds. I always go back to Reynolds. He's my fave. That blond hair, those muscles…" She shivered. "Let's see, who else? Oh. I've been Bana, Pine, Efron and DiCaprio, as well. DiCaprio is another fave. And another blond, for that matter. Maybe I have a thing for blonds."

Hopefully the barb cut its mark. Gideon had black hair underneath all that blue.

"Oh, and I'm not into girls," she continued, "but Jessica Biel could change my mind. Have you *seen* her lips? So yes, I've even been Scarlet Biel."

Gideon did that jaw-popping thing again. And if she wasn't mistaken, the anger had returned full force, burning away the last vestiges of amusement. "So very few pieces of candy," he remarked.

Apparently, she could push him pretty far. How had she thought him merely angry before? That was suppressed rage she was hearing in his voice…as well as deep thrums of arousal.

The latter was a sound she'd once known well and never thought to hear again.

Do not smile. "I like variety, what can I say? Maybe one day it'll even be my mission to bag and tag each and every one of them."

Steam practically curled from his nostrils. Yep, rage. He straightened, stepped forward, stopped himself, and retreated back into the doorway. "We aren't done with that topic for now," he snapped. He turned as if to leave.

"Wait." She wasn't ready to end the exchange. Not yet. "What about you?" she asked, shifting the focus off herself. *Careful.* "Any girlfriends I should know about? Or better yet, another wife? If so, I'll have to have you incarcerated for polygamy." There. No way he could guess at her desperation. At her clawing need to know.

Slowly he spun back around. "Yes," he said through clenched teeth, the word barely scraping its way free. Meaning no, he had none. "I have a girlfriend, and I'm married to someone else."

Scarlet released a searing breath she hadn't known she'd been holding. Gideon was single. A male whore who tapped any ass he could get his hands on, yes, but he was still unattached. She began shaking. Not in relief, she was sure, but in disappointment that she wouldn't get to murder someone he loved right in front of him.

So...we're done here.

She now had the info she'd wanted; she could ditch him. Except, she threw her legs over the side of the mattress and stood. Without knocking him down and running away. *Idiot.* "I'm taking a shower and you're getting me food. Don't even think about arguing or I swear to the gods I'll fill your next dreams with countless spiders." At least, she thought she would.

For some reason, Nightmares didn't like to torment him. She'd had to beg to get the demon to do so the first and only time, and the stupid beast had protested and whined every single moment. That had never happened before. Her demon was an equal opportunity tormentor.

Why did Nightmares like him? *Him,* of all people. Her demon didn't even know him, since she'd become possessed *after* Gideon had abandoned her. But her demon *had* endured her constant complaints about him, so she would have placed good money on Nightmares wishing Gideon was dead, just so Scarlet's complaining would stop.

"Well?" she demanded. "Why are you just standing there? Get moving."

Gideon's lips did that adorable twitching thing again. Trying not to grin? Odd man. Anyone else would have stomped away in irritation. Or threatened to stab her for such a haughty, commanding tone.

"Whatever you desire, my sweet."

Which meant he'd be doing nothing. She'd figured. He'd always been stubborn and had never taken orders well, and that was something she used to like about him. Still. She couldn't leave him feeling satisfied with the conversation.

Satisfaction belonged only to her.

Which meant it was time to throw him for another loop.

As she strolled to the bathroom, stripping along the way, she said over her shoulder, "Oh, and, Gid. I've been lying to you all along. We were never married."

DAMN IT, damn it, damn it! Gideon still couldn't detect when Scarlet lied, and that was really starting to *annoy* him. For some reason, every word out of her lovely lips still caressed his ears, and worse, that audible stroke was spreading to his entire body. How?

Fact: truth usually made his demon hiss. Fact: lies usually made the demon purr. With Scarlet *Pattinson*— he nearly punched a hole in the wall of the hotel room as Strider had done at the fortress as his *annoyance* escalated—it picked up only on her raspy voice, too lost in pleasure to care about truth or lie.

He was going to have to stop that. Otherwise, he might never get his answers.

Leave her, Lies demanded.

Go get her? *Hardly. I like my balls where they are, thanks.* The kind of woman who would punch you for trying to kiss her awake would knee your testicles into your throat for peeking at her naked curves while she washed.

Naked…curves… Hello, hard-on.

The bathroom door clicked shut, blocking every last inch of her from his sight. Bad, uh, *good* thing, too. She'd been down to her bra and panties. Black, both of them. With lace. The bra had clasped in the front, just asking to be separated. That testicle ascension might be worth it, he thought, already striding forward.

His mouth watered, a lick of flame dancing over his body, heating his blood to scalding. Somehow, he stopped himself before hitting the door. *Show some restraint, for gods' sake.* It was just, holy hell, she was beautiful. Like a portrait come to life, all pale, rose-dusted skin and a fall of silky black hair. All dangerous curves and lean muscle, two things that didn't normally go well together. On her, however, they did. And exquisitely so.

Exquisite. The perfect word for her back and its tattooed canvas. Around her waist were the words *TO PART IS TO DIE,* and around the words were flowers.

Lots and lots of flowers. Flowers of every color, shape and type, and he wanted to trace each of them with his tongue. Below the blooms, on her thighs, was a butterfly tattoo laced with all the jewel tones of a rainbow, glitter-bright and caught midflight, as if heading into those flowers.

Ex-qui-site.

That wasn't what had caught the bulk of his attention, though. *TO PART IS TO DIE.* He'd had those very words and the flowers surrounding them tattooed around his own waist. Why had he done something so girly? That's what all his friends had wanted to know after laughing their asses off at his expense. He'd told them he'd wanted to prove that nothing could lessen his appeal.

The truth was he'd done it because he'd seen those words and flowers in his mind, over and over again. They'd plagued him, and he'd known, *known* they meant something, but not *what* they meant. Now he knew he'd seen them on this woman. Which meant whether they were married or not, they had spent time together.

Why can't I fucking remember it?

I know, Lies replied, as if he'd asked the demon.

Shut up. I like you better when you're quiet.

The sound of water hitting porcelain suddenly reverberated through the hotel room. Scarlet was probably naked now, he thought. Probably soaked in that water and moaning as it slid down her luscious body.

He moaned, scrubbing a hand down his face and hoping to wipe away the naughty images flashing through his head. Didn't help. He closed the rest of the distance, arm extending for the knob. *Goodbye, testicles. We had a good run.*

Just as before, he caught himself in time. He growled,

backed away and planted his feet more firmly in place. No, no, and no.

At least he didn't have to worry about her escaping. Not successfully. While she'd slept, he'd placed tiny sensors on all the doors and windows and wired them to his phone. He'd know the moment she tried to leave. And she would. Soon. She wouldn't be able to help herself. Fighting was clearly part of her nature.

So was annoying him.

How was he supposed to handle a woman who picked her last name based on who she was currently lusting after? Which was fine when she was lusting after other females. Sexy, even. Something to be encouraged, too. But the males? Hells. No. Not if there was a chance they were hitched, and not until they had things settled between them.

Still. He knew how he *wanted* to handle her. Skin-to-skin. Every part of him longed to step into that shower, lick her all over, tasting her. Then, oh, yes, *then,* he'd sink deep inside her, feel her tug his hair and scratch his back. Feel her legs wrap around him and hold on tight. Hear her gasp his name and beg him for more.

Mini Me, his most beloved appendage, started weeping, and the twins begging, uncaring about potential loss.

Not gonna happen, men. Not yet, at least. She'd resisted him more intensely than he'd expected. Not that he'd tried very hard. Hard. Ha. But maybe that was a good thing. As Strider had reminded him, Hunters were in Budapest and out for blood. Now that they could kill the Lords and pair the demons with people of their choosing, now that the Lords were close to victory, the Hunters were more determined and vicious than ever. If Gideon seduced Scarlet, he would forget about guarding her.

He could have taken her to another city, he supposed, and seduced her there. That would have been safer. But, no. He couldn't leave his friends like that. They needed him more than ever. Maddox was consumed with easing his pregnant wife; Lucien's girlfriend was planning their wedding; Sabin's wife was visiting her sister in the heavens, so the warlord was pretty much operating on a hair-trigger of emotion; and Reyes's woman had enough shit to deal with. As the All-Seeing Eye, she could peer into heaven and hell, and the things she saw were often far worse than anything Scarlet could manufacture in her dream-world.

Not to mention, Aeron, until recently the keeper of Wrath, was still recovering from his interlude with death. For the first time in centuries, his mind was his own, his demon no longer a part of him. As expected, he hadn't yet acclimated to the change.

Gideon wasn't envious as some of the warriors were. He actually liked his other, darker half. Together, they were more powerful. Together, they were stronger, smarter, and no one but Scarlet could lie to him. Okay, fine. A few others could, but only when he let his emotions get the better of him. Which wasn't often.

But speaking of being unable to tell truth from lies… *I've been lying to you all along. We were never married*, Scarlet had said.

Damn her and her seductive wiles. Were they or weren't they? He had those flashes of her, yes, as if he *had* taken her to bed before. As if he had savored every inch of her and had already done all the things he now

wanted to do. But those could very well be urges he'd
had, mere fantasies, rather than reality.

Gideon sighed and strode to the bed where Scarlet
had lain. He lifted the sheets and pressed the still-warm
cotton to his cheek, the scent of midnight orchids wafting to his nose. Had he experienced this warmth skin-
to-skin? Did he know that scent?

Scowling, he dropped the sheet as his cock wept a
little more. *Get out of here before you forget your good
intentions and storm into that bathroom.*

His demon liked the thought of storming. *Don't enter
the bathroom. Don't enter the bathroom right now!*

Seriously. Shut it. Even though Gideon had told Scarlet in his roundabout, deceitful way that he wouldn't be
fetching her any food, which he'd meant at the time, he
left and locked the room, rode the elevator downstairs,
wrote out what food he wanted, then handed the receptionist the note.

Lies prowled angrily through his head the entire time,
hating the distance from Scarlet. Completely surreal.

The receptionist smiled and began typing. "Give us
an hour, Mr. Lord."

He *almost* corrected her and said Pattinson. Anything to connect him to Scarlet. Instead he nodded and
returned to the room. Scarlet was hungry. Therefore he
would feed her. Wife or not. Because bottom line, he
still had questions for her and she still had answers.

How he proceeded after this, as caveman or seducer,
would be up to her.

CHAPTER THREE

HAD SHE EVER felt this fantastically clean? Scarlet marveled as she brushed her hair.

Gods, this was nice. Not a speck of dirt marred her. She now smelled of the same apples-and-vanilla fragrance that coated the air, along with the usual floral scent that coated her skin. Courtesy of her father? She'd always wondered.

Her sore muscles felt revived, her spirits restored. Well, kind of. Why was she still here? Why wasn't she running, as she'd promised Gideon she would?

Nightmares didn't reply, the water having lulled the demon into a peaceful sleep.

Didn't matter. She already knew the answer. Gideon still intrigued her.

How many times do you need to be told? You can't let yourself develop feelings for him again.

Easy to think. Hard to actually prevent. Gideon had seen to everything. He'd placed a toothbrush, toothpaste and hairbrush on the sink. Oh, yeah. And a freaking blue bow for her hair. Clean clothes had rested on the toilet lid, though they weren't what she would have chosen for herself. He'd picked a flowing, barely there blue dress rather than pants and a T-shirt. High heels rather than boots. He hadn't given her a bra. Just blue panties.

Clearly, he had a fascination with blue. Why?

She should know, and hated that she didn't. Was this a recent development?

Wasn't like it mattered, she told herself next. His thoughts and reasoning weren't her concern.

"I'm so happy waiting for you," he called through the door.

The sound of that rumbling voice caused goose bumps to break out over her entire body. She imagined him pacing back and forth in front of the door, and she wanted to grin. Patience had never been his thing. She'd always liked that, mostly because he'd been so eager to be with her.

He used to rush to her cell after every mission, kiss her face, hands roving, desperate to relearn her curves.

"I missed you so much," he'd said. Every damn time.

"Don't leave me again." Always her reply.

"I'd stay in this cell with you if I could." A fleeting, sad smile, offered the very last time they'd had this exchange. *"Maybe one day I will."*

"No." She hadn't wanted that for him, no matter how much she craved being with him. *"Just...make me forget you were ever gone."*

And he had. Oh, had he.

If he could have removed the collar that had been permanently anchored around her neck, he'd always said, he would have done so and run away with her. But he hadn't possessed the ability. Only a few of Zeus's chosen had. So the golden collar had remained, seemingly glued to her skin and keeping her weakened, her demon's powers muted.

Besides, only a select group of immortals were able to

flash—to travel from one location to another with only a thought—in and out of Tartarus, and Gideon hadn't been one of them. He would have had to sneak her through the entire realm, past the guards and to the gate. One, on its own, would have been difficult; together, they were impossible, even without the collar. But he'd still wanted to try.

With the thought, she felt herself softening. Damn it! *Fight it. You can't survive another heartbreak, and that's all he has to offer. Heartbreak.*

She dropped the brush on the sink and as it clattered ominously, tugged the dress over her head. The soft material stroked her skin, and she moaned. She'd never dressed herself this way, but maybe she should have. So decadent... The panties were equally soft, which elicited another moan. The heels, she left alone, donning her old boots instead. Better to beat a heartless man into submission with.

Finished, she turned, shoulders squaring, determination rising. One last encounter with Gideon, and then she was ditching him. But that was it, the end. She'd finally have closure. For surely that's what she needed, what she lacked. Once she had it, she would return to the life she'd begun building for herself. A life as a human mercenary. Or rather, a jack of all wicked trades.

Do it. Get it over with.

"Are you kidding me with this?" she said as she stomped from the bathroom and held out the bow. A cloud of sweetly scented steam followed her.

Immediately his electric gaze raked her, lingering on his once-favorite places. Something dark entered his eyes, and he gulped. "What?" The word was a croak.

"I thought it was ugly." Meaning he thought it was pretty.

And he wanted her to have pretty things. How... sweet.

Damn him!

He stood in front of a wheeled square table that hadn't been there before, arms once again crossed over his chest. To keep from throttling her?

"So you like women who dress like schoolgirls." She ignored the thundering of her heart and the heat spreading through her veins. "I didn't realize you had such innocent fantasies," she said, then wanted to curse. She'd sounded breathless. Maybe because her statement had raised a very naughty question. What did he fantasize about nowadays?

How did he like his sex? As gentle and consuming as he once had?

How did he like his women? As sweet as she'd once been? Most likely.

He'd shown only a few signs of attraction to her since discovering her inside his dungeon, and she was as hard as stone.

She had to be. Her life didn't allow for dresses like this one. She had to be prepared to fight, always. She was a child of Rhea, the god queen, and she would make an excellent hostage to ransom. Not that her mother would pay it. More than that, she had many enemies, for killing her would remove her half-mortal self from the line of succession.

The scent of fresh baked bread, chicken and rice suddenly hit her nose and her mouth watered. Forget the bow. Forget closure. Her hand fell to her side. "You brought me food," she said, dazed.

Another sweet gesture, the jerk.

"Nope. It's all for me." He eased into the chair behind him. Steaming plate after steaming plate littered the surface of the table, that steam wafting around him and creating a dream haze. "That color looks terrible on you, by the way."

She licked her lips. Over the food, she told herself. Not because he liked the way she looked. Which was good. "Payback is a bitch, you know. And you can count on the fact that I'll put *you* in this dress sometime soon."

He shrugged, drawing attention to the wide girth of his shoulders, then held out one of the plates. The one with chicken, rice and veggies. She was walking to him, hands outstretched, before she realized what she was doing. After she claimed the plate, she plopped into the seat across from him and dug in.

So. Good.

"So…why don't you sleep during the day?" he asked. "When the people here aren't awake."

That, she didn't mind sharing. Even though she could guess his plan. Start her off with something light. Get her talking while she was distracted with food. "Somewhere in the world, people are asleep when I am, and the demon finds them. Besides that, every day I fall asleep a single second later. And every night I *awaken* a single second later. The time always varies ever so slightly, ensuring we're able to target *everyone* at some point." *In other words, fear us.*

"Not good to know." A pause, then, "I don't want to know why you got the tattoos. I don't want to know who gave you those tattoos. And I most definitely don't want to know how things ended between us."

Yep. She'd been right. "I told you we weren't really married." She chased a deliciously flavored bite of buttered carrots with a glass of red wine. *Even. Better.*

"And I believed you."

She shrugged, mimicking his nonchalance. "I've answered enough of your questions tonight. And I know that's why you brought me here. To relax me, lower my guard and find out everything you're dying to know so you can lock me back up." And worse.

"You're wrong," he said, reaching out and cupping her hand with his own. He brought it to his lips and pressed a soft kiss into her suddenly burning flesh. "I just wanted to spend time with you, to get to know you, the world around us forgotten."

Softening...again... They were words she'd longed to hear so badly she'd often ached physically. Hearing them now...

And realizing they were a lie...

The softening instantly ceased. Suddenly she wanted to remove the invisible knife he'd left in her back and stab him with it. Since he wasn't crumpling into a heap of pain, as she'd heard he did when he spoke the truth, she knew he'd just told a whopper.

He was playing her, and she'd almost let him. *Harden up. You're a bitch. Act like it.*

"That's easy for you, isn't it? Forgetting the world around you, I mean." Bitterness crept through her tone, and there was nothing she could do to defuse it. "Your poor, sad memory."

He frowned, and his hand fell away.

She wanted to shout. With frustration. With a demand that he touch her again. With fury that she *wanted* him to touch her again. Instead, she remained quiet and finished her meal, consuming every last crumb, every drop of wine, and leaving nothing for the man across from her.

"Why are you so…not stubborn about this?" he asked with what seemed to be genuine curiosity. "About keeping me in the light?"

Because she'd spent thousands of years wondering where he was, what he was doing and who he was doing it with. Wondering if he ever thought of her, wondering why he never returned for her. Wondering if he was even alive. Each day had been worse than the last, a constant churning in her mind, her emotions rolled out, flayed and left raw.

But she'd known with gut-wrenching intensity that he loved her, so she'd finally had to accept that he hadn't returned because he'd been killed. Death was the only thing that could have kept him away. So she'd mourned him, crying so forcefully, so intensely, she'd actually shed tears of blood.

And when she'd finally discovered that he lived… Oh, the pain. Pain that still haunted her, a constant shadow in her heart.

In contrast, he'd been wondering about her for a few weeks. He didn't cry himself to sleep about it. He didn't throw up because the worry and the heartache were too much to bear.

Her hands clenched so tightly, the glass she held shattered. Beads of crimson sprang up all over her palm, but she didn't flinch at the ensuing sting. This was nothing compared to what she'd once endured. *Nothing.* She no longer cried about *anything.*

Gideon sighed and wrapped his fingers around her

wrist, inspecting the damage. "Love to see you injured. Don't want to make it all better."

Truth.

When he had strode into his fortress's dungeon and she'd seen his beautiful face, the only thing she'd truly felt at the time was awe. He was alive. He was with her again. But then the anger had sparked. Followed by the resentment and the consuming urge to hurt. None of those compared to what she felt just then, however.

Rage. So much rage.

How dare he. How fucking dare he care about such paltry wounds! He was sitting there, calm as could be, poking at her emotions like a child with a stick because he could. Because she was a big, fat question to him. That was all. He wanted answers. Not her. Not her forgiveness. He couldn't care less about easing her *real* injuries and making her "all better."

Had she been nothing to him, even all those centuries ago? Yes, he'd wed her, but he'd left her soon after. Left her, she now knew, to steal and open Pandora's box. She also knew he'd been paired with his demon and shoved out of the heavens soon after that. But she'd been possessed that same day, still locked inside her cell.

After those centuries spent in darkness—what oddly seemed like a mere blink of time for her whenever she looked back—had passed and she'd once again had control of her mind, she'd remembered Gideon. Realized he'd been given a demon, too, and figured he had gained control of himself, as well. So she'd waited for him to return for her. And waited. And waited, for so damn long. Then all those questions began swirling in her head. And then the worry had set in, followed by the grief that he hadn't survived.

And in that grief, she'd done things that had shocked even her demon. Terrible things. None of the gods and goddesses sharing her cell—the one she'd been moved to, away from the *tender* hand of her mother—had survived her rampage.

The Greeks had nearly executed her for those actions, but in the end, Zeus had preferred to parade her in front of Cronus, his own father and greatest foe, enjoying the fact that she was proof Rhea had cuckolded him. Anything that tormented the deposed Titan king was worth keeping alive, the Greek sovereign had said, no matter how dangerous that thing was.

And then the Titans finally won their freedom. Cronus and Rhea would have liked to leave her behind, she knew, but they'd needed her skills to help defeat the Greeks.

Once the screams had faded and the blood had stopped flowing, she'd scoured ancient scrolls for information about the Lords of the Underworld, hoping to find them and ask how Gideon had perished. Where his bones rested. She'd intended to give him a proper burial, pray over him, say goodbye.

Instead, she'd discovered her husband was still alive.

Her relief had known no bounds. But then, neither had her upset, for that's when other questions had begun plaguing her. Why hadn't he come back for her? Why hadn't he sent word that he'd survived?

She'd sought him out to ask him. And yes, to throw herself back into his arms. To feel him surrounding her, sliding in and out of her, once again. Finally. The way she'd been dreaming about for so many years.

She'd found him in that bar in Buda. She'd walked

past him. Except, he hadn't noticed her. Glanced at her, yes. Moved his gaze away as if she were of no consequence, yes, that, too. He'd been too busy crooking his finger at a human female, and then having sex with that female right there in the club.

Scarlet had left, heartbroken all over again. As she did her best to learn about modern human society by watching TV, all the while secretly hoping Gideon would find her worthy when she did so—her, a woman who had been raised among criminals, who had never been wanted by her mother, had never known her father, and who had a wretched demon trapped inside her— she'd kept her ear to the ground, always curious about Gideon and what he was doing.

Maybe she'd purposely allowed the Lords to capture her. Without consciously admitting that she craved a moment like this. A moment to see what a shit Gideon truly was. A moment to finally, blessedly cut him from her thoughts. Which, even now, was completely against her nature and something she'd sworn never to do. Captivity was something she despised. Yet she'd stayed in that fucking dungeon and hadn't tried to escape. For this man who didn't remember her. A man who had no problem using her. Hurting her. Tearing her down.

He. Needed. To. Suffer.

Scarlet jumped to her feet, plate in hand. A plate she tossed at Gideon without warning. It crashed into his face and shattered just as her wineglass had done. And just as her hand had beaded with blood, so did his face.

Not enough.

Scowling, he jumped up, as well. "That was nice. Thanks!"

She'd already launched another plate, and this one slammed into his chest. It, too, broke apart, slicing past his T-shirt.

"What don't you think you're doing?"

"I'm not kicking your ass. I'm not hating your guts. I'm not thinking you are the biggest ass the gods ever created. How's that? Did I speak a language you can understand?" *Kill him. She wanted to kill him.*

"I may remember you, Scarlet," he bellowed, backing up when she grabbed her fork and held it out like a dagger. She'd murdered men with less. Even immortals. "But you haven't haunted me." Motions stiff, he raised his shirt. Amid the cuts, above his heart, was a tattoo of eyes. Dark eyes. Like hers. "Don't you see? You... haven't...haunted...me."

It was a lie, like him. It had to be.

"That proves nothing! Thousands of people have dark eyes."

He slanted his head and brushed the hair from the back of his neck. There, she found a tattoo of bloodred lips in the shape of a heart. Like hers. Then he turned and raised his shirt again. On his lower back were flowers, all kinds of flowers, and the words *TO PART IS TO DIE*.

It was an exact replica of her own tattoo. He'd shown it to her once before, the first time he'd entered the dungeon, but seeing it again was still like being punched in the chest.

"I just want to make no sense of this," he added softly. He pivoted, facing her once again. "Don't help me. Please."

Seeing those tattoos didn't lessen her fury. No, seeing them increased it. He'd imagined her, but he'd still slept with all those other women. He'd still continued on with his life, not seeking out the source of those images.

"You think that makes everything better, you uncaring bastard? While you were down here whoring around, loving life, I was in Tartarus, a slave to the Greeks." One step, two, she eased around the table and approached him. Warrior that he was, he remained in place. "What they wanted me to do, I had to do. Whether I wanted to or not." Parading around naked for their enjoyment. Fighting with other prisoners while they bet on the winner. Scrubbing other people's filth on her hands and knees. "Yet you left me there. You never came for me. You promised you'd come for me!"

Seething, panting, she stabbed the fork into his chest and twisted with all her strength.

Surprisingly, he didn't try to stop her. Didn't try to defend himself. Rather, he stood there, his eyes narrowing. In his own fury? And if it was in fury, who was he pissed at? Her? Or the Greek gods who had forced her to do those vile things?

Didn't matter. This was just the beginning of his punishment.

"And do you know what else?" Her fingers clutched the fork so tightly, her knuckles screamed in protest. "After I came here and saw you with another woman, I gave myself to another man. Willingly this time. And then another." Lies, all lies. She'd tried. She'd wanted to hurt him that way, but she hadn't been able to follow through.

And oh, how she hated herself for that failure. More than wanting to hurt him, though, she'd needed someone to make her feel as he once had. Protected, loved, cherished. Like a treasure. That, too, had failed miserably.

She'd walked away from both encounters feeling hollow and sad.

Gideon's shoulders slumped, and all that dark emotion seemed to drain from him. "I'm not sorry. I love that you felt the need to do such a thing. I don't want to kill the men you were with. Even though I remember everything about our time together. You still somehow do *not* affect me."

He was sorry, he loathed that she'd done such a thing and wanted to destroy the men. Pretty words. For him. But she was having none of it. He was far too late. With a snarl, she jerked the fork out of his chest, the prongs dripping crimson, then stabbed him anew and twisted.

He grunted.

"Again," she snarled, "do you think that makes everything better? You think the fact that you've forgotten me makes your actions any less painful?" *Shut up, shut up, shut up.* She didn't want him to know how much he'd damaged her.

"I don't—" He frowned. Then he reached into his jeans pocket and withdrew his phone. His gaze quickly scanned the screen, and when their eyes next met, there was smoldering rage in those electric depths. "We don't have visitors."

"Friends of yours?" She didn't ask how he knew. She could guess, loving modern technology as she did.

"Yeah. I adore Hunters."

She could have struck him again, quickly jabbing both of his eyes, leaving him to deal with the uninvited guests injured and blinded. But he was hers to hurt, not theirs.

"How many?" she demanded, removing the utensil

and switching the focus of her rage. *Wake up, Night-mares. Your skills might be needed.*

The demon stretched and yawned inside her head.

"I know," Gideon said.

So he was as clueless as she on that score. "Which door did they enter?" she asked.

"Not the front."

She performed a quick inspection. There was a door-way that led out of the bedroom-slash-kitchenette into a vestibule. That vestibule branched into three hallways. No matter which direction the intruders came from, they'd have to enter it. Perfect.

You ready, baby? Because Mama was wrong. No maybe about it. You're needed.

A purr of anticipation rumbled through her. *Gonna be fun.*

I'll handle the final blow. Okay?

Greedy.

Yes. But then, she needed *some* outlet for the growing darkness inside her. *And leave Gideon alone. I don't want him to see the things you show his enemies.*

That earned her a growl. *I would never hurt him.*

It was a declaration she'd never thought to hear, even with the creature's reluctance to scare the warrior in his dreams. Had the circumstances been different, she would have demanded to know why. Not that it would have done her any good. Nightmares was as generous with answers as she was.

"Get on the bed," she commanded Gideon. "I've got this."

"Hell, yes," he said, unsheathing a sharp, gleaming knife and a small revolver from the waist of his pants. He'd been armed this entire time, yet he hadn't defended himself against her. "I relish the thought of you battling such sweethearts alone."

Macho men. They considered women a liability in situations like this. But this one would soon learn. She wasn't the same girl he'd known in prison. Or rather, the same girl he couldn't recall.

"They're here. I know they're here," someone whispered. A whisper, yes, but her ears registered every word as if the person were right beside her. A skill she'd developed in prison. A skill that had saved her life on countless occasions.

"If we take him the girl, they'll have to let us in," another said.

"And the guy?" Yet another.

"Dies."

As Nightmares laughed, more than ready to begin, Scarlet shoved Gideon back into his chair. He landed with a huff as she lowered her internal guard and unleashed her demon. Darkness exploded from her, thousands of terrified screams threading through the impenetrable thickness. Even Gideon, powerful immortal that he was, wouldn't be able to see through it. She, however, would have no trouble drinking in every sparkling detail.

"I'd cover your ears, if I were you," she suggested.

"Scar," he began, as close to her name as his demon would apparently let him get, a hint of anger in the undertone. And oh, was his expression stony. He hated this. But whatever he meant to say was cut off as Scarlet pressed a finger against his lips, a silent command for no talkie-talkie. The enemy would hear.

A moment passed. The stiffness never left him, but Gideon nodded. He was graciously bowing out of the fight and letting her handle things. His surrender was completely unexpected. Why hadn't he jumped to his feet and foolishly demanded to help her?

Ponder it later. Frowning, she turned to face the intruders. There were four of them, all male, and all holding weapons.

Only four? They must think themselves stronger than they actually were. Or consider her and Gideon weaker than they really were. Or perhaps this was just the beginning. Most likely others were posted throughout the hotel, watching, waiting for the right time to strike.

As the men entered the bedroom, they encountered the darkness and the screams and stumbled to a halt, trying to orient themselves and figure out what was going on. But it was too late for that. Nightmares wove around them, a swirling, dark dancer, as graceful as he was lethal, holding them in place, even floating to their ears and whispering their deepest fears.

Pain.

Blood.

Death.

Soon they were clutching their heads, moaning, images of the Lords of the Underworld strapping them down, torturing them as the Hunters had often tortured others, becoming all that they could see.

One of Nightmares's talents was sensing hidden fears and exploiting them. That's how they'd known about Gideon's fear of spiders. Only problem was, they had no way of knowing what had *caused* those fears. And she was beyond curious about Gideon. He hadn't seemed to care about the bug while with her in Tartarus. He'd even flicked the creatures off her when they'd invaded her cell.

"Make it stop, please make it stop," someone pleaded.

"Enough!" someone else shouted.

No. Not nearly enough. Cold, uncaring. That's how she had to be. And really, she enjoyed this as much as her demon did. Enjoyed hurting those who thrived on suffering. For too long, she'd been a victim herself. But no longer. Never again.

Smiling, she strolled toward the men, fork still in hand. She reached the nearest, his terrified moans like candy to her ears, and brushed his hair from his face. The soothing touch startled him, yet he leaned into it, as if seeking comfort anywhere he could find it. As if he assumed she was a friend.

Without any more warning, she jammed the fork into his jugular. He screamed, but that scream blended with all the others floating from her. A chilling but welcome music. Warm blood spurted from him, coating her hand as he collapsed. She eased to the next man, gifted him with that same gentle touch, the calm before the storm, then stabbed him, as well.

More blood sprayed, a river of the deepest scarlet, the very essence of her name.

She finished off the other two just as quickly and efficiently. Just as ruthlessly. Perhaps she should have played with them a bit. Oh, well. Next time.

Once the moans and movement ceased, she closed her eyes and tugged the shadows and screams back inside her. There they whirled like a tornado until she blocked them from her awareness, something she'd learned to do over the years. Otherwise, she would have tumbled into insanity a long time ago.

Perhaps it was a blessing that she and Gideon would

never be intimate again, she thought then. When she lost control of her body's sensations, she lost her hold on her demon, allowing the beast to have free rein even though she was awake. What she'd done to those boys—Hunters?—would be done automatically to her lovers. Not the cutting, but the absolute dissolution of light, the cries of the damned ringing in their ears.

For a man, it was hard to stay, well, hard during something like that. Watching fear and disgust contort Gideon's features while his cock was buried deep inside her might just end her. Her pride, surely. Her will to live, maybe. Already, she existed on only an instinctual level. Breathe, eat, kill. That was it.

Mind on the task at hand. Gideon was sitting exactly as she'd left him. Only, his expression was blank, a guarded mask as his gaze raked her, taking in the blood coating her hands. He traced his tongue over his teeth before looking at the men.

"Harmed?" he asked, still without any hint of emotion.

"Dead," she replied. "You're welcome." Would a thank-you have been too much to ask? She'd saved him from suffering a single injury. Well, besides the ones she'd given him.

Blue eyes snapped back up, pinning her in place. "Yeah, I was talking about them. Not you."

Oh. He wanted to know about her? Shocker. *No softening.* "I'm fine. Not a scratch on me. But we should probably go." *Our separate ways,* she silently added, ignoring the pang in her chest. "I'm sure more Hunters are on their way."

He offered no reply.

Do it. Leave, she commanded herself. She didn't. She

remained in place like the idiot she was. Closure must not have been achieved yet. Not really.

What would it take?

"Are you just going to sit there?" she threw at him.

He stood, but still he didn't sheath his weapons. "You and utensils make a bad team."

Another pang speared her chest. "No more compliments, or I'll give you another firsthand demonstration." Just to taunt him, she held up the dripping fork and waved it through the air.

"Yes, please. Another demonstration would be nice." He bypassed her, unafraid, and crouched in front of her victims. With quick proficiency, he searched their bodies, even under their clothing. "All of them are marked."

Her arm fell heavily to her side. Hunters tattooed themselves with the symbol of infinity, their way of proclaiming they wanted a forever without evil. That these boys didn't bear the mark… Huh. "Maybe they're just recruits. When they entered, one of them said something about being let in. Maybe he meant being let in to the Hunters Are Assholes club."

Gideon nodded as he stood, a lock of cobalt falling over his brow. "That makes no sense."

"Because I'm smarter than you are." She fought the urge to smooth the hair into place. Still no closure, but she forced herself to say, "I guess we're done here, then." For real, this time.

"Sure." He closed what little distance there was between them, putting them nose-to-nose, his heat enveloping her, his musky cologne fuzzing her senses. "Don't listen carefully. I'm upset you're okay." His lashes fell,

oh, so slowly, before stopping, lingering, and she knew
he was peering at her lips.

Thinking of kissing her?

She gulped. No. No, no, no. "Gideon."

"Keep talking." Slowly, still oh, so slowly, he leaned
toward her, as if he did intend to kiss her.

No. No, no...yes. Yes, yes, yes. Every muscle in her
body tensed, waiting, ready. The blood inside her veins
sizzled and snapped. Would he taste the same? Feel the
same? She had to know. *Then* she could leave him. Then
she would have closure and wouldn't ever have to look
back and wonder.

But just before their lips touched, his fingers circled
her wrist with a soft clink. No, not his fingers. Too stiff,
too heavy and too cold. Frowning, she glanced down and
saw that he'd handcuffed them together. Understanding
dawned.

That...bastard...

A red haze shuttered over her vision. Not dots, but a
full-on cloud. Tricked. The bastard had tricked her. Had
never meant to kiss her. Had used her obvious desire for
him against her.

"I hope you're proud of yourself." That was all the
warning she gave him. She jabbed the fork into his chest
and rather than twist, she slammed her palm into the
handle, pushing it deeper. This time, he couldn't contain
his grimace. "And I hope you know this will seem like
child's play when I'm done with you."

"As long as we're apart," he gritted out, "I'm
happy."

As long as...as long as... He needed to be together to
be happy? Though part of her suddenly wanted to grin
sheepishly, perhaps bat her lashes, she scowled up at

him. Stupid softening heart. He'd just betrayed her, and she almost melted when he tossed a few flattering words at her. Flattering words that meant nothing, because he still only wanted answers.

"Tell me. Does this make you happy?" She kneed him in the balls.

He hunched over, gasping, but amid those gasps, she managed to make out a single word: "Yes."

Good. "So where are you taking me?"

"Heaven." Another gritted admission.

Still. She easily translated. He planned to take her straight into hell.

CHAPTER FOUR

AFTER THE swelling went down in his balls, Gideon phoned Lucien, keeper of Death, asking for cleanup at the hotel, then dragged a protesting Scarlet outside, through the glass-covered atrium and along the brightly lit city streets to the Escalade he'd hidden in a parking garage a few blocks away. Night was in full swing, the star-sprinkled sky framing the golden half-moon. Though he was prepared for anything, there were no other Hunters—or recruits, as the case may have been— waiting to attack.

He wasn't sure how those four kids had followed him. Especially if they'd had no training. He'd made damn sure he'd lost any tails. If there had been tails, that was. Which he would've bet every cent of his, uh, Torin's money that there hadn't been. So either a god or goddess was watching him and reporting his whereabouts or the boys had simply gotten lucky and had happened to be at the hotel when he checked in.

He didn't believe in coincidences, so the first was most likely. Cronus was helping the Lords and Rhea, the god queen, who was at war with her husband, had teamed up with the Hunters. But why would she send recruits to fight him, rather than actual Hunters? And would Gideon's location be compromised no matter where he went?

Probably.

His hand clenched on the steering wheel as he threw the vehicle into Reverse, Scarlet's arm moving with him.

"What's got your panties in such a twist?" she asked conversationally.

He wasn't fooled. She was still pissed as hell at him.

Silent, he maneuvered them through the gloomy garage and back onto the city streets. Late as it was, traffic was light. His gaze kept returning to his rearview mirror, though, just in case.

"You're begging for another fork in your chest," she muttered.

Again ignoring her, he shouted, "Cron!" *Stop. You're ticked at him. There has to be another way.* But Gideon knew better, and wouldn't lie to himself. Not now of all times. "I don't need you!"

In the passenger seat, Scarlet stiffened. "Cron. As in Cronus?"

He nodded.

She hissed in outrage and jerked at the cuffs. "What the hell do you want with him? I hate him!"

Did she have a beef with everyone? "Not answers, okay?"

"Well, you can let me go and *then* chat with him." There was an edge creeping into her voice. One he'd never heard before, even when she'd stabbed him. Her struggles increased, and then she was kicking at the passenger door to pop it open.

Was she…*scared* of the god? Couldn't be. Scarlet had faced down four potential Hunters without any hesitation.

"My reasons for…avoiding him are…not urgent."
His stomach twisted. He'd almost spoken the truth. Had
almost told her that his reasons for summoning the god
were indeed urgent. He'd had to force out the lies. "And
those reasons aren't life-and-death."

"I don't give a shit!" Slam, slam, boot against plastic.
Crack. "I don't want him here."

Oh, yes. She was scared. Why?

Rather than ask—he knew she wouldn't tell him if
he did—he changed the subject to give her a moment
to calm down. If she kept pulling at him, he was going
to lose a limb. Again. "Did you have to leave those kids
alive?" She'd killed them without any hint of mercy.

He would have done the same, sure, but he was a
guy. Weren't girls supposed to be softhearted and shit?
Well, besides Cameo, keeper of Misery. She could kill
an enemy while filing her nails.

"Yeah." Scarlet's frantic bid for freedom slowed, then
ceased altogether. She peeked at him over her shoulder.
"So?"

"Why? We could have pleasured them for information."

Her lips twitched as if she were suddenly fighting a
grin. "Why, Gideon, I didn't know you swung that way.
They were cute, though, weren't they? Especially the
blond. Is that who you were imagining sexing up?"

Now *that* tone he recognized. Sugar-sweet and irritat-
ing as hell. But yeah, the blond had been cute from what
he'd been able to tell, and he hated that she'd noticed.
Actually, he hated that she preferred blonds. His wife
should— *You don't know that she's your wife.*

Not mine, Lies piped up. *Not mine.*

Meaning Lies was claiming her? Hardly. If anyone claimed her, it would be Gideon. *If* they were married.

And then what? he wondered. He still planned to return her to the dungeon, no matter what. Which meant she was going to hate him. As if she didn't already. As poorly as she'd treated his man-parts, he suspected that she did.

His guilt returned, filling his nose, his lungs, then sweeping through his bloodstream. *Has to be this way.*

Yes. She's not mine.

Zip it.

"Why did you leave them alive?" he insisted.

Scarlet's seemingly delicate shoulders lifted in a negligent shrug. "They were there to hurt us. If I had let them live, they would have had the opportunity to come back for us. To poison others against us. And their determination would have been greater than ever."

What she said made sense, but it also caused his stomach to clench. The absolute conviction in her voice had given him a searing glimpse inside her psyche. One she would undoubtedly prefer he not have. Once, she'd let an enemy go rather than kill him and that enemy had returned for her. Had hurt her. With others in tow.

How had the bastards hurt her? Raped her? Beat her? The steering wheel whined as it bent, nearly snapping in half, and Gideon forced himself to loosen his hold. If, after he'd been kicked out of the heavens, he'd gone back for her, as he once might have promised her, would such a fate have been prevented?

Gods. His guilt became a cancer, eating at him, leaving him raw and agonized. Again, he wanted to ask her for an explanation, but again, he knew she would tell him nothing. Until they reached their destination and he seduced her. Which he *would* do, guilty or not. Before their uninvited guests had arrived, she'd looked ready to accept his kiss. Hell, she'd looked ready to return it with equal passion.

He wanted that. Needed it.

"Nothing to say?" she asked. "No lame reply?"

Lame? He did the best he could, damn it. *She's just frustrated, lashing out.* But really, this wasn't entirely his fault, he reminded himself. Something had happened to his memories. Not that the knowledge eased his guilt.

Actually, his memories were another thing to discuss with Cronus.

"Cron!" he found himself shouting a second time.

And just as before, Scarlet began struggling for freedom. "I told you I don't want him here. I told you—"

But the rest of her words were lost to him. One moment Gideon was at the wheel, cuffed to Scarlet and motoring down the long, winding roads, the next he was in the heavens, puffy white clouds surrounding him, Scarlet nowhere to be seen.

Trying not to panic, he spun, wild gaze searching for her. Only more of those clouds greeted him. There were no roads, no buildings and no freaking people. "Scar," he shouted, heart ready to burst from his ribs. He had to find her. Couldn't let her—

"Rest easy, Lies. Time has momentarily ceased for your female. When I return you, all will be as you left it."

Another turn, and he was peering over at Cronus. His heartbeat slowed, even as he tried not to gape. The king looked younger every time Gideon saw him, but this… this… *Too young,* he thought with a shake of his head.

Gone was the silver hair. In its place were startling locks of honey-brown and pale gold. Gone was the wrinkled skin. Now he was unlined, his complexion smooth and sun-kissed.

A white robe that appeared as soft as the clouds draped him, and sandals wrapped around the veined, scarred feet of a warrior. He exuded so much power, Gideon felt the weight of every compelling wave hammering at his shoulders. Remaining standing required power of his own. A lot of it.

"Why did you summon me?" the king asked.

"Lastly—" first off "—I don't want your vow that all will be as you didn't say." Confusing, even to him, but important.

Like Scarlet, Cronus knew him well enough to discern what he was truly saying. Confusing or not. "You have my word. She isn't going to crash. She isn't even going to know you were gone unless you tell her." And, thankfully, Cronus wasn't upset by his demand. "Happy now?"

A little irritated, perhaps, but not upset. Good. "No. Not happy." Every muscle in his body released its vise-grip on bone. "No, thank you."

"Does this mean you've forgiven me for not telling you how to find Aeron's spirit?"

No. Never. Rather than admit that to the king, however, he remained silent. Better silence than punishment. Even he was smart enough to know that. But the question explained the king's sudden patient benevolence.

"What I did," Cronus said, a little stiff now, "I did for your own good."

Making Gideon beg and then denying him what he begged for had been for his own good? Yeah. Right.

"You are an immortal, not a god, so your understanding is limited. One day, however, you will thank me." As the words echoed between them, Cronus's nose wrinkled in disgust. "I cannot believe I'm explaining myself to you. It's sickening, really, the way I must baby you. Where is the fearsome warrior I was told to expect?"

Gideon barely stopped himself from rolling his eyes. Baby him? Ha! "You are not a—"

"Watch your tongue, Lies." Eyes of the darkest obsidian sharpened. How odd. Usually those eyes were the purest gold. "Otherwise, you'll lose it."

He gave a rigid nod. Perhaps he wasn't so smart, after all.

"Better." Cronus clicked under his tongue, clearly satisfied his charge had been properly subdued. "Now, I ask again. And for the final time. Why did you summon me?"

To demand your wife's head on a dinner platter. No need for silver, either. Any metal will do. Not that he could say such a thing aloud. "Just so you know, your wife…she's a real prize." He braced himself, expecting immediate punishment. Though he couldn't stop himself from reaching for a dagger. Instinct allowed nothing less.

"If you prize garbage," the king replied dryly, "then, yes. We agree."

A truth, even spoken in so disparaging a tone. Lies spat in distaste.

Gideon returned the dagger to its sheath. Astonishingly, he and the king were on the same page. "This isn't the thing. I don't suspect she's watching our every move. I don't suspect she's having us followed. And I don't suspect she's sending humans to kill us."

"I know. I've known for a while." Again truth. Cronus pinched the bridge of his nose, a man at the end of his rope—without a blade. "Damned female. She's always been more trouble than she's worth."

"How can we encourage her?" *To stop,* he silently added, wishing like hell he could just say what he wanted. "She's not causing all kinds of grief, and she's not going to have us murdered before we can save your ass from Gal." Or rather, his head from Galen.

Danika, Reyes's woman and the All-Seeing Eye, could do more than peer into heaven and hell. She could predict the future. She claimed Galen was going to behead Cronus. Which was the only reason Cronus was helping the Lords.

No, not true. There was another reason, one Gideon had only recently learned. Cronus was possessed by a demon. By Greed. Like Scarlet, he'd been a prisoner of Tartarus and one of the lucky few chosen to host the "extra."

Back and forth Cronus paced in front of him, the power he emitted intensifying, crackling the air. "After what happened to your cohort Aeron, I had amulets made. One for each of you. When worn, they will prevent her from watching you."

Truth. And wasn't that just a little bit of awesome? "Don't give me." Now, now, now.

The pacing continued without pause. "Only problem is, they will prevent *all* gods from watching you."

Meaning himself. Bastard had to have his fingers in everything. "Here's an unworthy news flash. The cons far outweigh the pros. So, don't give me," he repeated, holding out his hand and waving his fingers.

A portion of his impatience stemmed from a desire to be hidden from the Powers That Be. Finally. But mostly, he just wanted to return to Scarlet. He didn't like being away from her, he realized.

Still the pacing continued, even gaining speed. "Wait just a minute. *If* I do this, I'll need daily reports. And if a single day passes without someone telling me what's going on down there, I will personally raid your fortress and remove the amulets from around your necks. After I remove your heads."

Gideon didn't point out that taking their heads would free their demons, possibly sending the crazed fiends on a ferocious rampage, something even Cronus would be cursed for doing. Which was why the king had let the warriors live when he'd first assumed control of the heavens. Even though he'd desperately wanted to destroy them.

And it was weird, thinking of the king of kings as being curseable. But, yes, it could be done. Apparently, Cronus wasn't the most powerful god in town. That honor belonged to the mysterious being who had saved Aeron's life. The being that had long ago defeated even death. The "One True Deity," Olivia called him.

Although, there was a chance Cronus wouldn't be punished for freeing the demons from their hosts, for they now knew a new pairing could be made. That's what had happened to his friend Baden's demon, Distrust. A new pairing.

Baden was dead, and Distrust now resided inside a Hunter female. A female Gideon wasn't sure he'd be able to kill, even if she had a dagger pressed to his throat.

Not that he minded killing women. He'd done it before. Under Sabin's leadership, it was kind of mandatory to treat females as equals. In all things, even war. What bothered him was that a part of Baden swam inside that woman's body.

How could he play a role in his good friend's *second* defeat?

"Lies! Are you listening to me? I asked if you understood."

Wait. What? Gideon pulled himself from the dark mire of his thoughts. "Please don't repeat yourself."

Red suffused the god's cheeks, and the color wasn't from embarrassment. No, it was fury that decorated his expression. "I will not repeat myself. You will either give me the daily reports I demanded, or you will not receive those amulets. Do you—" black eyes blazed "—understand?"

The reports, the amulets. Of course. Was the temper tantrum really necessary?

"No, I don't understand."

Finally Cronus stilled, nostrils flaring as he tempered his breathing. His golden gaze locked on Gideon. Gold again, he realized. Why the continual change?

"Very well." Cronus held out his hand, empty palm up. Azure lights sparked, pinpricks that dotted the endless expanse of white, before something began to crystallize against his skin. Two somethings, actually.

Gideon leaned forward for a closer look. He saw two silver chains, both with a butterfly dangling from the center. Studded throughout those jagged wings were small rubies, sapphires, a piece of onyx, ivory and even an opal. Each jewel or stone seemed alive, swirling with an inner fire he usually saw only in his dreams.

Pretty, but… "I'm gonna look *so* manly." The words were out before he could stop them.

A growl escaped the king, far more menacing than any that had come before. "Is that a complaint, Lies? Because I can—"

"Yes, yes. No apologies. I don't want them." He snatched the necklaces before they could be taken away and anchored one around his neck. The metal was hot—hot enough to blister his skin—but he didn't remove it. The other he stuffed into his pocket. Somehow, he would trick Scarlet into wearing it. "What about my enemies?" *My friends.*

"I'll visit the fortress and hand them out."

Truth. How accommodating the usually morose god was being. There had to be a reason, one that didn't bode well for Gideon. Still. He'd take what he could get. "No, thanks," he said again.

"If that's all—"

"Don't wait." The king had given him an opening, intentionally or not, and he jumped on it. "Scarlet didn't tell me that we were wed and I wasn't wondering if—"

"Scarlet?" The gold once again disappeared from his eyes, the obsidian like a living entity. "Rhea's daughter?"

Gideon blinked. She was *Rhea's* daughter? She was a fucking royal *princess?* Did that mean… "Are you not her father?" he croaked out. That might explain their matching black gazes.

"No!" So much disgust poured from that single word, Gideon could have drowned in it. "Never speak such a blasphemy again or I will unleash a torrent of suffering the likes of which you've never known."

Why the disgust? Why the warning? She was a beautiful, intelligent, brave female, damn it, and the bastard should be proud to call her daughter. Gideon's hands fisted, even as he told himself he wasn't angry. He was relieved that Cronus wasn't his father-in-law. *Possible* father-in-law, he hastily added.

Sabin's wife was Galen's daughter, and Gideon had seen the problems that little family connection had caused. No, thanks.

"Her father was mortal, and her mother is a whore," Cronus continued, the disgust far from waning. "*That's* who's in your vehicle? Seems I haven't been paying enough attention to you lately, Lies. I knew you had the girl in your dungeon, but had not realized you had taken her out. *Without* my permission. I should punish you."

Again, truth. *Careful.*

She's not mine, his demon suddenly piped up. A warning to the king. One Cronus couldn't hear, thankfully.

Not now. Don't push. "No apologies, Great One." That he wasn't bombarded with pain for the "great one" comment shocked him. Cronus had to know he meant the words as an insult. "As I wasn't saying, she didn't tell me that we're wed. Something I remember. I didn't want to trick her into thinking I was softening toward her so that she would tell me more. And I didn't plan to return her to the dungeon once I had those answers."

"Wed? You and Scarlet?" Cronus frowned, head tilting to the side as he pondered. "Everyone knew she was interested in you the first moment she saw you, but there was no hint that the two of you were seeing each other. Much less willing to wed each other."

She'd *always* been interested in him? Suddenly he wanted to puff out his chest and bang on it like a damned gorilla. She liked the look of him, and always had. Despite her purported adoration of blonds. *Thank the gods.*

Surely he could sneak past her rage and ignite that interest again. Somehow, some way. "Do you know of anyone who didn't have the power to erase thoughts of her from my mind?"

A pause, almost oppressive in its intensity. Cronus licked his lips, suddenly uneasy. Then uttered a hesitant, "No."

Gideon's demon purred. A lie. Cronus had just told a lie. He did know someone who possessed that kind of power. Who? "Why—"

"No more questions." The command was snapped, his tone aggravated now. "Just…be careful with her. She's feral. Otherwise, I would have taken over her care myself."

You will not touch her, he wanted to scream, even as his demon gave another purr. Another lie. What had the king lied about this time, though? That she was feral, or that he would have taken over her "care"? Or both?

Didn't matter if she was feral. She was Gideon's wife, for gods' sake. Maybe. But either way, he *was* going to bed her. If that didn't return his memory of her, nothing would. At least, that made sense to *him.* And what if, afterward, she was willing to help him and his friends in their ongoing war with the Hunters?

Yes, of course. If she would help, he wouldn't have to return her to the dungeon, even though he'd told Cronus he would. The king wanted to win the war, didn't he? Scarlet could destroy the enemy while they slept, eradicating the need for bombings, stabbings and gunfights.

That would be total win-win. No downside. Well, except for one, but it was minor, so it hardly bore mentioning. *Thought you never lied to yourself.* Gideon bit his tongue until he tasted copper. Fine. The downside was huge. Devastating. He would never be able to trust Scarlet because his demon couldn't read her. And after what he'd done to her, she would never want to help him.

Therefore, she had to return to the dungeon no matter how much she softened toward him.

"I grow tired of your wandering mind," Cronus said on a sigh.

So did Gideon. The results sucked. "Don't have one last thing." Hopefully the god realized he had something else to discuss after this. "In prison, did anyone not... hurt her?" The last was croaked from him.

Something hard shuttered over the king's eyes, not just erasing their color but shutting down his expression and blocking all hint of his emotions. "We're done here. You have things to do. I have things to do. So..."

Clearly, he wouldn't discuss Scarlet anymore. Damn him. Though everything inside Gideon screeched in protest—including Lies—he quickly switched the subject before he was sent away. "There wasn't something else I needed to know. Olivia didn't mention that you have Sienna." Sienna was Paris's woman. A woman who had died in the man's arms. A woman he still craved, apparently.

Gideon felt like he was always the last one to know these things. Paris certainly hadn't told him. But Olivia loved sharing the details of her life, as well as the details of everyone else's, and Gideon adored spending time with her. She had mentioned that Cronus had taken

Sienna's spirit, kept the girl near him, and then, when Wrath was split from Aeron's body, the god had placed the demon inside the girl.

The pain she must be in right now...the utter mental agony. That demon was probably urging her to do all kinds of despicable things. Things she would do; she wouldn't be able to help herself. Things that would haunt her for the rest of eternity.

"I have her," Cronus admitted reluctantly.

Truth. Lies hissed.

Tread carefully, he reminded himself. "May I not look upon her?" And report to Paris.

"No." No hesitation. "You may not. And now, we truly are done. I have shown too much leniency already, and look what it's gotten me." Cronus waved his hand through the air, and the next thing Gideon knew, he was back at the wheel of the Escalade, Scarlet cuffed to his wrist.

The change was so jarring, he accidentally jerked the wheel. The car swerved to one side, tires squealing. Another car was approaching from the other lane, headlights bright. Another quick swerve, and the car missed his. Barely.

Scarlet gasped. "What the hell are you doing? Our conversation wouldn't be over just because I went flying through the windshield, you know."

His demon gave a contented sigh. *Not mine.*

Gideon evened out, but didn't mention what had just happened in the heavens. As much as she disliked Cronus—why?—he couldn't be sure of her reaction. However, every woman liked receiving gifts, and now seemed the perfect time for a distraction.

Don't mess this up. "So, uh, I would hate if you reached into my pocket."

There was a suspended beat of silence. Then a dry, "I don't think so."

"I don't have a present for you."

Interest lit her dark eyes, but she remained still. Even suspicious. "The present wouldn't happen to be a hard cock, would it? Because if it is, I would have to return it. Minus a few inches."

His lips twitched as he fought his amusement. And yes, his cock hardened. He only had to be near her for an erection to happen. Or hell, think of her. He liked her dirty sense of humor. "Yes, it is, but you won't find that, too."

Now *her* lips twitched. That had happened before, yet he'd never seen her smile.

Truly smile. And he wanted to, desperately. She would glow. He knew she would, could see her beautiful, smiling face inside his mind, lush red lips curved at the corners, teeth straight and white. Her eyelids would dip a little, but the wicked glint in her irises still would be visible.

He sucked in a breath. Was that a memory? A memory of her smiling over at him? Happy with him? Well-loved?

"Fine," she grumbled, but she couldn't hide the trembling in her hand as she reached into his pocket, careful to avoid the very thick length of him. Another gasp left her as her fingers clasped the too-hot metal. She even jerked.

Gideon had to press his mouth into a tight line to cut off his moan of pleasure. Her touch… She was so close to Mini Me, she had only to angle her wrist to reach it. And he wanted her to reach it as desperately as he'd wanted to see her smile. But all too soon, and without angling her wrist, she removed her hand and studied the amulet.

"What is it?" Was that disappointment in her tone?

"Not a match to mine, that's for sure."

Her gaze moved to him as he flicked his own amulet out from under his shirt.

"Oh." The disappointment, if that's what it had been, disappeared. "Wh–why do you want us to have matching necklaces?"

Now he couldn't tell if she was happy, upset or wistful. Or maybe she was simply a combination of all three. Like, the gift made her happy because it meant he'd been thinking of her. Like, the gift upset her because he was giving it to her now, when he didn't remember her. Like, the gift made her wistful because he seemed hopeful of a future together.

"Well?" she prompted gruffly.

He forced a shrug, because he couldn't answer. Not without hurting his cause. To admit—in his way—that he hadn't bought it for her would hurt her. To admit that it wasn't a symbol of what they'd once shared and could maybe share again, would, what? Hurt her.

"When did you get it?"

Again, he shrugged.

Angrily, she hooked the necklace around her neck and he wanted to shout with relief. There. Done, it was done. She was protected from prying eyes, and he hadn't had to force the issue. The night suddenly seemed brighter.

"You look stupid wearing yours, by the way. In fact, you look like a girl."

Or not. The words confirmed his earlier fears, but deep down he knew that she was merely lashing out, again, because she didn't understand him. How like her.

You know her so well, do you? He didn't have an answer for himself, either.

"So where are we going?" she grumbled.

Yet another shrug. He honestly didn't know. He had three and a half days—no, nights—left to woo and win her. To learn about her and his past. So, someplace romantic would be best. But where?

Clearly, he *didn't* know her, because he had no idea what she would find romantic. A secluded cabin? A fancy hotel? He sighed. "Don't tell me about someplace you've always wanted to go but haven't—"

"Oh, you want to talk now?" she said, cutting him off. "I don't think so." Eyes narrowed, she turned on the radio and cranked up the music, a hard, pounding rock, before settling back in her seat and facing the window.

Message received. He could suck it. And not the good way.

CHAPTER FIVE

HOURS PASSED in silence. Well, not silence. The radio continued to blast Scarlet's favorite heart-pounding rock. Gods, she missed her iPod. With the buds in her ears, she could have closed her eyes and pretended she was at home. Not that she had a permanent home, but anyplace was better than such close quarters with the man she'd both loved and hated for centuries. A man she still craved with such intense longing she couldn't deny it anymore.

Almost didn't want to deny it. But she would. No way would she give him another chance to shatter her so completely. To pleasure her and forget her.

Shamefully, she *had* almost caved, though.

He'd given her a gift. The most beautiful butterfly necklace she'd ever seen, and one that matched his own. When she'd first reached into his pocket, she'd been disappointed that he *hadn't* really wanted her to fist his cock. Then she'd seen the necklace, and well, she'd wanted to leap into his lap and kiss every inch of his beautiful face. She'd wanted to lick each of his piercings and thrust her tongue against his. Wanted to feel his arms wrap around her and hold her tight. As if she meant something to him again. Wanted to hear him gasp his version of her name.

But he'd seemed almost…uncomfortable about the

whole thing. Guilty, even. Why? Only reason she could think of was that he hadn't wanted her to read too much into the gesture. Hadn't wanted her to leap into his lap and kiss every inch of his beautiful face.

That seemed likely. Especially since the bastard hadn't tried to turn down the music and talk to her again. Maybe he was even *relieved* that she'd closed their channels of communication. Which was dumb. He'd sprung her from prison to talk to her, hadn't he? He should try harder. Not that she'd cooperate. The moment she did, he'd try to take her back to the dungeon and she'd have to ditch him as planned.

Actually, she'd do that tomorrow. His friends would probably be pissed that he'd lost her, but that wasn't her problem. He'd also have to make it back to a city littered with Hunters without her aid, but again, that wasn't her problem.

She had enough problems to deal with.

One of which was fast approaching.

Gideon was still driving when the sun began to rise. She stiffened in her seat, dreading what came next but helpless to stop it. First, lethargy beat through her, draining her strength, making her limbs feel heavy and her head loll. Then her eyelids closed of their own accord, her lashes seemingly glued together. Then darkness wove through her mind, an incessant spiderweb—spiders, Gideon hated spiders, funny that she thought of them now—followed quickly by dissonant screams that overshadowed all else.

Her demon took over from there.

Laughing gleefully, Nightmares propelled her into a dark, misty realm where human and inhuman minds were like doorways. When a door was open, that meant the person was asleep and the demon could enter at will. Location didn't matter. Distance didn't matter. Time zone didn't matter. Adults, children, male, female, that didn't matter, either. Nothing mattered to the demon but feeding on terror.

With only a glance, she and the demon would know who each doorway belonged to, what kind of person they were and what they feared most. Like with Gideon and his silly fear of spiders, she thought, smiling again. He was a big, bad warrior who had killed thousands of people without a jump in his heart rate. But he almost peed his pants when an insect scampered toward him.

She supposed she couldn't blame him. She *hated* the creepy little bugs. They'd constantly invaded her cell in Tartarus, crawling from every shadow and wall crack. And every time she'd awoken from her impenetrable sleep, she would find herself covered with bite marks.

Not to mention the bruises her cellmates had left behind. Until she'd started invading *their* dreams.

Whatever she'd done to them in this dark realm, real life had parroted, and they'd awoken in puddles of their own blood, often missing limbs. Some had never awakened at all.

Who do we want? the demon asked her. The most frequently asked question between them.

Over the years, they'd learned to work together. They even liked each other, relied on each other. At times, the demon had been her only friend.

"A Hunter would be nice," she replied. Maybe they could scare the guy to death. That always put Nightmares in a stellar mood. Besides, she owed the Hunters. Not because she cared that they wanted to hurt

Gideon, but because they'd ruined a perfectly good meal for her.

This will be fun. More gleeful laughter as the demon whisked them forward, the doorways blurring at her side.

When they stopped, they stood in front of an open doorway that was far larger than any she'd seen before. Moans of pleasure echoed from inside, a decadent mix of male and female. There was a slap of flesh against flesh. Murmurs of "more" and "please."

An erotic dream, then.

"Who is this?"

Galen. Leader of Hunters. Keeper of Hope.

Galen. She scowled. The warrior had led his army against the Lords because they were demon-possessed, and yet Galen himself carried a demon. The contradiction was baffling, but it didn't surprise her.

Galen had always struck her as more snake than man. A few times, he'd helped Gideon bring a prisoner into Tartarus, and he'd been all smiles while Gideon faced him, but the moment Gideon had turned away, Galen's glower had bored into his back.

When Gideon had told her that he'd found a way to curry the gods' favor thanks to his pal Galen, and that for his reward, he would request her freedom, she had begged him not to do it, whatever he planned. Of course, he hadn't listened. He'd been too assured, too hopeful, of his success.

She'd wanted to "thank" Galen for his part in Gideon's failure for a long, long time, but hadn't allowed herself to do so. That would have helped Gideon, and she hadn't wanted to do that, either.

Now, however, with that necklace burning against her chest, she no longer minded the prospect quite so much.

Ready?

Slowly she grinned. "Let's do this."

They stepped through the entrance, a phantom unseen by the dreamer, and suddenly Scarlet was viewing the evidence of what she'd heard. Galen was tall and muscled, with blond hair and blue eyes. Eyes that were peering down at a beautiful, pale-haired female. A female he had anchored against a bathroom sink, his majestic white wings outstretched, enclosing her in a feathered haven.

The woman's shirt was pushed to her chin, bearing her large—really large—breasts. He feasted on them eagerly. Her pants were around her ankles as Galen pounded inside her, hips shifting to produce maximum pleasure.

His pants were merely opened at the waist, so Scarlet saw very little of him. Too bad. She could have taunted Gideon with the size of his enemy's cock and the hardness of his ass.

So many fears, Nightmares said with awe.

"Tell me." She spoke aloud, knowing dream Galen couldn't hear her unless she wanted him to.

Being alone. Being defeated. Helpless. Ineffective. Overlooked. Forgotten. Dead.

Weird. He carried the demon of Hope. Shouldn't he be more optimistic? No matter. Scarlet walked through the dream bathroom, Galen as oblivious to her presence as he was to her voice, and allowed Nightmares to repaint the scene.

"Make him sorry he was ever created."

My pleasure.

Suddenly, the writhing, moaning girl became a man. A human.

Galen stopped pounding. Even yelped and jumped away, wings shuddering with the movement.

Scarlet laughed. Oh, this was going to be fun. "More."

The bathroom was replaced by a long, dark tunnel, and the human disappeared. Galen spun, wild gaze searching his new surroundings, the tips of those wings grazing the walls and scratching.

"What's going on?" he rasped. "Where am I?"

His words echoed, but that was it, the only sound. Desperate for answers, he kicked into gear, racing forward. The tunnel stretched forever, no end in sight. His panic doubled, tripled, hot breath rasping from him and sweat pouring from his body.

Delicious. Nightmares laughed. *Tastes so good.*

"More," she said again.

Do you want the honors?

Sharing was caring, she thought. "Yes. Please."

Lead him to the edge, and I'll show him what might one day happen to him. Oh, his fear...none of the others will compare.

Scarlet allowed herself to materialize, though she didn't show the formidable warrior what she truly looked like. The image she projected was one of a little girl she'd met inside Tartarus. For the single day the child had been allowed inside a cell. A little girl named Fate.

Everyone had been frightened of her, because everything Fate had spoken had come true. *Everything.* That's why the Greeks had so quickly put her to death, the poor thing.

But for that one day, she had been Scarlet's friend.

"If you believe what you see, you'll lose your husband," Fate had told her during their only conversation.

Of course Scarlet had believed what she'd seen— Gideon's absence—so of course Scarlet had lost him.

Many, many years had passed. Perhaps Galen would recognize Fate, perhaps not.

Either way...*let the games begin.*

As Fate, Scarlet wore a robe streaked with dirt, had big blue eyes, so innocent, and a mouth forever dipped in sadness. Red hair hung in tangles all the way to her ankles.

She appeared a few feet in front of him. "Come," she said gently, and held out her small, mud-caked hand. "You must see what awaits you."

He tripped over his own feet but stopped before he hit her, still panting, still sweating. "Who are you?"

As forgetful as Gideon, then. But sometimes ignorance served her best. What people imagined was often far worse than anything she could tell them.

"Come," she repeated. "You must see."

"I— Yes. All right." Galen shakily placed his palm against hers.

Down the corridor she ushered him, Nightmares practically jumping around in her head. Finally, because she willed it, a light appeared, and the significance of that light was not lost on him. Once again, his fear spiked.

He even tried to pull away from her, but she tightened her grip, stronger than she appeared. "You must see," she told him. "You must know."

They reached the light, which just happened to be a cliff ledge that overlooked a battlefield. On that battlefield was man after man, woman after woman, an ocean of death and destruction, for each body was bloody, motionless. And on each of their wrists was a tattoo of infinity. The mark of the Hunter.

There, in the center, was Galen. He was still standing, though he, too, was bloody and wounded. His white-feathered wings were outstretched but clearly broken. His strength was drained, his knocking knees threatening to give out.

"No. No!" Beside her, a shaking dream Galen *did* drop to his knees, dust pluming around him.

On the battlefield, Gideon strode toward him, as menacing as ever. His blue hair danced around his face in the strong wind, and his piercings gleamed in the sunlight. There was a trickle of blood at the corner of his mouth where his lip ring had been ripped out. In one hand, he gripped a long, sharp sword. In the other, he clutched a gun.

Laughing, he pointed the latter at Galen and fired. The leader of the Hunters flew backward, landing on his ass, unable to rise as Gideon continued to bear down on him.

"No!" the Galen beside her shouted again. "Stand up. Fight him! I didn't survive that demon girl's poisonous bite only to die at the hands of my enemy."

He didn't, allowing Gideon to raise his sword and strike. Galen's head detached, leaving his body behind.

"No! *No!*" Sky-blue eyes found her, a well of despair. His face was pale, the blue veins underneath his skin arrestingly evident. "Tell me I can change this. Tell me this isn't my fate."

"You wish me to lie?" she said in that sweet little-girl voice.

His hands fisted at his sides, useless weapons against what awaited him. "Why did you show me this, then? Why?"

"Because—"

Scarlet came awake with a jolt, sitting up, panting as Galen had done in the dream realm. Damn it. She hadn't finished with him, but her time there had ended. And there would be no going back for twelve hours.

At least Nightmares was satisfied. The demon had fed on Galen's terror, terror so much more intense than what humans experienced, and now retreated to the back of her mind.

"Not good. You're asleep."

Gideon.

His voice floated over her, into her, burning her up. With anger, with lust. Goodbye fun dream world, hello hated reality.

"Where are we?" she demanded, studying her new surroundings. She'd fallen asleep in his presence— again—and he'd clearly taken full advantage of the situation.

"Someplace shitty."

Rather than a hotel room, she found herself in a forest, the sun setting in a violet sky. She rested atop a cool bed of moss, and there was a natural, bubbling spring beside her. She still wore the dress he'd given her, but at least he'd removed the cuffs.

Before she'd jacked up the music in the car, he'd tried to ask her what she found most romantic. She hadn't replied, so he'd obviously taken a guess. And to her consternation, the bastard had guessed correctly. This was amazing. Night birds were chirping, the scent of wildflowers saturated the air and Gideon was gloriously bathed in that violet-tinted light.

Right now, he was sitting in front of her, only a few inches away, leaning against a tree trunk. A lock of hair had fallen onto his forehead, and just as before, she had to curb the urge to brush the strands back in place. His baby blues were all over her, perusing, lingering, savoring. Trying to remember?

His hands were fisted on his lap. Was he trying to stop himself from reaching for her?

Gods help her, but she knew exactly what this man could do to her body. With his hands, his tongue. He could have her writhing, begging, in seconds.

Fight his appeal. "You might as well let me go." *Or you yourself could, I don't know, finally ditch him.* "You're not going to find any pleasure with me."

"I'm sure you're right."

Sweet heaven. He truly thought to bed her. Was utterly confident in her capitulation. Why, oh, why was that so damn sexy?

She narrowed her eyes, lest he see the desire surely banked there. "You sprang me for answers, so why are you trying so hard to soften me romantically? You'd have better luck working me over with your fists." Good. She'd sounded angry rather than breathless.

"Didn't think about that already."

He'd thought about hitting her? That—that—

"And I could absolutely bring myself to do it."

Sweetheart.

Gods, she really was an idiot, melting like butter because he'd decided not to beat her up. Next she'd be hearing angels sing because he decided not to fork her

jugular. "No matter what you do, you're going to fail."
Fingers crossed that wasn't a bluff.

"Even if all I want us to do is relearn each other?"

Yes. No. Argh.

Hey. No more softening. "Nothing wrong with *forgetting* each other, either."

He was grinding his teeth as he moved his legs, trapping her knees with his ankles and placing her feet dangerously close to his—hard, *growing*—penis. Tragically—er, thankfully—his pants prevented her from experiencing skin-to-skin contact. Therefore she despised—loved, damn it—those low-slung jeans.

"So who aren't you today?" he asked, wisely changing the subject.

Hurt him. Make him stop this slow seduction. "Scarlet...Reynolds." She shivered as if the thought delighted her. "Yes. I'm in the mood for a little Rye-Rye today."

Gideon popped his jaw, teeth bared for a second. "Are we not married?"

"Sure we are," she said. "But in my mind I'm cheating on you with Ryan."

Now the pink tip of his tongue peeked out from his lip, as if he meant to chew it off. "You're so freaking funny."

"Who said I was joking?"

Before she could blink, he was on her, pushing her into the moss, his chest pressed against hers, his weight pinning her. "You do *not* annoy the shit out of me."

A tremor skipped down her spine, her nipples straining against her dress, trying to reach him. She could have knocked him off; she was strong enough, skilled enough, but she didn't. She fisted the collar of his shirt, holding him in place. Craving… "Well, if you hadn't guessed, you *do* annoy the shit out of me."

In and out he breathed, nostrils flaring. "Keep talking, I don't dare you."

Shut up, he meant. "Or what?" He smelled so damn good, like musk and alluring spice. Warmth radiated from him and enveloped her, slinking around her in a sly embrace.

"Or…" His gaze dropped to her lips. The anger seemed to drain from him, something hotter, sultrier taking its place. Those rasping pants never slowed, and in between them, he said, "You're so unbelievably… ugly." The last was offered hesitantly, as if he feared she wouldn't understand what he was trying to tell her. "You don't make me ache. You don't make me hunger for so many things. Dirty things. Wicked things."

Kiss him.

No, don't you dare.

A war raged between body and mind. If she kissed him, she wouldn't be able to halt what was sure to follow. Once his lips met hers, she would be lost. His taste drugged her, his body addicted her. That's the way it had always been with him.

And now, she would want but she couldn't have. Not truly. But for one blissful night, she would belong to him again. *Any* price was worth that. Added bonus: she could forget her troubles, forget the lonely future that awaited her.

Forget. Wrong word. She stiffened, no longer having to talk herself into resisting. "Get off me."

"I want to hurt you," he whispered, heated breath dragging over her skin. "Tell me to stop."

Meaning, he wanted to pleasure her and all she had

to do was give him the go-ahead. She shook her head in a desperate attempt to prevent what she still wanted, needed, but could never afford. "No. I won't."

Wait. No, she wouldn't tell him to stop? Argh!

Slowly he smiled—*so wicked*—as if that's exactly what he'd hoped she would say, no matter her meaning. "Too bad," he said. And then he fed a sizzling kiss straight into her mouth.

CHAPTER SIX

SWEET GODS ABOVE, Gideon thought, dazed. This woman—his woman—tasted like perfectly ripe berries, felt like caged lightning against him, and the sounds she made as his tongue rolled and thrust against hers, those little catches of breath, were like heroin mixed with ambrosia. Addictive, mind-fuzzing, overwhelming.

He had her pressed into the ground, his legs between hers, his erection resting against the apex of her thighs. He wanted to knead her breasts. Gods, did he want to knead her breasts. But that would be too much too fast. For her, at least. So he did the only other thing he could. He captured her wrists and pinned them over her head, effectively pinning his own movements, as well.

Mistake. That, of course, arched her lower back and closed all hint of distance between their chests, muscle to soft, luscious breasts. Her nipples were hard, so wonderfully hard, and they created the most delicious friction against his chest, catapulting him to a new level of awareness.

A dangerous level where her enjoyment and happiness were more important than his own.

He didn't release her, though. It was too late for that. He had to have more. So if he couldn't roll those nipples between his fingers, if he couldn't tongue them, he'd have to settle for continuing to rub himself against them.

As an added bonus, every little movement rammed his shaft into her core, causing them both to shiver and groan.

Kissing usually did nothing for him. Maybe because he could never ask for what he wanted; he had to lie and demand the opposite. He had to ask for sweet, innocent. He had to ask for gentle, tender. Yet, with Scarlet, he didn't have to ask for anything. She simply gave him hard and wet. Deep and intense. She bit at him, sucked on his tongue, scraped at his teeth. And he couldn't get enough.

He kissed her forever. He kissed her while the insects sang and the moon fought for its place in the sky. He kissed her until he lost his breath. Kissed her until she was writhing against him, her legs wrapped around him, squeezing him, her teeth nipping at him as she silently begged for more.

And yet, through it all, she seemed distanced. As if she weren't truly there with him. As if she held a part of herself back.

Hell. No.

Distance, he wouldn't tolerate. He might not want to push her too far, but by the time this kiss ended, she would think of no other man but him. She would be happy she was wed to him. She would dream of him, crave him more than any other.

Was this what it had been like between them, all those centuries ago? Consuming need dipped in fervent heat then twined with unquenchable aches?

He released one of her hands, and she immediately tunneled her fingers through his hair, nails digging into his scalp. Enough to make him bleed. Yes, yes. More. Maybe he could push her a *little* further. But to do so, he'd have to sacrifice the kiss. With their mouths pressed together like this, he couldn't think properly.

Moaning, Gideon wrenched himself away from her lips. She had her eyes sealed shut, as if she were in pain. Those lips were swollen and red, moist. Unable to help himself, he licked that moisture away before hiking her dress up to her neck, baring her panties, her stomach and lastly her breasts. He hadn't given her a bra. Too much had he liked the idea of her sitting next to him, a thin piece of cotton all that rested between his skin and her nipples.

Her breasts were perfectly sized, a little less than a handful, and those nipples were as red as her lips. His mouth watered as he lowered his head. And dear gods, sucking one of those little berries into his mouth was a religious experience. The moment his tongue made contact, his entire body felt as though it went up in flames from the inside out. His blood turned his organs to ash. His ashed organs liquefied his bones, and those liquid bones scorched his skin, leaving blisters.

She must have experienced the same melting sensation, because a scream of pleasure exploded from her. An honest-to-gods, I'm-losing-my-mind scream of pleasure. He loved it, reveled in it. Except a thousand other screams followed hers. And those weren't forged by pleasure. Those reeked of fear and pain.

"Gideon," she rasped.

Once again, he raised his head. Her eyes were still sealed shut, only now her mouth was pulled tight in an agonized line. Thick black shadows were seeping from her ears, her mouth, and swirling around her head.

Her demon, he realized.

Since Gideon had gained control of his body and

his actions all those centuries ago, Lies had been like a ghostly companion. There, but hardly noticeable. Well, until recently. Before Scarlet, the demon had rarely spoken to him outright or asserted its presence physically. Rather, his demon had mostly led him through compulsions.

This wasn't a compulsion for her. This was an all-out manifestation. And he had no fucking clue what to do.

"How can I make this worse, devil?" He tried to pull away from her, to ease her in any way he could, even if that meant no longer making out with her. But her eyelids at last popped open, her irises glowing bright red, and she grabbed his shirt, jerking him back.

"What the hell do you think you're doing?" The words were a harsh growl, and all those discordant screams layered the undertone, a tide of malevolence. "Hear us well. If you dare stop, we will punish you."

Us. We. Her demon was *that* involved? That much a part of her? O-kay. Not his first three-way, but certainly his strangest. There was no time to marvel, however.

Scarlet dragged a finger down the center of his shirt, ripping the cotton, exposing his chest. She flattened her palm against his pierced nipple and licked her lips. "More," she moaned, arching into him.

Her cleft brushed his shaft, and the rest of the blood left his brain. The moist tip of his cock even pushed past the waist of his pants. The fact that the shadows were still drifting from her, the fact that those screams were still echoing between them, failed to faze him. His desire for her was simply too great. He, too, had to have more.

Not sex, he told himself. Not yet. He still thought it would be pushing her too hard and too fast. And he wouldn't have her crying foul later, claiming he'd taken advantage of her and using that as an excuse to distance herself further.

"You're just sitting there. Hurry!"

Complaints about his performance already when she was clearly passion-drunk. He'd like to say that was a first, but couldn't. Many women had complained about his *get in as fast as you can, get and give an orgasm and leave* mentality.

"Gideon! Obey."

"Sure, sure. Don't show me what you want first." He didn't leap into action, of course, but watched as Scarlet began kneading her own breasts, exactly as he'd yearned to do. Strands of her silky black hair fell down her shoulders and curled around her fingers, as if tickling her.

Her eyelids closed to half-mast, and her teeth chewed at her bottom lip as she reached down with one hand, past her pretty blue panties and into the wet heat of her. Gods, she was sexy. Her stomach hollowed into the most sensual navel he'd ever seen, and her thighs stretched into the hottest legs.

"That good enough for you? I showed you, damn it, now keep up your end of the bargain."

Finally, he moved. He reached out and fisted her dress, lifting the material the rest of the way over her head and then tossing it aside. "Press your knees closer together," he croaked out.

At first, she obeyed and closed her legs to him. When he applied pressure to her knees, urging them farther apart, she realized what she'd done and dropped them open. Spreading herself, eager for him. Her hips arched forward, back, beseeching him to do something, anything.

For a moment, he luxuriated in the image of her. He'd seen her like this before. He knew it, to his very soul he knew it. For this image didn't seem new, but somehow a part of him. Deep inside, hidden but there. Yet, when he tugged those panties aside, pushed her fingers from the place *he* wanted to be and lowered his head, when he traced his tongue up the slick heat of her, the taste of her *was* new. He had absolutely no memory of it.

And what a shame. Nothing had ever tasted as sweet, as heady. She filled his mouth, invaded each of his senses, branded his every cell.

"Gideon. Please. Please, please, please." Scarlet. *"More. Now!"* Her demon. Funny that he could tell the difference between them already.

But he needed no more urging. He lay on his belly, his face right between her legs, and did everything his fevered brain had been imagining since he'd discovered her in his dungeon. He licked, he sucked, he nibbled, he tongued her in the sweetest possible way, sinking deep, savoring every drop of her.

When that wasn't enough, his fingers joined the play. First one, then two. Three stretched her, and he was afraid he was hurting her, so he took his time, letting her become used to him. And when she did, she rode those fingers with complete abandon, arching into him, tugging on his hair, clawing at his scalp. Again, he loved it. Couldn't get enough. Wanted it to last forever.

Wanted to do more. Do everything. Things he'd only ever dreamed of doing to others but hadn't been able to do because of his demon. Wicked things, things most women would probably shy away from. Hell, things most men would probably shy away from. But he was a warrior who had seen and done things most people couldn't comprehend. He'd lived for a long, long time and normal had grown yawn-inducing.

Perhaps Scarlet would have let him do everything he wished. Perhaps she even would have enjoyed it. She'd lived a long time, too. But with her past, having spent so many centuries as a slave, she might have hated it. Either way, now wasn't the time, he reminded himself.

This was about getting each other off while reassuring her that he wouldn't do more until she was ready. Mentally as well as physically. That she could trust him. With her body. Her secrets.

A lie? Suddenly, he didn't know anymore.

"Gideon, Gideon. Yes, like that. Don't stop. What you're doing…gods, I love it."

More decadent words had never been spoken. She was getting close, her body tensing, readying for completion.

Not without me, he thought. Though he wanted her hand wrapped around his cock, stroking him, maybe even cupping and pulling at his testicles, he fisted himself. As he began licking her once again, he worked his shaft up and down, his grip strong, the glide sure and wet from *her.* Gods, yes. That was good.

He sank his tongue deep, just as he had done with his fingers, and just like that, she erupted. Her inner walls clamped down on him, holding him captive. Her knees squeezed his temples, hard, and he thought his skull might crack. He didn't care. He'd done that to her; he'd given her that pleasure. He'd pushed her over the edge of control.

Pride and possessiveness poured through him as he tasted the sweetness of her orgasm. His strokes on his cock increased in speed, in intensity, and he shot up, over her, keeping himself from crushing her with one hand flattened beside her shoulder. Her eyes were still at half-mast, and she was panting. Sweat glistened on her brow, and there was a trickle of blood seeping from the corner of her swollen mouth. Her nipples were still hard, even though an air of absolute satisfaction radiated from her.

Mine, he thought, and then he, too, was hurtling over the edge, jetting hot seed onto her stomach. Perhaps he should have angled away from her, but he wouldn't have been able to turn away if a sword had been poised at his throat. His gaze was too busy drinking her in, and yeah, he liked the thought of his seed on her. Like a brand. It was only fair, after all. Her essence was inside him, swimming through him.

Now he collapsed on her, crushing her, unable to help himself, the last drop having emptied him out completely. He had no energy left. He couldn't quite catch his breath, and the only thing his mind wanted to do was to relive what had just happened. The sights, the sounds, the taste, the feel.

It was probably the same for her, her mind caught up in what had happened, her heart softening toward him. He could ask her anything now, and she'd tell him the truth; he was sure of it.

"Get off me, you big lug," Scarlet said, shoving him aside.

Wait. What?

Surprised by her vehemence, he rolled to his back, looking up at her as she stood. The shadows were no longer pulsing around her, and the screams of pain had died. She kept her back to him as she marched to the bubbling spring. It was too dark to see the nuances of her tattoos.

Next time, I'll kiss those tattoos. But oh, he could see the contours of her ass, and damn. Three words: *Per. Fec. Tion.* Firm, made for cupping. *Why didn't I cup her?*

He'd concentrated on her fun zone, and lost focus on everything else. *Next time,* he thought again.

Without a word, she entered the water and sank to her shoulders. That's when she finally faced him, though her gaze never quite touched him.

"You've got a, uh, slow recovery time," he told her. He sat up and scrubbed a hand through his tangled hair.

"Well, there wasn't much to recover from," she replied tartly.

His eyes widened in surprise, then narrowed in affront. The little brat had really gone there, not so subtly telling him the experience hadn't been good for her. She was lying. Of course. And he didn't need his demon to tell him that. (Which the bastard did not.) She'd enjoyed the hell out of herself. She'd writhed and screamed. She'd begged for more, damn it.

Scowling, he jumped to a stand—and pretended he'd tripped when his knees almost gave out. Apparently, *he* hadn't recovered. Motions stiff, jerky, he removed the tattered remains of his shirt and shoved his pants to his ankles.

Shit, he thought, seeing himself. His anger drained. He was still wearing his boots. What kind of lover wore his boots when tasting a woman for the first time?

He kicked those off, nearly falling on his face again, and stepped out of his jeans. He removed his weapons, too, all ten thousand of them, it seemed, strapped over every inch of him. Naked, unabashed, he strode to the spring and settled in beside her. Steam rose, the mist like glitter as it danced in the air. The hot water caressed his tired muscles.

"What are you doing? You weren't invited." Scarlet swam to the other side, putting as much distance between them as she could. Yet nothing could have separated their gazes. They were now locked together in a heated clash of wills. At least her eyes were black now, rather than red.

"I could have done a lot less to you, you know," he grumbled. "Where's my no thanks?"

"Your no thanks is right here." She flipped him off with absolute relish. "And yes, I know you could have done a lot more to me." Her hand fell back into the water, and her head tilted to the side, her study of him intensifying. "Why didn't you?" Soft, whispered.

A loaded question, and far worse than "Do I look fat in these pants?" There was no way to answer without damning himself. *You weren't ready* would be met with *How do you know what I'm ready for; you don't even know me.* Or the lie *I didn't want to do more,* which was what he'd have to give her, would be met with *Neither did I* or a thousand questions about whether or not he now remembered her.

Time to change the subject. "Why don't you stay there?" As he spoke, he crooked a finger at her.

Stubborn, she shook her head. But she said, "I will, thank you."

A muscle ticked below his eye. He wanted to hold her, damn it. Wanted to wrap his arms around her and snuggle her close. He wanted to, well, bask in her. Because that would thaw her out. Of course.

"You didn't know what I meant, Scar."

"Look," she said, strength weaving itself into her tone. Her butterfly necklace sparkled as a ray of amber moonlight fought its way past the canopy of leaves above them. "What happened, happened. We can't undo it, but we can take steps to ensure it doesn't happen again."

He could only gape at her. Why the hell would they want to do that?

"We just don't need to go down that road again," she continued, as if she were reading his mind. "It didn't end well the first time and it would only end worse the second."

"You can know that for sure." He straightened, meaning to close the distance himself and shake her. She was too determined, too sure of herself.

She kicked out a foot, flattening it against his chest, and stopped him. "Stay where you are." The red reappeared in her eyes, matching the glimmering ruby in her necklace.

So. The demon wasn't too far from the surface now, after all. But Nightmares had seemed to like him, and had certainly wanted him. Did that mean Scarlet was battling her body's—and her demon's—needs, even now?

Pensive, Gideon settled back against the rocks. But when Scarlet tried to remove her foot, he grabbed her by the ankle and held on.

"Let me go. Oh, gods. Don't let go. Don't you dare let go."

He'd pressed his thumb into her arch, massaging. If he couldn't shake her without a fight, he'd settle for disarming her. Her head fell back against the rocky wall behind her, and the harder he worked, the more she gasped.

"I'm not trying here," he told her. Damn, but he'd never tried so hard. "To remember, to make amends, to make something work."

While continuing to gasp in pleasure, she said, "You don't want me. Not really. You want answers."

He couldn't deny it. He did want answers. But with every second that passed, he wanted her more. "To part is to die," he said, and because it was a lie—though he almost wished it wasn't—he wasn't struck with pain and weakness.

"Stupid words that mean nothing."

He felt that way, yeah, a little bit, but her memories were intact. She shouldn't. He tried not to let his irritation and frustration show. "Give me nothing." Something. "Just a little nothing." Anything.

A long moment passed in silence. He continued to rub her foot, and she continued to enjoy, but she didn't speak. He thought she meant to ignore him. But then, finally, she sighed, so many emotions tangled in that heavy exhalation.

"Once, you were delivering a prisoner to Tartarus. An immortal who had tried to kill Zeus in order to claim the heavenly throne for himself. Before you could get him locked inside one of the cells, you noticed that I was fighting a goddess." Her brow furrowed. "I can't remember who it was, only that she was tall and blond."

That could be any one of thousands. "Please, don't go on."

"She was…winning." The furrow deepened, and

Scarlet frowned. "That doesn't feel right. I mean, in my mind I can see her holding me down and scratching me, but the image feels…wrong. I'm not making any sense." She waved a hand through the air, droplets of water dripping off and splashing. "Anyway, you noticed us and released the prisoner to rush to me. While you pulled the goddess off me and helped me to my feet, the new prisoner tried to escape. You ran after him, and all the gods and goddesses inside my cell tried to escape, as well. I held them back while you captured the male because I didn't want you to get into trouble."

Wow. She could have run herself, but she hadn't. For him, she'd stayed. The knowledge was…humbling. If she spoke true, that is. Why the fucking hell couldn't Lies tell with her? "And what didn't the gods and goddesses do in retaliation?" They wouldn't have let that kind of betrayal go. She'd stopped them from gaining their freedom; they would have punished her. Severely.

She shrugged, deceptively cavalier. "I told you one thing, as you asked. That's all you get."

Damn it. The story had only whetted his appetite for more. "Seems like you haven't endured a lot of pain to be with me. Why would you not do that?"

"None of your business." Once again, she didn't pretend to misunderstand what he was saying and his respect and admiration for her grew. Along with his frustration.

"Don't tell me, and I won't give you a boon. Anything you don't want." Without a doubt, she'd ask for liberation. He'd give it to her, because damn, he just couldn't lie to her anymore, and then he would catch her again. Lock her away as planned.

It was necessary, he reminded himself. She was dangerous, could destroy him and everyone he loved. He'd remind himself of those facts until the word *necessary* was simply a part of him, as vital as breathing.

Her interest perked. "A boon to be named later?"

"No."

She tugged her foot from his clasp and gave him the other one. He tried not to smile as he set to work, massaging this arch in turn. So quietly demanding. So adorable.

Necessary.

"All right, yes," she said. "I'll tell you." She licked her lips, averted her gaze and peered up at the heavens. "Just…give me a minute."

"A minute" turned out to be eleven. Not that he was counting every damn second.

The suspense was killing him, though he suspected what she was going to say. *I risked punishment because I loved you.* Part of him wanted to hear the words, even if that made him a sadist. The other part of him *really* wanted to hear the words. Even if that made him a masochist. She didn't feel that way now, and it wouldn't end well for her if she did. A thought that left him hollow and sick.

Fucking necessary.

"Are you sure you want to know?" she finally asked, hesitant yet hopeful. "The knowledge will change you, and not for the better."

Couldn't be "I love you," then. Her expression was so troubled, he'd never seen its like. Dread coursed through him and his fingers stopped moving. He sat up straighter, his gaze trying to burrow into her soul. "No. Don't tell me. Don't tell me *now*."

She gulped. "Gideon. We…you and I…we had…a son. We had a son, and his name was Steel."

CHAPTER SEVEN

AMUN, KEEPER of the demon of Secrets, lounged in a plastic lawn chair in the middle of the thriving green forest surrounding his home. He had a battery-operated mister in front of him and a cooler of ice-cold beer beside him. Alcohol didn't do much for immortals, but he liked the taste anyway.

Overhead, the sun was shining so brightly, a few thousand amber rays managed to seep through the thick treetop canopy and directly onto his skin. And yeah, he had a lot of exposed skin. He'd come out here clad in his swim trunks and a smile.

When he closed his eyes, it was easy to pretend he was on a beach. Alone. He did this as often as possible; it was his time away from people and the secrets they could never hide from him, no matter how hard they tried. Secrets his demon was always desperate to unearth, always prowling through their heads to find, listening to their thoughts. Thoughts Amun then heard himself.

That was hard enough, but bearable. If that had been his only ability, he thought he might have been able to live a normal life. But his demon could also *steal* those memories, each new voice joining the thousands of others already floating through his head, increasing in volume until finally blending with his own, so that he could no longer distinguish which were truly his.

It was as if *he* had lived the life of the person whose memories he took. Whether that life was good—or utterly horrific.

Swiping thoughts was something Amun hated to do, but sometimes it was necessary. Learning what your enemy knew and had planned could win a battle. Making that enemy forget could win a war. So, though he hated it, he would use his demon in that way without hesitation. And had, over and over again.

A woman's giggling snagged his attention, and he opened his eyes. He didn't have to see her to know who was approaching his hideaway. Olivia, the angel. Aeron was in hot pursuit of her.

Amun could already hear their thoughts.

Gods, her laugh is sexy as hell.

If I use my wings, he won't be able to catch me, and I really want him to catch me.

Almost…got…her…

He's almost got me!

A panting, grinning Olivia broke through the bush, spotted Amun and grabbed the dagger strapped to the outside of her thigh beneath her robe. When she realized who he was, she stopped, relaxed and waved.

Not expecting her sudden pause, Aeron rushed through the bush a second later and slammed into her, propelling them both to the ground. Aeron twisted midway, taking the brunt of the fall. But Olivia's glorious white wings spread and flapped, easing their momentum, and they settled gently on a bed of leaves.

"Got you at last, sweetheart," Aeron said with a mock growl, attempting to kiss her.

"Aeron," Olivia protested, gaze darting to Amun. "We have company."

"Company?" The warrior popped to his feet, already reaching for his own weapon, as well as flipping Olivia to her stomach, doubtless to protect her vital organs. When he saw Amun, he, too, relaxed. And, if Amun wasn't mistaken, he blushed. "Hey."

Hey, Amun signed. He would have loved to greet his friend properly, would have loved to talk with him, but Amun knew too well the dangers of opening his mouth while all those voices fought for release. One word, and they would overrun him. They would smash through his defenses and become all that he knew. Everyone around him would then hear what he was forced to listen to on a daily basis.

He loved his friends too much to subject them to such poison. Besides, he was used to it. They were not.

Aeron helped Olivia to her feet and brushed the leaves and twigs from her gleaming white robe. "What are you doing here?"

Again, Amun signed his reply.

Aeron just watched him blankly. The warrior was learning the language, but wasn't proficient yet. "Slow down, please."

"He said he's on a mini-vacation," Olivia supplied.

Amun nodded to let Aeron know the female was correct.

"We'll go, then," Aeron said.

Stay. Please. Olivia had no secrets, no sins, something Amun adored about her. She was the most open, honest and innocent person Amun had ever met. And Aeron, well, Amun already knew all of his secrets. They were nothing new to his demon, therefore his demon remained dormant while in the warrior's presence.

Their thoughts, though, were another matter. Amun was helpless to do anything but listen to what went on inside their heads. To him, it was as if they were speaking aloud.

Aeron thought, *How can I get out of here without hurting his feelings?* And Olivia thought, *How sad Amun looks. I should cheer him up.*

"We would love to stay with you," Olivia replied, and clasped Aeron's hand.

The former keeper of Wrath scowled at her. Clearly, he'd wanted to spend the next few hours rolling around with her, naked, not talking with Amun.

Amun tried not to grin. If there was one thing he enjoyed more than this time alone, it was teasing his friends. He didn't get to do it often, as quiet as he had to be, so he worked with what he was given.

Thank you. I would love to spend time with you.

"Then we shall spend as much as you'll allow us," Olivia responded happily.

Aeron's scowl deepened, and Amun fought a laugh. As Olivia tucked her wings into her back, she led the shirtless warrior toward Amun's chair and gave him a little push.

He settled with a heavy sigh, his many guns and daggers clanking together. Once, Aeron's entire body had been a canvas of tattoos. Dark tattoos of death and violence to remind himself of the things he'd done, and the things he might do again if he wasn't careful. But not too long ago, Aeron had been killed and miraculously brought back to life. His resurrected body was tattoo-free.

Or had been.

Aeron had already begun decorating himself again. This time, however, the images were almost comical. Olivia's name claimed the spot just above his heart, and her face was etched in perfect detail on his wrist. He even had black wings tattooed on his back, reminiscent of the wings he'd lost during his transformation.

"Oh, is that beer?" Olivia clapped excitedly as she settled on Aeron's lap. Her dark curls bounced around her shoulders, intermittently hiding and revealing the glittery flower petals woven throughout. "I've always wanted to try beer."

Amun shoved the cooler away from her, even as Aeron shouted, "No! No trying beer." Then, more calmly, "Sweetheart. No. Please."

Too well did they recall the last time Olivia had indulged with alcohol. Without a doubt, she was the world's saddest drunk.

A huff escaped her. "Fine. I won't taste it."

Aeron relaxed. Maybe because he had no idea she planned to guzzle it instead of taste it.

Before she could reach for a bottle, Amun clapped for her attention. *You look very pretty today.* And she did. Her cheeks were rosy, and her sky-blue eyes bright. Love radiated from her.

"Thank you," she replied, beaming up at him.

"What'd he say?" Aeron demanded.

"He thinks I look very pretty."

The warrior's lips pursed. "I told you that a few minutes ago and you ran from me."

"But I was going to reward you when you caught me."

The warrior's narrowing violet eyes landed on Amun.

Why'd you have to be here? he thought, knowing Amun heard. *Now I have to wait for my reward.* "So. Do you come here often?" he said aloud.

Trying to appear somber, Amun nodded.

That violet gaze shifted, perusing their surroundings. "I can see why. It's nice here. Peaceful."

Which was one of the reasons Olivia had chosen to lead him down this path. She'd wanted her man to forget his troubles, if only for a little while, and simply enjoy.

A paradise, certainly, Amun signed.

"But aren't you worried about Hunters sneaking up on you?" Olivia asked, and seemed to sink into herself. Hate was not part of her makeup, he knew, but she didn't like the pain those men had brought her man.

Were you?

She blushed, and Aeron choked on what seemed to be a bout of laughter. That, he'd apparently understood.

Actually, with the iron fence around the property and Torin having this place monitored 24/7, I'm not worried about anything but relaxation.

Torin, keeper of Disease. The poor man couldn't touch anyone skin-to-skin without infecting them with some sort of sickness. Of course, that sickness wouldn't kill immortals, but it *would* infect them and they in turn would infect everyone *they* touched. Therefore, Torin spent most of his time alone in his room.

Well, not so alone anymore.

Amun had picked up on his thoughts, as well as Cameo's. Cameo was keeper of Misery, and the two had been engaged in a passionate affair of You-can't-touch-me-but-you-can-watch-me-while-I-pretend-you-are for weeks. Both knew it wouldn't last, but they were enjoying the hell out of each other right now. So much so that Amun often wanted to cut off his own skull and dig out his brain, just for a few moments of peace.

"We really didn't mean to intrude on your relaxation time," Aeron said. "So we'll just be on our—"

What's mine is yours.

Aeron's shoulders slumped, and Amun fought another laugh.

"Yeah, but my darling is right. You deserve to relax in peace. So why don't you take half the forest, and we'll take the other half? No, that won't work," she rushed on. "We'll just stress about the dividing line."

Silly woman.

"Oh, I know. We can work out a schedule." Olivia grinned, proud of herself. "Something like, you get Mondays, Wednesdays and Fridays, and we get Tuesdays and Thursdays."

Or I get every day, since I've already staked a claim. And you can visit me upon occasion.

"Or you thank us for allowing you even those three days," Aeron retorted when Olivia translated. "Otherwise, we might spill *your* secret and then every last person living in the fortress will start coming here."

Amun flipped him off, a sign that needed no interpreting.

The booming laugh that next escaped his friend was like soothing balm to his ears. Before Olivia, and the events that led to Aeron's death, Aeron had never exhibited such merriment. He'd been very much like Amun projected himself to be. And, truthfully, most often was. Somber. Sorrowful. Almost grief-stricken.

What's it like? Living without a demon? So many centuries had passed, Amun barely remembered how it had been, living in the heavens, carefree and without interference.

"Honestly?" Aeron leaned back until his shoulders were resting against a tree trunk. He pulled Olivia with him, and helped her curl herself around him. "Amazing. There's no voice in the back of my head, beseeching me to do terrible things. There's no urge to hurt or maim or kill. But it's also…odd. I hadn't realized how much I'd come to rely on the bastard, uh, fiend—sorry, sweetheart—for information about people. I'm having to relearn how to read people's intentions."

Amun knew that, because of Wrath, the warrior had sensed a person's sins the moment he'd neared them. He'd then become filled with a need to punish them, hurting them the way they'd hurt others.

You'll adapt.

"Soon, I hope."

"The good news is that he's not as moody," Olivia added.

Lips twitching, Aeron kissed the tip of her nose. "All thanks to you, sweetheart."

"You're welcome."

Amun's heart gave a little lurch. In happiness for what his friend had found. And yes, in jealousy. He wanted a female of his own. Desperately. He'd found one he could have enjoyed, too. Kaia, a Harpy. She was a liar and a thief, but she was open about it, her sins there for everyone to see. She kept no secrets.

But she'd also slept with Paris, keeper of Promiscuity and one of Amun's closest friends. Not that Paris wanted her again or could have her even if he did. Once Paris slept with a woman, he couldn't get hard for her again. That was part of his curse. But while Amun knew the

little Harpy was intrigued by him, he also knew she
would not be settling down anytime soon. And Amun
wanted forever.

With other women, human women, well, it was too
difficult. He knew what they were thinking every minute
of every day. He knew when they found another man
attractive. He knew when they said something nice to
him but were thinking something cruel.

Aeron sighed, drawing his attention back to the
present. *I'm here. I might as well ask him,* the warrior
thought.

Amun straightened. He'd known Aeron would approach him sooner or later with the coming question,
but hadn't known how to respond. He still didn't. *Don't
ask me,* he signed. *Not yet.*

A muscle ticked beneath his friend's eye. "I hate when
you read my mind."

Then conceal your thoughts. He didn't think there
was a way to do so, though. No one had ever managed
such a feat.

"I can't," Aeron confirmed. "Which means you already know that Olivia and I are leaving tomorrow."

Actually, no. That wasn't true. Aeron planned to
leave Olivia behind, she just didn't know it yet. The
warrior was desperate to keep her safe. Which, in his
mind, meant leaving her here, even though she would
be pissed.

Where are you going? he asked, though again, he
already knew the answer.

"To hell," Aeron replied. It wasn't a metaphor, either.
The man meant exactly what he said. "We want you to
come with us."

Legion, the little demon Aeron viewed as a daughter,

was currently trapped in the fiery realm, and Aeron had ever intention of rescuing her. Had the warrior asked Amun to go anywhere else, he would have said yes without hesitation. But hell…he shuddered. His demon had lived there, once upon a time. That same demon had fought to escape, had succeeded, and had been punished for that success.

But the memories of that place had never faded. The heat, the screams, the rank odors of sulfur and rotting flesh that permeated the air. Disgusting. Add in the vile thoughts of the demons still living there and the tormented thoughts of the souls suffering there, and it was a new kind of hell for Amun.

What about Baden? he asked. Another of Aeron's pressing burdens.

Aeron arched a black brow. "You know about that, too. Great."

Baden. Once their best friend. But thousands of years ago, Hunters had beheaded him. Unlike Aeron, he hadn't been given a second chance at life. He hadn't done anything to deserve one, apparently. But Aeron, who had recently spent a little time in the afterlife, had seen him. Talked to him.

Baden was out there. Baden could be freed, returned to them like Aeron. They just had to find a way to convince any deity who would listen to bring him back to life.

Aeron had kept this information to himself. But then, that was a habit they shared. Aeron liked to weigh all the facts, find any possible solutions, before mentioning a potential problem to the others. That had never been more evident than now. Aeron no longer suffered but all the others did, and he didn't want to add to their suffering until he could offer a resolution.

"Once Legion is safe," Aeron said, "I'll tell the others about Baden. We can then concentrate on freeing him. But Legion has to come first. She's suffering. He is not."

And the Hunters? The artifacts? Pandora's box? Will you forget those? Now that you're without a demon, they must not concern you anymore.

A scowl darkened Aeron's face, shadows seeming to seep from his eyes. "You're wrong. They concern me greatly. I don't want to watch my best friends die because I allowed my enemy to find the artifacts. I don't want to watch my best friends die because I wasn't there to protect them. But I love Legion, too. She's being tortured down there and I can't stand it. I have to free her, or I'll be no good to anyone."

Even after what she did to you?

"Yes," Aeron replied without hesitation.

Olivia nodded. "Yes. Me, too."

Amun expected such forgiveness from Olivia. She was an angel and, as he'd already realized, didn't know how to hate. She couldn't even hold on to a good anger. But Aeron? Forgiving a female for making a bargain with the devil, nearly ruining his life by almost killing his angel? Shocking. But maybe forgiveness came more easily to him now that he was without his demon's need for vengeance.

"The sooner we find her, the sooner we free Baden, and the sooner I can concentrate on the artifacts and the Hunters," Aeron added.

Many reasons to go, yes, but none overshadowed

Amun's reasons for staying behind. *Are you asking anyone else to go with you?*

The back of Aeron's head banged against the tree, once, twice, and he peered up at the ocean of sky. "No. I hated even asking you. I don't want to leave the fortress unprotected or task the warriors with something else to do."

So, why me? Aeron had never thought the answer outright, and Amun had never pulled it from his friend's mind, so he honestly didn't know. The other warriors were just as strong as he was, just as skilled at warring and killing.

"Secrets," Olivia said with a sad little sigh. "Your demon will be able to learn where Legion is being held."

That made sense, and Amun nearly moaned. Because it meant they needed him specifically. Not for his brawn, but for his demon. No one else would do. How, then, could he tell them no?

He couldn't.

He scrubbed a hand down his suddenly tired face. Though everything and everyone inside him began screaming in protest, making him wince, he nodded. *If I agree to do this, you'll have to ask one more.* To take Olivia's place and better their odds of success.

"Who?"

William.

William was an immortal of some sort, though none of them knew exactly what he was. The man liked to think of himself as a sex god, that much Amun knew. He'd sleep with anyone—and had. A man of few standards, no question. But he loved fighting almost as much as he loved sex, and he wasn't possessed by a demon.

Therefore, the darkness of the underworld wouldn't frighten him. And if Amun fell as he suspected he would, there would be someone there to help Aeron leave.

"I will," Aeron said. "I'll ask him."

Amun sighed, as sad as Olivia had been. *Then count me in.*

CHAPTER EIGHT

THE BLOOD…the girl saw it in her mind, dripping, flowing, rushing. The screams…she heard them in her ears, agonized, evil. The darkness…it surrounded her, closing in tighter and tighter, nearly suffocating her.

How long this had been going on, she didn't know. Time had ceased to exist for her. There was only pain and chaos. And fire. Oh, God, the fire. She could smell the fumes, the scent of rotting bodies and brimstone.

Tears leaked from the corners of her eyes, scalding her cheeks. She was lying in a bed, knees drawn up to her chest. Over and over she shivered from cold, and yet, she was still burning up inside. Someone had carried her here. She couldn't remember who. She only knew that the moment he had set her down, she had attacked him, unable to help herself. So badly she'd wanted to bathe in his blood. She'd wanted to hear his scream join all the others.

If he'd survived, she didn't know. Didn't care. Would have actually welcomed another victim, and she hated herself for it.

"How are you today, pet?"

The words were barely audible through the screams, but she understood them all the same. And she didn't have to open her eyes to know who now stood beside her bed. Cronus. King of the gods…her master.

Can't hurt him. Can't allow myself to hurt him. He would punish her. Again.

Hurt him, another beguiling voice whispered through her head. It would feel so good.

Can't. Any more pain, and she would crumble. Forever lost.

Once she'd been known as Sienna Blackstone. Once, she'd been human. Once, she'd been a Hunter. Then she'd fallen for Paris, keeper of Promiscuity, and slept with him to strengthen him. Big mistake. The empowered warrior had decided to use her—as a shield. He'd abducted her just as she'd once abducted him, allowing her own people to gun her down.

At the time, she hadn't thought it was possible to feel such agony. Liking a man, only to discover he couldn't care less about you. Bullets, slicing into flesh. Life, slipping away. She laughed bitterly now. How foolish she'd been. That hadn't been agony. That had been a massage. *This* was agony.

Her back felt as if it had been dipped in acid and salt. Two hard *things* were growing between her shoulder blades, sprouting from the ruined flesh. Horns, perhaps. Or maybe wings. Every so often, she thought she felt them flutter.

"Answer me. Now."

Punish, that beguiling voice commanded. *Take all that he claims as his, and then take his head.*

Though her head was already filled with more evil than she could bear, new images began taking residence. She saw all the things Cronus had stolen over the centuries: artifacts, power, women. She saw all the lives he'd taken—and exactly how he'd taken them. So many. Oh, there were so many lives cut short because of his greed.

Not just his enemies, but his own people. Even humans. Anyone who had gotten in his way. Blood flowed, and the screams reached a new crescendo.

Oh, God. Moaning, she pressed the heels of her palms into her eyes. Had she known what awaited her in the afterlife, had she known what kind of person he truly was, she would not have allowed him to lead her to the heavens.

She would have stayed with Paris. A man she'd thought she hated with every fiber of her being.

That hatred for him must have anchored her to his side, because her spirit had followed him for several days after her body died. He hadn't been able to see her, hadn't sensed her in any way. She'd watched as he'd given her a warrior's funeral; that had surprised her. She'd watched as he'd cried for her; that had confused her. She'd watched as he'd mourned for her; that had, unexpectedly, touched her.

Her anger with him had begun to drain. She'd thought: *even though he used me, he must have truly cared about me.* And if he was capable of caring, he must not be the evil creature she'd been led to believe.

But then his body had begun to weaken and Sienna had been forgotten. To regain his strength, he'd slept with some random stranger. And then another. And another. He hadn't cared about a single one of them. He hadn't cared that they'd wanted more from him than a mere bedding. He'd walked away afterward and never looked back. Just as he would have done to her if she hadn't captured him for her boss.

Her anger had returned, hotter than before.

That's when Cronus had appeared before her. "Come with me," he'd said, "and you will live again."

"I don't want to live again." The life she'd led had not been the stuff of dreams. After her younger sister was abducted from her home, her father and mother had checked out. They'd wanted nothing to do with anything, even their remaining child. Fighting the Lords of the Underworld had become Sienna's cause, her sole purpose. There would be no evil in the world, no more abductions, if Pandora's demons were destroyed, she'd been told.

Cronus, though, had not given up.

"You can avenge your death, then," he'd replied.

"I don't want to do that, either." She'd just wanted to pass quietly into the afterlife, the world and its inhabitants forgotten. Perhaps there she would have found her sister.

"You don't know what you want. But I can see your desires in your eyes, whether you admit them or not. You're desperate for a second chance. You want what you were denied. A family. Someone to protect you, to cherish you. Someone to love you."

She'd swallowed the lump in her throat. "And how will I get that with you?"

"I'm creating an army. A holy army of warriors the likes of which you have never seen. You can be a part of that."

That's how he planned to find someone to protect, cherish and love her? "No, thank you."

"I cannot do this without you."

Why? She was too frail to win a physical altercation and had always been a little too timid to call anyone on their shit. That's why Dean Stefano, her boss, had always used her in the office, researching demon lore.

She'd been flabbergasted when he'd asked her to seduce Paris and at first, she'd said no.

Then she'd seen his picture. No man was more exquisite, sensual in ways no mortal could ever hope to be. Her heart had raced and her palms had actually sweated, desperate to touch him. As plain as she was, no one like him had ever paid her any notice. As beautiful as he was, she hadn't understood how he could house such evil.

The desire to meet him, to see that evil for herself, had become an obsession. So she'd finally said yes. She'd arranged an "accidental" meeting in Athens. He'd been interested in her, which had made her feel special. She almost hadn't drugged him, had almost sent him on his way. But then she'd noticed the red tint bleeding into his eyes, glowing, broadcasting his malevolence for the entire world to see. There'd been no denying his origins then.

He *was* evil, even though he kissed like an angel. And maybe, just maybe, if she helped destroy him, the world really would become a better place to live. Maybe child abductions really would end. So she'd done it. She'd drugged him.

And she had died for her efforts.

And, terribly enough, what did she regret most? Not enjoying him, fully, completely. Just the two of them, worries forgotten. What came in only a distant second? Not killing him.

"Join me," Cronus had added, "and you'll meet Paris again. I swear it. He'll be yours to do with as you please."

His words were proof that he did indeed know what she wanted, whether she would admit it aloud or not.

See Paris again? Have the warrior at her mercy? Yes! And yet, it hadn't been enough. "No."

"But more than that," he continued as if she hadn't spoken, "I will ensure you see your sister again."

She'd nearly grabbed him and shook him, so great was her shock. "You know where she is?"

"Yes."

"And she's alive?"

"Yes."

Thank God. Thank God, thank God, thank God. "Then yes," she'd said without hesitation. "Yes, I will help you. Now. Hurry. *Please.*"

"You are saying that you will be mine, my soldier. Yes?"

"Yes. *If* you take me to my sister."

"I will. One day."

Her sense of urgency intensified. "Why not now?"

"Your mission comes first. Do you agree?"

No. But she'd said, "Yes." Anything to see her precious Skye again.

"Then it is done." He'd grinned slowly, satisfaction radiating from him, and whisked her to this palace in the heavens.

Had she gotten to see her sister yet? No. Had he trained her to fight? No. Had he sent her on that mission, whatever it was? Again, no. He'd simply kept her here, alone unless he visited or summoned her, with nothing to do but think. And hate.

She'd tried to leave, but she couldn't. She was bound to Cronus in a way she still didn't understand. A way she couldn't refute or disobey. Whatever he asked of her, she did, compelled by a force she could not defeat. Even though she'd tried to do so, countless times.

"I asked you a question," Cronus said now, drawing her from her memories and straight back to the pain pulverizing her. "How are you?"

"Worse." A whimper.

He sighed. "I had hoped otherwise, for I'm eager to use you."

"What's wrong with me?"

"Oh, did I forget to tell you?" He laughed, the sound carefree. "You now carry the demon of Wrath inside you."

Everything inside her stilled. The screams. Her spirit's heartbeat. Even the darkness ceased swirling. The demon of Wrath was…inside her?

No. No, no, no! She was not one of them. *Couldn't* be one of them. "You're lying. You have to be lying."

"Hardly. It's trying to make itself at home in your mind, and its wings are sprouting from your back."

Panic built, spread. Wings, he'd said. Exactly as she'd suspected.

"I'm sure you can hear its thoughts by now, urging you to do things you wouldn't normally want to do."

Oh. God. He had. He'd truly done it. He'd paired her with a demon. *Noooo!* This time, the word was a wail inside her. He'd made her the very thing she'd fought against. The very thing she'd hoped to destroy.

A sob burst from her. "You bastard! You've cursed me!"

He huffed and puffed, insulted. "How dare you take that tone with me? I've *blessed* you. How could you fight for me as a mere human, a lost soul? The answer is simple. You could not. And so I gave you a way to do so."

The tears streaming from her eyes burned as if they

were carving grooves into her cheeks. "You ruined me in the process."

"One day you will thank me," he said confidently.

"No. *No.* One day I'll kill you for this." A vow.

Heavy silence slithered between them, a hungry snake ready for its meal. "You threaten me even though I brought you a present." He *tsked.* "Someone you were *dying* to see."

Skye?

Not daring to breathe, Sienna forced her eyelids open, and through the blur of her vision she saw that there really was a female standing next to the god king. The girl reached his shoulders, had a mane of dark hair like Sienna's own and olive skin. Her facial features were obscured by shadows, but that didn't stop Sienna's heart from thundering inside her chest.

Trembling, Sienna reached out. "Sister?"

There was a rustle of clothing as the pair moved away from her. "You don't deserve a present today, pet. Therefore, you will not get one."

"Skye!"

Silence. The two turned away and marched off. The girl never uttered a word of protest.

"Skye!" she shouted again. "Skye! Come back. Talk to me." The last choked from her, tangling up in the hard knot forming in her throat.

Again, there was no response.

Sienna collapsed against her bed, new sobs racking her. How could Cronus have done this to her? How could he be so cruel?

He must pay. He must suffer.

The deep voice whisked through her head, and she

jerked in shock and revulsion. *Shut up, shut up, shut up. I know what you are. I hate you.*

The insult had no effect. *He must pay. He must suffer as you suffer.*

Expecting the voice this time, she didn't jerk. She stilled. She even began to ponder. The demon of Wrath was inside her. And helpless and sick as she was, there was nothing she could do about that. Yet. So why not use it? Just once? Just to balance the scales and make things right?

"H-how? How do I make him suffer as I now suffer?" Oh, God. She was talking to a demon. *Stop!* It was weird and wrong…yet oddly freeing. There would be no stopping. Cronus had to pay for this.

You must steal that which he values most.

"And that is?" Whatever the answer, she would do as the demon suggested and steal it. She would not hesitate. Cronus had thrown her into this terrible fire; he could burn with her. "His wife? His children?"

His power.

"All right." Another vow. But just how was she supposed to steal power from a god?

He will pay. He will suffer.

Yes. Gradually, her tears dried and her heartbeat calmed. The lump in her throat dissolved. Cold seeped through her, filling her up, consuming her. "He will pay. He will suffer."

"VISIT HELL? No damn way."

Amun stood in front of the large plasma screen in the entertainment room, facing William. This had been the only way to get the man's attention. Whenever Amun had knocked on William's bedroom door, he'd been told to go away. Whenever he'd followed William into town, the warrior had ignored him as he plundered his way through the female population, one—or two—at a time. Sometimes the bastard had even done his business with Amun standing there.

Now, William was a captive audience. Because Amun had brought in reinforcements. Anya, the goddess of Anarchy. As powerful and vindictive as she was, she could make anyone do anything she wanted at any time.

Especially William.

The two were best friends and loved to torture each other. Which was why Anya had stolen some book that belonged to William. A very important book, apparently, and one the warrior needed to save himself from some curse. The two were always careful to keep those details buried behind inane thoughts while in Amun's presence.

He could have sifted through their minds to gain the answers, of course, but hadn't. He didn't need any more secrets, thank you very much.

He did know that whenever William acted like a "good boy," Anya returned a few pages to him. So when Anya challenged William to a game of "Guitar Hero," along with Gilly, a teen who now lived at the fortress, William had accepted. The three were positioned around the TV, where Anya had stated they would remain until Amun had said his piece. Or signed, as the case was.

We need your help rescuing Legion, Amun began.

"Sorry, but I have plans elsewhere," William said darkly. "I'm leaving tomorrow morning, and I'll be gone for a few weeks."

"What plans?" Gilly demanded, fingering the butterfly necklace Lucien had given her earlier. A necklace exactly like the one Amun, Anya and William also wore. They had been told to wear them always, to block their actions from the prying eyes of the gods. "Why didn't you tell me you were going somewhere?"

Whoa. What was that? Pure possessiveness had layered her words.

You're mine, he suddenly heard Gilly think. *We belong together, not apart.*

O-kay. Amun massaged the back of his neck. He hadn't needed to know that.

Expression tight, William tossed his drumsticks in the air, caught them and twirled them. "Doesn't matter why I kept you in the dark. I'm going and that's final."

And wow. William usually joked about everything. He took nothing seriously. That he was in this temper...

I've got to stop this, William thought. *This can't go on.*

Good. That was good.

"This trip is final, you said?" Anya arched a brow at her friend, her lips curling in challenge. She was engaged to Lucien, keeper of Death, and was one of the most beautiful females Amun had ever seen. Not surprisingly, Lucien indulged her every whim. "You didn't yet clear this trip with me, either."

"You can't go without me," Gilly said.

"I can and I will. And don't threaten me, Anya. This is one thing I will see through no matter what you do to my book."

Her expression a storm cloud of fury, Gilly tossed her bass guitar on the floor. The plastic cracked. Exactly as she imagined her heart was doing. "You promised to protect me always. How can you protect me if you're gone?"

She had straight brown hair and big, beautiful brown eyes. She was average height, but had more curves than any seventeen-year-old girl should have. And William was clearly doing his best not to look at her.

He was failing. *Must…stop. Why can't I make it stop?*

As though a book of his own opened up in Amun's mind, with everyone's secrets filling the pages, Amun suddenly knew exactly what was going on. Gilly thought she was in love with William. William was attracted to the girl and horrified because of it. She was too young for him.

But while William could do nothing about his desire for Gilly, he *could* do something about his thirst for justice. Gilly had been terribly abused as a child, and William had tracked down her family with every intention of killing them in the slowest, most painful of ways. That's where he was going. To Nebraska to have his revenge. Wouldn't be difficult, either. The mother was a housewife and the stepfather a doctor.

"I didn't lie to you. I will always protect you," William told her gently. He stood, reached for her, but realized what he was doing and dropped his arms to his sides. "You have to trust me on this."

Amun clapped his hands for their attention. *Help me help Aeron and then I'll help you with the girl's family.*

William's attention had already wandered. He hadn't watched Amun's hands and had no idea what Amun had said. As Anya realized what Amun was implying, her blue eyes widened. Rather than voice the words for him in English or Hungarian, allowing Gilly to understand, she spoke to William in the language of the gods. The rough sounds were music to Amun's ears, reminding him of the carefree years he'd spend in the heavens.

"I don't need help," William growled in the same language. Stiff, he tangled a hand through hair the color of the darkest night. "Actually, I *want* to do this alone. And besides that, Legion annoyed me. I'm glad she's gone. I think it's safe to say I wouldn't rescue my own mother from hell. If I had one. I wouldn't even rescue Anya."

"Thanks," the goddess said with a roll of her eyes. "But listen. Aeron isn't glad she's gone." Her voice was gentler than Amun had ever heard it. "Which means Lucien isn't glad. Which means I'm not glad."

William remained unmoving. "Don't care."

"Lucifer is afraid of you, Willy. In hell, you'll be able to do things and go places Aeron and Amun can't."

For a moment, William's mind opened, gearing up to recall exactly why Lucifer feared him. But then he shut down the memory, which meant that Amun couldn't read it, not without digging, and that still wasn't something Amun wanted to do.

"Again," William said with a shrug. "Don't care."

Just as stubborn, Anya persisted. "William, think about what you're turning down. When you're with Gilly's family, you won't know what they're thinking, what they fear, what other terrible things they've done. But Amun will. He can tell you. And you can do more than hurt and kill them. You can terrorize them."

Gilly tossed her hands in the air. "Will someone please speak in English and tell me what's going on? Someone? Please?"

"No," Anya and William said in unison.

"God! You guys are *so* lame. You want to act like I'm not here? Fine. I'll do you one better. I'll leave. I don't know why I hang around you, anyway." With that, Gilly flounced out of the room.

Scowling, William jabbed one of his sticks through his drums. "Fine. Count me in, Amun. I'll go to hell with you and Aeron. Afterward, you'll help me deliver hell to my humans. Got it?"

For better or worse, Amun nodded.

CHAPTER NINE

WHEN SCARLET sat up and opened her eyes to a brand-new evening, she had no idea what to expect. After her "we had a son" bombshell, Gideon had basically gone into shock. He'd been silent, withdrawn, and she hadn't forced a confrontation because she'd wanted him to have time to absorb the astonishing news.

Before he could do so, however, the sun had risen and she'd fallen asleep, lost to her demon. She'd been too distracted to participate in their usual terror games and didn't even know who they'd targeted.

"Were you lying? Don't tell me!"

The words whipped at her, and she quickly focused. Gideon hadn't moved her from the forest. Trees still surrounded her, birds and insects still sang. The spring still bubbled, and mist still wafted. There was no waning sunlight, no violet sky, only a thick blanket of dark, heavy clouds. A storm was brewing.

In more ways than one.

Gideon was bathed in shadows. Shadows her gaze had no trouble penetrating. His blue locks were wet and plastered to his brow, his cheeks, yet were still a gorgeous frame for the upsetting lines of tension that spread from his temples to his mouth. His eyes were like lasers, boring past the mental shields she surrounded herself with. His expression was tight, fierce, his lips pulled back from his teeth in a scowl.

He stood in front of her, a dagger in each hand.

Breath suddenly trapped in her throat, she swept her gaze over her body. There were no cuts on her arms or legs, and her dress was in one piece. There wasn't a single spot of blood to indicate he'd injured her.

Okay. So. He hadn't attacked her in fury. Did that mean he could get away without saying, "Who aren't you today?" Did that mean he could get away with not kissing her awake?

Gods, his kiss. She reached up and traced her fingertips over her mouth. A mouth that still tingled. His tongue had plundered and taken and given. Taken so much passion. Given so much pleasure. His hands had been everywhere, touching her, learning her. And his body, so hard and hot against hers, had transported her back to the heavens. Locked up, helpless still, but uncaring because she had her man. A man who loved her.

It had been so long since she'd given in to the demands of her body. So long since she'd lost control. Gideon hadn't seemed to mind that loss. No, he'd seemed to enjoy it. He'd come on her belly and marked her as if they still belonged together.

Afterward, she'd wanted to cuddle up to his side. She'd wanted to kiss his neck and breathe in his musky scent. She'd wanted to spill every secret, talk about everything they'd once shared.

But she knew him, knew this man who had no clue about what she'd once meant to him. And she'd known beyond any doubt that that's what he had planned. He'd taken her from prison into paradise, simply for answers.

Answers he would attempt to unearth through fair means or foul.

He'd always been that way. When determination set in, Gideon was more stubborn than she was. It was as annoying as it was wonderful. For once he'd decided that she was to be his bride, he'd moved heaven and earth to make it happen. Despite the odds against them.

She wouldn't be used in that way, however. She wouldn't let him think he could fuck her—or almost fuck her—and get his way.

"Scar. You're not pissing me the hell off. Don't pay attention to me." He tossed one of the daggers with a lethal flick of his wrist. "Don't tell me what I don't want to know."

Scarlet whipped around, following the movement of the blade. The tip was now embedded in the tree trunk, vibrating. And there were hundreds of grooves in the bark. He'd been tossing that thing all day, it seemed.

"No," she said softly, facing him again. "I wasn't lying." Steel was not something she would lie about. Ever. For any reason. He had been—was still—the most important person in her life.

A ragged breath left Gideon. "You didn't say *was*. His name *was*. That means he's…he's…"

"He's dead," she whispered hoarsely. "Yes."

Absolute agony contorted Gideon's features. Maybe she shouldn't have told him about the boy. Sometimes she wished *she* didn't know; it was just too painful. But part of her had thought, hoped, that Gideon would have retained knowledge about his own child. Knowledge that might have led to memories of his wife.

"All of it. I don't want to know all of it." As he spoke,

he sank to his knees, the knuckles wrapped around the second blade leaching of color. "Please."

Seeing such a strong warrior reduced to such bleakness tore at her, and she had to blink back a rush of stinging tears. If she told him now, it wouldn't be because of sex. It would be because he'd begged. At least, that's how she rationalized this new need to share. Everything.

"All right, yes," she said, no less hoarse as her harsh, jagged breath scraped against her chest cavity. "I'll tell. Tell you everything about his life and his death, but you can't speak. If you interrupt me with questions I may not be able to continue." Emotion would choke her. She would break down, sob, and no way would she allow Gideon to see her like that. This was going to be hard enough. "Got me?"

A moment passed, Gideon remaining still, silent. What danced through his head, what made him hesitate to agree, she didn't know. All she knew was that talking about Steel wasn't something she did. Ever. Again, it was just too painful. Even if Gideon remained quiet, she wasn't sure she would be able to get through this. Definitely not without crying.

Pretend it's a story you made up. Distance yourself. Yeah. Right.

Finally Gideon worked through whatever issue he had with her demand for silence and nodded. His lips were pressed in a thin, mulish line, cutting off any words he might have wanted to speak.

Scarlet inhaled deeply, searching for fortification. She didn't find it. The words simply wouldn't form.

She pushed to shaky legs and strode to the tree with the dagger. Gideon didn't try to stop her as she removed the tip with a jerk. Then she began pacing, tapping the sharp metal against her thigh in a steady, hopefully calming rhythm. A cool, damp breeze fragrant with earth and sky wafted around her, while twigs and rocks cut at the soles of her feet.

Just say the words. Pretend, pretend, pretend. You'll be talking about someone else's life. Someone else's son. "I told you I was pregnant and you were happy. You petitioned Zeus for my release into your custody. He said no. So you arranged for my escape. Only, I was caught. I was given twenty lashes before you realized I'd failed. They had thought to break me, to force me to tell them who had aided me. I didn't." She would have died first.

"The pain was manageable, at least, but I was so afraid of losing the baby. My cellmates tried to hurt me, too, but I fought harder than I'd ever fought anyone and was soon given a cell of my own permanently, not just for our...interludes. That's where I eventually gave birth to our—" her voice caught on the word "—to a beautiful little boy."

As the image of Steel flashed through her mind, that sweet boy sleeping on her chest, looking like an angel, she tripped over her own foot. She was shaking as she righted herself.

True to his word, Gideon remained silent, waiting.

The first few drops of rain fell, almost as if nature was crying for her. For all she'd lost.

Pretend. "You visited me every day. And every day you stayed a little longer and were a little more reluctant to leave. I feared you would have yourself committed to the prison just to remain at my side." And she was ashamed to admit she'd liked the idea. "Then one day you came to me, told me you had a new plan to gain my freedom, though you didn't give me the details at the time. That plan was, of course, to steal Pandora's box. So needless to say, you never returned."

At her sides, the trees began to blur. Her chin trembled, and her cheeks heated, the rain falling more steadily now. *Do it. Keep going.* She wanted to look down at Gideon but didn't. His expression, whatever it was, could be her undoing.

"Then I was possessed by Nightmares, as you know, and I wasn't a fit mother. So the Greeks took him. Took Steel." And she'd blamed Gideon more and more for the separation. If only he'd come back for her, for them, how different things could have been. "When my head cleared and I realized what had happened, I begged to see him but my cries went unheeded. I tried to escape every day. And every day they whipped me anew."

A choking sound left Gideon, but still Scarlet didn't allow herself to look at him.

"Finally, I noticed how Tartarus, both the prison and its warden, were weakening. At last I managed to escape and made my way to Olympus. And I…I found our baby." This time, the choking sound left *her.* "But he was a baby no longer. Centuries had passed, but he was only a teenager, his immortality slowing his aging process, I guess. And he…he had no fucking idea who I was."

Rain, tears. Both drenched her.

Pretend, damn you. "He had grown horns and fangs, his eyes were red and patches of his skin were scaled. That's when I realized they'd given him a demon, too. Which one, I still don't know. But he was beautiful, damn it." The last was screamed, identical to a banshee's wail, but she couldn't help herself.

Silence. The cool wash of water.

Finish this. "They had made him their whipping boy. They laughed at him, kicked him, abused him vilely. There was no happiness in his eyes. Just resolution. He was enduring, proud, strong. A determined warrior. And that just made it worse, you know? I had failed that precious boy in every way, yet he was still everything I could have wanted in a son."

Tears continued to leak, tendrils of acid, scorching her cheeks. She wiped them away with the back of her wrist, shaking violently now. *Pretend.* "I erupted at his treatment. I unleashed my demon in the most horrendous show of violence the heavens had ever seen. By the time I finished, the gods and goddesses around him were driven to insanity, which ultimately aided Cronus in his own escape.

"But I digress. When the darkness cleared, I realized Steel was afraid of me. He even fought me when I tried to abscond with him. I didn't want to hurt him, so I let him run from me. He went to Zeus, the only father figure he'd ever known, and together they chased me down. Not that I tried to hide. I wanted Steel to find me."

She swallowed the serrated lump growing in her throat. "To Steel's surprise, Zeus chained us in front of each other. He told Steel that I was his mother, and Steel…he…" Once again she had to fight past those blistering tears, not even the chilly rain cooling them.

A sliver of rock sliced the sole of her foot, and she welcomed the sting. "He was distraught. He cried. Begged me to forgive him. I tried to reassure him. He could have killed me, and I wouldn't have cared. But Zeus was determined to punish me for the trouble I had caused. He took…he took Steel's head in front of me."

Deep breath in, deep breath out. "I fought so fervently against my chains, I lost a hand that day. But I didn't free myself in time. He was…gone. He was gone, and I was thrown back into my cell. And I stayed there until the Titans managed to overthrow the Greeks for good. But you know the worst part? He'd planned it. Zeus had planned to kill him all along. He'd had someone there, waiting, a new host for Steel's demon."

Again, silence. No, not true. Her choppy inhalations blended with Gideon's uneven exhalations and mixed with the patter of the storm.

There. He knew everything now. Every painful moment of Steel's life. Scarlet's failure. His own failure. What could have been, what hadn't been. Why she hated him so damn much. Why she could not possibly ever forgive him for leaving her behind.

"Scar," he whispered brokenly. "I—I—"

Still she couldn't face him. She felt too exposed, too raw, as if she'd been scraped with a razor from the inside out. "What!" A scream.

"I understand, I do." Meaning, he didn't. "That sounds like the…man I knew. A king who—"

"Don't talk to me about that bastard! You liked him, I know. You respected him, admired his strength. Before your possession, he was even good to you. As much as he was capable of." And that wasn't much. So the fact that Gideon defended him in any way… *Suffer!* "How did he treat you afterward, huh? He cursed you and he banished you! But you know what? He was never good to me and he was never good to your son." The words were coming in gasping rumbles now, slashing at him.

She had to stop. Her sobs were threatening to escape. But how dare he question the validity of her tale? He should be pleading for absolution. Shouting to the heavens. Cursing. That he wasn't...

"I'm leaving you," she said. Though she'd tried for a calm, this-is-how-it's-gonna-be tone this time, her own suffering was evident in every nuance of her voice. "You owe me a boon, and I'm redeeming it by asking that you don't come after me. You've done enough damage."

With that, she did it. She at last walked away and left her husband behind. She didn't look back.

Closure sucked.

YOU'VE DONE ENOUGH DAMAGE.

The words echoed through Gideon's mind. Everything inside him screamed to jump up, to chase Scarlet down, to bind her to him in whatever way necessary, to do something, anything to soothe the wounds inside her, but he didn't. He remained crouched on the ground, shaking, hot tears streaming down his already soaked cheeks.

She was right.

He *had* done enough damage. At first, he hadn't wanted to believe her. He'd scrambled for any possible scrap to disprove her. But the pain in her eyes had been too real, the wounds in her voice seeping crimson. Which meant not only had he abandoned his wife, he'd also abandoned his son. An abandonment that had eventually led to his son's murder.

A murder Scarlet had been forced to watch, helpless.

Why couldn't Gideon remember? Why?

Rage beat through him, harder than fists of iron. Whatever he had to do, he would find out.

With a roar, he ripped off his necklace and tossed it aside. "Cronus," he shouted to the treetops. "Cronus! I command your presence."

It was the truth, but he couldn't stop the words. Didn't want to stop the words. Immediately, his demon screamed and pain slammed into his chest. Pain that doubled him over. Pain that spread through every inch of him, turning his blood to acid and his bones to bubbling liquid.

Pain he deserved.

Soon he couldn't move, could barely speak. But over and over, he called, "Cronus. Cronus. Come to me. I need you."

An eternity seemed to pass, the rain finally dying, though the moon never broke through the clouds and the sun never appeared. Where was Scarlet? Had she made it someplace safe to await the coming morning? Probably. The girl was resourceful. Well able to take care of herself. Look at everything she had survived.

She was stronger than he was, that was for sure.

Gods, no wonder she was done with him. She had to hate him. *Did* hate him. The emotion had drenched her final goodbye. He didn't blame her, either. Just then, he hated himself. He'd left his own child to die. His own child.

He should be beheaded.

The tears stared flowing again, and he squeezed his eyelids shut. Darling Steel, saddled with horns and fangs, even scales. The ever-fastidious gods and goddesses had probably made him feel ashamed of those features. Features Gideon would have loved and fawned over. Cherished.

Scarlet had been right about something else, too. At one time, Gideon had liked and respected Zeus. The former god king might have been selfish and power-hungry, but in his way, he'd been good to Gideon. Until the Pandora's box fiasco. After that, the Greeks had ignored Gideon and his friends, and as time passed, Gideon had found contentment with his new life.

Not his wife and child, though. They never had. Zeus had never been good to them, and for that, Zeus would suffer.

I will destroy the bastard. Once, Gideon had done everything in his power to protect his king. And how had he been repaid? His greatest treasures were taken from him. *I will avenge my son. My wife.*

Pandora's box be damned. Vengeance came first. Now. Always.

"Tsk, tsk," a male voice suddenly said, the quiet sound exploding through Gideon's head.

He pried open his eyelids.

Cronus crouched in front of him, disappointment shadowing his ever-more-youthful features. "You are a fool, letting yourself decline like this. And for what? A single moment of truth?" He sighed. "Why did you summon me? Again. I just spoke to Lucien and received my daily update. I do not require another."

"Zeus," Gideon gritted out. "I want him."

Lies screamed.

Another bout of truth. Another bout of pain, fresh and searing.

Cronus blinked in surprise. "Why?"

"I want him," Gideon repeated, panting. He would not

discuss Steel with Cronus. If the god were to remember the boy, were to bad-mouth him in any way, Gideon would be out for *his* blood, as well, and right now he needed the king as an ally.

"No." Unwavering, certain. "You cannot have him."

Gideon clenched his jaw as his gaze fogged over. *Fight this.* "He's your enemy. Let me slay him for you." He was so used to speaking deceitfully, he should have stumbled over the truth. At the very least, he should have had to think about what to say. Yet he didn't. The truth flowed from him, already a part of him. Zeus would die by his hand.

"Why would you want to?" Cronus asked, genuinely curious.

"The fact that he's breathing offends me."

Lies whimpered. *More, please more.* Stop, please stop.

The king's expression hardened. "Only after he has endured thousands of years of confinement will he be allowed the sweet taste of death. If even then. And I will be the one to deliver it. Now, is that all you wished to discuss with me?"

If Cronus wouldn't help him willingly, the king would just have to help him unintentionally. All Gideon needed was passage into Olympus. Or whatever Cronus was calling the place. From there, he could hike into Tartarus. He'd spent centuries doing so and still knew the way.

That was one thing he hadn't forgotten.

"I want to go to the heavens." Amid his demon's renewed screams, he gritted his teeth. Gods, the pain. Any more, and he would finally pass out. *Just a little longer, and then you can sleep.* "Let me recuperate there, so that the Hunters won't find me in this condition and hurt me."

Finally, a lie. That didn't ease his suffering; it was too late for that, but Lies did sigh with a kernel of relief.

"A boon, then? From me to you."

Gideon nodded as best he was able.

"If I do this, you know you will owe me."

Another nod. "I'll do…anything you…want." For Steel. And for Scarlet. And maybe, while he was sneaking his way into the prison and removing Zeus's head, he could figure out what the fuck had happened to his memories.

"Very well." Slowly Cronus grinned with satisfaction. "You may stay in the heavens until you have recovered. No longer, no shorter. And in return, I may call upon you at any time with my request for payment, and you must heed that request above all else."

"Yes." Another truth, more pain, more hissing.

The deal was struck.

As Gideon closed his eyes, the ground beneath him disappeared. After centuries of banishment, he would finally return to the heavens.

CHAPTER TEN

"THAT STUPID, stupid man. That pig. That jerk. That raging asshat!"

As Scarlet stomped through the forest, slapping tree trunks along the way, she called Gideon every vile name she could think of.

"That shithead. That brainless caveman. That... father."

Goodbye, steam.

She stilled, panting, sweating, palms stinging. He hadn't known he was a father. She'd thrown the information at him, then left him to deal with it on his own. And too well did she know how impossible it was to deal on one's own.

For months after Steel's death, she'd done nothing but cry. She'd stopped eating, had even stopped speaking. Maybe, if she'd had someone there to care for her, to pick up the shattered pieces of her soul, she would have recuperated sooner.

Much as she hated—no, *hate* was too strong a word just then. And she didn't know why. Still. Much as she *disliked* Gideon, she didn't want him wallowing. He was in the middle of a war. He couldn't afford to wallow.

One more night with him, Scarlet thought, hating herself. And it wasn't too strong a word when directed at herself. She turned around and stalked back to Gideon's camp. She'd heard him shouting to Cronus, the god king who had despised her all her life because she was the evidence of his wife's betrayal. Evidence his peers could see.

Had Gideon thought to ask him for confirmation about Steel, like her word and pain weren't good enough? Or had he been seeking vengeance against Zeus, as she once had?

If that was the case, she would have to stop him. The former sovereign suffered more locked away, his power taken from him, the knowledge that his greatest rival was controlling his throne a constant in his mind, than he ever would have suffered if she'd killed him.

Too quick. Too easy.

Still. She couldn't leave Gideon alone. So she would stay with him for what remained of the night, comfort him as best she was able. Not that he deserved it, but hell, she'd always been a giver. But after this, she was done with him. For real this time.

Only, when she broke through the final wall of leaves, she saw that he'd already left the camp. So soon? She hadn't heard him take a single step. Where the hell had he gone?

Scarlet spun, searching for any sign of him. All she found was a bag. Scowling, she stalked to it. Along the way, something hard, hot and thin hooked around her bare toe, and she stopped.

Her scowl became a frown of confusion and then irritation as she bent down and lifted…his butterfly necklace. Why had he left it? Because he was done with her and didn't want to match her anymore?

She popped her jaw, removed her own necklace—

how stupid she'd been to wear it—and clenched them both tightly in her fist. Metal crunched against metal.

"Rotten scum." She drew in a deep breath and caught a whiff of godly majesty. It was like a cloying perfume, pungent enough to sting the nostrils. She'd endured that scent most of her life, and had been ecstatic to finally escape it when she'd left Tartarus.

Cronus had been here, she realized. Son of a bitch! Where had the king taken Gideon? Had the god hurt him or helped him?

She had to know. And there was only one way to find out...

"Mother!" she shouted. Gods. She'd sworn never to do this again. Leaving Gideon helpless to Cronus's cruel whims was not an option, however. And yeah, maybe the two got along and Gideon was happy right now. She'd still do everything in her power to separate them.

Without a doubt, Cronus would try to poison Gideon against her. That shouldn't have mattered since she planned to take off tomorrow, but some part of her couldn't accept such an outcome.

Several minutes passed, but nothing happened.

"Gonna play difficult, are you?" she muttered. "Fine. So can I."

First, though, she would prepare. Surely Gideon had a few weapons in that bag. She closed the rest of the distance and pulled the zipper. Inside she found T-shirts, jeans, sweatpants and yep, weapons. A semiautomatic, a few blades and an axe. Most surprising? An unopened packet of Skittles.

Scarlet quickly changed into a T-shirt and sweats. The sweats she had to roll at the waist and ankles, but at least they stayed on. Then she stashed the weapons all over her body. The necklaces she stuffed into one of the blade sheaths.

Now. Time to try again.

"Mother! Answer me or I swear I'll find a way back into the heavens. I'll move in with you. I'll be your constant companion. You won't be able to see anyone without my presence. You won't be able to do anything without me by your side. Do you hear me? This is your last chance, Mother, before—"

"Enough! You are not to call me by that hideous name. How many times have I told you that?"

Thousands. And Scarlet cared as much now as she had every other time. Which meant she cared not at all.

The voice had come from behind her, so she turned. Slowly. As if Rhea wasn't strong enough to fear having at her back. To be honest, she simply didn't relish seeing the woman who had given birth to her. Even though she needed her.

When their gazes finally met, Scarlet barely contained her gasp of surprise.

Last time she'd seen Rhea, the woman had been greatly aged. Her silky dark hair had become a frizzy gray, and her unlined skin had turned into something akin to dry, wrinkled parchment. Now, her hair was a perfect mix of salt and pepper and her skin had smoothed out, only a few lines remaining.

From crone to cougar, Scarlet thought. *Bitch*.

Rhea wore a revealing golden robe, the top veeing to showcase her ample cleavage, the bottom so sheer Scarlet could tell she wore matching panties.

"Do you plan to stare at me all night, Scarlet darling?" Each word was sneered. "I know I'm beautiful, but I still deserve respect. Tell me why you summoned me and let's be done with this."

Collect yourself. "Surprise! I wanted to present you with a Mother of the Year award," she said dryly.

Black eyes so like her own narrowed. "I have better things to do with my time than argue with an ungrateful upstart."

Ungrateful. Right. Scarlet simply refused to cater to the demanding woman's every whim. For good reason. No good would ever come of it.

Once, Rhea had loved her. Had treated her like a jewel. But as Scarlet matured, Rhea had begun to see her as a threat. As competition. For men, for the throne if they ever managed to escape, which they had always planned to do. Love had turned to jealousy, and jealousy to hatred.

That hatred...gods, Scarlet had wanted to die when she'd realized her own mother would be happier if she were dead.

Had it not been for Alastor the Avenger, a Greek god who had been attracted to the young, blossoming Scarlet, Rhea and Cronus would have had Scarlet killed long ago. But Alastor had cursed both of the former sovereigns as only an avenger could. Every time they attempted to kill her, they would physically age.

Needless to say, they'd still tried many times. And they had indeed aged, just as Alastor had promised. Finally, their attempts had ceased and Scarlet had lived as normal a life as a girl in prison could. Meaning, no privacy, fighting for ever scrap of food and being prepared for anything.

Would have been nice to have Alastor by her side now. Rhea would do anything Scarlet desired. Without complaint. But sadly, Alastor had been killed when the Titans escaped, freeing the godly sovereigns from his curse.

Now is not the time to reminisce. Her chin jutted as she squared her shoulders, an attempt to disguise her loathing. "Your husband was here. What did he do with Gideon?"

Rhea frowned, though she couldn't hide the edge of satisfaction clinging to her expression. "I'm afraid I have no idea who this Gideon is."

Like hell. Scarlet's mother might not have known that Scarlet and Gideon had married—no one did—but everyone had known of Scarlet's interest in the warrior. More than that, everyone had known of Zeus's army. Well, known of the warriors who had visited the prison, and Gideon had been a part of that. "Come now, *Mother.* I know you're helping the Hunters. I also know your team is losing."

Red bloomed in Rhea's cheeks, erasing the satisfaction. "You know nothing, you foolish girl."

But Nightmares homed in on the queen's sudden spike of fear, stretching, purring, wanting to invade her mind and exploit every drop of it. "One last chance to tell me what I want to know, and then I start looking for Gideon on my own. And each night that I fail to find him, my demon will find you. You won't be able to close your eyes without seeing your defeat. Without seeing every way you can die."

Rhea's chin lifted, her fear falling away, speculation taking its place. "Well, well. I could almost be proud of you at this moment. We should join forces and—"

"Where. Is. He?" Never would Scarlet aid her mother. Not in any way. The things this woman had done to her…stabbing her, sending men to try and rape her, demeaning her at every turn. No. Never.

A moment passed in silence. Then Rhea's eyes narrowed, creating tiny slits of undiluted loathing. "I could kill you for such impudence, you know. There's nothing to stop me from doing so now. No curse to age me."

"Try." Scarlet almost wished she would. Not that she would succeed. Scarlet was well able to take care of herself now. In fact, she'd killed many of the Titans who had hurt her in prison. Rhea had to know that. Rhea had to know what she was capable of.

When the god queen remained in place, Scarlet almost smiled. Oh, yes. Rhea knew. There would be no challenge issued today.

"Gideon has promised Cronus a boon," her mother said stiffly. "I will take you to him if you promise me you'll ensure that boon is never granted."

Trying to force her hand. She should have known. "Done." But in this, Rhea wouldn't get her way. Scarlet abhorred Cronus as much as she abhorred her mother, so preventing him from getting something he wanted wouldn't be a hardship. And besides that, Gideon was a liar. If Gideon had promised the god king something, he'd never really meant to see it through.

Therefore, there would be no boon to divert.

Win-win.

"Come then. Let's get this over with." Rhea waved a delicate hand through the air and the next thing Scarlet knew, she was standing inside an unfamiliar bedroom. Red velvet draped the walls, and crystal hung from the ceiling like twinkling stars. Every piece of furniture was polished mahogany, and made for seduction. A four-poster bed with rumpled covers, a lounge for two, bookshelves filled with naked photos rather than books. A dresser littered with bowls of fruit.

"Where are we?" Scarlet asked, unable to mask her awe.

"The royal court." Rhea looked around with disgust. "Cronus used to keep this secret room for his mistresses." She uttered a tinkling laugh. "Well, he did until I torched the entire chamber. But then Zeus had it restored for *his* mistresses. I came here after gaining my freedom from Tartarus, just to see what had been done. You remember, don't you? You tried to enter, but we denied you." She laughed again, but this time it was a cruel sound. "Perhaps Cronus and your Gideon are having an affair."

As if. Gideon didn't swing that way. If she hadn't already known, his kiss would have assured her of that. He liked women. Liked them more than he should, but whatever.

"Where is he?"

"Cronus? I'll have you know I don't watch his every—"

"You try my patience, Mother. Where is Gideon?"

The queen ran her tongue over her teeth, waves of resentment pouring from her, before pointing to the lump in the center of the bed. "You'll find him there."

"If you're lying…" Scarlet allowed the threat to hang unfinished.

She approached the bed, trembling, and sure enough, Gideon was there, half-hidden by the covers. But her relief was short-lived. His pallid body shook, and sickly sweat poured from him. His teeth were digging into his bottom lip, and he was moaning.

That mop of blue hair was plastered to his forehead

and temples, his skin was welted and his eyes squeezed closed. What was wrong with him? She wanted to tend to him, but didn't permit herself to move another inch. Not yet. Not with an audience.

Rhea appeared at her side. "He's not very attractive like that, is he?" she asked conversationally, and Gideon's lids popped open. His eyes were bright red, glowing, and he couldn't quite focus on either woman. "That blue hair, those piercings. All that pain. A real warrior wouldn't acknowledge it, much less succumb to it."

"Spoken like a woman who's never known true pain." Her nails bit into her palms. *No one speaks poorly of him but me.*

"With you as a daughter, I've known my fair share. Believe me."

Ouch. Scarlet might not like this woman, but those kinds of comments still cut.

Maybe because, for a long time, even after her mother had begun to belittle her, purposely distressing her, she'd tried to be a good daughter. She had been Rhea's own personal little slave girl, catering to her every whim.

Her mother wanted extra food, so she'd stolen it. Her mother thought a goddess was too pretty, so Scarlet had broken the female's nose. Her mother wanted time outside her cell, so Scarlet had bought it for her. Doing whatever a guard wanted her to do.

That had been the worst, giving herself to men she hadn't liked and who hadn't liked her. But she'd cared so little about herself. She'd felt worthless without her mother's love and had been determined to earn it back. Until the first murder attempt. Rhea had distracted her before going for her throat.

"They all watch you. They all crave you. You, a little nothing," Rhea had screamed as the blood dripped.

Cronus, who had also been in their cell, had come at her next. *"You might be my wife's child, but you are not my heir and you will never have my crown."*

Alastor had been walking by, had seen Scarlet fall. He'd entered the cell, shoving Rhea aside and scooping Scarlet up. *"You have no crown,"* he'd told the former king. *"Nor will you ever again."*

After doctoring her, he'd escorted Scarlet back to her prison. Where Cronus and Rhea waited. By then, Alastor had already cursed the pair. But that hadn't stopped them from trying. Again and again. Actually, months had passed before they'd noticed how much they were aging. Only then had they stopped.

Sometimes, though, their words still haunted her.

She laughed bitterly. Those echoes of the past were her own personal little nightmare.

"I'll let you know when my end of our bargain is met," she said, keeping all emotion from her tone. Which would be, oh, never. "You can go now."

Of course, her mother remained where she was. "I never knew what you saw in him, why you watched him so covetously. Paris, Lucien and Galen were the pretty ones, though one could hardly call Lucien pretty anymore." Rhea's face scrunched with disgust. "Sabin was the strong, determined one. Strider the fun one. Any of them would have been better than *him,* the wild one who *enjoyed* fighting."

Like that was a crime. Still, Scarlet clenched her jaw to keep her rebuke inside. One, she didn't want her mother to know how much Gideon still meant to her. Not that he meant a whole hell of a lot, she assured herself. Defending him would be like shouting her feelings (small as they were) from a rooftop. Two, she hated that anyone, especially Rhea, was seeing him like this, weakened and hurting, and prolonging the discussion would only encourage the goddess to stay.

"Now they're all evil and in need of extermination," her mother continued.

"Funny that you say that, since you're just like them. *Strife*." Oh, yes. Rhea was possessed by the demon of Strife. She might deny it, but Scarlet knew the truth.

Rhea stiffened, a predator who'd spotted prey after a too-long fast. "Utter that word again, and I'll entice your lover into my bed. I could do it, you know, and there would be nothing you could do to stop me. I grow prettier every day."

Do not react. Not to the jealousy suddenly beating through her, or the consuming fury. Again, that would only encourage the goddess. "Do whatever you want. Later. For now, just leave us," she said, knowing the order would grate on Rhea's nerves. "I have a few things to discuss with him and *then* you can have him." There. That should throw her mother for a loop.

At first, Rhea didn't obey. She sauntered to the other side of the bed and ran the sharp tip of a nail up Gideon's leg, stomach and then throat. Gideon latched onto her wrist and growled. She laughed that tinkling, dead laugh.

"Bitch," he croaked, and then hunched over on another moan.

"You know, I think I'll have him anyway." With a smile that returned every bit of her satisfaction, the queen disappeared, leaving Scarlet alone with her husband.

Finally Scarlet was able to climb up the bed as she'd wanted. Very carefully, she settled beside him, her pulse hammering at the base of her neck. "Are you a prisoner?" she asked, smoothing the hair from his damp brow.

He leaned into her touch. "Yes."

A lie, she knew, because his answer wasn't followed by another moan. "Why are you here?"

"Not to...find...Zeus."

Some of the ice around her heart melted; she couldn't stop it. So. He *had* meant to seek revenge. "Killing him won't make you feel any better," she said softly.

Their gazes met, a heated tangle. "Not willing to... find out."

"Cronus won't allow you to do that. So why did he bring you here?"

Gideon's smile was brief yet still pained. "He doesn't need my help with the Hunters. I didn't ask him to bring me here so I can recover from the truth I spoke. I don't plan to make my way to Tartarus."

"You spoke the truth? In the forest?" Scarlet flattened her palm over his cheek, thumb tracing the bruise under his eye. "Stupid man. Believe me, if I thought it would ease my pain, I would have found a way to kill Zeus long ago."

"Scar." He reached up with a shaky hand and cupped her nape. His grip was weak, but she knew what he was doing. Offering comfort. Comfort she had been denied for so long.

Tears suddenly burned her eyes.

Dangerous. Too dangerous. She couldn't allow this. Couldn't rely on him like this. Not for anything, even something as simple and wonderful as comfort. What would happen the next time she needed consoling and he wasn't nearby or didn't want to offer it? She would need it, wouldn't know how to cope without it.

She straightened, and he was too weak to follow her movement. His arm thudded back on the mattress.

You are hard. Uncaring. "It's treacherous here in Titania," she said coldly. "You jailed many of these Titans, and they'll be all too happy to kick you while you're down."

"Care. I do."

He might not, but she foolishly did. "We should return to Earth."

"Sure, sure."

Sweet, resisting man. "Gideon—"

"What if Zeus wasn't the one to take my memories of you and Steel? What if he didn't remove them to keep me from kissing him?"

That…that made sense, she realized. Zeus had been so powerful, he very well could have removed Gideon's memories to prevent the warrior from killing him for Steel's death. Although the gods and goddesses of memory were usually the only ones capable of such a thing. Zeus could have paid one of them to do it, however.

With each new thought, rage sparked inside her. The same rage she'd born in her cell, the same rage she'd carried with her since her escape, but stronger. So much stronger. Zeus might have stolen more than her son. Zeus might have stolen her future.

Why she'd ever been content to let him languish, she didn't know. It was so unlike her. Perhaps someone had screwed with *her* mind, as well.

"I'll help you reach him," she said with such deadly

calm even she was scared. Rivers of blood would flow. Screams would echo into a thousand midnights.

She wanted to go now, this second, to finally act, but morning was fast approaching and she would fall into that undisturbed sleep, unable to care for herself.

In this, she realized she did need Gideon and she *would* allow herself to use him. Tomorrow... Oh, yes, tomorrow. Vengeance.

"He will suffer," Gideon said on a ragged breath, mirroring her thoughts. Once again, he moaned in pain, but his next words rang out clearly. "I swear it."

CHAPTER ELEVEN

ZEUS'S MENTAL doorway was closed and locked with a *Do Not Disturb* sign draped on the knob.

For hours, Scarlet waited in front of that doorway, clawing and kicking and pounding, something that usually bathed the target in fatigue. Even gods and goddesses. Yet the entry remained closed.

He was awake and fighting the lethargy with a strength he shouldn't have possessed. Not with his slave collar. But he would have to sleep eventually. Everyone did, even deposed god kings. And when he did, she would be there.

However he'd convinced her to allow him to suffer from afar…she might never know. The fucker had killed her son in front of her, and had likely taken Gideon's memories of her. He was the reason her heart had withered and died. He was the reason she had cried herself to sleep so many nights. And he could very well be the reason she'd felt abandoned, alone, forsaken and used.

None of that mattered to her demon, however. *Must feed,* Nightmares said.

She understood, knowing well the consequences of denying her other half what he needed. He wouldn't want to, but he would be forced to feed on her.

So, though she would have preferred to stake out the Greek for all of eternity, she approached Galen.

And, to be honest, hurting him would calm her down. Somewhat.

Thankfully, *his* doorway was open. His dream was as turbulent as before, only this time it was all his own. Over and over he relived what she'd shown him. His helplessness. His weakness. His defeat at Gideon's hand.

Nightmares drank in his terror, luxuriating in the emotion even though the demon hadn't caused it, before scenting someone else's fear and moving on. And then another. When the demon was finally sated, Scarlet steered them toward Gideon's doorway. It, too, was open.

Her warrior slept. What thoughts drifted through his mind?

Walk away. A command from her sense of survival.

Can't. A cry from the most feminine part of her.

She was trembling as she stepped inside, and what she next saw left her gasping. There she was, wearing a beautiful red gown, yet chained in front of a strong, struggling boy who appeared half human, half demon. Zeus stood behind the boy, a curving knife in hand, glinting silver. Around them was a crowd of people cheering.

Not a memory, she realized, because Gideon had some of the details wrong. He was simply creating a scene from what she'd told him.

For a long while, she debated: show him the truth or leave him to the illusion. An illusion that would be much easier to digest than reality.

He needs to know. Who spoke to her this time, she didn't know.

Did he, though? Sometimes she would prefer not to know herself.

He needs to know. For Steel. Steel deserved a father who knew how he'd lived—and died.

With that, Scarlet's reservations vanished. For Steel, she would do anything.

Trembling, she reached out and waved a hand over dream Scarlet's gown. That was the easiest correction to make and a good place to start. The material disappeared as if her palm was an eraser. Then, with another wave of her hand, she repainted her clothing. A dirty white robe, stained with blood. Ripped at one shoulder. She added cuts and bruises to her face and arms.

Gulping, she eyed the crowd. Using both hands, she wiped them away, leaving herself, Steel and Zeus, and a figure cloaked in darkness. A being whose feet didn't quite touch the ground, the hem of his black robe blowing in a wind no one else could see. The being who would accept and cage Steel's demon.

Without the cheers, a near-deafening silence took over.

Next, she changed the surrounding hippodrome where Zeus had often hosted his chariot games to an abandoned temple. White alabaster columns rose all around, dewy green ivy climbing their beveled lengths. There were steps that led to a cracked marble altar, each stained crimson from the many sacrifices that had taken place there.

That done, she turned her attention to Zeus. Her fingers curled in as her mind shouted *avoid!* She might snap. But she didn't stop. His gold and purple robe was the first to go. In its place, she painted armor. Silver. Etched with jagged yet beautiful butterflies that matched the tattoo on her back, as well as the tattoo on Gideon's right thigh. Between each of the butterflies was a glowing bolt of lightning.

The knife the Greek sovereign held became a serrated machete crafted for maximum pain. With it, he didn't just slice. He ruined.

Do it. The rest. Gideon had gotten the god's facial features correct. Eyes that mirrored the thunderbolts adorning his armor, snapping, sizzling, glowing. A blade of a nose. Thin lips, but a strong jaw that more than made up for the shortcoming. Zeus had thick, pale hair that curled to his shoulders, the perfect accompaniment to skin the color of bullion. Sometimes, when you looked closely enough, you could see the streaks of lightning shooting through his veins.

Good. Survey done. Only, it wasn't relief she felt. One last detail to change...

Finally, she moved her attention to Steel. Tears instantly burned her eyes, and her shaking increased, nearly toppling her into a sobbing heap. All the while, she could feel helplessness churning inside Gideon. He wasn't here, was merely watching with a mental eye, but his emotions were completely engaged. Everything he felt here, he would feel later, when he awoke.

Do it. Just do it. She shaved Steel's horns down, hating the action, hating herself; the Greeks hadn't wanted the boy to use them as the weapons they'd been. She added patches of scales along the right side of his body. *So beautiful.* His teeth, she sharpened so that two fangs protruded over his bottom lip. *My baby.*

Humans would have found the boy grotesque... beastly. She found him lovely. Her heart lurched, so badly did she want to urge him to her chest and hold on forever. *My angel. Taken too soon.*

Finish it. Gulping again, chin trembling, she lengthened the boy's eyelashes and changed his eye color from black, like hers, to electric blue, like Gideon's. She added several years to his age. Gideon had pictured him as a young boy of eleven or twelve. He'd appeared closer to sixteen, a teenager who had never had the chance to date or make love. A teenager who had never felt worthy or loved, and oh, she knew that feeling well.

In actuality, though, she didn't know if he *had* dated or loved anyone.

Her tears began to fall freely as she covered him in dirt and bruises, broke his arm, his leg, and added thick scars to his back. *Hundreds* of them.

There. It was done. For good or ill, it was done. The scene was painted.

And now...now it was time for Gideon to see how things had truly unfolded.

Unsure whether she could live through this again— *for Steel, anything for Steel*—Scarlet nodded, arms falling heavily to her sides, and each image jerked to sudden life.

"Please don't do this," dream Scarlet begged. "Please. I'll do anything you want." The cut on her lip split, and blood seeped down her chin. "Just leave him alone. *Please*."

Zeus's hard expression never wavered. "Countless times you've tried to escape, and yet you expect me to offer you a boon? Surely even you couldn't be that foolish."

"He's just a boy. He did nothing wrong. Punish *me*. Kill *me*. Just let him go. *Please*."

"He's *not* just a boy. He's centuries old."

"Please. Please, Your Highness. Please."

Through it all, Steel kept his head bowed and his eyes averted. He wasn't trembling, he wasn't crying. He was silent, still. Expectant. As if he *deserved* everything that was to be done to him.

"As long as he lives, you will continue to defy me," Zeus said. "Therefore, he must die. Simple, really."

"I won't try to escape again. I swear it. I'll return to prison and quietly rot there. *Please*."

"You had that option, daughter of Rhea. Once." Gaze never leaving her, the god king tossed his blade in the air, caught it by the handle. "But I must admit, I do like the thought of your head rolling. Perhaps I was too hasty in selecting who should die. What do you think, Steel? Shall I kill your mother or shall I leave that honor to you?"

At that, Steel finally looked up. Shock curtained his features, overshadowing the acceptance and shame. "M-mother?"

Such a sweet voice, with hints of smoke and cloud.

Scarlet offered him a watery smile. "I love you." The very words she'd yearned to say for so long. "No matter what happens, Steel, I love you. I've always loved you and always will. I didn't give you up, my darling. You were taken from me." Choked now.

"Yes, she's your mother. Yes, you were taken from her," Zeus confirmed as the teen turned to him in stunned confusion. "You may offer your thanks now."

Steel's shock gave way to horror, liquid red bleeding into his azure irises. He was the reason she was chained, after all. Thinking she was an enemy to the crown, he'd led Zeus straight to her. "Mother," he said again, and this time, there was pain in that beloved voice. "I—I—"

"Don't blame yourself, sweet boy. You are everything I wanted you to be. Strong. Lovely. Intelligent. You did exactly as I would've done had the situation been reversed. I love you so much." She couldn't speak quickly enough, knowing that at any moment—

"Enough," Zeus barked, just as she'd feared. "I asked a question and desire an answer. So which is it to be, Steel? Will her death be delivered by my hand or yours?"

"I—I don't want you to kill her." Steel's watery gaze drank her in greedily, as if he were memorizing every little thing about her. "And I do not wish to kill her, either. Let her live. Please." His plea mirrored all the ones she'd given before.

Scarlet fought with every ounce of strength she possessed. She had to reach him. Couldn't bear to see him pained. "I'll be fine, darling. Let him do it. It's fine, I swear to you." She would rather die herself than allow a single scratch to befall Steel.

"I will not be merciful," Zeus said.

"I don't care," Scarlet told them both. Better she suffer now than Steel suffer in the coming centuries because he'd murdered her.

Silence. Terrible, terrible silence. But then, something far worse. "Kill me instead," Steel said. "I am nothing. No one."

"No!" Scarlet screamed.

But Zeus nodded, stroked his jaw and ignored her, focusing on her son. "You're right. She's much too valuable to dispose of. As the bastard daughter of Rhea, she is an embarrassment to Cronus and thus a priceless weapon to wield against him should the need arise."

She calmed. A chance. Hope. Zeus considered her a tool to be used against his enemies.

"Still. She must be punished for her actions. Whatever shall I do, then?" he asked, seeming genuinely pensive.

Hope dwindling... "Send Steel away," she pleaded. "That will punish me. I'll wonder where he is and what's happening to him. Please. *Please*. Nothing would hurt me more than that. You know this is true."

Slowly Zeus grinned. He nodded. "An excellent plan. I'll send him elsewhere."

Hope renewed, flooding her. "Thank you." Her shoulders sagged, her breath emerging shallowly. Her son would be safe. He would live. He would grow into the man he was meant to be. "Thank you so much, great king." Thanks continued to pour from her lips. She was babbling, she knew she was, but couldn't stop. "Thank you."

But she'd spoken too soon.

"I'll send him to the afterlife," the god added, at last silencing her. "As I originally planned."

As he'd always planned, she realized. He'd never considered letting the boy go, had only been toying with her.

Steel's eyes widened. In fear, in regret, then fixed on hers in resolve. "I'm sorry. Mother."

Scarlet screamed, the force shaking the temple, shattering her own eardrums. "No! *No!*"

"Yes." With no hesitation, Zeus raised the blade and struck.

GIDEON AWOKE with a roar and bolted upright. Tears were streaming down his cheeks in streams of acid. With a shaky hand, he reached up and wiped them away. Dear gods. He'd just seen Zeus slit his son's throat. He'd felt Scarlet's pain and helplessness. Her desperation.

That's how it had happened, he knew it was. Scarlet had shown him. He'd sensed her in the dream. Her sweet scent, the intensity of her emotions. She truly would have done anything to save that boy. *Anything.* That's how much she'd loved him. And she'd had to recover from his loss alone.

Gideon wouldn't have been able to do so. He was barely holding himself together now, and he *still* couldn't remember the boy. That beautiful boy. How strong Scarlet was. How resourceful. She was a survivor to the marrow of her bones.

His respect for her doubled. His desire for her tripled.

She deserved to be pampered. She deserved to be fought for as the prize she was. So pamper her he would. Fight for her he would. He couldn't make up for the past, but he could give her a better future.

Lock her away again? Never! He'd been a fucking idiot to think otherwise. Dangerous or not, she was his. He would kill anyone, even his friends, if they threatened her.

He'd have to find her, though. A difficult task, surely, considering she wouldn't want to see him. And—

His gaze had been circling the bedroom, ensuring no enemies lurked nearby, a habit ingrained from centuries of war. Now he stopped abruptly.

Scarlet. Here. Sleeping. *Surreal.*

She was cuddled up beside him, her legs straight,

one hand flattened over her heart, the other draped over her forehead. That mass of silky black hair was splayed around her shoulders, gleaming like polished ebony. She was a feminine feast, made to love and be loved.

He reached out, realized his shaking had increased—damned truth-telling weakness—and caressed a fingertip down her nose before his muscles gave out and his arm flopped uselessly at his side. *Need to touch her.* Always.

For the moment, he would have to be satisfied with the knowledge that she was here. How? Why? Did it matter? *She was here!* They could talk, and he could begin that pampering. Foot massages every day, her enemies' heads delivered to her doorstep like the morning paper.

Come on, baby. Wake up. Through the windowed doors that led to a balcony, he could see that the sun was muted and falling, darkening. That pampering could begin sooner rather than later. Any moment now and Scarlet would—

Her eyelids popped open and she bolted upright just as he had done. Her head slammed into his chin, and he winced.

As she rubbed the point of contact, their gazes met. Her eyes…so dark, so mysterious. So filled with pain and hope and regret. A treasure as priceless as this woman should only ever look satisfied.

She licked her lips and slowly eased back onto the mattress, twisting to her side to face him. Her mouth floundered open and closed for a moment, as if she were searching for the right words to say. He didn't want her to bring up the dream. Not yet. That was a heavy subject and right now they both needed to relax. Or rather, he needed to comfort her as he hadn't done before.

"So, who aren't you today?" he asked, lying down so that they were eye to eye.

There was a flicker of relief on her face. "Scarlet... Long," she replied.

Long. As in Justin. A man with black hair and brown eyes. Gideon almost smiled. Sweet progress. Hopefully, she'd never pick a blond again. And one day, maybe she'd even call herself Scarlet Lord.

Did he want that? Yes, he did, he realized almost immediately. He liked the thought of this woman belonging to him. *Truly* belonging to him in a way that all the world would recognize.

"How are you feeling?" she asked softly.

"Worse."

A lengthy breath escaped her. "Good. That's good."

With the last of his strength, he settled his arm over the curve of her waist. She didn't rebuke him for so intimate a gesture, and he took heart. "When I'm even worse, I don't want to hit Cronus's bedroom." He needed to get his hands on a slave collar. That way, the doors to Tartarus would open right up for him. Those collars were like keys to the gate. To get in, that is. Getting out would be a different matter entirely. "But damn. I've got my necklace, so I can roam freely." Without it, Cronus would know where he was and what he was doing. The god king could stop him and send him back to Buda before he set a single foot in the prison realm.

One of Scarlet's brows arched. "You're saying you don't have your butterfly necklace, so you can't move freely around this palace?"

He nodded, trying to gauge her expression.

She pulled both chains from a knife sheath at her waist, letting them dangle from her fingers. "I've got them. I found where you'd tossed yours like garbage." She sounded almost bitter. "So they aren't just pretty decorations?" Now she sounded…disappointed.

He'd made her think the necklace was a present from him. And when she'd found his, she had thought he'd "tossed it like garbage." As if *she* were garbage. He wouldn't allow her to think such a thing.

I will never lie to her again, he vowed. Then blinked. Wait. He would never purposely mislead her with his lies. Better. "They don't prevent the gods from watching us. From listening to us."

As he spoke, her eyes widened. With that widening, she should have been even easier to read. Only, those orbs offered no hint of her emotions. "The necklaces are blocks, then."

At least she hadn't erupted at his deception. "Exactly wrong."

"Good. Smart." She moved to anchor one around her neck, but he shook his head, stopping her. "But why wait?" Okay, now she looked ready to erupt. Her eyes were narrowed, almost…fiery, and her teeth bared in a fearsome scowl.

"I'm too strong to leave right now—" too weak "—and we shouldn't wait until we're ready to sneak out of the palace to fall off Cronus's radar." They absolutely *should* wait. The moment Cronus lost his connection to Gideon, he would suspect the truth and do everything in his power to stop Gideon from succeeding.

"So you're going to sneak out to—"

Again, he nodded.

Anticipation wafted from her. The two of them were going to Tartarus, and they were going to kill Zeus.

"How long till you're recovered?" she asked.

"Not another day." One more day.

Blink. "So what are we supposed to do in the meantime?"

Kiss. Touch. Relearn each other. Make love. "Not talking."

She rolled her eyes as if he'd just made a funny. "You and me? Talk? I don't think so. We've said all we need to say to each other. We'll work together in this, because we're stronger as a pair, but that's all we're doing. Working together. Killing together."

Great. She was falling back into stubborn mode. But he didn't mind. She could say anything she wanted, do anything to him. He planned to stick to her like pasties on a stripper.

"And anyway," she continued, resolute, "let's be real here. I don't have to wait around. I can sneak through the palace and kill any god or goddess I stumble upon. I'm actually doing you a favor."

A growl rumbled low in his throat, rose, lashed out. The thought of Scarlet traipsing through the palace halls alone did not sit well. She wouldn't be up against humans, but immortals. Stronger, more violent immortals. Pure male instinct wanted her safe, happy and *not* in fucking constant danger.

Calm. He would just have to keep her busy. And if she wasn't interested in talking, that left only one other option. What he'd wanted to do in the first place.

He'd considered himself depleted, but the thought of having her rallied his cells, muscle and bone, allowing him to roll on top of her. She gasped at his weight, but he didn't shift away. No, he pressed himself down, giving her more.

"Talking it is, then," he said, and as he'd done the last time he'd needed to soften her, he meshed his lips into hers.

CHAPTER TWELVE

SCARLET STARTED to utter a protest. She'd already kissed Gideon once, and now had his intoxicating taste seared into her mouth, her body, after centuries of fighting to remove it. Centuries of fighting to forget his weight, his heat, his strength. She didn't need to do so again, didn't need another reminder. Didn't need the cravings to return.

Not that they'd ever stopped.

She thought to push him away. He was weakened right now, and wouldn't be able to stop her when she scrambled off the bed and out of the bedroom. He wouldn't be able to draw her back into his arms, hold her close, overshadowing pain with pleasure.

But then his tongue rolled against hers, so damn sweet she could have wept. *Then* he whispered "Scar" as if the nickname were a prayer, and rather than protest, rather than push him, she cupped the back of his neck with one hand and tangled her fingers into his hair with the other, canting his head.

The kiss deepened, from languid to shattering in a single second. A match lit, thrown. An inferno. Raging. Thoughts derailing. Nothing mattered but here, now. The man, the passion. The past fading.

Thoughts struggling to form.

What are you doing?

Mouths claiming. Feasting. Breath mingling. Warm, then hot, then scorching. Tearing her down. Building her back up.

A glimmer of reason.

Don't just start *to protest. Do it! Protest. Don't just* think *to push him away. Do it! Push.*

Fire, cooling. Ice, crystallizing. Yes, yes. That's what she needed to do. Protest, push. She wouldn't lose herself again. She was smarter than that.

Prove it.

Scarlet wrenched her lips from his. Panting, she said, "You want to talk, we'll talk." Her body shrieked a protest all its own. Still, she continued. "I'm the daughter of Rhea, and I was born inside Tartarus. For thousands of years, it was all I ever knew." The words rushed from her, laced with desperation. Surely this topic would douse her passion completely.

Gideon stilled. There was disappointment in his bright eyes, but also thrums of eagerness. Finally, he was getting what he'd really wanted. Information. "Don't go on." He didn't move off her, though, and she foolishly didn't insist that he do so. "I don't want to know everything about you."

How easy she was. Another declaration like that, and *she* might kiss *him.* "At first, Rhea loved me, cared for me. But then, as I grew older, she began to see me as a threat. She wanted me dead. Real bad."

This topic should have dulled her passion, but it didn't.

Every muscle in Gideon's body tensed. And not in desire.

Great. The distraction ploy had worked. Only, it had worked on the wrong person.

"When we were freed, the Greeks defeated, I tried to follow her to this palace. I hoped to make amends with her, make use of the libraries." To search for information about Gideon, but Scarlet kept that to herself. "She had me barred from entering." Bitterness trickled from her voice, but again, it didn't dull her passion in the slightest. He was on top of her, and all she had to do was open her legs. "She told me I wasn't worthy to walk the halls."

His eyes narrowed dangerously. "How'd you get her to keep you out this time?"

Knowing what he meant—how had she gotten her mother to let her in—Scarlet said, "I bargained with her." Would he be pissed about that? "I have to stop you from giving Cronus whatever it is you promised him. What did you promise, by the way?"

No. No anger. Surprising. "We didn't agree to discuss it at a later date," he said.

Ah. The old you'll-owe-me-a-favor-of-my-choosing-at-the-time-of-my-choosing. "You lied to him, of course." It was a statement, not a question.

Gideon hiked his shoulders.

She'd take that as a resounding *yes,* and wished she could trust herself to flatten her hands on those wide shoulders, feel the muscles bunching and straining underneath. "So there you have it. What you didn't know about my life in a dirty nutshell."

He peered down at her for a long while, silent, searching. So many emotions played over his features. Regret, sorrow and the anger she'd looked for before. "I'm…not sorry for all you've endured. I'm…not sorry for my part in it. Damn it!" The anger clearly won, and he pounded the mattress with his fists, bouncing them both. "I really

love that I can't tell you what I really mean without setting us back a few days."

His apology weakened her as nothing else could
have. His vehemence delighted her. Combined? They
slayed her. "Hey, don't worry about it," she offered, at
last giving in to the desire to touch. Her fingers traced
up his arms, learning every ridge of muscle and sinew.
"Gideon Speak is kinda fun."

Like that, the anger drained from him, wonder overshadowing everything else. "You aren't too good for me.
In every way. No, thank you, devil. For everything."

He thought she was too good for him? *Slayed. Her.*
"No welcome," she replied softly.

He licked his lips as his gaze fell to hers, and suddenly she knew his passion hadn't been extinguished,
after all. "I—I—"

"Want to kiss me?"

He nodded. "I'm not *dying* to do so."

Don't admit it, don't you dare admit it. "Me, too."

One more time, she thought dazedly. She would enjoy
him one more time. Sex, though? No, she wouldn't go
that far. But kiss him, continue touching him? Oh, yes.
She needed to pass the time, anyway. At least, that's
the only reason she would cop to just then. Besides, it
wasn't like she truly would have left him here, helpless
against any god or goddess who entered the room. For
the moment, he was still her husband and she would
protect him.

"If we do this, the shadows and the screams will
return," she warned. "I won't be able to stop them.
They're part of me, part of my demon."

"I dislike anything that's a part of you. I don't want
to experience everything you have to offer."

Melting… "Then kiss me," she commanded. Then his sweet words would cease, and she could begin to rebuild the ice. That needed ice.

Gideon needed no other encouragement. His lips were on hers a second later, kissing her as if he needed the air in her lungs to survive. He moaned as if he'd never tasted anything more delicious. Kneaded her breasts as if nothing, even weakness, could prevent him from enjoying them.

Once again, her blood heated in her veins, a growing inferno that liquefied her bones. Her nipples hardened, ever-ready for his mouth, and her skin tingled, a plea for more.

"Want you clothed," he rasped.

Only time she ever had to translate his demon's lies was when they were in bed, her mind on other things, so it took her passion-fogged brain a moment to realize that Gideon actually wanted her naked.

Sex? she thought again. If she got naked, he would be inside her. She might even beg for it. *Beg…yes…* Hopefully, though, she had a little too much pride for that. "No," she managed.

He paused, lifted his head. Their gazes met, his eyes so bright a blue they rivaled a king's ransom in sapphires. He licked his already moist lips, breathing careful. "How about we don't negotiate?" His voice was rough, as if each of the words had been rubbed with sandpaper.

Negotiate, huh? "All right." Never let it be said that she was unreasonable. "Shoot."

"All rather than half."

Reality: he was willing to remove half her clothing rather than all. A concession, yes, when he could have insisted on full nudity. Eventually, she would have caved. "And in return I get…?"

"Definitely not an orgasm."

Her lips quirked at the corners. "Do you want me to remove the top or the bottom?"

"Top." Lightning fast, no hesitation.

He wanted her pants off, and gods, she wanted to take them off. "Deal," she said with a nod. "You can take my top off." Better that way.

Too bad she hated "better."

His lips quirked as hers had done, because he knew she'd purposely misunderstood. "As if you didn't know I wasn't lying," he said, calling her on it. "As if I don't know you meant to say *pants*."

With a strength she wouldn't have thought him capable of in light of his demon's curse, Gideon shoved the sweats and panties from her waist to her ankles, then off completely. A gasp left her, cool air suddenly caressing her. He didn't give her time to complain or even encourage him. He crawled down her body. And there was the moment to stop him…gone. He pushed her legs apart. Another moment…gone again. He licked the most aching part of her.

"Yes!" Her back arched as she cried out, her hands already in his hair, holding him close.

She rode the waves of pleasure with abandon. No, no, not abandon. Had to keep the shadows and the screams inside. Gideon didn't mind them, he'd said, but she wasn't yet ready to share him. She wanted this moment all to herself, that fiery tongue working her, loving her.

"Don't want more?" he rasped.

"I—I—" *Can't admit it. He'll say something sweet, and more of that ice will melt.* "More. Please."

"No more it is." He continued to lick, his teeth scraping perfectly, making her shiver. Soon his fingers joined the play, one sinking in and out, then two. Three. The shadows pulled, and the screams tugged.

"Gideon." She released him and grabbed the headboard, hips arching in a fluid, desperate rhythm. Felt so good, so damn good. Was propelling her so close to the edge...

"Terrible," he muttered, eye closed to half-mast, lips curled in a half-smile. "Just terrible. Had my fill. Will always have my fill."

He likes it, she reminded herself. *Wants more. Wouldn't ever get enough.*

Ice...melting. Heating...

Don't care, she realized suddenly. She *wanted* the blaze to grow, consume.

Scarlet draped her legs over his shoulders, the heels of her feet digging into his lower back, her thighs squeezing his temples.

"But something I do like...you're not holding out on me." A muscle ticked below his eye as his lashes lifted and he pinned her with a hard stare. "Where are the shadows and the screams you didn't promise me?"

"I don't...I can't... Don't stop now!"

"Don't let them go, and don't show me our wedding," he said, and then sucked her clitoris between his teeth.

She screamed, she shook, she almost came, the pleasure was so intense. But she wasn't quite there. Just a little more, and she'd fly to the heavens. "Please."

"Scar…wedding…I don't want to see it." His voice was strained, as if he had to force the words out.

"Now?" she panted. While he was…while she was… "We're a little *busy*."

"Can't you do it while I'm sleeping?" He blew a puff of air against her warm, moist folds, and as sensitive as she currently was, she was thrust ever closer to satisfaction.

It was wonderful and terrible, gratifying and frustrating.

"Yes," she grumbled. "I can do it while you're awake." She could project images into his mind at any time. Nightmares was just as able to invade daydreams, after all. But just then Scarlet wanted Gideon concentrating only on her aching body. On the here and now.

"Then, nope. I want you to do it later."

"Why?" Why couldn't he wait till after? Because he feared she'd leave him? Because he thought she'd deny him? "Never mind. But be warned. The ceremony was short, we couldn't risk something longer, and kind of somber." She'd give him what he wanted, though. "Just know that the moment you stop, I stop." There. Bargaining, just as he liked.

"My displeasure," he practically purred, tongue flicking out and darting back and forth over her clit.

Once again, her back bowed. Okay, maybe demanding he continue hadn't been the most brilliant of plans. Her thoughts were fragmenting again, her blood heating yet another degree, her organs blistering before erupting into more of those decadent flames, her bones melting, wanting only to pour over him.

In a burst, the shadows and the screams escaped her

hold, swirling around Gideon and filling the room. Just as well. She could use them to create the daydream.

Concentrate. Scarlet dug through her favorite mental files—files she'd buried and thought to never consider again—and found the one Gideon desired.

Instantly the scene opened up in both their minds.

Late at night, while the prisoners of Tartarus slept, Gideon roused Hymen, the imprisoned Titan god of Marriage, and brought him to the cell they used for making love.

For Scarlet, Gideon had arranged a lingering bath a few hours before, and had given her a clean white robe. Only, that robe was composed of lace and that lace conformed to her curves. She'd never felt lovelier, before or since.

When the two men stepped into her cell, she threw back her hood in eagerness, and her long, dark hair cascaded over her shoulder, brushed and silky for once. Gideon reached out, pinched a lock between two fingers, and brought the strands to his nose. He breathed deeply his gaze perusing her.

"Hideous," the Gideon between her legs breathed just as the Gideon in the dream rasped, "Exquisite."

A blush stained her cheeks, then and now. But she wasn't the exquisite one, and she knew it. There was no more gorgeous sight than Gideon. His black hair rose in spikes, his blue eyes were bright, the midnight lashes framing them like feathered fans, and his lips still swollen from her earlier kisses.

He possessed a shadow beard, sharp cheekbones and a strong jaw. There wasn't a flaw to him. He wore the thin silver armor she'd shown him in his dream of Steel, as directed by Zeus, and that armor was etched with jagged butterflies exactly like the tattoos they now bore.

"Are you sure you want to do this?" she asked nervously. Back then, her voice had lacked the...hardness of today, and even Scarlet had to acknowledge how sweet and innocent she sounded.

"I've never been more sure of anything in my life, sweetness."

Her blush intensified, and ever shy, she cast her gaze to the ground, lips curling into a happy smile. "I'm glad."

"Well, I'm not sure about this," Hymen said. He cleared his throat, drew his hood around his face to keep his features hidden in shadow. "If anyone learns of my part in this, I'll be executed."

Gideon's arm wrapped around Scarlet's waist, a clear gesture of possession. "I told you. No one will learn of it, and besides that, you've already been handsomely rewarded."

"But I—"

"Discovery is the least of your worries," Gideon barked then. "Marry us or feel the sting of my blade. Those are your only choices. And, Hymen. If you feel the sting of my blade, it won't be only once. No one will recognize you when I'm done."

Hymen shifted from one foot to the other, his fear palpable. "Of course, of course. We'll start now." The words rushed from him. "Gideon of the Greeks, tell Scarlet of the Titans why you wish to wed her."

Those piercing blue eyes met her dark black ones, and he took her hands in his. "From the first, you enchanted me. You are more than beautiful. You are smart and strong and determined. When I'm with you, I want to be a better man. I want to be worthy of you."

As he spoke, this long-ago Gideon, more ice melted around Scarlet's heart. But he wasn't finished.

"I want to provide for you. I want to give you the life you deserve. One day, I will. Because I know, deep in my soul, that to part is to die."

Tears flooded Scarlet's eyes.

"Scarlet of the Titans," Hymen said, a little choked up himself, "please tell Gideon of the Greeks why you wish to wed him."

While her knees knocked together, Scarlet struggled to find adequate words. Words that would tell this man exactly how she felt. "From the first moment I saw you, I was attracted to you and hated myself for it. But how could I have known that underneath your beautiful exterior was an irresistible mix of courage, passion and tenderness? You quickly proved your worth, and taught me mine. I was a slave, but you made me a woman."

His eyes were filled with tears as well, she noticed.

"You are my everything," she whispered, chin trembling. "My past, present and future. My heart. My life. To part is to die."

Hymen swallowed audibly. "Kiss now and forevermore seal this union."

Gideon didn't hesitate. He wrapped his arms around her, drew her close and pressed their lips together. Their tongues met, twined, his breath filling her lungs and her breath filling his.

They were one.

In the present, Scarlet allowed the image to fade. She realized she'd never released the headboard, and the metal was bent. Realized Gideon had stopped pleasuring her, but she hadn't noticed, so lost had she been in the memory. So lost, in fact, that real tears were now streaming down her cheeks.

They were streaming down Gideon's, too.

Their gazes met as they had inside that cell, and she saw the emotion swimming in those baby blues.

He was the same, yet so completely different. And the differences weren't physical, though his hair was now as bright a blue as his eyes. He was harder, harsher, more distanced. Before, he'd had an easy smile and had delighted in soothing her with his biting observations of both the Greeks and Titans.

"Do you know why this prison is so big?" he'd once asked her. "Tartarus is overcompensating for the size of his dick."

She'd nearly swallowed her tongue, she'd gasped so hard at his irreverence. She'd always wanted to insult her captors, but had been too scared. Gideon had given her the freedom to do so, to finally vent, even in so small a way.

Now, he opened his mouth, but no words emerged. Perhaps he didn't want to lie just then, and she was grateful. She was too raw, too vulnerable, as if her heart had been cut out of her chest and presented to him in a ribboned box.

Slowly he climbed up her body. Still not speaking, he kissed her. Again, she didn't protest. She simply opened to him, accepting everything he wanted to give. She tasted herself, sweet and warm, but also him. Wild and minty. Before, his hands had been all over her. They'd kneaded at her, both taking and giving pleasure. Now, he cupped her cheeks, infinitely gentle. Giving all, taking nothing.

And like that, the icy shell she'd spent centuries erecting stopped melting. It simply tumbled down, brick by frosted brick.

"Not going to…won't…don't trust me, devil." Gideon unzipped his pants. "Not going to…" Again, he didn't finish. He simply pressed his erection between her legs, hard and unbelievably thick, unyielding male to weeping female, and hissed. He didn't sink inside but rubbed… creating the first bloom of a fever. A slow burn, but all the hotter for it.

Trust him not to take what she hadn't offered. But really, she wouldn't have stopped him if he'd poised himself for penetration. Still. He never did. He contented himself with the rubbing and the kissing, tongues rolling, savoring, simply basking in all that she was, as she did with him.

For a moment, she pretended they were back inside that cell. That this man really was her husband. A husband who loved her, who placed her needs above all things, even himself. She pretended that he would return to her tomorrow as well, love shining in his eyes. She pretended their only obstacle was her imprisonment.

"Gideon," she moaned.

Perhaps he'd been doing the same, pretending, because the sound of her voice snapped him from that steady pace. His movements toughened, sped up. Became more frantic. He'd always been so gentle with her, treated her like a porcelain doll, but now…he was dirty and wanton, consuming, the friction sparking.

She drank him in greedily, luxuriated. And it was easy, so easy to do. To give herself. To lose herself. Even though he was different now. Maybe *because* he was different.

"Not…my Scar. Not my Scar. Don't touch me," he pleaded. "Please, don't touch me."

Touch. Yes. Must. She pried her fingers from the headboard, her hands falling on him, nerves tingling back to life as her nails grazed his skin, leaving welts. He roared, a song of absolute contentment tinged with utter despair. The past and present, discordant yet soothing.

"You…you…" he said, then stopped himself. "Scar." A prelude, a waiting storm. "Don't come, don't come for me, don't you come for me." With every word, his cock pressed against her clit.

Every muscle in her body stiffened, pain in its most exquisite form. The shadows danced faster…faster… the screams grew louder…louder…until hers joined the symphony, the edge of completion rushing to meet her halfway.

She hurtled over, shaking, shouting, clutching at the man responsible. "Gideon!" *My Gideon.*

Soon he was shaking as well, roaring again, louder this time, and warm seed was jetting onto her stomach. That only increased her pleasure, spiraling her into a deeper awareness of her body. He was on top of her, weighing her down, all over her, his semen on her skin, branding her.

A marriage of the flesh, base, instinctual. What she'd craved, had never thought to have again. What she'd needed, despite the repercussions.

What would surely be the death of her.

An eternity later, they collapsed together, Scarlet into the mattress, Gideon still on top of her. As the shadows and screams dispersed, neither of them moved. They lay there for a long while, trying to catch their breath, still completely lost in the moment. This was, perhaps, the only relaxed, contented moment they would ever have, because she couldn't allow this again, she realized.

She had to replace the ice.

There was no other way to protect her fragile heart. A heart she couldn't afford to give away. Not again. She barely had any pieces of it left. But there *were* pieces. And that was just as shocking.

Save yourself. Hurry! She shoved him off her and sat up, not trusting herself to look at him. "Get some rest," she said coldly. "I'll make sure no one enters the room."

Last time they'd fooled around, he hadn't complained about the abrupt change in her. He'd simply done as she'd ordered. Mostly. This time, he latched onto her arm and jerked her backward, twisting her so that she landed on her stomach.

Before she had time to protest—*so you'd give one now?*—he raised her shirt and planted a soft kiss on her lower back, where her tattoo rested. *TO PART IS TO DIE.* The action was so unexpected, so astonishing and secretly welcome, she pressed her lips together to cut off her sob. Damn him. *Damn him to hell!*

"Don't stay next to me. Don't let me hold you," he whispered. "Please."

Resist. You have to resist. But she found herself nodding and whispering back, "All right." *Idiot.*

With a sigh, she curled closer to him. *I'll patch myself up tomorrow.*

CHAPTER THIRTEEN

IMPATIENCE RODE Strider like a damn carnival pony.
Several days had passed since he'd last received a text
from Gideon. Last Strider had heard, Gideon was leaving his hotel due to a Hunter infestation. Understand-
able. But Lies had one more day to check in or return,
and then Strider was supposed to search for him. Hell,
Gideon might be in trouble and counting on that.

Except, Strider had to remain in the fortress. Some
bad shit was about to go down.

What a cluster. Amun, Aeron and William had left
a short while ago to perform a search and rescue in the
fiery pits of hell. Yeah, a real party in a box. Strider
would've liked to go with them, though. At the very
least, to trail behind them and offer what protection he
could. But he wouldn't be doing that, either.

Instead, he found himself standing inside Torin's
bedroom. The keeper of Disease was seated before a
wall of monitors, each revealing a different location in
the fortress, the mountain outside it and the surrounding
city as the warrior typed away on a keyboard.

Normally Torin was nonchalant, irreverent and un-
ruffled. Today he'd tangled his hand through his white
hair too many times to count, causing the strands to
stick out around his head. His neck-to-toe clothes were
wrinkled, and the gloves he wore every minute of every

day were frayed in a few places. His expression was dark and somber, and lines of tension bracketed his eyes.

"Where are the Hunters posted again?" Strider asked.

"There, there, there and there." Torin motioned to different monitors with a tilt of his head. "They're in large groups, and they're surrounding the fortress full-circle."

"How were they able to amass and approach without our knowledge?" Torin's eagle eye usually missed nothing. Helped that he could hack into any system, even the city's, the government's, and study areas from *their* cameras.

"They fucking appeared out of nowhere," the warrior mumbled. "Which means someone flashed them. Lucien can only flash those he touches, so whoever did this is sickeningly powerful. I've summoned Cronus, but he—"

"Is here," a hard voice finished.

Both Strider and Torin turned to find Cronus towering in the far corner. The god king strode forward, the hem of his alabaster robe dancing around his ankles. Interesting.

There'd been no flash of light, as the sovereign usually preferred. Like the Hunters, he'd simply appeared.

Was everyone off their game today?

Like Torin, he was in a state of disarray. His dark hair, now minus any gray, was a mop around his head. His tanned skin, no longer marred by wrinkles, was tight with his frown.

"What's going on?" Strider asked. He didn't mind fighting Hunters. In fact, he loved it. Lived for it. His demon did, too. Every victory was like injecting heroin straight into his veins, a high, an addiction. But this…

Some of his friends were gone. The fortress was filled to bursting with women. Some of them delicate, and in need of serious protection. Hell, Maddox's female was pregnant. How was Strider supposed to win this battle *and* keep everyone safe?

Cronus stopped behind Torin, closer than anyone had dared get to the warrior in years. "Galen is out of commission for the time being, so my…wife—" he sneered the word "—is dealing directly with the humans. And she's commanded them to storm this fortress, destroy it and everyone inside then steal your artifacts from the rubble."

Damn. Damn, damn, damn. He couldn't even rejoice that Galen was out of commission, for whatever reason. This was bad news, all the way around.

A growl rose from Cronus. "Her daring…offends me."

"Kill her, then," Torin suggested, deadly serious.

Strider seconded that motion.

Never had the god king appeared more wistful. "No. I cannot."

The absolute conviction in his tone surprised Strider. "How about I do it?" Killing females wasn't his favorite thing, but he'd had to do it before. Hunters were fond of using women to distract the Lords, to learn about them and ultimately betray them. He did what was necessary to protect his friends. Always had, always would.

Cronus shook his head, though he hadn't lost his pensive glow. "No."

What the hell was holding him back? "Do you love

your wife or something? Even after all she's done to you?"

"Love that whore? No!" A denial spat as if the greedy bastard had just been asked to abdicate his throne.

Kings, man. Worse than females. "Then let me end her."

Cronus rounded on him, fury flickering black and gold in his eyes, and gripped a fistful of Strider's shirt. "You will not touch her. Do you understand me?"

All systems go.

This was a challenge. One Strider couldn't ignore. His demon roared to life, happy, eager to attack. There would be no saving the god queen now. Not without Strider suffering. And that's exactly what happened when he lost. He suffered. And he would do anything to prevent such an outcome. He wanted the heroin.

The king must have realized his mistake. He released Strider, palms out. "My...apologies, Defeat. Do whatever you wish." Though he didn't sound apologetic, the words had the desired effect.

Defeat's eagerness deflated. Challenge over, systems shut down. Disappointed, Strider nodded and smoothed his shirt. "So, you wanna explain? You don't love her, but you want her alive. She's causing you nothing but problems, yet you don't want to end her. I'm drawing a blank on this one."

He could imagine his head separating from his body in the ensuing silence.

Then, "If Rhea dies, I—" Cronus scrubbed a hand down his suddenly tired face. "What I'm about to tell you does not leave this room. If it does, I will know and I will retaliate."

Strider and Torin shared a look, then both of them nodded.

Cronus closed his eyes. Several more minutes ticked by in that lethal silence. Then his shoulders slumped, and he sighed, facing them. "If Rhea dies…I die. We are…connected."

Strider's first thought after absorbing the news? Oh, shit, no. Not good. Not good at all. The Lords needed Cronus. For the moment, anyway. Bastard he might be, but that bastard was helping them in ways they hadn't known they'd needed. He'd provided them with ancient scrolls that listed all the immortals possessed by one of Pandora's demons, giving the Lords a chance to capture them before the Hunters did. He was able to whisk them wherever they wished to go—like the fiery pits of hell. He had given them necklaces that prevented other gods from being able to spy on them.

Strider fingered the necklace in question. A butterfly with blade-tipped wings, exactly like the one tattooed on the left side of his hip, dangled from the center of an unbreakable chain. What would they do without Cronus's aid?

Return to a life of being ignored by the gods? Sounded good in theory, but what if someone else, someone who didn't want them to succeed, took an interest in their cause?

Torin stopped typing and swiveled in his chair, peering up at the king. "But Rhea's helping Galen. And Danika—" the All-Seeing Eye "—predicted Galen would kill you. If Danika was right, Galen will also be responsible for Rhea's death. So why would your wife aid him?"

Good point. They'd known for months that Galen

would make a play for Cronus's head, but they hadn't known why. Until a few weeks ago, when Strider and a few of the others had finally gotten the surly deities known as the Unspoken Ones to cough up some answers. Whoever presented the Unspoken Ones with the god king's head would be given the Paring Rod, the last of the artifacts needed to find Pandora's box.

Only problem? Each of the Unspoken Ones was part man, part animal and all venom, and he didn't trust them.

They were slaves to Cronus—slaves that would be freed upon his death—and would say anything to gain release. Hell, they may not even know where the Rod was.

Besides, there was no telling what kind of havoc they'd wreak if they were loosed. They liked to eat humans, after all. As in, chomp them out and spit out their bones.

The Rod wasn't worth risking the end of the world. Yet.

"Since Rhea flashed the Hunters here," Strider said to Cronus, "can you flash them elsewhere?" He could have patted himself on the back for that one. Someone should probably dub him Master Strategist.

A shake of the king's head dashed his hopes for such a prestigious (and brilliantly invented, if he did say so himself) award. "She'll simply flash them back. Perhaps *inside* the fortress next time."

"Okay," Strider replied, thinking aloud. "Currently we're missing a chunk of our forces. Which means we won't have an edge if we fight these Hunters. Which means we could lose. Which means it'll be best if we split up. I can take one of the artifacts. Reyes can take

Danika, and Lucien and Anya can take the remaining artifact. We'll all go in different directions. The Hunters won't be able to track us all. And with our new necklaces—"

"I prefer manlaces," Torin said, sounding more like his old, irreverent self.

"Fine." Damn. Why hadn't *he* thought of that? "With our new manlaces, even Rhea won't know where we are."

Cronus stroked his chin, seemingly lost in thought.

"What about the others?" Torin asked, clearly recognizing a phenomenal idea when he heard one.

Strider started designing a Master Strategist plaque for his room. "Maddox can take Ashlyn somewhere. As protective of her and that bun in her oven as he is, he's probably already built a bomb shelter in the city. Now that Gwen's back from her trip to the clouds, she and Sabin can take care of themselves. They aren't in any danger. Aeron's off on his mission to hell and Olivia's taken Gwen's place in the sky, from what I can tell. The others, well, Kane, Cameo and Paris, can stay here with you and defend our home. Gideon can help when he returns." *If he returns.*

He will. Strider wouldn't believe otherwise.

A moment passed in heavy silence, but at least there was no cutting edge to this one.

"What about the fourth artifact?" Cronus asked, returning to the conversation. "Who's going to look for it?"

Bottom line was, they couldn't allow the Hunters to get it. Even at the expense of Cronus's head. "I can," Strider said. "I'll take the Cloak of Invisibility with me.

That way, I won't have to fight anyone if I find it. I can just grab it and go."

Torin arched a black brow at him, green eyes glowing. "Do you have any idea where to start looking?"

Yeah. He did. The Temple of the Unspoken Ones.

Cronus must have realized the direction of his thoughts, because he gave another growl.

"I'm not going to betray you," Strider assured him, palms raised in a mimic of Cronus's earlier gesture. Like Gideon, he could easily lie. Whether he was lying or not, though, he didn't yet know. "I'll remain invisible and listen. If the Hunters arrive, if the Unspoken Ones mention anything about the Rod, I'll be there. I'll find it first."

Cronus relaxed somewhat. "Very well. You may go with my blessing."

"And, uh, we had best get everyone on the same page and on their way," Torin said, his voice hard once again. "The Hunters are on the move."

Strider's gaze returned to the monitors, and sure enough, the groups of Hunters were closing in on the fortress. "You tell everyone what's going on," he said to Torin in a rush. "I'll grab the Cloak and kill as many of those bastards as I can on my way out."

Defeat sat up again, once more happy and eager.

Happy and eager himself, Strider palmed a blade and a semiautomatic, his favorite weapon combination. One stunned, allowing him to close any distance, and the other destroyed up close and personal.

This, he thought with a grin, was going to be fun.

DEAR…GODS. The heat was unbearable, the smells of sulfur and rot thick in Amun's nostrils. Thousands of screams assaulted his ears, each more tortured than the last.

Why had he agreed to come here?

Oh, yeah. To save Legion. For Aeron.

Like Amun, Aeron and William were seated in the small but sturdy boat Cronus had summoned for them after flashing them here. Of course, they'd had to promise to do the bastard a favor in return for the flashing as well as the boat.

They were currently navigating the River Styx, careful to remain as still and steady as possible. One drop of that liquid upon their skin, and their life force would begin to drain.

"So, why is Lucifer afraid of you?" Aeron asked William, cutting through the silence as he gently rowed.

The warrior, who was reclining at the stern of the boat, plucking at the tip of his blade, merely shrugged. "Just is."

"There's always a reason," Aeron insisted.

"Yeah, but that doesn't mean I'll always talk about that reason."

William made sure to keep his mind blank, Amun noticed, preventing Amun from reading his thoughts.

Such a delightful journey already. And this was only the beginning.

They had to follow the river to where it merged with the four other rivers flowing inside this vast lair. Phlegethon—the river of fire. Acheron—the river of woe. Cocytus—the river of wailing. Lethe—the river of forgetfulness. And they had to do it without disturbing Charon, the boatman of the underworld responsible for carting the dead to whichever section of hell their lost soul had been condemned to. The fires, the endless pits, the persecution caverns.

Until recently, they wouldn't have had to worry about Charon at all. But upon Cronus's release from Tartarus, the god king had returned this realm to its original state, including the rehiring, so to speak, of its guardians.

Charon, if Amun's sources were accurate, was nothing more than a walking skeleton. He viewed living beings as abominations and strove to wipe them out. To the dead, however, he was courteous.

I would help you with the coming trials, Cronus had told them, just before disappearing, *but I must return to your fortress 'ere my wife does more harm.* Then he'd added, *I bid you good luck, for you will greatly need it. You bested Lucifer, Aeron, and now he wants revenge.*

That "besting" was the reason Legion was trapped here. She had broken a heavenly law and bound herself to Aeron. Lucifer had planned to use that bond to possess her body and escape the underworld. Only, to save everyone he loved, Aeron had allowed Lysander to take his head and break the bond, returning Legion here and ruining Lucifer's plans.

Olivia upset that you left her behind? Amun signed, and William translated, his gaze then roving over the dark, misty water in search of another boat.

A muscle ticked below Aeron's violet eyes. Eyes he, too, was moving over the water. "Yes."

"How'd you manage it?" William asked, sounding genuinely curious rather than cheekily blithe for once. "I know women, and that one is more determined than most. And, well, you've got no backbone where she's concerned."

Aeron ignored the jab. "Lysander helped."

Lysander. An angel. An elite angel, at that. He was Olivia's mentor, the one who'd killed Aeron, and the only man powerful enough to keep a resourceful female like Olivia from following her man.

"She'll hate me when this is over," Aeron added morosely.

Amun caught the bulk of his thoughts. Aeron had nearly called this trip off to prevent such a thing from happening, and that had filled him with guilt. Olivia was his life, his future. He loved her more than he loved himself, more than he loved his friends. She was his everything. But he wouldn't be the warrior she'd fallen in love with if he'd left Legion here to die. Yet he hadn't been able to tolerate the thought of bringing innocent Olivia into this dark, evil place.

She'd been here before, and several demons had attacked her and ripped off her wings. The memories still troubled her at times, and Aeron never wanted her to have to relive those helpless moments. So he'd tricked her into staying with Lysander, who now held her captive in the sky.

In spite of everything, part of him wanted to go back for her and bring her here if that's what she wished. Anything to stop her from hating him.

"Yeah, you're probably right," William replied after some thought involving knives, scissors and a tub of honey. He showed no mercy. But then, he never did. "Women aren't known for their forgiveness. Especially women who've been spending quality time with the minor goddess of Anarchy and a bunch of bloodthirsty Harpies."

Aeron scowled at him, and the warrior just laughed.

That laughter caused Aeron's aggression to spike and his paddling to increase in velocity. Gently, Amun removed the oars from his hands and took over.

Because of the thickness of the mist, he could see very little in front of him. However, he began to see what looked to be pinpricks of orange-gold light. A crackling fire, perhaps? Were they close to the River Phlegethon?

He turned just as slow and easy as he paddled to silently ask the others to verify. But as he moved, he spotted several ripples in the water. Ripples that weren't coming from their boat. His blood heated, and it had nothing to do with the two-hundred-degree temperature.

Amun smoothly locked the oars in their holders and grabbed his guns. Aeron and William caught the significance of his gesture and followed suit.

"What do you see?" William whispered as his gaze scanned the area.

Aeron crouched on his belly, peering intently into the night. A moment passed, silent, taut. "There's another boat," he whispered back. "Several yards ahead."

Amun opened his mind, allowing his demon to search for any incoming streams of conscious thought. All he heard was *Must die, must die, must die.*

Charon, he realized, just as the other boat came into view. A figure wearing a long, black cloak stood in the center. He had flames instead of hair, and a face that was composed only of bone. Worse, with only the barest (yet still earth-shattering) glance, Amun realized Charon's eyes were deep black holes where thousands of souls seemed to dance…or writhe in pain.

"Let me take care of this," William said.

"By all means," Aeron replied.

William stood, and the vessel rocked. "You know me, old friend. It is I, William the Beloved," he called. "We mean you no harm. We just want to pass through."

Old friend? William the Beloved?

Charon lifted both hands and pointed a bony finger at Aeron and William.

Oh, shit. William's thoughts invaded Amun's mind. *Guess I shouldn't have bagged his wife last time I was here.*

Wonderful.

"What does being pointed at mean?" Aeron demanded softly.

"It means we're on his hit list," William responded, sounding grimmer than Amun had ever heard him. "Be afraid. Be very afraid."

Amun, the guardian had ignored. Which made no— The answer hit him, drifting to him from the creature's thoughts. Charon sensed the demon inside Amun and didn't care if he entered hell or not.

Just as, this very morning, he hadn't minded if Galen entered. The memory washed through Amun's mind.

"You demand payment, this I know," Galen had said just before tossing a severed human head into Charon's boat.

Charon had nodded in acceptance, and swept his arm behind him so that Galen could pass. Only, Galen remained in place, jaw hardening. He looked over his shoulder, forward, over his shoulder again.

Again, Charon swept his arm back to usher Galen along.

Galen scrubbed a hand down his face. "I can't. Not yet. There's something I have to do on the surface first."

His hands fisted. "Someone I have to kill before the bastard kills me. But I'll be back. And when I am, you'll remember that I've already paid for my entrance."

"Uh, Amun, man," Aeron said, dragging Amun from his troubling vision. "You listening? Any ideas about what we should do? William says we can't look into the bastard's eyes without losing our own souls, and we can't touch him, either. If we do, he'll be able to compel our gazes to his."

Charon's boat was inching forward, Amun saw, and sparks were now igniting over his fingertips. *Kill, kill, kill,* the boatman was thinking. The obsessive concentration he displayed didn't bode well.

Options? Payment wouldn't work, not for them. Aeron was no longer possessed by a demon, and William was merely an immortal. Charon wouldn't let them pay to pass unless they were dead. Or missing their souls. And the boatman planned to do whatever was necessary to ensure either outcome.

The first thing he planned? Splashing them.

Thank the gods Olivia had supplied them with a vial of water from the River of Life. Found only in the heavens, a single drop could counteract the effects of *this* water. Only problem was, once they ran out, they were out. There'd be no more. Ever.

Better for one man to use one drop than three men to use three drops. More than that, Amun's soul was tied to his demon, so Charon wouldn't want it. Which meant Amun was the only one who could look at and touch the guardian without consequence.

Which meant Amun had to be the one to act.

Have an idea, Amun signed. *On my signal, propel our vessel to the shore.*

"Great. Someone else will be the hero for a change. But what's the signal?" William asked.

This. Amun leaped at Charon, throwing them both into the river. Sizzling water enveloped him, practically burning away his clothing and peeling away his skin. But he held tight to Charon, caging the bony creature within his arms. Perhaps the water negated a little of the creature's ability, because Amun felt no compulsion to gaze at him. Most of his power remained, however. Skeletal hands pushed at him and those hands were a thousand times hotter than the water, like jolts of electricity straight to his heart, causing the organ to stutter to a halt.

Still Amun held on.

Soon, lack of oxygen began to fuzz his brain. He opened his mouth, accidentally swallowed a mouthful of that terrible, rotting liquid and gagged. Death crawled through him, destroying him cell by cell, filling him with decay. Weakening him.

Charon wiggled loose.

The boatman kicked his way to the surface. Though Amun's vision was dotting over with black, he fought his way up, too. Before he could discover whether Aeron and William were safe, Charon batted him back under with a hard elbow to the top of his head. Stars flashed behind his eyes. More of that disgusting water slid down his throat and into his stomach. A stomach now churning and burning with nausea.

Again, Amun fought his way up. The moment he broke the surface, he sucked in as much air as he could. Good thing, too. His boat was out of sight, and Charon was pissed and now determined to end *Amun*. Demon or not.

As Amun treaded water, their eyes met. The souls were swirling, faster and faster, white blurs that hypnotized. And yet, Amun didn't lose *his* soul. Somehow, his demon kept him grounded.

Punish, punish, punish, the creature was thinking. He grabbed Amun by the hair and shoved him under. This time, Amun wasn't strong enough to free himself. He could only flail, sucking in gulp after gulp, dying a little more with every second that passed.

Dear gods. Was this it for him? His muscles seized, preventing all movement. Yes, this was it. The end. His body was shutting down. He'd lived so long, he should be happy about that. But he'd never fallen in love, cherished anyone the way his friends cherished their women, and found that he mourned the lost opportunity.

Inside his head, Secrets roared. Roared so loud and long his muscles twitched back to life. *Can't give up. Can't. Give. Up.*

His demon had never spoken to him before.

Though it required every last bit of his strength, Amun kicked Charon in the chest, shooting them apart, and swam up and away. He glanced left, right, and spotted the shore because William was holding some type of glowing stick and waving him over.

Determined, he breast-stroked toward the light. Until Charon grabbed hold of his ankle and stopped him. Secrets roared for a second time. *Must...fight...*

Secrets even reached a mental claw toward the boatman and unleashed a stream of images inside his head. Good images. The few happy secrets Amun possessed. Secrets that had saved human lives. The giving of money. The giving of organs. Love from afar.

Charon released him and clutched at his own bony

temples. Panting, still dying inside, Amun worked his way to the shore.

William reached for him, but Aeron stopped him. "You can't touch him. You'll weaken, too."

Amun fell upon the ground, sharp rocks digging into his bare, blistered back.

"Open your mouth," Aeron commanded. He was thinking: *Never seen a man in this condition. Will the water be enough to save him? Oh, gods. How could I have brought him here? If he dies, it'll be my fault.*

Amun didn't have the strength to obey. The cool water Aeron tried to pour into his mouth dribbled over the side of his face. And damn it! That had been more than a drop.

"Open, or I'll do it for you," William growled. He meant what he said.

Amun finally managed to unhinge his jaw, prying his lips apart, and a second later a cool stream was dripping into his mouth, slowly chasing away the weakness and the burn.

"That's enough," William said. "There's hardly any left."

"Is he—"

"He'll be fine. Look, the charred areas of his skin are weaving back together."

"Yeah, but how long—" Abruptly, Aeron stopped talking.

A few yards away, voices cackled. Amun didn't have to see to know multiple pairs of red eyes peeked around a bloodstained boulder. He could already hear their thoughts: *Fresh meat.*

CHAPTER FOURTEEN

BACK ON MY FEET and in fighting form, Gideon thought the next night. Well, perhaps "fighting form" was too strong a phrase. Barely-hanging-on-but-forcing-himself-into-action was a much better description. He led Scarlet through secret passageway after secret passageway in Cronus's palace, stumbling over his own feet every couple of steps.

"Sure you're good?" Scarlet asked, squeezing his hand.

"Of course," he lied smoothly. No way he'd turn around and go back to that bedroom. One, he'd make love to her. There wasn't time for that, and worse, she'd have to do all the work and he'd look like a jerk. More of a jerk than he already was. And two, vengeance waited.

"Great. You're doing horribly. We should turn around and—"

"Yes."

"Argh! You're so frustrating. Well, are you sure you know where you're going?" she asked next.

She wasn't a woman to suffer in silence.

"Nope." Thousands of years had passed since he'd last been inside this heavenly citadel, but he remembered these hidden hallways. Gods knew he'd once used them enough, having been one of Zeus's trusted elite. He'd had to sneak the king to his mistresses and the mistresses to the king, all the while listening for plots against his majesty and watching for spies. Then and now, it helped that many of the walls were made of two-way glass.

"Beautiful," Scarlet suddenly gasped out, tugging at him, trying to get him to stop.

"We'll gawk at everything later." No, actually, they wouldn't. They'd be too busy torturing their son's murderer. *Don't think about that until you find the bastard.* The rage would consume him, and he'd use up what remained of his energy.

She knew what he'd meant, knew they wouldn't be coming back. "But I...I've never seen anything like this."

That's right, he thought with a pang of regret. Even though she was the daughter of a queen, she'd been treated like a slave her entire life, denied her birthright not only when all the Titans were imprisoned, but after they were freed, as well. Fuckers! He slowed his steps, allowing her to take in the stardust chandeliers, the glistening marble waterfalls, the orchids blooming straight out of the walls.

How could her mother have kept this from her? How could the woman who'd given birth to her have treated her so poorly?

Like you treated your own son?

Gideon popped his jaw. *Someone stole my memory of him, damn it.*

That didn't ease his guilt. He should have remembered that precious boy. Some part of him should have, at the very least. Yet, of all the times Gideon had seen flashes of Scarlet in his mind, he'd never seen flashes of Steel. He didn't have a single tattoo to represent and honor his dead son.

I'm the worst fucking father in the world.

Lies had nothing to say on the matter; it was as if the demon didn't care about the boy, living or dead, truth or lie, on any level.

But Steel couldn't be a lie. No one would fake the pain Scarlet had projected upon his murder. Not even the actors Scarlet liked to eat with her eyes.

With his free hand, Gideon scrubbed at his scalp. Even now, he couldn't remember his life with Scarlet. Couldn't fucking remember, even though their wedding was the most beautiful thing he'd ever witnessed. She'd glowed. Oh, had she glowed. With love, promise…hope. Just thinking of it, he was humbled.

And yeah, he wanted her to look at him like that again. He didn't deserve it, but he couldn't stop the desire.

He fingered the butterfly necklace once again clasped around his neck. Thank the gods Scarlet had found it and brought it to him. Even though she had every reason to hate him, she'd thought of him, looked out for him.

She truly was far too good for him.

"Can you imagine living here?" she asked with wonder. Wonder tinged with regret and sadness. "I mean, I've been forced to live in caves and crypts and *this* was my legacy. Wow. Just wow."

"Believe me, I don't prefer to live below." Here, he was one of a thousand others who were just as strong as he was. If not stronger. There, he was a man of power.

He wanted to be all-powerful in Scarlet's eyes. He wanted to be well able to provide for her.

Hell, he might just buy her a palace of her own. Actually, no. He'd build the bitch with his bare hands.

"Amazing." She tugged free of his hand, stopped and pressed her palms to the glass. Her own necklace clinked. "People actually read in those chairs?"

He paused beside her and sighed. "Take your time. We don't need to reach Cronus's room, like, ASAP. He won't be returning for me soon, and we don't need to be long gone by then."

"I know that, but why venture into his bedroom?" Her gaze was glued to the heavy velvet drapes and the gold-inlaid tables that filled the empty sitting room. No, not empty, he realized. Someone—a tall, blond male—was striding to the bookcase. "Can he hear us?" Scarlet whispered.

Did she want him to? "Yes."

"Oh. Good. So we can drool in peace."

He didn't recognize the god, but that didn't stop Gideon from hating the male at first sight.

"Anyway. As I was saying," she continued. "Why can't we just head to the prison?"

"We don't need a slave collar to open the gates of Tartarus."

"Hell, no! I'm not wearing a slave collar. Not ever again!"

"We have to wear it, smartie, not just hold it. Now. Do you not know who that is?" *So I know the name of the next man I kill.*

"Of course I do. That's Hyperion, Titan god of Light. Gorgeous, isn't he?"

Damn her and her attraction to blonds. "I might have known the face, but I don't know the name. I also don't know that Hyperion is a sociopath. He doesn't enjoy setting immortals on fire just to watch them burn and hear them scream."

"Sexy."

"You didn't meet him in prison?" he gritted out.

"Met, yes. We didn't share the same cell, though. Unfortunately."

If Scarlet thought to kiss another man the way she'd kissed Gideon, if she thought to allow another man to touch her the way Gideon had touched her, burning to death would be the least of her worries. Right now, she belonged to Gideon. She was his wife. He didn't share. At least, not anymore.

Scowling, Gideon grabbed her hand and tugged her forward. "Not enough of that." His steps were clipped, his boots thumping into the onyx floor. They snaked a corner and another room came into view. A ballroom. Glittery sprites were darting throughout it, dusting and polishing the entire area.

Around another corner, the hall tilted at a steep incline, and though his still-tired thighs hated the burn, he didn't slow. His growing anger gave him strength. Anger, not jealousy. He didn't do jealousy.

"So who aren't you today?" He hadn't asked yet, he realized. But as always, once he wondered, he could think of nothing else. *Say Lord. You had better say Lord.*

"Scarlet…Hyperion. Yes, that has a nice ring to it."

Enough! At the top of the incline, Gideon stopped and spun. When Scarlet slammed into him, he grabbed her by the shoulders and shook her. She kept her gaze averted and…was that…was she… Sure enough. Her lips were curling into a smile. She was fighting laughter, the witch.

Gideon released her, his anger draining. Anger, not jealousy. "You're not begging for a spanking, you know that?"

"I—" Her words cut off as she gasped. Once more she pressed herself against the glass, her amusement forgotten. "That's Mnemosyne. My aunt."

Knee-mah-zee-knee. Odd name. He followed the direction of Scarlet's gaze. Inside an opulent bedroom of cherrywood and gold-threaded marble, a slender blonde sat upon a ruffled pink bed. Her hair curled innocently to the middle of her back. In contrast, she wore a slinky black dress that was slit up both thighs.

"No hurry, remember?" He wrapped his arm around Scarlet's waist. He hadn't dared before. She would have rebuked him, and he'd known it. But she had teased him a moment ago, and she was distracted now; he wasn't above using either to his advantage. He wanted to touch her. All the damn time.

"I have to talk to her, Gideon. Please." Dark eyes flicked briefly up to him, imploring. "She's the goddess of Memory and she might know who messed with your mind. Or how they did it, at the very least. Gods, I can't believe I didn't think about asking her before."

It was the first time Scarlet had asked him for any-thing, and he found, even as urgency raced through him, that he could deny her nothing. "Sure you can't trust her?"

Frowning, Scarlet's head canted to the side. Her gaze swept past her aunt, past the room, to someplace he couldn't reach. "She was always kind to me. Wait. At least, I think she was. She used to hug me when I was sad. Again, I think. My memories of her are fuzzy."

Fuzzy. That wasn't like Scarlet. She remembered every-freaking-thing.

Her gaze met Gideon's, lingering this time, and her frown deepened. "Wait. What was I saying?"

She couldn't remember that, either? "We weren't discussing your aunt."

"My who?"

He blinked down at her. She couldn't recall a conversation from two seconds ago? Weird. And wrong.

His attention returned to her aunt. The goddess of Memory, huh? Gideon had never dealt with the woman; she'd been locked up before his creation and he'd never heard any gossip about her. Good or bad.

Scarlet followed his gaze. "Oh, look, Gideon! That's my aunt Mnemosyne." Eagerness practically buzzed from her as she jumped up and down. "She's the goddess of Memory. Maybe she'll be able to tell us how your memories were taken."

O-kay. "Scar. Don't look at me."

Slowly her head turned, and her eyes clashed with his. "What?"

"Who's not in that room?"

She blinked in confusion, just as he had done a moment ago. "What room?"

He cupped her chin and turned her head back to the glass, so that she was once again looking inside the chamber. She gasped. "Gideon! Do you know who that is? She's the goddess of Memory, and she might be able to tell us how someone screwed with your mind."

His stomach clenched. Clearly, someone—Mnemosyne herself?—had screwed with *Scarlet's* mind. Because if she wasn't looking at her aunt, she couldn't remember the woman.

Could Mnemosyne have taken Gideon's memories, as well?

There was only one way to find out.…

Fury. So much fury. "Just…don't give me a minute to reason out the best way to approach her. Okay? And stop watching your aunt, no matter what."

"I— Okay." She tried to turn her head toward him, but he placed a hard hand on top of her head and held her immobile. "Fine. I'll be still. But why do you want me to keep looking at her?"

"Just don't do it." He didn't want her to forget again.

His arms fell to his sides as he considered their options. There was a doorway from the secret passage that led into the bedroom. Actually, there was a doorway to every room in the palace. But he didn't want to exit that way and reveal the passage to Mnemosyne, just in case she didn't know about it. As long as it was secret, he could use it as a way of escape. Which left only one option, really. Waiting.

Obstacle one. He and Scarlet would have to wait until the goddess left the room, sneak in and then wait for her to return. That could cause all kinds of problems since they needed to reach Cronus's room before the king realized they were missing.

Cronus could have stored the slave collars somewhere else, but Gideon highly doubted it. The king would want them close at hand, easily reachable if he decided to enslave someone new.

Obstacle two. Scarlet would need to sleep soon, and that would force them to remain for another twelve hours. At least. That was a little more waiting than he wanted to do.

On the plus side, Cronus wouldn't be able to find them. They could hide anywhere. But that didn't meant they could escape.

"Why are you doing this again?" a female voice suddenly asked from the bedroom. Only, Mnemosyne hadn't moved her lips. Peering closer, Gideon saw that a second woman had just exited the closet. A servant?

"With Atlas gone," the goddess replied in a bored tone, "I needed a lover."

Atlas, Titan god of Strength. Once, the god had attempted to escape Tartarus and Gideon had helped hunt him down and re-cage him. And it hadn't been easy, either. No one had ever fought so forcefully.

Where had the god of Strength gone?

"But Cronus?" A pair of black stilettos dangled from the servant's fingers as she approached the bed. She was tall and thin, with short brown hair that curled around her head. Plain blue cloth covered her, and not a single piece of jewelry did she wear. "You've only been his mistress for six days, and already he kicked you out of your quarters in favor of a man."

"I don't need a reminder," the goddess snapped.

"Have you learned who the man is yet?"

"No, but I will."

"Is Cronus…?"

"Experimenting with a male lover? Who knows? I'll learn that, too, and eliminate the bastard if so."

The female sighed. "Your sister will never forgive you for taking her place at the king's side."

Mnemosyne laughed, the sound carefree. "Oh, Leto, you ignorant fool. My sister won't bother me. No matter what I do."

Ah. He knew the name. Leto was the minor Greek

goddess of Modesty. She'd been one of Hera's personal attendants yet had given birth to two of Zeus's children, and when the former queen learned of Zeus's infidelity, she had hated Leto for it. Hera had also tried to kill her, which was why Leto had been incarcerated with the Titans and had later, most likely, helped Cronus regain his throne.

Leto bent in front of Mnemosyne and strapped the shoes to her feet. "But how can you be sure?"

"Insurance."

"But—"

A frowning Mnemosyne stood. "You're bothering me now. Leave."

Color bloomed in Leto's cheeks, but she straightened and strolled from the room.

Mnemosyne strode to the full-length mirror just in front of Scarlet and Gideon, heels clinking, and twirled, watching herself as long as possible.

"Perfect," she breathed, her satisfaction clear.

Scarlet reached out and traced the glass, just along the woman's jaw. "Her tone with Leto…that isn't like her. She's gentle. She's unerringly kind. I…think. I mean, even though everything inside me tells me she used to hug me and whisper sweet words into my ear, in the back of my mind, I can see her pushing me down. Yes. She did. She pushed me down. I can see it now."

"Are your memories fuzzing more?" Clearing up, he meant.

She understood. "Yes. The more I watch her, the more solid they become. She didn't just push me, she…yes, she actually kicked me while I was down."

First, the bitch was going to pay for that. Second, Scarlet was regaining her memory with surprising speed.

Gods, he wished it were that easy for him. Just think about something and boom, it was all there. Every last detail. So badly he wanted to relive his every moment with Scarlet and Steel.

"Worry, Scar." *Don't worry.* "You won't get to talk to her."

"Thank you." Such intense longing radiated from her, his chest started hurting. "There's a lot I want to ask her about. The pushing and the kicking. You. What if…what if *she's* the one who hurt you?"

What if. Yeah, he had questions of his own. And damn it. While he could wait for answers, he didn't want Scarlet to have to. There had to be another way inside that room.

He looked down the passage, where they had yet to go. Several more doorways loomed. "Stay here," he said, an idea hitting him. *Come on.* He pulled her with him. The next room was occupied by several servants, but the chamber after that was empty. Perfect. They could exit the secret passage with no one the wiser, backtrack to her aunt's room and enter through the front door. That way, if a quick escape became necessary, running back into the passage would still be an option.

Gideon twisted the knob, relieved when the door opened soundlessly.

Inside the new quarters, he closed the door and watched as the paneling blended into the mirrored wall. Then he faced Scarlet and placed a finger at his lips. *Quiet.* This room might be empty, but he hadn't forgotten that the one next to it was not.

She nodded in understanding.

Avoiding the immaculate feathered bed was tough—he could just imagine Scarlet on top of him, grinding on his always-hard cock—but he managed to place one foot in front of other. Eye on the prize and all that shit. As planned, they backtracked. In the hall, several sprites bustled past with their cleaning supplies. Gideon acted as if he belonged there and they ignored him. With all the immortals that passed through this palace, they were probably used to strangers.

Mnemosyne's door was closed. And damn, he was growing tired of trying to pronounce that name, even in his mind. He'd never be able to say it out loud, anyway, thanks to his truth-curse. NeeMah would have to do instead. Besides, Scarlet thought she remembered this woman pushing her down, so that made the bitch an enemy, as far as Gideon was concerned.

"Let me do all the talking," he said.

"Thank gods. I wasn't going to say anything to you, but since you mentioned it…she wouldn't understand you, so you'd be doing everyone a favor, letting me take over."

He pressed a hard kiss on her lips, a silent thank-you. Then, with his free hand, he palmed a dagger and burst inside.

The goddess gasped as she spun to face him, a hand fluttering over her heart. "What—"

"Hello, Auntie," Scarlet said at his side. "Did you miss me?" He was proud of her. There was iron-hard determination in her tone.

Blue eyes widened. "S-Scarlet?"

"The one and only."

"How did you get up here?" She couldn't mask her outrage. Or her fear. "Your mother—"

"Doesn't matter," Scarlet said. "We have questions, and you have answers. Answers you *will* give us."

Good girl.

NeeMah gulped. Laughed shakily. "Yes, of course. And of course I missed you. I love you so much. You know that. I would do anything for you, just as I did when you were a child. Do you remember?"

A moment passed. Scarlet's head tilted to the side, and she rubbed her lips together as if she were pondering something important. Her warrior-stance relaxed. "I— Yes. Yes, I do. You were so kind to me."

Gideon squeezed her hand. *Don't lose focus now, sweetness.* She was looking at the goddess; her mind shouldn't be fuzzing. Should be clearing. Right? That's how it had worked in the hallway.

"I'm so glad you remember." NeeMah's arms opened, the very picture of love. "Now come over here and give your favorite aunt a hug."

Scarlet tugged from his hold and rushed forward. "I'm so sorry we scared you. We're not going to hurt you, I swear."

Gideon tried to grab her, but she danced out of reach, threw herself at her aunt, and he was forced to watch as smug satisfaction filled the goddess's eyes. Definitely a bitch, he thought. Besides that, his demon was suddenly going batshit crazy. In a good way. The demon *liked* her.

Pathological liars always had that effect.

"I'm just so happy to see you," Scarlet continued, oblivious. Looking at NeeMah must not matter when you were in the same room with her. Or when she purposely wove a deception.

"And I'm so…happy you're alive."

Lie. Both he and his demon recognized it.

The bitch would pay for playing with his woman. He'd thought it before, but now, now it was a need.

"Now. Tell me about the man you brought me." The goddess's gaze landed on Gideon, intent, studying this time. Recognition—followed by shock—claimed her features. "You. Wh-what are you doing here? With Scarlet? What questions do you have for me?"

He ran his tongue over his teeth. Such a telling reaction. She knew him, and she had expected him to stay away from Scarlet. "Scar, devil," he said, waving her back to his side. "Don't ask her if she screwed with my memory."

Suddenly panic overrode every other emotion on the goddess's face. She straightened, stiffened. "Scarlet, my sweet. Your friend is being very rude. And sadly, he's acted this way before, hasn't he?" She caressed Scarlet's temples, rubbing her thumbs in circles. "Even though you try so very hard to instruct him with his manners."

"Gideon," Scarlet admonished, releasing her aunt and turning to him. Her eyes were glazed but narrowed. "How dare you treat my favorite aunt that way? You know better. I've told you and I've told you to treat my family with respect."

Uh. *Excuse me?*

NeeMah remained behind her, taller than Scarlet and towering over her shoulder, but using her as a shield nonetheless.

"Don't ask her!" he shouted.

Scarlet blinked, the glaze fading from her eyes. "Ask her…"

A now-trembling NeeMah laid a hand on Scarlet's shoulder. "Scarlet. You know I love you. You know I would never hurt you. And now you know, much to my regret, that Gideon used you to get to me. He and I were lovers, and he's always wanted me back. Isn't that right? We've talked about this."

Liar!

And yet, power hummed from each of her words, and *Gideon* almost believed he'd used Scarlet to reach this point. That he'd wanted to kill Scarlet and her aunt all along. Because if he couldn't have NeeMah, no one could.

Lies laughed, a giddy sound, and an image popped into Gideon's head. Small, fuzzy, but there. An image of Gideon pacing back and forth, planning. And the more he studied the image, the more the details filled in. He'd been in his bedroom in Budapest, and he'd—

Again, Lies laughed. *Hate it, hate it, hate it.*

This time, he was jarred from his thoughts. If Lies "hated" the images so much, that meant they were fabricated. And if they were fabricated, that meant NeeMah had planted them. And if NeeMah had planted them…

"You used me," Scarlet gasped out. Absolute betrayal filled her eyes as she stared at him.

Had the same false images floated through her mind? Of course they had, he thought. NeeMah was more powerful than he ever could have realized. "Devil, you don't have to believe me. I wouldn't kill your aunt if you were in front of her." *Come on, darling. Move away from her and I'll end her.*

"How could you do that to me?" Scarlet croaked. "How could you use me to win back my aunt after everything you *already* did to me?"

"I never—" Shit. He couldn't say it. Couldn't speak

the truth. "Your aunt is beautiful to me." *Understand what I'm saying, please understand.* "You're not the only one I want."

Grinning now, fear gone, NeeMah backed away from Scarlet. "I'll go get help, my sweet." Despite her expression, her tone was still sad. "You keep him here. Whatever it takes."

"Yes." Scarlet widened her legs, balled her fists. An attack position. And this time, her warrior-stance was directed at him.

What the hell? "Scar, this isn't—" he began, but before he could utter another word, Scarlet had launched herself at him, her intent to kill more than obvious as she slashed at his throat.

CHAPTER FIFTEEN

BETRAYED AGAIN, Scarlet thought darkly. By the same man. And she couldn't fully blame him. She kept letting it happen because she was attracted to him. Well, no more. She wouldn't kill him, she decided just before contact, though part of her knew that was the only way to truly end the madness inside her. But she *would* beat him senseless and hold him here until her beloved aunt returned.

Whatever happened to him after that, she wouldn't care.

She *didn't* care.

As they hit the ground, Gideon arched back to avoid her nails in his jugular. He also took the brunt of the fall. The back of his skull slammed into the floor, and he winced. Must have cracked him good, because blood splattered. To her surprise, he didn't try to fight her off as she straddled his chest and glared down at him.

"I should never have trusted you," she snarled. "Trusting you always destroys another piece of my life."

His hands—hot and hard and callused—flattened on her thighs, as though he was holding her to him rather than pushing her away. "That woman was telling the truth. I did this to you. She didn't. She wasn't lying. She wasn't manipulating your memories and weaving fake stories inside your head." The words escaped him in a rush.

Mnemosyne lie to her? Ha! "You're the only liar here." She drove her fist into his nose, and more of his blood spurted. "That's for forgetting me," she spat. She'd wanted to do this for a long time. Nothing would stop her now. She punched his face again. More blood. "That's for abandoning your son."

Stop, Nightmares cried inside her head. *Don't hurt him.*

Decided to wake up, did you? Well, you can just shut the hell up!

Don't hurt him. Please. He's telling you the truth.

Defending the bastard? You're my demon. Not his. Now do what you were created to do and frighten him. Cover him with spiders.

No.

Fine. She would destroy him on her own. Except, when she raised her fist for a third punch, Gideon didn't turn away. He waited, his expression resigned, even expectant, and she paused. He was letting her hurt him, damn him. Scarlet tried to catch her breath. There was no satisfaction in his acceptance. Only shame.

"Don't think about this, devil."

Devil. His version of *angel* or *sweetheart.* This wasn't the first time he'd used the endearment, and just as before, her heart squeezed in her chest. "*You* don't get to call me that. You don't have the right." Not anymore. "Besides that, there's nothing to think about. You were using me to punish my aunt."

"Godsdamn it, you aren't the most exasperating creature I've ever met."

"You think so?" Scarlet popped to a stand and kicked

him in the stomach. No mercy. She couldn't show him any mercy. "That's for sleeping with her. Actually, that's for sleeping with all your bimbos while you were married to me."

Stop. Nightmares again. Despondent. *You must stop.*

No mercy. *Not until he's dead.* But her own mind rebelled at that. *I thought you'd decided not to kill him.*

Demon red flickered in the depths of Gideon's eyes. "Don't you dare listen to me, to what I'm really saying. I slept with her. I did. Okay? All right?"

There was something about his claim, something she should be considering, but at the moment, she couldn't make rational thought matter. All she could see was Gideon's naked body wrapped around her aunt's, the two lost to their passion. All she could hear were Gideon's moans of pleasure.

He'd wanted Mnemosyne all along.

Scarlet's hands balled, her nails cutting skin. "You're going to regret ever meeting me. That's a truth you can take to the bank. Or better yet, the grave."

"You are *so* not stubborn," he gritted out, remaining exactly as he was. Splayed, hers to abuse. "I will always betray you. Don't you understand? Always. Betray. You."

"I know!" Another kick.

Breath exploded from his mouth. He closed his eyes for a moment, lines of frustration branching in every direction. "Don't think about this," he repeated. "I'd met your aunt a thousand times before. There are many reasons—"

"Shut up! There's nothing for me to think about."

Scowling, she paced around his prone body. Another kick. But again, satisfaction proved elusive.

Growls suddenly filled her head. Nightmares had stopped pleading and was now worked into writhing fury. *Stop, or I'll make you relive Steel's death. Over and over again.*

"You don't know me better than anyone," Gideon burst out on a wheeze. "*Why* would I need you to win her back, when I'd met her so many times? *How* could I touch her if I wanted you?"

Those questions made absolutely no sense. Why was he— Wait. He was Lies, she reminded herself. He couldn't speak truth. Translation: why had he needed Scarlet to win a woman he'd never met, and how could he have touched Scarlet if he'd wanted Mnemosyne? That's what he was really asking.

She raised her fist.

Last warning.

"Because you—" She stopped, frowned. Good questions. She considered her options, her demon panting, waiting for her to strike, to finally unleash a tidal wave of grief over her. A tidal wave that would *not* stop her. "Because you…needed me to make her jealous." Yes, that was it. The knowledge solidified as she pulled the memories of her recent time with Gideon to the forefront of her mind.

Every time he'd kissed and touched her, he'd been distanced. He hadn't made love to her, hadn't tried to penetrate her. Because that would have been taking things too far when he loved another. Yes, yes. The more she considered this, the more everything made sense. The more *right* her aunt seemed.

"Yeah, that's totally my style," he said dryly.

Style or not, it just made sense. "You…bastard! I wasn't good enough to fuck, is that it? You were saving your precious cock for *her*." Scarlet swung her fist down, intending to knock him in one ear and cause his brain to fly out the other.

An image of Steel, cut and bleeding, *dying,* took residence inside her head, and she whimpered.

In the blink of an eye, Gideon was sitting up and gripping her wrist. His eyes narrowed, his lips pulled tight. "You don't want penetration? I won't give you penetration." With a sharp tug, he had her on the ground. Before she could protest, he rolled on top of her, pinning her down with his muscled weight.

Nightmares removed the gory, hated image and moaned. *Yes!*

No way Gideon would—oh, yes. He would. He worked at the waist of her pants, trying to jerk them open and down.

"Stop," she said on a trembling breath. What was happening? "Stop."

More, her demon demanded.

The warrior stilled, but he was panting as he glared down at her, reminding her of herself a few moments ago. When she'd been furious and jealous and…irrational? Surely not. She was thinking clearly for the first time in centuries. Wasn't she?

"You can't accuse me of being a lot of things, Scar, and wanting you more than air to breathe isn't one of them."

Another translation was needed: she could accuse him of a lot of things, and wanting her more than air was one of them. So…he did want her. Proof: he wasn't writhing in pain.

Scarlet gulped back the sudden lump in her throat. He. Wanted. Her. So why had her aunt— Wait. That was the something she'd been trying to remember a short while ago. He had to speak in lies or he would hurt. Savagely. And he'd said, *I slept with her. I did*. Her, meaning Mnemosyne. Yet he hadn't screamed, passed out or grown weak.

So he *had* been lying. He hadn't ever slept with her aunt.

This was…this made no sense.

"I need to think," she said softly.

Gideon eased off her, but didn't move away. She lay there, struggling to put the rest of the pieces together.

First, Mnemosyne had accused him of trying to make her jealous. But what had he done to make her aunt jealous? Nothing, that's what. He'd come up here to find Zeus and avenge Steel. Scarlet had followed him, and he'd been genuinely surprised to see her. Which meant he hadn't planned for her to follow him.

She'd told him about her aunt, and he hadn't acted as if he knew the woman. Granted, that could have been a lie. But then, why would he have arranged for Scarlet to see her if he'd wanted to keep their association secret? The jealous thing, sure, but he hadn't put his arm around Scarlet while Mnemosyne watched. He hadn't tried to kiss Scarlet or seduce her in front of her aunt, either. He'd just yelled at her, commanding her to find out if her aunt had messed with his memory.

That's when Mnemosyne had placed a warm hand on Scarlet's shoulder and told her about Gideon's plan. *Told* her. Yes. The moment Mnemosyne had spoken, the first image of Gideon and her aunt rolling around in bed, naked, had appeared in Scarlet's mind. That image had been fuzzy at first, but the more Scarlet had believed it possible, the clearer the image had become.

"T-tell me you desire my aunt," Scarlet said, focusing on the man above her.

There was a hard glint in his eyes. "I desire your aunt."

Not a flicker of pain.

Not daring to hope, she said, "Tell me you used me to win her."

"I used you to win her."

Again, no pain.

Her aunt had lied to her.

Scarlet closed her eyes. Anything to hide the burning relief most likely banked there. Gideon hadn't betrayed her. *Gideon hadn't betrayed her!* The knowledge was part soothing balm for her battered heart and part kindling for her sudden, raging guilt.

"I'm sorry for kicking you," she said on a groan. "And punching you. And screaming at you."

At last, Nightmares calmed.

Slowly Gideon eased the rest of the way off her. "You're not forgiven." The words offered absolution, but there was no emotion in his tone.

Scarlet cracked open her eyelids, only to see that Gideon had already turned, presenting her his back. Still angry? Hiding his expression? "She's powerful. To have made me believe in your cruelty, and so strongly, so quickly..." Scarlet shuddered. "I can't believe the sweet woman I remember did that to me."

"Yeah, she's a real sweetheart." Gideon flicked her a glance over his shoulder as he stood. Nope, he hadn't been hiding his expression; it was as empty as his tone. "And I'm sure all of your memories of her are correct."

Correct equaled wrong. Every muscle in Scarlet's body tensed. He was right. The image she had of her aunt didn't fit with the woman she'd just encountered. *Of course* Mnemosyne had manipulated her perception at some point.

Mnemosyne had certainly had plenty of opportunities. For centuries, they had shared a cell. A simple touch, a spoken word, and *boom*. Scarlet's life was completely altered.

Dear gods. How many times had Mnemosyne screwed with her head? How many of her memories were fake?

Which memories were fake?

Air burned her nose, her lungs. Suddenly Scarlet didn't trust *anything* she believed. Even…her wild gaze landed on Gideon.

"We don't need to get out of here," he said, extending a hand.

Don't think about this now. You can't afford the panic. Gulping, she twined their fingers and allowed him to tug her upright. As before, when he'd gripped her thigh, his skin was hot, hard and callused. Shiver-inducing. "Enough time has passed that I doubt Mnemosyne went for help. She ran. Is probably hiding. Otherwise, guards would be in here, weapons pointed at us."

Strong shoulders lifted in a shrug. "Better sorry than safe."

"We can't leave, though. We have to find her. I need to…talk with her, find out what other lies she's convinced me of."

Gideon shook his head, resolute. "What Zeus did is—"

"A lie, maybe." The realization hit her and she gasped, her free hand flying to cover her mouth. Maybe Zeus hadn't truly murdered Steel. Maybe someone else had. Or maybe Steel had never been killed. Maybe Steel was alive. Maybe he was out there, waiting for her to find him.

Hope bloomed inside her chest, filling her with a joy she hadn't known since the last time she'd held Steel in her arms. "We have to summon Cronus." She fisted Gideon's shirt. "We have to find out if he knows anything about Steel."

His expression gentled, and he cupped her cheeks. "Scar, devil…"

Devil. There was that endearment again. She rose on her tiptoes and pressed a quick kiss to his lips. Lips still swollen from meeting her fist. Lips that were bleeding and missing a ring. Had she tugged it loose? "I'm sorry" wasn't enough.

"Please, Gideon. I think…I hope… What if he's still alive? What if our baby is out there?"

He opened his mouth. To protest? Then he shook his head violently, scales flashing underneath his skin. "Oh, sweet sunshine and roses, I can absolutely believe I'm doing this," he muttered, releasing her to jerk his necklace from around his neck and stuff the chain into his pocket.

Wow. That was the vilest curse she'd ever heard him utter.

"Cron!" he shouted, fist raised and pumping in the air. "I don't want to talk to you."

A moment passed in silence. Scarlet could barely

contain herself; she felt ready to jump out of her skin. Knew she wouldn't last much longer. Soon she would start shouting threats. Dismemberment, the removal of the king's cock.

"Cron!"

"Manners, Lies. Manners. You're in my home. You do not bellow for me. You ask nicely."

The voice came from behind them, and they swung around in unison. Cronus was perched at the edge of the bed, his lips pinched in displeasure.

Who cared about his displeasure? He was here! Scarlet's shoulders sagged with relief. Answers were within her grasp, hope a living entity inside her.

"No thanks for coming," Gideon said, bowing his head in deference. He'd never done such a thing before, and she knew he did so now for her benefit. Because she was desperate, and he was taking no chances.

Ice...melting. Again.

"Well, well," Cronus said, gaze roving over her warrior. "We've regained our strength, I see. I didn't expect you to recover so quickly. But what are you doing in Leto's bedroom?"

Pleasantries? Now? "I'll do the talking," Scarlet told Gideon before facing off with the king. Knowing him as she did, she knew she couldn't just jump into her demands. "We've learned something disturbing about Mnemosyne. She—"

"Why. Are you. In Leto's. Bedroom?" Cronus asked again. His attention never veered from Gideon.

Argh. "Your mistress was here. We wanted to talk with her."

One dark brow arched, but that was it. His only reaction to her words. Damn him! After the aging curse was cast, after failing to kill her over and over again, he'd decided to ignore her, to pretend she didn't exist. She was an embarrassment to him, after all. Proof his wife had cheated on him.

Like he could cast stones, though. His mistress was his wife's sister.

Gideon sighed, and there was an angry twinge to it. On her behalf? Her guilt returned. She never should have punched him. So many times. "Your mistress wasn't here."

"Which one?" the king asked smoothly.

Just how many did he have?

"Not Mnemosyne," Gideon said.

A curtain fell over Cronus's features, obscuring his emotions. "And?"

"And she didn't try to fuck with Scarlet's memory."

"And?" the king asked again.

"And we don't want to talk to her," Gideon snapped.

Cronus's head tilted to the side as he studied the warrior. "She came to me. Told me you were in here. Tried to convince me you were here to kill me, but what she hasn't yet realized is that her tricks do not work on me. She's currently locked in my chambers while I figure out her game."

"Let me help you with that," Scarlet said, determined. She had a few ideas about how to extract information from her aunt. Needles were involved. So were hammers.

Again, Cronus ignored her. "I want Secrets to interrogate her, but he's otherwise occupied at the moment."

"And you don't expect me to fetch him for you?" Gideon asked through gritted teeth.

"I expect you to return to your fortress and summon me the moment *he* returns. *That* is the boon I require of you as payment for the time you've spent in my palace."

A muscle ticked in Gideon's jaw. Hers, too. Rhea's "requirement" for Scarlet was to *stop* Gideon from summoning Cronus when Amun returned, and she nearly roared in frustration. If finding Amun was the only way to gain information about Steel, she wouldn't stop Gideon. No matter what she'd promised her mother.

No matter what that might cost her.

She'd heard stories about what happened to those who broke their promises to the gods, and those stories had never ended favorably. The liar was always weakened, curses were always heaped and death was always the end result.

Dying before holding her son again…hell, no!

Perhaps *she* could summon Cronus, she thought next, and grinned. Hello, loophole. Her grin quickly faded, however. What if the king ignored her? And what if her promise to her mother was *still* considered broken?

"You're unwell?" Gideon whispered in her ear, drawing her attention.

You're good, he meant. "I'm fine," she replied. Her inattention must have worried him. "Thank you."

"If Mnemosyne is aiding Rhea," Cronus continued, "she must be destroyed. If not…" He shrugged. "I haven't yet grown tired of her and the way she vexes my wife. So either way, I don't think I'll allow you to speak with her."

Scarlet had to fight the urge to launch forward and slam her fists into Cronus's face. To break his nose, his teeth, and introduce his penis to her knee. Multiple times.

Gideon must have sensed the direction of her thoughts because he twined their fingers and squeezed. To comfort her?

"Doubt me not," she said harshly. "I will confront my aunt. And if she lied to me about my son's death, I'll kill her whether she betrayed you or not. Whether you want her alive or not."

Cronus blinked at her, looking at her for the first time since entering the room. "Your son?" His astonished gaze returned to Gideon. "What's she talking about?"

"Steel, damn you," Scarlet shouted. "The child I gave birth to when we were still in captivity. Is there a chance he's still alive?"

Silence. Thick, unwanted silence that slithered through her like a snake, ready to bite, to poison.

Then, "Scarlet," the king said, and his tone was suddenly, shockingly gentle. "We were locked in the same cell from the time of your birth until we managed to escape. You never gave birth. You were never pregnant."

CHAPTER SIXTEEN

THIS WAS THE FIRST time Gideon had ever seen Cronus exhibit any type of compassion. And that he did so toward a female he hated…well, Gideon could now forgive him for his earlier treatment of Scarlet, ignoring her as he had. And yet, Gideon wished there was no need for such compassion.

You were never pregnant. The words, though meant for Scarlet, hit Gideon, and he knew. Knew. *Truth.* Cronus spoke only truth. That meant only one thing. It hadn't been Gideon's memory that had been tampered with; it had been Scarlet's.

No wonder Lies liked her so much, yet hadn't been able to tell if she spoke true. She was a living falsehood, but didn't know it. They'd never had a son. They'd probably never been married.

Which sucked. He'd grown used to thinking of Scarlet as his wife.

Perhaps they *had* married, though. In secret, as she'd said. After all, the first time he'd seen her, when she'd told him they had once wed, he'd had flashes of her in his mind, flashes of the two of them, naked and straining toward release. He'd thought those flashes were memories. And yeah, they could have been.

Because the fact was, he'd seen her in his dreams, too.

Before he'd ever met her. That had to mean something. Right?

Steel, though…he'd had no flashes of his son. Not a single one. That, too, had to mean something. And yet, he didn't have to wonder about his feelings for the boy. Now that the fury over Steel's supposed treatment was gone, he realized he possessed a spark of love for what might have been. He truly mourned his child's loss.

And if he mourned, when he'd had only that one glimpse of Steel, the glimpse Scarlet had given him, how much worse must *she* feel?

Scarlet's gaze darted between the king and Gideon, Gideon and the king. She was shaking her head continuously, trembling, gasping for breath. His heart actually wrenched inside his chest, scraping against his ribs. He hated to see her like this. So torn up and vulnerable.

"You're wrong. You have to be wrong. I held my little boy. I *loved* him." The last was said angrily, as if daring the king to contradict her.

Frowning, Cronus rose from the bed. "There are too many eyes and ears here." He waved his hand and their surroundings simply disappeared, leaving only a wide expanse of thick, white mist. The air was cool, fragrant with the sweet scent of ambrosia.

Gideon breathed deeply, savoring this moment of calm before the coming storm. The mist thinned, cleared, and he saw that they were in the heart of an ambrosia field, the tall flowering vines rising from the ground, pink flowers reaching toward the glowing sun.

Sun. Shining. His attention whipped to Scarlet. He expected her knees to collapse and her eyes to close as sleep claimed her, but she remained standing. Awake. Not even yawning.

How?

"This is a realm where night and day are one," Cronus explained, as if reading Gideon's mind. Hell, he probably was. Some immortals could do so. Gideon knew that Amun could. "Besides that, Scarlet's demon operates on a time scale, not the rise and fall of the sun."

Didn't bother him when Amun read his mind. Cronus, though, bothered him greatly. What he was feeling for Scarlet and Steel was private. His. He didn't want to share. Not because he was embarrassed about the softer emotions running rampant through him, but because he wanted every part of them all for himself. Real or not.

Not important right now. Your woman is all that matters. He wrapped his arm around Scarlet's waist, intent on soothing her the only way he could, but she jerked away from him, still shaking her head, her trembling becoming violent.

"My son was real. My son *is* real."

"In your mind, no doubt he is." Cronus pivoted on his heel and eased forward, forcing Gideon and Scarlet to follow. His fingers brushed the tips of the vines as he said, "Here's how Mnemosyne works. She places her hand on you, for contact increases the power of her suggestions. She then tells you something. If it's something you want to hear, your mind accepts it more readily. If not, she'll tell you something else, then something else, until she's woven a tapestry inside your mind."

Scarlet tripped over a vine, and Gideon grabbed her by the T-shirt, hefting her up and keeping her on her feet. She didn't seem to notice, kept striding forward, remaining close to Cronus and glued to his every word.

Gods, she was lovely in the sunlight. Even lost to sorrow and confusion, she seemed to soak up the rays and glow from within.

"Do you understand now?" Cronus asked.

"No. Her methods don't explain anything," Scarlet lashed out. "I know every detail of Steel's life. *Every* detail. My aunt could *not* have created so complex a tapestry."

"She can and obviously did. Once Mnemosyne makes a suggestion, the seed of a memory is planted. The more you consider that seed, the more it's watered, and the more it will grow. As it grows, your mind begins to fill in the blanks, so to speak, making the memory plausible. Making it as real to you as if it truly happened."

Gideon kept his gaze glued on the endless sea of green and pink in front of him. He didn't dare glance over at Scarlet again. She was the strongest female—or rather, person—he'd ever met, but he doubted even she could withstand this type of devastating news without breaking down. A breakdown she wouldn't want anyone to witness.

"I—I—" Her voice quivered. Was drenched with an agony so overwhelming he had never encountered its like. To her, this must be like watching Steel die, helpless to save him, all over again.

Just then, Gideon would have willingly died to give the boy life.

"I can't talk about Steel right now," she said in a tragic tone that rivaled that of Cameo, keeper of the demon of Misery. "Just tell me if Gideon and I were... were..."

Slowly, so slowly, Cronus shook his head. "You were not."

Truth.

Lies roared, furious, disbelieving. And Gideon wasn't sure whether it was because the demon hated truth, or because the demon wanted those words to be a lie.

Gideon hissed in disappointment. He desired Scarlet more than he'd ever desired another, and he liked having her with him. Most of all, he loved knowing she belonged to him and no other man.

Perhaps…perhaps he'd wed her now. For real this time. It was worth considering, at the very least. Because damn, he *hated* the thought of being without her.

No, Lies said. *No.* Yes, yes.

"Why would Mnemosyne not do something like that?" Gideon asked. He was surprised by how rough his voice was, as if his throat had been scrubbed raw with sandpaper.

Cronus sighed. "I can guess. Scarlet's mother. Shortly after Rhea and I were cursed with an aging spell, Scarlet grew unexpectedly happy. Not because we were aging, she hardly seemed to notice that, but because she clearly had a secret. Looking back, I realize Mnemosyne must have begun weaving those memories of you at Rhea's behest, to punish her daughter for the spell. You see, any time Rhea tried to kill her, the queen aged a bit more."

And if the queen had looked anything like Cronus when they'd come out of Tartarus, she had tried many, many times to off his sweet Scarlet. Again, Gideon wasn't opposed to killing females, and he added Rhea's name to his Must Die Painfully list.

"The sisters had noticed how Scarlet watched you," the king continued. "Everyone had. There was absolute longing in her gaze. That's why, I'm sure, it was so easy for Mnemosyne to plant the suggestion of a marriage when in fact, the two of you had never even spoken."

"Oh, gods," Scarlet gasped, tenting her hands over her mouth. Her horrified gaze landed on Gideon. "I—I—"

She had desired him, even then, and the knowledge filled him with pride. But she didn't like that he knew, that much was clear, and he found that he wanted to ease her, even in this.

Gideon stopped, grabbed her by the shoulders and shook her. "Don't recall that even before I met you, I didn't see you in my mind. Don't recall that I didn't even tattoo myself with your eyes, with the same tattoo you bear. We may have married, and we may have met, but I did not notice you, too." *Understand me, sweet. I craved you, even then.*

As he spoke, however, several questions claimed his attention. How had he known about the tattoo? How had he seen it before he'd actually met the woman? Had they been connected somehow?

She'd begun to relax, to nod, but then she stiffened and jerked from his hold. Cold infused her eyes. "After our…fake marriage, after my possession, after I gained control, I entered your dreams until your doorway disappeared. Another reason I thought you were dead. I never used my demon against you, I simply watched over you. That must be how you saw me."

Well, another question answered. And once again, he was filled with pride. So much desire… But not her. There was no pride, no joy. Her horror had only grown.

"You didn't want me in prison," she said, tears forming, spilling over. "You didn't notice me then."

Those tears nearly dropped him to his knees. "Devil." He reached out, meaning to force her to accept his embrace. He would comfort her, damn it. He may not have noticed her back then, but he noticed her now.

She darted out of reach, and several tears splashed onto his hand. "I hated you," she spat. "For so long, I hated you for abandoning me. I even blamed you for Steel's death, and I wanted to punish you. I *dreamed* of punishing you. Then I entered your life, and I did hurt you. In your dreams, I presented you with your greatest fear. And I was glad. I liked doing it. Liked hurting you. Then, today, I punished you again. Yet you had done nothing wrong. You had never done anything wrong." She choked on the last word, a sob bubbling from her parted, trembling lips.

"Devil, you did everything wrong. Blame yourself. I wouldn't have done the same thing." *Please understand.* It had never been more important for a person to understand what he was truly saying.

Shaking her head, she swiped at the still-falling tears with the back of her hand. "I'm sorry. You'll never know how sorry I am for everything I did to you. I—I—I have to go. Send me home. Please." Her gaze swung to Cronus. Or rather, to where Cronus had once stood.

The god king was nowhere to be seen.

"Cronus. Cronus!" Scarlet shouted.

In the next instant, the fields disappeared and walls of gray stone rose at Gideon's sides. Gideon whipped around, taking in his new surroundings. His bedroom, he realized. His bedroom in Buda.

Moonlight seeped from the window, illuminating his furnishings. A platform bed with a brown-and-white comforter. Two nightstands, both marred by the knives he constantly tossed at them. One balanced a red lamp that had a chink on its left side. One held a bowl of candy bars.

There was his dresser, his scuffed leather chair. His closet stuffed with more weapons than clothing. The doorway to his bathroom.

Home. He was home. But it didn't feel like home without Scarlet. Where was she? Had Cronus left her there, in that field? Alone with her grief? He roared as Lies had done earlier, enraged, helpless, desperate. He would—

Calm.

Scarlet appeared in the center of his room, and Gideon breathed a sigh of relief. Except...

Her tears were gone. Her horror and hurt, vanished. Her face was a blank canvas, completely devoid of emotion.

"Scar," he began, rushing toward her.

Her gaze met his, and she held up one hand to ward him off. "I wish you a safe and happy life, Gideon. Nothing more needs to be said." She tried to pass him, but he latched onto her arm, stopping her.

"Where aren't you going?"

"Away."

No way in hell. He knew her, knew she planned to hunt and torture her mother and aunt for what they'd done to her. "We'll kiss them together." Kill them together. "No?"

"No." Something in her eyes hardened. Like liquid cooling and solidifying into steel. Steel was the perfect name for any child of hers. She was stubborn to her very core. "*I'll* take care of my mother and aunt."

His grip tightened, and he jerked her into the

inflexible line of his body. She slammed into him with a huff, but refused to look up at him. Her gaze remained on the wild pulse at the base of his neck.

He was panting, he realized. In fear that he wouldn't be able to reach her. In arousal. She smelled of the ambrosia fields and radiated warmth. "You must have heard me correctly. We'll kiss them *together*."

Finally, her gaze lifted. Pinpricks of red flashed every few seconds, as if her demon was ready to break free. "After I kill my aunt, I'm going to find a way to remove my memories. All of them. I want a fresh start, a clean slate. Because right now I have no idea what's real and what's fake. I don't know, and it's killing me. Do you understand? It's *killing* me."

His own anger draining, he kissed her forehead. "I'm not sorry. So not sorry, devil. You can't let me help you kiss her, okay?" The other thing, well, he'd die before he allowed Scarlet's memories of him to be taken.

A tremor rocked her; she gulped. "How can you want to help me after everything I've done to you?"

"I don't…like you. I don't miss him, too."

He didn't have to elaborate. She knew who "him" was. Once again, tears pooled in her eyes. He'd never thought to be glad to see a woman cry, but her sadness was much easier to take than her emotional barrenness.

"He wasn't real," she whispered, hands clutching Gideon's shirt and twisting.

"You're right. He wasn't."

"I know— Wait. What?" She blinked in surprise. He could only speak in lies, so what he'd said should have felled him. But he was still standing, still strong.

"Steel wasn't real. To the two of us, in our hearts, he wasn't real."

The tears spilled down her cheeks.

"We won't make them pay for this, devil. I just need you to...not trust me." *Trust me, please.*

"They manipulated me," she said, the melted metal he'd seen in her face bleeding into her voice. "Laughed at me all these years. Why? What did I ever do to them?"

"They aren't monsters." They were. Far greater than any demon he had encountered. "It had everything to do with you." *Nothing* to do with his darling Scarlet. With his free hand, he threaded his fingers through her hair, once again offering what comfort he could. He didn't dare release her at any point or she'd bolt. "They didn't get one thing right, though. As far as I'm concerned, we aren't really married."

Her brow furrowed, but the rest of her sagged. "You're saying you consider us married?"

Rather than try and explain in Gideon Speak, he nodded.

"Hell, no," she said vehemently. She pounded a fist into his chest. "No."

Not the reaction he'd expected. Or wanted. The words had flowed of their own accord. Natural, meant to be. He'd considered it before, but now he knew. He *would* have her, in every way. Whatever it took.

"The two of us?" she continued. "We're done. We're over. Not that we ever got started."

Hardly. "You're right."

Her eyes narrowed, wet lashes nearly fusing together. "Now you listen to me. We're lucky we escaped an eternal pairing. We're terrible for each other. All wrong." She laughed and the sound reminded him of a harbinger's bell. A sound some immortals heard just before they died. "No wonder you didn't notice me the night I first sought you out."

He arched a brow. *What night?*

"You were at a club," she answered, though he hadn't spoken the question aloud. "And you nailed a human female in a shadowed corner, where anyone could have seen you. Where *I* saw you."

Once, public sex had been a usual occurrence in his life. So, he shouldn't have been able to isolate a single night in his memory and know, *know* Scarlet had been there. But suddenly he could.

An evening like any other, ambrosia-laced alcohol and sex his focus. Yet there'd been a thick cloud of darkness next to his table, one his eyes hadn't been able to pierce. He'd thought his excess had addled his mind. Especially when the scent of orchids had wafted to his nose. When Lies had tried to jump out of his skull. When his cock had throbbed unbearably.

"I didn't sense you," he said. "Didn't take someone else, thinking *she* was responsible for the lust I was feeling when in truth, she was—" *not* "—and you weren't." *Were*.

"I—I— Still." Color bloomed in her cheeks, twin pink circles of embarrassment. "We're still wrong for each other."

"Right again." And suddenly, all he could think about was her earlier words about how he couldn't possibly want her because he'd never tried to penetrate her.

That's what he got for being considerate. For giving her time.

Well, bye-bye consideration. He was taking what he wanted. *All* of what he wanted. He was going to have this woman, and she was going to accept him. She was going to admit that they belonged together. That they were perfect for each other. Everything else could be figured out later.

Was there anything to figure out, though? She amused him, delighted him, set his blood on fire. She never backed down, didn't fear any part of him. Even his demon. She met him challenge for challenge. Was probably stronger than he was.

More than that, they both needed comforting right now, and there was only one way to achieve it. In bed.

Without a word, Gideon anchored both of his hands on Scarlet's waist and tossed her atop the bed in question. She bounced on the mattress, but when she finally stilled, she didn't scramble off; she just peered over at him, confused.

"What are you doing?" she asked in a husky voice.

"Finishing this," he said, advancing on her. Finally, he was beginning it.

CHAPTER SEVENTEEN

WIN, WIN, WIN. Have to win.

"I know." Sweat poured down Strider's face and chest as he rounded a corner, slowed his sprint to a frantic walk and pressed into the shadows cast by a looming column. Thankfully, he'd realized he had tails—four of them, to be exact—before reaching the Temple of the Unspoken Ones. So he'd changed directions and now found himself in the historic district of Rome, miles from the island, a gawking crowd around him, eyeing the towering white remains of the Temple of Vesta and taking pictures so they'd always remember the moment. Blending in was kind of a problem. He was taller than everyone around him and thicker with muscle.

But he would have liked to gawk, as well. He had helped build that temple, after all. *After* he'd helped destroy the one that had been erected before it. Not that he'd ever be given credit. Not that he wanted credit.

Good deeds could ruin a man's rep. 'Cause really, a sensitive warrior would not elicit fear inside the hearts of Hunters.

Fear was sometimes the only thing that kept those Hunters at bay.

Strider had been warring with them for thousands of years. In the old days, they'd followed him from one city to another, blood and screams and death in their wake. Buildings had been razed, history tainted. He and his friends had retaliated so savagely, so brutally, he'd thought his enemy exterminated.

Several years of peace had followed. Years his demon had basked in, high from victory. But of course, the hiding survivors one day forgot their fear and rose again. Attacked again. The war resumed as if it had never ceased.

Win, win, win, the demon of Defeat chanted inside his head. *Must win.*

"I fucking *know.*" But the Cloak of Invisibility was currently in his possession. He couldn't chance being injured and immobilized in a fight. Which meant he had to run.

Gods, he hated running.

If he could just find a moment alone, he could drape himself with the stupid Cloak and disappear, then forget this had ever happened. That he'd ever been spotted, shot at, and now, cornered.

Only thing that stopped him from withdrawing the thing that very second was the possibility that the Hunters following him didn't know he had it. No reason to show it to them and add fuel to their determination.

He tried to be gentle with humans as he pushed his way through them. Some muttered about his rudeness, others turned to yell at him only to zip their mouths when they got a glimpse of him. Dark as his expression was, he probably looked capable of murder.

Fitting. He was.

Had the Hunters found Lucien and Anya, wherever the couple had gone? Had they found Reyes and Danika? Soon as he was safe, he was going to call them, warn them that the enemy could be near.

The soles of his boots thumped against the paved streets of the Forum. Birds squawked and flew away. Sunlight speared the ground and bounced up, and he had to blink rapidly to wet his stinging corneas. If he could make it another few blocks, he would reach the Aedes Divi Iuli. He could lose himself in the ruins, something the Hunters chasing him couldn't do.

At least, he didn't think so. He knew this land because he had once lived on it. They hadn't.

Pop. Whiz.

Silencers. "Shit!" The curse flew from his mouth as a sharp sting lanced the back of his shoulder. Accompanying the sting was a warm rush of liquid. Finally, they'd nailed him. As many times as he'd been peppered with bullets in the past, he knew the feeling.

Shit. Shit!

Win. Win!

"I will." Perhaps he should have gone to the States. Bigger crowds, larger land mass. Easier to lose oneself. But he'd wanted to chat with the Unspoken Ones. See if he could convince them to change the terms of their bargain. Like, rather than bring them Cronus's head, freeing them and most likely endangering the entire world, maybe they would be happy ruling over their own realm or something. If he could get them to agree, he could go to Cronus and present the option.

Thankfully, he'd noticed his tail before he'd reached the temple and headed for the Roman Forum. The damage he could have caused had he unintentionally allowed his enemy to hear his plan was too vast to consider just then.

WIN!

"Give me a minute." What to do, what to do. He

was wearing that fucking butterfly necklace, so Cronus wouldn't know where he was or what was going down. Which meant Cronus wouldn't be popping in and saving the day. And Strider couldn't take the necklace off because *Rhea* could then pop in and *ruin* the day.

Pop. Whiz.

Another sharp sting, this one in his calf. He stumbled, but kept moving.

Win.

"I told you. I'm on it." Looked like he'd have to use the Cloak of Invisibility, moment alone or not.

Strider reached into his pants pocket—damn it, his hand was shaking—and withdrew the small square of gray cloth. Surprised him every time he saw the thing. How could so powerful an artifact come in so small a package?

Someone stepped into his path, and Strider simply barreled through him. Another *pop* and *whiz* rang out. Humans might not recognize the muffled sounds, but they recognized danger and raced for cover.

Strider spun to the right just as a bullet soared past him. Plumes of dust and debris rained around him as the bullet lodged in rock.

Defeat laughed like a kid who'd just opened his Christmas present early and found out he'd gotten exactly what he'd asked Santa for. *Winning!*

Quickening his steps, he tossed a glance over his shoulder. There were four Hunters, three males and one female, racing after him, spreading out to engulf him from all sides, darting through the crowd as if they had done so a million times before.

A plan began to form in Strider's mind, and he grinned. He wouldn't need the Aedes Divi Iuli, after all. He took the next corner as if his feet were on rails and shook open the Cloak. The more he shook, the more the Cloak unraveled. The more it unraveled, the bigger it got. Soon, it was large enough to cover his entire body.

"Did you see that? He's got the Cloak!" one of the males shouted.

"Kill him!"

"No mercy!"

Win, win, win.

More pops. More whizzes. So many he couldn't keep track. A few weeks ago, Hunters would've done everything in their power to keep him alive. Capture him, yes, but also ensure he lived. They'd feared freeing his demon and unleashing its evil upon an unsuspecting world. Except, Galen had found a way to pair the freed demons with new hosts. His plan? To pair them with people of his choosing. Humans who would follow his every command.

Pop. Whiz.

A bullet lodged in Strider's lower back, another in his thigh. He stumbled, slowed. Shit. At this rate, he'd bleed out before he got the cape around his shoulders.

Win, win, win. A whimper now, pained and unsure. A pain that radiated through Strider.

"Don't give up yet," he muttered. "I've got this. I promise you." Both arms shaking now, he managed to drape the Cloak over himself and jerk the hood in place. In the next instant, his body disappeared from view and even he couldn't see it. An odd sensation.

He leaped from the path he'd been taking, stopped abruptly and turned. The Hunters slowed, each frantically searching the thinning crowd for any sign of him.

They'd put distance between themselves, but now edged closer to each other.

"Where'd he go?" one rasped.

"He used the Cloak. Damn it! We'll never find him now."

"Think he's still running or do you think he's waiting nearby, planning to follow us?"

Winning! Defeat said again, happy once more though not completely satisfied. No one had died.

"He's a demon coward. He's running."

"We can't know that for sure. Which means we can't return to base."

"And we shouldn't talk, either. Damn it!"

None of the Hunters had looked to their feet yet. Had they, they would've seen the blood that left the protection of the cape and materialized on the stones. Strider eased to the dirt, careful to avoid bumping into anyone and giving away his location.

"So what do you want us to do?" the female asked, speaking up for the first time. Husky voice, a hint of smoke.

"Split up," the tallest of the group said. He was clearly the leader. He had dark hair, dark eyes and dark skin. And he looked so much like Amun, Strider was momentarily struck senseless. Surely he was merely seeing things. "Just roam the city until I call you and tell you otherwise. But move as fast as you can. He's injured, and won't last long out there."

Each of them nodded, broke apart and kicked into gear. Well, except for the leader and the girl. They shared a loaded glance. Silent. A muscle was ticking in the guy's jaw.

He leaned down, pressed a quick kiss to the girl's mouth, muttered, "Stay safe," and moved away from her.

Interesting. And profitable. Clearly, the two were lovers. The leader would probably do a lot to get his female back.

Rather than find shelter and patch himself up, Strider followed her. *New challenge,* he told his demon.

Win.

I will. She was petite with shoulder-length blond hair. Mixed into the blond were streaks of bright pink. She wore a white Hello Kitty tank top and ripped jeans. Weapons were probably hidden all over her curvy little body. There was a silver stud in her eyebrow that matched the gray of her eyes, and one of her arms was sleeved with tattoos.

There was something familiar about her. Something that caused a wave of...hatred to hit him. Yes, hatred, he realized with shock. There was no mistaking the dark emotion for something else. How odd. He didn't remember meeting her. Not in any of the battles he'd had with Hunters. That didn't mean he hadn't met her, though. Only that she'd been insignificant at the time.

Why the hatred, then?

Win. Win!

Worry about who she is later, asshole, he told himself. Short as she was, she was able to move faster than he would have expected. He wouldn't be able to keep up, as weak as he was becoming.

Win.

I told you. I will. She's as good as mine.

When the girl wound around a corner and headed toward a crowded building, Strider grabbed her by the hair and jerked. A low blow, but necessary. As she fell, she yelped in surprise. A second later, though, she was on her feet, two daggers palmed.

"Bastard," she snarled. "I knew you'd come after me, the perceived weak link. Well, that was your first mistake."

Several humans turned to stare at her, obviously wondering who she was talking to.

Strider didn't reply. Just darted behind her and smashed his hands against her carotid, cutting off the blood supply to her brain. And shit! She was cold. Like a block of ice. He almost pulled away. Almost.

"So what was my second?" he asked smugly.

At first, she struggled, tried to spin. "What the—" But then her knees buckled, and her eyes rolled back into her head.

Just like that, she was out.

We won. We won!

Too easy. Still. As the pleasure began to wash through him, Strider grinned. The grin only widened as he picked up the girl, shivered—because *damn*—then hid her within the confines of the Cloak and carried her away.

SIENNA DRAGGED herself from her bed, the chains around her neck, wrists and ankles rattling, cutting. When she stood to shaky legs, those chains pulled taut, cut deeper, preventing her from moving away.

There was a red film over her eyes, coloring her vision, painting everything she studied in crimson. Fitting, since she wanted everything in the room to be bathed with blood. Hers, Cronus's. She craved it. Dreamed of it. The velvet curtains, the flowers blooming from the walls, the polished wood and the alabaster statues of too-tall men with too many muscles…

…all dripping…

Enough! Must reach Paris, she thought. Or maybe the thought belonged to the demon. Wrath. The enemy inside her. The enemy she should despise but couldn't; just then, Wrath was her only link to vengeance. And salvation.

Paris will help. This time, she knew exactly who the words belonged to: the demon. *Paris can guard you until you're strong enough to attack Cronus.*

Maybe Paris would guard her. Maybe not. Moments before she'd died, she'd told him how much she hated him. And she had. Hated him. She was pretty sure she still did. Or didn't. God, she was so confused. The more the demon spoke about Paris, the more her dislike faded.

Paris will help.

"I heard you the first time," she snapped.

Part of her—the human part—thought she might try to kill the warrior when she reached him. Part of her—the female part—thought she might kiss his beautiful face. Only thing she knew for sure was that she *was* going to find him, and she *was* going to use him, as Wrath had suggested. He, too, was possessed by a demon, and while he guarded her—if he would—he could teach her how to control this new, darker side of herself.

And once that happened…bye-bye Cronus.

Determined, urgent, she stepped forward again. Or tried to. Those damn chains yanked but held steady. Her body burned with rage, with hate, and the wings still growing between her shoulder blades flapped wildly.

Each emotion gave her strength. She jerked again. And again. Skin sliced open and vessels burst. The pain, the pain, the pain… *Paris*, her mind shouted, giving her strength…and finally, one of the chains cracked…

AMUN STUMBLED through the smoky cavern, William and Aeron holding him up and keeping him from kissing the bone-laden ground. They'd fought countless demon minions to get here, to this forgotten valley of death. They were as injured as he was. He shouldn't add to their burden, but he couldn't help himself.

Crunch, crunch. Sweat poured from him, draining him. His skin was sliced like a Christmas ham, but that wasn't the worst of his torment. Too many secrets…they were bombarding him, consuming him. Evil secrets, vile secrets. Thefts, rapes and murders. Oh, the murders.

The souls decaying in this underground prison had killed their brethren in the most heinous of ways, enjoying every bit of torture they inflicted. And now, the demons who lived here were enjoying every bit of the torture *they* inflicted. Retaliation, they found it so sweet.

The demons, at least, didn't keep secrets. They were happy to share the disgusting details of their lives. But Amun could also read their minds and knew their basest thoughts. He could feel their desire to steal, to rape and murder. Could see through their eyes as they did so.

Never had he felt so dirty, and he doubted he would ever be able to cleanse himself of this. Secrets loved it, though. Loved every moment of it. Was humming, soaking up each new revelation like chocolate through a straw.

"Nothing on Legion?" Aeron asked for the thousandth time.

He shook his head and winced at the ensuing ache.

"We can't keep roaming this place blind," William said. "We're each cut up and bleeding from our last go-round with those minions. They're small, but damn, they're wily. I thought I was going to lose my balls."

Lucifer might be afraid of the warrior, but his servants were not. They'd attacked William as staunchly as they'd attacked Amun and Aeron.

"You're going to have to steal a demon's memories," Aeron told Amun grimly. "It's the only way. William's right for once. The longer we're here, the more we're forced to fight and the weaker we become."

No, Amun thought, even as he nodded. He'd known it would come to this. He'd hoped otherwise, and had resisted for as long as he could. If things were bad now, they were going to be impossible after he stole a full set of demon memories. There would be no purging himself later.

They would be a part of him forever.

Why are you doing this again? he wondered. Because he loved Aeron. Wanted his friend happy and knew his friend couldn't be happy any other way.

And what of your happiness?

He ignored that question. He might talk himself out of what he was about to do, and couldn't allow himself to do such a thing. *Find a demon,* he signed. *Bring it to me alive. The higher up the caste system it is, the better.*

"You want a High Lord?" William asked, incredulous. A High Lord was what possessed each of the Lords. They were the most powerful of the demons and the most knowledgeable of what was happening down here, but there were only a few left within these depths. A few that hadn't tried to escape with the others.

Like Secrets.

Amun nodded. *If possible.* They would also be the hardest to capture.

His friends led him to the shadowed mouth of the nearest cave and eased him down. Every muscle in his tired body sighed in relief, basically liquefying. He closed his eyes. Rest, he'd rest for a moment.

Someone patted his shoulder. Someone placed a gun in his hand. Then footsteps sounded. How long he sat there, weapon gradually slipping from his too-loose hold, he didn't know. All he knew was that the next time he opened his eyes, his friends were back.

Aeron and William stood before him, panting, barely managing to maintain their grip on a wildly bucking demon. The creature was as tall as they were, with green scales over portions of its body and a face composed only of bone. Several horns protruded from its spine and even its feet.

"Not a High Lord, but close enough," Aeron gritted out. There was a new gash on his forehead and blood was seeping into his left eye.

"Do your thing," William commanded. "Before it's too late."

Though it required every ounce of his strength, Amun managed to reach out and place his hands on the creature's skull. The bucking intensified. Frantic screams escaped. Twice, Amun's sweaty palms slid out of place, but he eventually made the mental connection and his hands were no longer needed.

Memory after memory flooded him. A lifetime of

rage and pain and torture. All inflicted upon others. The creature was second in command to the High Lord Pain, Reyes's demon. Upon Pain's escape, this creature had taken over. And oh, had it enjoyed hurting others. In every way imaginable and even some Amun had never considered.

This one had even hurt Legion. And now her shrieks were trapped inside Amun, her terrified expression the only thing he could see. Gods, he wanted to vomit. And did vomit, the moment the connection was severed.

William and Aeron released their burden, and it collapsed to the ground, useless now, brain wiped clean.

A hand settled atop Amun's head and caressed down, stopping at the base of his neck and massaging. A comforting touch meant to soothe. Nothing could soothe him, however. Not ever again.

"Do you know where she is?" Aeron asked gently.

Amun nodded, tears burning his eyes. Those shrieks… the blood…too much…

The hand on his neck stilled. "Where? Tell me, Amun. Please."

Amun raised his gaze, ready to vomit again. *She's given to a new demon every other day. She's beaten, tortured…and worse. In between those days, she returns to Lucifer, who entertains his minions with her screams. Today, she's with him. And he…he…he knows you're here. He plans to kill you in front of her.*

CHAPTER EIGHTEEN

SCARLET DIDN'T move or speak as Gideon crawled up her body. He took his time, too, removing her boots, socks and pants along the way. She could have protested. She didn't. She needed this, she realized. Just once. A moment of beauty and pleasure to overshadow a lifetime of hate and regret. Of sadness and pain. Of deceit.

Funny, Gideon was keeper of Lies, yet he'd been the only person ever to be honest with her.

So this moment? Yes, she would take it. Cling to it. Anything else with him...no. As long as her mother lived, as long as her aunt could manipulate her mind, she was a danger to him.

A danger he didn't deserve. He was blameless of every crime she'd ever tossed at his door.

Gods, she was a fool. Deserved only punishment. She should leave, not luxuriate in her own selfishness by stealing this moment. She owed him that, at the very least. But she couldn't force herself to pull away from him. *Just once,* she reminded herself. She'd have him. He seemed to want her, too, so really, *leaving* would make her selfish.

"So ugly," he whispered, reverently tracing his fingertips along the inside of her thighs.

Goose bumps broke out over her flesh, but when he

realized what he'd said, he froze and looked up at her with budding panic.

"I know what you meant," she told him softly. He'd left her in a T-shirt and panties, so he couldn't see the hard tips of her nipples. Couldn't see how much she already desired him.

Slowly, he relaxed. "I'm not amazed by you, devil." His thumbs dabbled at the indentation behind her knee, caressing her, tantalizing her. "Don't tell me you know that."

How could he be so gentle with her? How could he stand to touch her? After everything they'd just learned? *If you're going to enjoy this, you have to stop traveling down that thought path.*

But she couldn't stop. The thoughts lanced at her, sharp and undeniable. She had built fantasies around this man. *She* had. All on her own. Her aunt had merely made the suggestion that they'd been married, and Scarlet had created a full-blown history. She was humiliated. She was remorseful. Vulnerable. Raw. Humiliated. Had she mentioned that?

Mostly, she was mourning. Her beautiful wedding had never happened. She'd never lain in this man's arms, hopeful and sated. She hadn't given him a son. Her chin trembled as white-hot tears flooded her eyes.

"You don't have to do this." She might not want him to end it, might want this one moment with him, but she had to offer him a way out. If he was doing this out of pity, well, she couldn't handle any more embarrassment and that would embarrass her more than anything else. "You aren't really my husband."

"Keep talking," he muttered, lifting her shirt, bending down and laving at her navel. "I'm loving what you have to say."

A tremor moved through her, sultry and hungry. "Keep talking" equaled "shut up" in Gideon Speak. Who would have thought she'd enjoy hearing those words? "All I'm trying to say is that you don't owe me anything." Was that breathless voice hers? "If anything, *I* owe *you*."

He stilled, raised his head again, his eyes narrowing, lashes tangling together and blocking that gorgeous ocean-blue. "You owe me lots." There was unrestrained fury in his tone. "That's exactly what this is about."

O-kay.

"I don't want you desperately," he said tightly. "Do you not understand? My body doesn't ache for yours. I haven't dreamed of being with you since the first moment I saw you. The past matters. It does."

Several tears splashed over and trickled down her cheeks. *Embarrassing* tears. But still she couldn't move away. The past didn't matter to him? "Really?" How could she dare to hope?

He nodded, his unrelenting gaze never leaving hers. "You aren't mine."

She was his. And just like that, something snapped inside her. The resistance she'd fought so hard to build against him, perhaps. All that remained inside her was desire. So much desire. She would have him. *Just this once,* she reminded herself a second time. She would hold nothing back. Would give him everything.

What would happen to her heart afterward, she didn't know. *Liar! What's left of it will shatter.* She wouldn't worry about that until absolutely necessary. Right now,

Gideon was with her. He wanted her. That would be enough.

Though she'd wanted to jump him every time he'd neared her, she'd never allowed herself to be the aggressor with him. Her resentment and pride had hindered and muted every sensation. But not this time.

Slowly Scarlet sat up, forcing Gideon to do the same, until he straddled her thighs. Her hair tumbled to her shoulders. The strands weren't long enough to shield her cleavage, and that irritated her for a moment. Such a thing would have been sexy, and she wanted to be sexy for this man. In every possible way.

She wanted him to want her with the same intensity she'd wanted him all these years. All these centuries.

He sucked in a breath. "No more."

More. "Not yet. I want to see you." She gripped the hem of his shirt and jerked the material over his head.

Now she was the one to suck in a breath. Gods, he was magnificent. Perfect in every way. His skin was golden, his stomach roped with unparalleled strength. The black eyes and red lips he had tattooed on his chest and neck caught her gaze and she traced them with a fingertip. She even traced an imaginary butterfly on his right shoulder, nail scraping lightly, leaving an imprint of red. They might not be married, but the symbol connected them.

"Cools so bad," he panted.

Burns so good, he meant, and that thrilled her. She moved her touch to the indigo loop piercing his nipple, then the sapphire stud in his navel. Blue again.

"Why do you like blue so much?" she asked just before flicking her tongue against the nipple ring. Cold metal and hot skin, a delicious combination.

A moan escaped him. "You don't want to talk about this *now?*" He curled a hand over the erection straining over the waist of his pants and rubbed up and down. "There's not something better for us to do."

And she'd thought him magnificent before. Silly her. Here he was, at his most primal. A warrior who saw what he wanted and took it, damn the consequences. But… "Yeah. I do want to talk." Knowing him was just as important as being with him. *Only this once.*

That time, she despised the reminder.

Gideon's hand fell away, and he sighed, placing her desires above his own. He didn't edge away from her, but cupped her ass and urged her forward, until the core of her covered him. Hard, hot. She bit the inside of her cheek to stop a reckless groan from forming.

He licked his lips. "There wasn't this kid in Tartarus, and he wasn't the ugliest little thing I'd ever seen. One day I didn't deliver a new prisoner into his cell and the kid didn't ask for a game. Only thing I couldn't find was paper and a crayon. Wasn't blue. When I didn't hand them over, the kid didn't smile the sweetest smile I'd ever seen and tell me that blue was the bestest color in the world, like the sky he'd heard about but had never seen. That day, blue didn't start to represent…freedom to me."

As he'd spoken, Scarlet had ceased breathing, the tremor sliding the length of her spine too intense. "This boy," she managed to say. "Did he have a shaved head and black eyes?"

Frowning, Gideon tilted his head to the side. "How did you—" He went rigid. His gaze widened, and his attention zeroed in on her face, studying intently. "It wasn't you," he gasped out. "But you—"

"Had a shaved head like a boy, yes." Perhaps that was how he'd known her eyes, but that didn't explain how he'd known her lips. Had he seen them when she invaded his dreams, as she suspected? Had he truly been that aware of her? "It was one of the few kindnesses I remember from my mother. Most of the prisoners knew I was a girl, but it was best not to remind them. It was best to look as…unattractive as possible."

"Did anyone…"

She arched a brow. "Tartarus was filled with gods and goddesses used to getting their way. Used to exerting their power anytime they wished. They were angry, frustrated and desolate. What do you think?" She could have lied. Made herself seem pure, untouched. Yet, she wanted only honesty between them.

Oh, the irony, she thought.

A muscle ticked below his eye. "I didn't go to Zeus and ask for the boy's release, you know. I wasn't denied." Each word was harsher than the last.

"Thank you," she said, and she grinned. "That was sweet of you." So they *had* spoken inside that prison. That was real. A real memory. And they'd shared it. Together. No wonder she had adored this man from the first. "I'm done talking now. I hope you are?"

"Yes," he said gruffly.

But he was still clearly considering the past. Still angry about her treatment. She wanted him focused on her now, and only her. "Gideon?"

"Mmm-hmm."

"I'm going to have you now."

He huffed, but remained still as she unfastened his pants. Black briefs, tenting with his arousal. Her mouth watered. Before the night was over, she was going to have that hard, thick shaft inside her mouth *and* body. She wasn't letting Gideon leave this bed until they'd both climaxed a dozen times. At least. She would make the most of their night together.

Quickly she worked both the pants and the underwear off his legs and tossed them to the floor. He'd already kicked off his boots and socks. If he'd even been wearing them. She couldn't recall. And now, finally, he was bare. Now, finally, he was all hers.

She sat at his ankles, admiring the rest of him. His legs were long, lean yet perfectly muscled. There was a smattering of dark hair on his calves that thinned on his thighs and thickened again around his shaft. His testicles were heavy and drawn up tight.

"Don't touch me," he croaked out. "Your stare isn't killing me."

So he thought he was dying, did he? "Then I feel sorry for you. I haven't even begun to torture you yet."

A groan. Of anticipation? She hoped so.

Scarlet traced his real butterfly tattoo with her tongue, then worked her way up to his sac. He uttered another groan, this one far more hoarse. Just to torment him further, she blew on the moisture she'd left behind, warm breath that would cool against his skin. Yet another groan, even a bowing of his back as he sought closer contact.

"Grip the headboard and don't let go," she commanded, lest he decided to pump into her mouth and end things too quickly. He'd made her work for her first orgasm with him. She could do no less for him. "Do you understand?"

He stiffened.

At first, she thought she'd pushed this dedicated

warrior used to control too far. He stared up at her, uncertainty in his eyes. But then, his arms flew above his head and his fingers wrapped around the top of the wood. Holding so tightly his knuckles blanched.

His uncertainty hadn't stemmed from a reluctance to follow her orders, she realized, but from trepidation. He was afraid to believe she'd actually take over.

And that meant…he *wanted* control taken from him. Wanted to lose himself to the passion without worrying about anything but the sensations. Of course. The humans he'd been with wouldn't have known because he wouldn't have been able to tell them. Never mind that Scarlet wanted to kill those humans for having touched and tasted him.

"Tell me what you want from me." She needed to hear him say it. Needed him to know that she and no other understood his true meaning. "Admit it. In your way."

"I—I—" He licked his lips again. There was no shame in his brilliant eyes, only more of that woeful trepidation. "I don't know what you're wanting me to admit."

Yes, he did. "Say it, Gideon, or I walk away. This ends." Could she follow through with that threat? She didn't know. Hopefully, he wouldn't make her find out. Already she was damp and aching, hungry for him.

And she wondered, would he be the lover she'd created in her mind? Or something more?

"I don't want you to be in charge," he whispered, as if he feared she would take him at his word.

"Good. That's good. Because in this bed, I decide your every action. In this bed, I *own* you."

The relief that curtained his features would thrill her for the rest of her days.

So she took the game to the next level. "If you hesitate to obey me even once, I'll leave you unsatisfied. You'll have to watch me pleasure myself, knowing you won't be allowed to climax. Understand?"

He nodded, unable to hide his eagerness. Even his cock twitched.

She'd never been this hard-core an aggressor—sexually, that is—but she would be lying if she claimed not to enjoy it. She wanted to be what Gideon had never had before. She wanted to be everything he needed, everything he yearned for.

"Don't move, not even a little," she told him as she lowered her mouth to his erection. She didn't touch him, though, only let her exhalations continue to caress him. For a moment, she thought perhaps he'd even stopped breathing.

"Devil," he finally gritted out. But he didn't move. Oh, no, he didn't move. "I can wait forever. Please, please don't...do anything. Please..."

Still she waited. Until her blood was molten in her veins. Until he was trembling. Until she felt ready to jump out of her skin, the darkness and screams swirling inside her, desperate for release. *Then* Scarlet licked him from base to tip.

He shouted her name, a prayer and a curse rolled into one hoarse entreaty. She twirled her tongue around his slit, tasting the saltiness of his seed, then bore down, taking him all the way inside. Until, long as he was, he hit the back of her throat. *My man.*

Up and down her mouth rode him, and still he didn't move. He wanted to, she knew it, for she could feel the tension in his muscles. He might not be her husband, but just then he did belong to her. She did own him as she'd claimed, owned his passion, and the knowledge was heady, fogging her mind, heating her blood yet another degree.

She gripped the base as tight as she could, and he cried out. Not in pain but in intensified pleasure. With her other hand, she cupped his balls and tugged. "Move now. You can move."

Whatever tether he'd had on his body broke, and he shuddered over and over, again and again, pumping his hips into her hands, trying to slide his cock in and out of her steady grip. But she never loosened her hold, never let him create a necessary friction, and no seed emerged. His cock remained hard as a lead pipe.

"Good boy," she praised huskily. "You deserve a reward."

His only reply was a ragged pant. Sweat glistened over his trembling body as she kissed her way up his stomach. She stopped and dabbled at his navel, then played at his nipples, sucking one, then the other. Soon, his trembling was so intense, the entire bed was rocking and the springs were squeaking.

Inside her head, Nightmares hummed.

When Gideon tried to arch his back, placing his cock into the apex of her slick center, still covered by her panties, she bit down on his nipple ring and tugged. He moaned, and the wood he held cracked, but he forced his hips to settle back on the mattress. His breath grew more ragged.

Scarlet sat up and straddled his waist. Slowly she removed her shirt and dropped the material beside his head. His white-hot gaze ate her up, devouring her breasts. As he watched, she palmed them, tweaked her nipples.

He lifted his head, trying to get to them.

"No." *Yes.* It was a scream from her demon and a plea from her body, but she shook her head. "Down."

Reluctantly, he obeyed.

Denying him wasn't a power play for her. Far from it. He'd given the control to her, had been eager to relinquish it, in fact. That meant he'd wanted someone to tell him no. To direct him. Any other woman would have allowed the action, but he didn't want what he'd always had. He wanted something different. And she would give it to him, no matter the opposition. No matter how much she wanted that mouth sucking on her.

"Devil," he moaned.

Darling. "Put your hand between my legs."

The headboard finally broke as he rushed to obey. Though she'd told him to use only one, he placed one hand between her legs, groaned as if in pain, then placed the other on her thigh and groaned as if in *agony*.

She didn't scold him. Yet. The action had probably been instinctual on his part, and was definitely welcome on hers. "Make me climax like this. Me, only me."

He was jerking the barrier of her panties aside in the next instant, his fingers sliding over her wet clitoris. Now *she* was the one to groan. Nightmares, too. *So damned good.* The shadows and the screams finally broke free, seeping from her, enveloping the bed, wrapping around them.

Like before, Gideon didn't seem to mind. And for a long while, he simply rubbed her. Rubbed her until she was moving with his touch, trying to force his fingers to sink inside her rather than torment her sensitive center. Gods, he was working her to a fever pitch, so when he finally, blessedly penetrated her with one finger, she instantly climaxed, squeezing him, holding tight.

Her head fell back as she rode the waves of satisfaction to the sky, stars twinkling behind her eyes. How long she floated, she didn't know. She only knew that when she came back to herself, Gideon was still, awe in his eyes, awaiting his next command, his body so tense she could have snapped him in two.

That wasn't good enough, though. She wanted him out of his mind with lust. She wanted him begging for it.

Now she scolded him. "Again," she gritted out. "You'll make me come again before you receive your own pleasure. And perhaps next time you'll heed my orders to the letter."

There won't be a next time.

The thought almost chilled her desire. Almost. But too much did she crave him just then.

"Sorry. Sorry," he babbled, which meant he wasn't sorry at all.

A second finger joined the first, sinking in and out of her. All the while Gideon's thumb played with that little bundle of nerves. Double stimulation, so good, so good, so damned good. More shadows, more screams.

"Don't come, devil, don't come." His hips moved in sync with his words, rubbing against her, electrifying her enjoyment.

Just like that, Scarlet was propelled back to the sky, twirling, free, so overcome she might never be the same. Might? Ha.

"Don't let me have you, please, don't let me have you. Please."

A plea he'd probably never uttered to another. And

that he didn't take her yet, that he waited for permission, spoke more of his intense need to relinquish control than his hesitant confession had.

That was why she didn't give him what he craved. Not yet.

"Rip my panties the rest of the way off, but don't enter me."

The blue scrap of cloth was torn from her and resting beside her bra in less than a second. Gideon gripped her hips, fingers wrapping around to her ass. He pressed so determinedly, she knew she would have bruises. Bruises she welcomed.

"Not now?" Lines of tension branched from his eyes, and he was worrying his bottom lip so forcefully with his teeth, there was a trickle of blood running down his chin. He was on edge, desperate, but still he waited.

That roused her yet another degree, as if she hadn't already climaxed twice.

"What have you fantasized about doing to other girls?" she asked him.

"Other girls? I remember all the other girls." A broken admission. Strained. "I can think of everyone but you."

He thought only of her. *My darling.* She couldn't make him wait anymore.

"Inside," she said, and he was lifting her, thrusting deep, roaring loud and long before the last syllable left her mouth.

Scarlet climaxed instantly, shuddering, her roar blending with his. Gods, he stretched her, hit her just right, and the orgasm was far more intense than any she'd ever experienced before. Even the screams and shadows shuddered. Even Nightmares bellowed.

Gideon, too, climaxed instantly, shouting her name, jetting hot seed inside her. Branding her, claiming her. Owning *her*. She could have basked in the sensations forever, could have remained one being, a part of Gideon, for eternity.

Or at least until his bedroom door crashed open and two angry Lords clomped inside the bedroom, weapons drawn.

CHAPTER NINETEEN

GIDEON HEARD the split of wood against metal, and knew his door had just been kicked down. Next he heard angry footsteps, a muttered, "What the hell?" from his friend Kane, and a growled, "Shit," from Lucien.

They had to be confused. Scarlet's shadows filled the room from one corner to the other, thick and dark and writhing. Worse, the screams that accompanied those shadows were louder than a bullhorn and more menacing than a war cry.

"What should we do?" Kane demanded.

Clearly, neither warrior could see through the gloom. Shit, neither could Gideon. But he didn't want either one of them shooting now and asking questions later.

"It's not me," he shouted above the noise, rolling Scarlet beneath him and jerking the covers over her naked body. Thankfully, she didn't resist, and his urge to blind anyone who might see her so resplendent receded.

If he had his way, no one would see her bare but himself. And godsdamn, he was going to do everything in his power to have his way.

"Who's there?" Lucien demanded.

"It's not Gid. I'm not fine."

"Gideon?" Kane's shock was clear. "Strider told us you'd left."

"Didn't return."

"What the hell's going on in here?" Lucien again.

"Don't give me a minute, and I won't take care of things. Oh, and don't stay put." Gideon raised an expectant eyebrow at Scarlet. Much as he wanted to keep her hidden, he couldn't. His friends needed to see her (covered), see how he looked at her, and know beyond any doubt that she belonged with him. That to harm her was to die. That simple.

"What?" Dragging the sheet with her, she squirmed out from under him and propped herself against the cracked headboard. Her expression was blank, though her color was high. Dark hair tangled around her beautiful face and she smoothed several strands away with a steady hand.

Steady.

He didn't like that. Not when *he* felt like an earthquake was even now raging through him. "As if you don't know."

"Fine. You want an audience for our afterglow, you'll get an audience." She closed her eyes, features hardening with her determination. A moment later, the shadows thinned and the screams quieted, both seeming to vaporlock around her before being sucked completely inside her.

While she'd straddled him, while he'd thrust his shaft deep inside her, he'd forgotten that they were there. Hell, he'd forgotten everything. Except pleasure, that is.

And gods, had she given him pleasure. Nothing like that had ever happened to him before. But he'd dreamed of it. Dreamed of being at a woman's mercy while she took what she wanted from him. That probably wasn't something most warriors dreamed about, but over the years he'd disappointed too many women to count and that had been hell on his ego.

He'd say something like, "Don't tell me what you want, I don't want to know," so the women wouldn't tell him and he'd have to guess and of course, he'd some-times—most times—get it wrong. Tonight, he hadn't wanted to think about his next move. He hadn't wanted to wonder if he was doing it right.

Scarlet had taken care of everything. Exquisitely.

Yeah, he'd shot like a fucking virgin the moment he'd entered her and was embarrassed as hell about that, but that only proved how much she'd aroused him. He'd known she was enjoying herself, that she was taking exactly what she needed, and that had increased his own enjoyment. Actually, everything about her had increased his enjoyment.

Her body fit his like a puzzle piece. Her scent was like nose candy and better than any ambrosia he'd ever snorted. Yeah, he'd been there, done that. Her skin was smooth, the perfect contrast to his callused hands, and her hair was perfect for fisting. Inside, she'd been wet and warm and tight enough to squeeze him.

But next time, *he* was going to be in control. He was going to demand, in his way, that she tell him exactly what she craved. She would know what he meant, and she would tell him the truth. Tell him what she really wanted him to do to her. And he would do it. Every damn thing. Nothing would be taboo. The dirtier the better.

Kane cleared his throat and shifted uncomfortably from one booted foot to the other, and Gideon realized he'd been quietly staring at Scarlet, who was still watching him with that blank expression. He tried not to blush like a pussy but failed.

"Who's she?" Hazel eyes brightening with amusement, Kane sheathed the two Sigs in his hands. He must not have seen Scarlet in the dungeon.

Gideon studied the warrior. His mix of brown, gold and black hair was shorter than when Gideon had last seen it. No doubt his friend had caught the strands on fire. Again. The man's demon, Disaster, fed off catastrophes, purposely drawing them. In fact, one of the wooden shards that had flown from the busted door was lodged in Kane's side, blood seeping from the wound and soaking his shirt.

"She's my wife," Gideon said, and even though the words were a lie, he liked saying them. Could hear the pride in his tone.

"Actually, I'm no one," Scarlet stated baldly. "I'm nothing."

Like hell, he thought, tossing her a glare. She was... everything.

Everything? His brow puckered. Surely that was an overstatement. He liked being with her, enjoyed her, had contemplated marrying her for real, *felt* married to her, and would even kill to protect her. But was she *everything* to him?

He could think of nothing he valued as much as he valued her. Not his war, not his weapons. Not even his friends. So, yeah. Maybe.

"She's Nightmares," Lucien said, his blades steadily pointed in Scarlet's direction. "Aka one of the few prisoners who's ever left our dungeons alive." Unlike Kane, his eyes weren't gleaming with amusement. His eyes—one blue that saw in the spiritual world, one brown that saw into the earthly realm—were calm and determined. He was possessed by Death, and could shred a soul in a single heartbeat of time. The blades were kind of overkill.

"I don't suggest you lower your weapons. I'm sure you'd love for me to threaten Annie that way, just as I love how you're threatening Scar."

Annie, real name Anya. Lucien's fiancée. The warrior's face was terribly scarred, and as he ran his tongue over his teeth, those scars seemed all the more puckered. He was iron-willed, loved rules and took no risks when it came to the safety of his loved ones. Especially Anya.

"You could be making the *suggestion* under duress," Lucien said. "So, I'll keep my weapons where they are, thanks."

"You're right. I'm under duress." *Now put those gods-damn weapons away, before I'm forced to do something we'll both regret,* he wanted to shout. Lucien was his friend, and Gideon didn't want to hurt him. But he would attack, no hesitation, to protect Scarlet. She'd been hurt enough.

Finally, the blades were sheathed. Reluctantly.

"Why aren't you here? Feel free not to tell me and then stay as long as you want." Which meant: *Tell me and get your ass out!* They'd seen Scarlet, knew she was important to him. Mission accomplished. He was ready to be alone with her.

Lucien massaged the back of his neck. "Kane texted me that something was going down in your room, and I flashed back to help since Torin and Cameo are the only other people left at the fortress."

"Where aren't the others?"

"We'll get to that in a minute. I didn't expect you

to be here. Strider told me you'd left with Nightmares. And great going by the way, putting everyone at risk by letting the girl run wild."

"She doesn't have a name." Why the irritated, offended voice? "And it's not Scarlet." He just…he wanted his friends to treat her right. To treat her with respect. Not like she was a nuisance or an enemy and he should watch his back whenever she was around.

"And ta-da." Scarlet splayed her arms in a how-am-I-still-sane gesture. "After all that running wild, we're back. Or he is. I'm about to take off." She kicked her legs over the side of the bed, dislodging the sheet. In the next instant, both exquisite breasts were bared. Both nipples hard like frosted cherries. "Nice seeing you again, though."

Two pairs of eyes widened before both men spun to give her their backs.

"Yeah, leaving's gonna happen." Where the hell did she think she was going?

Scowling, Gideon grabbed her by the nape and jerked her back down. Roughly, yeah, but she could take it, and he liked that about her. With his other hand, he drew up the sheet. Then he settled in beside her, his arms locking around her and holding her in place wrestler-style.

She was a warrior herself and could have fought him, but she didn't. And it wasn't because she cared about who saw her naked, he thought darkly. Obviously she wasn't ashamed of her body. Not that she should be, but still. He was ready to sandpaper his friends' corneas even though their weapons were put away. Now they knew what a perfect shade of red her nipples were.

"I have stuff to do," she said stiffly, "and you have stuff to do. It's time to say our goodbyes."

"Sure. 'Cause we did *not* agree to take care of that stuff together."

Like Lucien, she ran her tongue over her teeth. "I never agreed."

Maybe she had, maybe she hadn't. He still couldn't tell with her. Which was odd, now that he thought about it. They hadn't been married. Their pasts weren't intertwined. Well, not as much as they'd assumed, anyway. And they now knew her memories were false. So why could his demon *still* not tell when she spoke true?

"Can we turn around now?" Kane asked, his amusement making another appearance.

"No," Gideon said as Scarlet said, "Why would you want to? We're decent."

Both warriors pivoted on their heels. Lucien pulled at his collar and Kane clearly fought a grin.

"We need to talk," Lucien said, then glanced pointedly at Scarlet. "A lot has gone down while you were away."

"Say no more." Immediately she tried to dislodge Gideon and stand, though she never outright tried to injure him. Which meant she didn't want her freedom enough, he thought smugly. "I can take a hint," she added. "I'll give you guys some privacy."

He held tight, keeping her in place. "Whatever you need to say to me can't be said in front of her."

She stilled, and that was both good and bad. Her skin had been rubbing against his, and well, the material draping his lap was getting taller by the second.

Cheeks flaming for the second time in the past five minutes, Gideon lifted her up and settled her in front of him so that her body covered his growing erection.

Mistake. The thick length pressed into the crevice of her ass, and he had to stifle a groan.

She gasped as if he'd burned her, and tried to jump off him. "Gideon!"

His arms wrapped around her in a vise-grip, and he used his legs to frame hers. "Don't get comfortable. You're going somewhere."

"Gideon." Gritted this time.

"Scar."

"Fine, you stubborn jackass." With a sigh that sounded both frustrated and relieved, she relaxed against him. Even rested her head on the curve of his shoulder.

Unable to resist, he kissed her temple. *That's my good girl.*

"Well." She gave an imperious wave of her hand in his friends' direction. "What are you waiting for? Start talking. The sooner you start, the sooner this ends."

Both Lucien and Kane were too busy gaping to speak.

What had Lucien meant? Kane, Cameo and Torin were the only ones left at the fortress? Why? And why had Lucien had to flash back here? Where had he been?

"Sure you don't want to dress first?" Kane finally asked Scarlet, sounding as hopeful as he did regretful.

"Not sure," Gideon answered for her. One, his curiosity was now too high to take the time needed to throw on a shirt and jeans. Two, he didn't want either man getting another peek at Scarlet. And three, he didn't want to release Scarlet.

Maybe he was being selfish, placing temptation right under Kane's nose like this. The man hadn't had a lover in years, too afraid his demon would somehow physically hurt his females. Which wasn't an irrational fear. It had happened. Several times. Gideon remembered the screams. But just then, Gideon was really only concerned with Scarlet. If he let her go, she might run before they settled things between them.

"Don't take her advice and explain," he finished. "You can't trust her, I swear." After everything, Scarlet wouldn't betray him. He knew that, at least.

Though he'd never shed his reluctance, Lucien nodded. "We'll start with the basics. You might not know this, but Aeron, Amun and William journeyed into hell to retrieve Legion. No one's heard from them since."

Cronus had mentioned the boys were somewhere else, but not that the somewhere was actually hell. Freaking great. Gideon couldn't leave until he'd spoken with Amun, and he wasn't sure how long he could convince Scarlet to wait before slaughtering her despicable family.

Of course, she was supposed to stop him from contacting Amun, and he planned to let her do so, freeing her from her promise to Rhea, but she couldn't stop him if he couldn't find Amun. So again, he had to wait.

Unfortunately, he'd never been a patient man. He wanted this over and done. He wanted NeeMah at his mercy, aka the end of his sword. He wanted time to romance Scarlet. Time to prove to her that things could work between them. All of which had to be placed on hold.

"Ready for the rest?" Lucien asked, fighting a grin himself now. "You look distracted."

He would not blush. Again. "Don't go on," he said with a wave just as commanding as Scarlet's had been.

Lucien gave up and let the grin form full-force. "Hunters surrounded the fortress, apparently planning to steal our artifacts. We decided to split up. Anya and I took the Cage, Reyes took Danika and Strider took the Cloak. Paris decided to take a vacation."

"Are we no longer surrounded?" he asked, glancing at his closet. He had a case of weapons in there. He could do some damage, blow off some steam.

"Strider killed most of them on his way out," Kane said with pride.

Lucky. "Others?"

"Maddox didn't want Ashlyn near a potential battle-ground, so he took her away," Lucien said. "Sabin and Gwen took Gilly somewhere."

Yep, that left only Kane, Torin and Cameo. Could they hold the fort if other Hunters showed up and attacked? Yeah, there were all kinds of traps leading up the mountain and any intruders would be forced to first battle explosions, trip wires, rigged gunshots and metal clamps around their ankles. But that wouldn't stop hundreds. Survivors could make their way inside.

"Can I count on you to stay?" Kane asked.

Adding one more warrior to the mix wasn't a miracle cure, but it *would* help.

Gideon's head fell back and hit the tattered headboard. He closed his eyes. Damn it. If the fortress was attacked and he was injured before Amun returned, if that delayed his confrontation with NeeMah…he would just have to deal, he thought.

"No," he said. "You can't count on me."

Scarlet didn't react.

"Knew it," Kane said. "Thanks."

"Now. Stay here," he told the warriors. *Get lost.* "I don't need some alone time with her."

"Have fun," Lucien replied, still shooting off that sheepish grin.

"And try to control the…whatever we stumbled upon," Kane added. "That was just flat-out weird."

With that, both men turned and strode out of the room. One of them remained in the hall to try and refit the door in its hinges. When that failed, whoever it was propped the wood in the entrance so that most of the bedroom was blocked, only a long, thin crack of light visible.

Alone at last.

"Don't stay here with me," Gideon said to Scarlet, and once again he hated his demon. More than anything, he wanted Scarlet to stay with him and he was willing to beg to make that happen. Beg properly. Truthfully. But he couldn't allow his body to weaken just then. His friends needed him at his strongest. "I don't want to be with you. We can't do this, I know we can't."

"Why would you want to be with me?" she asked, finally ripping from his hold, standing and whirling on him with shining black eyes. Gods, she was glorious in her nakedness. Skin still flushed and pink, nipples beaded from the cool air, lean legs braced, stomach flat and navel dipped. "Why would you want to try?"

Let her leave. A plea from Lies to keep her here.

Working on it. But why do you care?

Not mine.

That's right, he shot back, doing to his demon what Scarlet sometimes did to him. Even though he knew the demon lied, he responded as if the fiend had told the truth. *She's mine.* And that wasn't up for debate. "You didn't promise your mother to stop me from helping Cronus," he said. "You don't have to—"

Her bitter laugh shut him up. "Guess what? I lied to Mother Dearest. Besides that, you and I don't have a past," she continued before he could respond. "We're attracted to each other, yes, but that will fade. Right now I'm just the shiny new toy who gets you and your sidekick, and that's got to be a relief for you. But we have different goals, and that's what matters. I'm going to kill my mother and my aunt, even if it takes an eternity. You're going to protect your friends."

Shiny new toy. Fuck that! He popped to his knees, dislodging the sheet completely. Yeah, his erection stretched toward her, and yeah, she noticed, even backed up a step, but he didn't cover it. Let her see what the *shiny new toy* did to him.

Don't grab her, Lies commanded.

Grab her? He'd lose an arm. *We have to finesse this.* "Clearly you're thinking this through rationally, Scar. You don't follow through with your promise, and you'll live happily ever after." One thing he knew. For immortals, a broken vow was fatal. He'd imprisoned many Greeks for just such a crime. Therefore, Scarlet would be following through. "Second, you face your aunt and she won't give you new memories. She won't beat you." Gideon, too, laughed bitterly. They both knew her ass would be handed to her. "She won't chain you to a leash of her choosing."

"I know what she can do now. I know what to guard against."

Oh, really? "Having trouble recalling what happened today?"

She squared her shoulders and raised her chin. "I told you. I'm prepared now."

"That'll make a difference." No fucking difference at all! Why couldn't she see that?

"Well, failure is a chance I'm willing to take."

Well, he damn well wasn't. "Don't stay here with me, and I won't help you defeat her." Then, whatever. "We're weaker together, you know we are." They were stronger. "I mean, I did nothing to help you come to your senses last time, right?" He'd done everything.

Fury sparked in her eyes as she crossed her arms over her chest. "And just how long would you expect me to stay?"

He didn't answer. He couldn't. He didn't know how long he'd need to guard the fortress and everyone inside. Didn't know how much time would pass before Amun returned.

"That's what I thought," she said and turned away. The elegant curve of her back had him sweating, and those tattoos...he'd never licked them, never given them the attention they deserved. One day. One day he'd devote an entire night to her back. If she let him. "You'd keep me here indefinitely, and that I won't allow. I'm going."

Yes. Yes, let her go. Stop her.

"Scar."

"I'm going," she repeated, but still she didn't storm off. "Yes. I'm going." One step, two. Hesitant. As if she warred with herself. Or perhaps her demon.

His own demon whimpered.

She took another step, still hesitant. And then silence, waiting. Maybe he'd gotten to her. Maybe—

She fisted her hands and strode into the closet. Clothing whooshed.

A growl. *Stop her,* Lies gritted out, and it was the first time in all their centuries together that the demon had told the truth. *Please.*

Gideon blinked in shock, even as the demon screamed in pain. Pain that radiated through his entire body. A grunt escaped him, his muscles seeming to rip from his bones, his bones seeming to pop out of his skin.

"No," he barked. "No!"

"Gideon?"

Stop...her...

Another grunt. Black winked over his vision. *Shut up! We have to stay strong.*

Stop...

The sweat poured from him, little rivers all over his body. "Don't give me...a couple days...to learn more about...what's going on and do...what I can to help...so I can't leave with...a clear conscience." He could barely get the words out.

She leaned out of the closet, brow furrowed. "What's wrong with you?"

"Nothing."

A moment passed as she waited for him to elaborate. "Are you in pain?"

"No."

Again she waited. Again he offered nothing more. He didn't want her pity. Didn't want her having to take care of him. He wanted her to view him as the warrior he was.

She frowned, looked away. "Listen. We both know the truth. You can't leave this place with a clear conscience. No matter how long I give you. And no, I'm not doing this to be cruel. Please believe that," she whispered, then ducked back inside, disappearing from view.

Stop...stop...

Shut up! Panting, almost wheezing, he said, "I have slept...with very few women." Many. "All of them made me feel...utterly satisfied." He'd been pleasured, yes, but always hollow and lonely. "But with you, it's all physical." It wasn't. "I don't admire your strength...and your courage and fuck, I don't want...to see your smile." He did. More than anything.

"You don't know me," she called, but there was a tremble in her voice.

"And I don't...want to." Fuck. He wouldn't be able to stay awake much longer. Took every ounce of strength he possessed to get to his feet.

"Shut up! Just shut up. I *have* to leave." A pause. A sniff. "I have to." Another whisper.

No! A scream.

Gideon roared as more of that awful pain raged through him. "Morning won't...arrive soon. Don't wait another day at least." *Stay forever.*

"Damn it, Gideon. What's wrong with you? Tell me this time." Soft black material hanging from her fingers, she once again leaned out. "Please."

"Don't stay," he gritted out.

A frustrated sigh met his words. "The moon is high. I've got several hours to find someplace safe. I'll be fine, so there's no need to worry about me if that's what you're doing."

Maybe he could stall her. Keep her talking until the sun rose and she drifted to sleep. "How did your demon...know I love spiders...so much?" It was the first question that popped into his head.

"My demon just knows. My demon always knows. Why *are* you afraid of them? I've wondered."

He liked that she'd wondered about him. Even about that. "Before my possession—" after "—and never… at random times—" always "—I wouldn't feel them… crawling all over me. I wouldn't bat them away…and many more wouldn't take their place."

She disappeared back inside the closet. Something clanked. There was a muttered curse.

What else could he ask her? His brain was fogged, clouded by the pain, but surely there was something. "So why…" Damn it. What? "Why—"

"Stop. Just stop. You've never been this talkative before, so I know what you're trying to do." A gun clicked, metal slid against leather, and then she finally emerged fully.

Her hair was anchored in a ponytail at the base of her neck. She wore another of his T-shirts and a fresh pair of his sweatpants. Both were rolled to fit her shorter, smaller frame. In several places, there was a telltale bulge. Looked like she was stealing…four of his weapons. Not that he cared.

Gideon wanted to close the distance, grab her up and remind her of just how good it was between them. Weakened and hurting as he was, though, his knees finally gave out and he collapsed to the ground.

With a cry of concern, she stepped toward him. Just before contact, however, she stopped herself. Backed away. "Please understand, Gideon." Cold, so cold, and that was far worse than her lack of emotion. "It has to be this way. Being with you…hurts. There's just too much in the way. I'm too much of a liability to you. And I know that isn't your fault, it's mine, but that doesn't change anything."

Every instinct he possessed yearned to tell her she wasn't a liability. But he couldn't. Truth or lie, she would know his meaning. NeeMah influenced her too easily. That didn't mean Scarlet wasn't worth the risk.

She was worth every risk.

But he wanted her to be happy, even if that meant upsetting himself, and she didn't think she could be happy with him. It *hurt* her.

The thought of her hurting utterly destroyed him. She'd endured far too much already.

"Besides," she continued in that cold, detached way. Frowning, she rubbed her temple, as if her head were aching. Or perhaps, as he'd suspected, her demon was as loud and upset as his own. "Like I told you, I'm going to do everything in my power to ensure my memory is wiped clean. If I have to break into Tartarus and abduct the Greek god of Memory, I will. And when it's done, I won't remember you, so there's no reason to start something that has no future."

No, no, no. From the demon *and* Gideon. And yet...

Cringing at the effort required to move, he waved his arm toward the door. "Stay, then." If she needed to leave to find happiness, so be it. But when he healed, when the fortress was fortified, he would go after her. Somehow, some way, he'd prove *he* could make her happy, too. Wiping her memory, though, wasn't going to happen. Ever.

"Goodbye, Gideon," she said, then hesitated only a moment before walking away from him and out of his room.

No! No! Mine. Come back! Lies shouted, and that was the last thing Gideon knew.

CHAPTER TWENTY

THE OLD MATTRESS squeaked as the punked-out female thrashed atop it, lost in what was probably a bloody, violent nightmare. *I'll have to thank Gideon's woman later,* Strider thought, just in case she was responsible. And he didn't feel bad for the lack of compassion.

He had studied his bounty while she'd slept. Every inch of her, even peeling back her clothes for a look at all the hidden places. Weapons could be stored anywhere. Some would say he had no scruples, and he would agree. He didn't. Not with this woman. Never with this woman.

He now knew who she was, and she didn't deserve leniency from him. She deserved the sting of his blade.

There, lying on the small motel bed, locked with him in this tiny room, was Hadiee, the woman who had led Baden, keeper of Distrust, to his slaughter. *She helped destroy my best friend!*

The beheading had taken places thousands of years ago, and she'd been human. Or so he'd thought. Yet here she was, as young as she'd been back then. Which meant she was now immortal. Right? How it had happened, he didn't know. But he would find out. He would be finding out a lot of things from the bitch.

It had taken him a few hours to place her, 'cause yeah, the tattoos, piercings and pink streaks in her hair had thrown him. She hadn't looked like this back then. Her hair had been several shades lighter, a tumble of snowfall, and her skin glowing from the sun's kiss. She'd dressed in the rough, conservative garb of a servant, but that hadn't detracted from her prettiness.

He never would have placed her if not for the score-board tattooed on her back.

Lords: IIII   Haidee: I

She'd split her back in two, one side for the Lords, one side for herself. He'd known exactly what the marks meant, too, because Baden had marked himself that way, as well. Bitch.

The four he and his friends had supposedly killed, he couldn't name. And yeah, he'd probably slain them. In all his many centuries, he'd slain thousands. The knowledge of that should have dulled his anger toward this woman. It didn't. Baden had been the best man Strider had ever known. The kindest to his friends, the most supportive and caring.

Being possessed by the demon of Distrust had changed him, of course, just as being possessed by such a dark force had changed all of them. But he'd been the first to come back to his senses. The one who had led everyone else to the light. He'd felt the guiltiest for the destruction the Lords had caused. He'd been the first to reach out, to try and make amends with humans.

He had also hated what he'd become more than any of the others. He'd hated that he distrusted himself, everyone around him, even his friends. Especially his friends. But that had only made Strider love him more. Baden had been Strider's salvation. Strider had wanted to be Baden's salvation.

Hadiee had destroyed that chance.

As the girl continued to thrash, eyes squeezed shut, sweat beading over her skin, arms and legs jerking at their ties, her cell phone rang. Strider grinned. He'd been hoping this would happen and didn't have to guess who was calling. The boyfriend. The leader of the Hunters who had been chasing him.

Strider reached out, swooped the cell from its perch on the table beside him and flipped it open. "Sorry," he said into the mouthpiece, "but your girlfriend's a little tied up right now and can't come to the phone."

There was a pause. A ragged breath and crackling static. "She's mine, you sick bastard! If you hurt her…"

Oh, yes. The boyfriend. "If?" Strider laughed with genuine amusement. "That's cute. Really it is."

Now there was a roar. "Which piece of evil shit are you?"

"Doesn't matter. All that matters is that this evil shit has your woman. And he isn't giving her back. Not unless it's in pieces."

More of that static crackled over the line, followed quickly by a loud boom, a curse. Loverboy must have punched the wall. "What do you want with her? What will you trade?"

"One thousand Hunter hearts. Oh, wait. Hunters don't have hearts. So I guess there's nothing I'm willing to trade for her."

"You dirty, filthy—" The human stopped himself, as if only then realizing Strider could punish his woman for everything he said. "She's a good person. She has a family. She—"

Anger blasted through him. "*I'm* a good person. I have a family." He could just imagine how the Hunter was gritting his teeth at that. "And yet she would have taken my head without hesitation. It's only fair that I reciprocate."

"You aren't good, and you know it. You're selfish and dark and ruined. You belong in hell."

Selfish? Dark? Yeah, no question. But ruined? Hardly. "I've done nothing but try to protect myself for thousands of years."

"And in that protecting—" the Hunter sneered "—you've killed my friends."

"Just as your woman killed mine." Now it was Strider's turn to punch something. He slammed a fist into the side table, splitting the wood. *Boom!*

A feminine gasp had his gaze moving back to his charge. He stilled. She'd stopped thrashing, was staring over at him through blazing gray eyes. "And believe me," he added calmly, "she will pay for that."

No reaction from Hadiee.

Her boyfriend, however, exploded. "She hasn't killed anyone! But I have. Trade her for *me*."

Did he not know her history? It seemed unlikely that the one person who'd succeeded in killing a Lord of the Underworld wouldn't have become the stuff of legend among her cohorts. "No, thanks," Strider said. "I like the hostage I've got."

The Hunter's fury overtook him, obliterating his common sense. "I *will* find you and I will kill you, you motherfucking son of a bitch!"

Slowly he grinned. "Now that sounds like a challenge. Good news is, I accept." Inside his head, his demon jumped up and down with excitement. "Find me and we'll have a little party."

Without removing his gaze from the girl, Strider

closed the phone, reveling in the fact that he'd had the last word. He stood. Hadiee's murderous expression didn't change as he walked to the bathroom. He knew phones could be traced and tracked and wasn't going to allow that to happen here. Whistling, he crushed the plastic and wires into as many pieces as he could and flushed them down the toilet.

When he rejoined her, reclaiming his chair at the foot of the bed, he stretched out his legs and anchored his hands behind his head, a pose of smug relaxation. "Feeling better after your rest, darling Hadiee?"

Surprise darkened those gunmetal eyes. "You know who I am." A statement, not a question.

He answered anyway. "Yes."

"Well, no one calls me that anymore. I'm Haidee now. A minor change in spelling, but a big stride in modernization, don't you think? *Defeat*."

So. She knew who he was, as well. How did she, but not the boyfriend?

"Or you could just call me Executioner," she added, a taunt.

Rather than strike her as he wanted, he arched a brow. "I'll just call you Ex, then. Since you and I are going to be intimate, an endearment seems appropriate."

Surprise was replaced with anger. Once more, she began thrashing atop the bed, jerking at her ties. Her lips pulled back from her straight, white teeth, and she hissed over at him.

"Touch me and I'll peel the skin from your body."

"As if I'd touch you that way." He shuddered. He was not attracted to this female. Not in any way.

"Like I'd be stupid enough to believe a demon."

"No, you're only stupid enough to murder one."

No shame. No regret. Only a smile, dark and wicked, that didn't quite reach her eyes. "You say stupid. I say brave."

"But as I was saying," he continued past his sudden surge of rage, determined to scare her again, "I plan to intimately acquaint you with my weapons."

Funnily enough, that seemed to calm her. "You can try" was all she said.

"I'll do more than that." Before she could reply, probably to him again, he switched the direction of their conversation. "You've changed."

Her gaze raked over him, and she grimaced in distaste. "You haven't."

"Aw. Thank you." He flattened a palm over his heart. "That means so much to me."

"That wasn't a compliment," she snapped.

Good. He was getting to her. "Of course it was. I'm gorgeous."

"You're also a coward," she snarled. "A real man would have fought someone his own size."

He almost grinned. He'd been called worse. Maybe that was why insults like that never affected him. "Actually, I'm a very smart warrior. I took the weak link, yes, but now the rest of the chain will wither. Think about it. With your death, the men will go crazy. They'll be ruled by their emotions. They'll make mistakes. Fatal mistakes. All I'll have to do is wait, swoop in and kill them."

She didn't flinch at his words. Either she didn't believe he would actually kill a woman, which was stupid, since he'd done so before and as a Hunter, she had to know that, or she thought herself infallible. Which was... possible, he realized with a sudden blast of dread.

"I know you're more than human." His head tilted to the side as he ran his gaze along her compact little body. "What I don't know is what you are and how you got that way."

"And you'll never know," she replied, staunch once again.

"Doesn't matter, I guess. Even immortals can be cut down."

A smile curved the corners of her lips. Smug and satisfied and taunting. And this time, the amusement reached her eyes. "I know."

Two simple words, but they built a fire inside him that crackled and smoldered, spread and raged. So badly he wanted to stand, stalk to her and choke the life from her. He wanted to hurt her, make her suffer endlessly.

And he would.

He'd always been a possessive man. What he considered his was his. Women, cars, weapons, didn't matter. He didn't share. Ever. And right now he considered this woman his property and her misery his mission.

She was his to do with whatever he willed.

Whatever we *will,* his demon interjected.

So. Defeat wanted a piece of her, as well. Maybe Strider could share, just this once.

He schooled his expression to reveal nothing but calm. He thought perhaps there were red flickers in his eyes, showing just how close to the surface his demon now was, because Hadiee, no, Haidee, no, Ex, paled, blue lines becoming visible beneath her skin.

Inside his head, Defeat laughed, almost giddy, loving that the woman had been intimidated.

"Capturing you was the easiest thing I've ever done," he said. "Not a challenge at all. You're not much of a warrior, are you? Which makes me wonder why the men keep you around. Because they like to pass you around? Because you managed to kill a Lord, something none of your kind has been able to do again?"

Her eyes narrowed. "Maybe I let you capture me. Maybe I'm still Bait, and now that we're together, I'll lead you into slaughter. But let the men use me? No. I'm with one, and he *will* punish you for this. You have my word."

"The word of a Hunter? Sorry, but that means nothing to me."

"If you think I'll beg you to let me go, you think wrong. If you think I'll cower at your feet, you think wrong. I *will* prevail."

"You can try," he said, parroting her earlier words to him.

Her teeth flashed in a scowl. "I'll do more than that. I'll give my man your head as a birthday present."

Most would have been crying by now. She was brave, as she'd claimed, he would give her that. "Clearly you don't know me well enough. To think you'll be alive for your lover's next birthday…well, you are a Hunter. I shouldn't have expected you to be intelligent."

Tendrils of mist drifted from her nostrils. At first, he thought he was mistaken. But no. That really was mist, crystallizing in front of her face. "Oh, I know you," she said. "You're Strider, keeper of Defeat. I've seen your picture, heard tales of your exploits. You burned cities to the ground, tormented innocents then destroyed their families."

The reminder caused a muscle to tick below his eye. "That was a long time ago."

She wasn't done. "You thrive on challenge. You can't

lose without pain. Well, guess what? I don't think you can keep me in this room without having to tie me. I don't think you're strong enough."

What. A. Bitch. She wanted to challenge him, did she? She'd soon learn the error of her ways. He stood, stalked to the bed and withdrew a knife. Surprisingly, she didn't flinch as he lowered it toward her. She looked...eager. Ready to die.

What an odd reaction.

With quick precision, he cut each of the ties. Immediately she tried to bolt toward the door, but he caught her by the waist and flung her back onto the bed.

As she gasped, he jumped on top of her, weight smashing her down. She struggled, oh, did she struggle, teeth snapping at him, hands pounding at him, knees whipping a direct pathway to his shaft. Fuck!

He held on through the pain and dizziness and nausea and soon she tired, panting, sweating, more of that mist wafting from her.

That chilly mist smelled of...ambrosia, thick, flowery. Addicting.

"You really should think before you speak. You haven't been fed or watered." Like the animal she was. "You're too weak to take me."

When she stilled completely, he grabbed her wrists and pinned them above her head. He locked her legs down with his own, and his middle fell more deeply into hers, her body offering him a cradle.

She was soft, chilled, almost like champagne on ice. And the scent of that ambrosia... He felt his cock thickening, elongating, and growled, suddenly pissed off beyond measure. "See? Easy," he told her.

She looked at him through the thick shield of her

lashes, those gray eyes steady, emotionless. "Round one is yours. That hardly matters."

"Says the loser."

His demon purred with joy. That joy sparked pleasure, and that pleasure washed through him. Ah. That was why he was aroused, he realized; it had nothing to do with the woman. Thank the gods. He wouldn't be able to live with himself if he lusted for a godsdamn Hunter.

"What now?" she asked in that calm, dead voice.

"Now," he replied. "We send a piece of you to your boyfriend, then send the rest of you to my friends."

BY THE TIME they reached Lucifer's palace, Amun was useless and he feared he'd weakened his companions. There'd been other battles with demons, yet Aeron and William had had to fight on their own while protecting him. Now they were bloody and bruised and forced to drag him along.

His friends would've been better off leaving him behind.

The new voice in his head...gods, it was worse than any other he'd ever welcomed. So many urges...kill, maim, destroy. Reminded him of his first years with Secrets. So many dark deeds done...so many memories infused with his own.

One of these new memories filled his mind even then. Three human souls were bared and chained before him, each trembling, crying, begging for mercy. He didn't have mercy, however. He was too eager for this. His claws sharpened to deadly points and he slowly raked each tip over the two males, sinking deep, cutting skin and hitting bone, letting the female see what would soon be done to her, increasing her fear. Both men screamed, for his claws were tipped with acid.

That acid burned through the human souls, rotting everything it touched.

Soon their skin turned to char, and that char spread. That's when he flipped them over, one at a time, that sweet scent of rot in his nose, and raped them. Their screaming increased, their thrashing increased, and he laughed. Laughed with true glee. Fun, this was always so much fun.

The woman watched every thrust, helpless, afraid, knowing she was next.

Soon, he promised her. Finally, he emptied into the second male and turned to the female, already hard again. He was always hard. Always ready. The more unwilling the victim, the better.

She tried to crawl away from him, but the chain around her neck stopped her. He laughed. *Can't run from me, little maggot.*

No, Amun screamed in his mind. *That's not me. That's not me!*

He leaned over and vomited, entire body spasming as bile blistered a path through his throat.

Strong hands patted his back, offering comfort. "That's it. Let it out," Aeron said.

Once he'd voided his stomach completely, he straightened. Or tried to. His knees finally gave out and not even his friends could hold him up. He was too heavy. A dead weight, boneless.

They managed to drag him to a gnarled tree and prop him against the jagged trunk. Trees in hell, he thought dazedly. Go figure.

"What can I do?" Aeron asked, crouching in front of him.

Nothing. Groaning, Amun forced his eyelids to remain open. The new voice continued to scream, to make itself known, and the pain in his head increased. But he'd rather feel that pain than see those terrible images.

He scanned his surroundings, searching for a distraction. The forest was composed of ash and withered foliage. There was no green, no colorful flowers. Only an endless sea of black. Souls had been tormented here.

He had tormented souls here.

Oh, gods.

"Take a moment to rebuild your strength," William said, motioning to the looming hill where Lucifer's palace rested. "We're almost there."

Amun followed the direction of his friend's gaze. Black brick rose from that monochrome sea, two crumbling towers connected in the center to form a giant skull. There was a staircase enclosed by pikes—pikes that held severed human heads—leading to the yawning mouth of that skull, where sharp, yellow teeth hung like a chandelier. He would never make it.

Just leave me here, he tried to sign.

He didn't think he'd succeeded, but William understood him nonetheless. "You have to go with us. If it becomes necessary, and I pray that it won't, only you can discover where Lucifer has hidden the girl."

And how much worse would Lucifer's memories be than this demon's? How much more could Amun take?

"You've been here before," Aeron said to the warrior. "Anya said Lucifer is even afraid of you. Why is that?"

"Anya misspoke." William had once again carefully blanked his mind, preventing Amun from reading the truth.

"I don't think so. Knowledge is power, and we need all the power we can get. Look at us." Aeron waved a hand down his bleeding body.

He was at the razor-edge of his patience, ready to erupt at the slightest offense.

"The reason doesn't matter," William snapped. He, too, was gearing for a battle. "He'll fight me, just the same as he'll fight you."

Arguing wasn't helping their cause. Amun held out a shaky hand to be helped up. His knees nearly collapsed again, but two strong arms banded around him, his anchors in the storm.

Once more, the three of them trudged forward. By the time they reached the top of the hill, they were panting, cursing. There were no demon guards posted at the entrance to the staircase, but then, Lucifer didn't want to keep them out. The prince of darkness was inside, and he was waiting.

Up the stairs they climbed, dust pluming at their feet. The door was open. After only the briefest of pauses, they stepped into a wide foyer, where piles of bones rested in each corner. The floor was stained red with blood and sticky with things he didn't want to contemplate.

Amun pulled from his friends' clasps, determined to stand on his own. He wouldn't hinder them any more than he already had. He was a warrior, damn it. He could do this.

"Be ready," Aeron whispered, blades already in hand.

"Been ready," William replied, gripping his own blades more tightly.

They'd already run out of bullets and had had to dispose of their guns.

Together, they stalked forward, straight ahead, Amun continually tripping over his own feet. But he did walk, and at the moment, that was all that mattered. Finally they reached a room, scalding orange-gold flames licking each of the walls and fanning heat in every direction.

His demon sighed. And, if he wasn't mistaken, uttered the word *home*. Sickness reclaimed his stomach. *Not home,* he thought. *Never home.*

Focus. There, in the center of the room, was a dais built from brimstone and atop that brimstone was a throne of twisted, jagged metal and horns.

The prince of darkness reclined in it, calm, unfazed by his expected visitors.

"At last," Lucifer said, sipping from a bejeweled goblet. He was well built, with black hair and orange-gold eyes. He would have had a handsome face, one females probably would have melted over, if not for the deadness of those eyes. They gave him away, revealed his evil for all to see. "You certainly took your time."

"Where's Legion?" Aeron demanded.

"What? No pleasantries? No 'how are you doing, dearest master'?"

"Certainly," William said evenly. "I'm doing well, thank you, reviled slave."

Lucifer popped his jaw before nodding in greeting. "William. I was surprised to hear you had returned."

"Just tell the man what he wants to know, and we'll

leave. Your blood won't have to be spilled. I know, I know. You're welcome."

Amun concentrated all of his energy on the prince, linking with his mind, staying tuned to his thoughts. At first, there was nothing. Only silence. But Amun continued to push, to dig deeper, and must have finally penetrated some sort of barrier. All at once, an intense wave of hatred hit him. Hatred and fear, as Anya had predicted.

Mine, mine, mine. You will not take what's mine.

"I'm sorry my minions treated you so shabbily," Lucifer said. His tone was just as easy as it had been from the first, as if he wasn't chanting in his head. "I will, of course, punish them. Though perhaps I'll be more merciful than you used to be."

A vein popped from William's temple.

He was still closed off, and Amun didn't have the strength to mentally reach him. Besides, that might have severed the link to the prince.

Lucifer's head canted to the side, and he grinned, his attention shifting to Aeron. "There's something different about you, Wrath." Thoughtful, he tapped his chin. "No, no. I can't call you that, can I? You are Wrath no longer. You are demon-free. Would you like to change that?"

"Either tell us where the girl is or fight us. You're boring me, and I have things to do," William said.

Lucifer's attention returned to him, eyes narrowing. "Oh, yes. I know exactly what those things include. Seducing the lovely Gilly. Your desire for her grows daily, doesn't it? *Brother.* And really, I'm surprised you didn't stop and visit your Horsemen. They miss you so."

Brother? Horsemen? The four Horsemen of the *Apocalypse?*

Aeron stiffened, shooting William a shocked and angered glance.

Lucifer laughed inside his head, utterly pleased with himself.

He's trying to divide you, Amun signed, unsure Lucifer had meant what he'd said. Not about Gilly, and not about the Horsemen, Amun knew both were true, but about the familial connection. Unfortunately, neither warrior noticed him.

"He's lying, of course," William said smoothly. Or tried to. His voice trembled just a bit. "I've never touched Gilly, and I never will. I'm not into jailbait. And the horsey comment doesn't deserve a response."

One dark brow arched in smug amusement. "Whatever you say. Now, let's begin with the night's entertainment and rid you of your boredom. Shall we?" He clapped his hands, the sound echoing through the surrounding blaze.

To the left, two demon High Lords entered the room. If their grins were any indication, they'd been waiting eagerly for their summons. Between them was Legion, shoulders hunched, pale hair in bloody tangles around her head. She'd been stripped and chained, and there were welts along her thighs where she'd been whipped.

Knowing he couldn't afford the distraction, Amun blocked her thoughts. But not before he caught a glimpse of them. Oh, the terrible things that had been done to her…so much worse than what the minion of Pain had shown him, for that creature had only witnessed portions of her torture.

She might never recover.

She was as cut and bruised as he was, and there was a desolation in her eyes that had never been there before. But when she caught sight of Aeron, she began to struggle, to scream, worried for him, hopeful for herself.

"Aeron! Aeron!"

The demons held tightly, and Aeron tried to stalk forward, but William gripped his arm and held him in place.

"That's what he wants."

Lucifer was watching Aeron, eating up his reaction, loving the paleness of his skin, the grinding of his teeth. "Nothing to say, warrior?"

Aeron nodded. "You will die for this."

"That's it?"

Another stiff nod, as if he didn't trust himself to speak again.

Amun felt the surge of disappointment that filled the prince. He'd wanted Aeron to rant and rave. But, no matter, Lucifer thought, and Amun almost pulled from the being's mind. He retained the connection, sick to his stomach, churning with dread. Lucifer wasn't going to be deterred. What he had planned was sure to drive Aeron to the brink of madness. Aeron, stupid Aeron, who had ruined his plans to possess Legion and destroy the Lords.

"Then let's get started with the festivities," Lucifer said smoothly. "Shall we?"

CHAPTER TWENTY-ONE

SCARLET WAS experiencing the five stages of grief. All at the same time. Denial—Gideon *hadn't* been writhing in pain when she left him. Anger—her bitch of a mother had ignored her summons, over and over again, so she hadn't made it back to the heavens to begin tracking Mnemosyne. Bargaining—*Let Gideon finally win his war,* she'd prayed to no one in particular, *and I'll forget about my revenge against my aunt.* He'd be safe and Scarlet wouldn't be a liability. Depression—she would never see the beautiful warrior again, she just knew it. Acceptance—she'd done the right thing, leaving him. He would be better off.

Tears burned her eyes, but she hastily wiped them away. Only a day had passed, but she missed him terribly. And like an addict in need of a fix, she was still in Budapest, close to him. Close enough to climb the iron fence that surrounded his fortress and saunter up to the front door, knock, grab him when he opened said door and kiss him.

Only reason she'd resisted was because she'd barely gathered the strength to walk away the first time. No way could she do so a second time.

Idiot. Frustration and desperation joined her other emotions. She would have tried to summon someone besides her mother for a ticket into Titania, but none of the gods, Greeks or Titans, liked her. Or if they did, she didn't *remember*. Fucking Mnemosyne.

Return to Gideon, Nightmares pleaded. *I'll be good, I swear.*

Her demon had experienced the five stages of grief as well, but kept returning to bargaining. *You've always fancied him. Why? I don't understand. You fancy no one.*

He...belongs to me.

She wished. *I'm no good for him.* But she wanted to be. Gods, did she want to be.

He might not be her husband, she might not have any history with him, but she had come to...like him this past week. And he had come to like her. She knew he had. He'd tried to talk her into staying. He'd told her that he wanted more from her than a single bedding. And oh, gods, hearing those words had nearly crushed her resolve to leave.

But in the end, she'd known leaving was her best and only option. She'd also known she'd had to close the door on them completely. Otherwise he might have come after her. Until her mother and aunt were dead, they had to remain apart. As long as Rhea lived, Gideon was vulnerable. As long as Mnemosyne lived, *Scarlet* was vulnerable. Or rather, her mind was.

And if her mind was vulnerable, that meant Gideon was in danger. She could be convinced to hurt him, kill him, or even be persuaded that he was determined to hurt or kill her. She would attack him, and he didn't deserve that.

He was a good man. A strong and gorgeous good man, and she'd caused enough turmoil in his life. But if, after her mother and aunt were dead, he still wanted to try to make a relationship work, she would be willing, she decided. However, she doubted he would want to try. There'd been frustration, desperation, anger and sadness in his eyes as she'd abandoned him. And pain. So much pain.

She'd cried as she'd exited the fortress. Cried harder as she'd slunk into this underground crypt. The moment she'd reached the bottom, she'd closed her eyes and entered dreamland. Still crying.

She'd been tempted to find Gideon. In fact, all of her strength had been needed to resist. Only thing that had saved her from doing so was, ironically enough, her aunt. Scarlet had forced herself to visit the woman and wait outside the doorway to her consciousness.

Though she'd waited and waited, the bitch had never fallen asleep, and by the end, Nightmares had been a writhing cauldron of hunger. Scarlet had then given the demon free rein, and a tormenting spree had quickly ensued, shaping the dark dreams of thousands. Including Rhea's.

That, Scarlet had enjoyed, taking special care to present her mother with her greatest fear: losing to her husband.

Now, sleep was upon Scarlet again, and she was again waiting outside her aunt's doorway. If she couldn't reach Mnemosyne this time, she was going to draw Mnemosyne to her. And have a little fun in the process. That's why she had removed the butterfly necklace Gideon had given her. So that she could be found. *Soon...*

She had to wait several hours, but this time Mnemosyne's door creaked open...only to snap shut so quickly she couldn't sneak inside. Well, well. Her aunt was fighting slumber. Soon, though, the goddess of Memory would lose. They always did.

All the while Nightmares's hunger grew more intense, just like before.

Just a little longer, she told her companion.

The fiend whimpered inside her mind, and the shadows and screams that had been a part of her for thousands of years, so much so she hardly noticed them until Gideon aroused her to madness, intensified, too. Seeking release. Seeking a target.

I promise, she added. If she had to allow another tormenting spree, she would.

Finally, though, the wait paid off.

Mnemosyne drifted, her doorway opening halfway and allowing Scarlet to dart inside before it could close again. Which it was in the process of doing. She latched onto the sweet, shining dream even then trying to form and tugged, dragging her aunt deeper and deeper into that state of bliss. Luring her...

The dream continued, her aunt now unable to wake.

Mnemosyne saw herself on the heavenly throne, queen to gods and mortals alike. She issued orders that were instantly obeyed, and poems were composed about her beauty. Though she was mistress to Cronus in reality, Cronus wasn't the man she truly desired. That honor belonged to the Titan god of Strength, Atlas. He was a handsome man with dark hair and eyes a darker shade of blue than Gideon's, and he sat at her right-hand side, worshipping her.

So tranquil the scene was, so hopeful.

Scarlet wanted to scream. Her aunt didn't deserve

such accolades, even in her dreams. Not after everything she'd done. Not after the pain she had caused.

Scowling, Scarlet held out her hands and began wiping away the background. Atlas was the first to go, then the golden throne, then the palace. Thorns and fire sprouted in their place. She placed Mnemosyne in the center of those scorching flames, watching as they licked her aunt's body, burning away her skin, her beauty.

Mnemosyne shrieked in terror, in utter agony. So real was the dream, her skin would be melting in reality. It wouldn't kill her, Scarlet wouldn't allow the flames to last that long, but it *would* horrify the bitch to see herself in the morning. To see her pretty looks gone and a revolting hag in her place. Yes, that skin would regenerate. But until it did… Scarlet laughed.

Nightmares danced inside her head, loving every moment of this. *More!*

"My pleasure." With only a thought, Scarlet dismissed the blaze.

Moaning, her aunt fell to the ground, her knees too weak to hold her up. Scarlet walked to her, unhurried, rearranging the scene with every step. The plain gray walls of Tartarus formed, followed by the many cots that had filled their shared cell. Next, Cronus and Rhea appeared, arguing in a corner.

Lastly, Scarlet added herself. Bedraggled, dirty, a slave collar around her neck, and hair in tangles to her waist. When she'd reached adulthood, her mother had stopped arranging for her head to be shaved. Allowing Scarlet to be pestered by other prisoners had been more important to Rhea than being the fairest in the realm. The guards hadn't wanted to help Scarlet, either, and getting her hands on a blade had been impossible. Cutting it had become a luxury and one of the first things she'd done upon her release.

In the vision, she pressed her back against the bars and peered down at her aunt.

"Remember this?" she asked. "Our centuries of slavery?"

Mnemosyne barely had the strength to look up, but look up she did, hate glinting in her eyes. She was laboring for every breath, and tears were streaming down her ruined cheeks. Those salty droplets had to sting.

"Either you find me," Scarlet told her, crouching down to her level and cupping her chin despite her aunt's flinch to avoid contact, "or I come to you every time you fall asleep. If you thought the flames were bad, wait until you see what I have planned next."

"Bitch," Mnemosyne choked out. Strands of hair were charred to her skull, her cheeks sunken, some of her bones visible. "Cronus will kill you when he sees what you've done to me."

Slowly she smiled. "Good. I look forward to his attempts. Meanwhile, enjoy your first taste of tomorrow's entertainment."

With that, Scarlet threw her aunt to the wolves. Literally.

GIDEON LASTED three days. Three damn days. Once he'd regained his strength, he'd helped fortify the fortress, had snuck into town on several occasions to hunt for Hunters, had found a few stragglers, interrogated them, hadn't learned anything, and had killed them.

Now, he was going after Scarlet.

Her memories of him were her own creation, and

yeah, she now knew they were false memories. Fake or not, though, she had constructed some really good times between them. And she had to want him still. Even though she'd thought he had left her in prison, even though she'd thought he had betrayed her with countless women, she had come to Budapest for him.

He could do no less for her.

The simple fact was, he loved her. Loved her with every breath in his body, every cell in his blood, every bone and organ he possessed. He loved her to the depths of his very soul. Had only taken five minutes after she'd walked away to realize it.

She was strong and courageous, she understood him in a way no one else ever had. She teased him and never seemed annoyed that he couldn't tell the truth. No, she was amused.

She was beautiful and fit him perfectly. He couldn't think straight when she was gone because he could only think of her. Could only wonder where she was and what she was doing. Wonder if she missed him, needed him, thought of the pleasure they'd brought each other and could bring each other again.

All he had to do was find her.

No, Lies said on a sigh of contented agreement. *No, thank you.*

No thanks needed, buddy.

Where was she? Determined, Gideon massaged the back of his neck. He could reason this out. Scarlet wanted to destroy the goddess of Memory; the last person to see the goddess had been Cronus. In the heavens. Only immortals who could flash or had wings could enter on their own, and neither applied to Scarlet. So she would have needed help.

She would have known Cronus wouldn't aid her. She would have then turned to her mother, as she'd done when looking for Gideon. Except, would the god queen help her again? Scarlet was now bent on her destruction, as well.

So, probably not.

Who did that leave?

Damn it. He could think of no one. Which put him right back at square one. She'd never mentioned a friend or ally.

Didn't matter, though. He was still going after her. If he had to tear the world apart, he would. And there was someone who could give him a starting place.

Gideon strode to Torin's room. Before he could raise his hand to knock, his friend called, "Enter." Cameras, he realized, and wanted to smack himself on the head. *Should have thought of this before.*

Excitement suddenly overwhelmed Gideon. Maybe tearing through the planet wouldn't be necessary. Shaking now, he twisted the knob and stepped inside, then shut the door behind him.

"Expected you before this," Torin said, swiveling in his chair. Twined hands rested on his middle, and that should have made him the picture of relaxed male. Only, his cheeks were flushed, his eyes were glassy and he couldn't quite catch his breath.

Behind him, one of the computer screens played a YouTube video titled *House of Witches—A Peaceful Night at Home.*

Gideon saw women. Lots and lots of sexy women. Some were drinking champagne—from the bottle—some were dancing provocatively, but all were laughing uproariously.

"Show 'em what you got, Carrow!" someone called.

A black-haired stunner with green eyes came into sizzling focus and simply lifted her top, flashing a buxom pair of breasts as she shouted, "Whoohoo!" Then she paused with her chest still bared and said, "Post this without sharing the profits, and I'll cut off your—"

"Damn it." Torin swung around, pressed a few buttons, and the computer screen went blank. "I thought I'd turned that off," he muttered as he once again faced Gideon.

I'm not even gonna ask. "So, uh, how isn't everyone today?" All the Lords checked in with Torin at least once a day, so Gideon decided to get business out of the way before he made his "I'm outta here" announcement.

"Alive. That's all I know. Though Strider texted me to say he would soon be coming home with a 'prezie' for everyone."

A present? His curiosity was piqued, but Gideon only nodded. "Listen, there's not something I need to tell you about—"

"Stop right there." Torin held up a hand. "No need to bungle through something in a language I'm still having trouble deciphering. Like I said, I expected you before this. I heard about your 'wife' and I'm honestly surprised you lasted this long. Kane, Cameo and I have got things under control here. Since Strider took a page from Gwen's book and played Goodbye Trachea with everyone surrounding the fortress, no one's tried to attack us, and I've seen nothing to indicate that anyone will in the near future. So go get your woman. If you can convince her to join us, everyone will stop running to me and begging me to talk some sense into you and lock her up. It's not like she's tried to hurt us, anyway, you know?"

Relief speared him so intensely he almost dove into his friend for a bear hug. "I hate you, man. You don't know that, right?"

Torin grinned, all pearly whites. "Now *that* I have no trouble deciphering. I hate you, too. But get all thoughts of hugging me out of your head. Yeah, I can tell you want to. I'm not the hugging type. I really will kill you with kindness."

Might be worth it. "I wouldn't, you know," he said in all seriousness. "Hug you, I mean. Wouldn't plant a big wet one right on your lips, either." Which meant he totally would. Because really, he would still be able to kiss Scarlet. Yeah, he'd be infected and that would infect her, but neither of them would die from it, and then neither of them would ever be able to touch anyone else.

He liked the thought of having Scarlet all to himself.

The keeper of Disease puckered up. "In that case, don't let me stop you. It's been a while, so I'm desperate. Even you look good at this point."

Gideon wasn't sure Torin had *ever* been kissed, but found himself grinning, as well. "You are—"

"Lies!" a hard voice shouted from outside, echoing from Torin's speakers. "Lies! I know you're in there. Come out right now. Come out and face me, you mangy coward!"

Amusement fading, Torin swung around and eyed the computer monitors. Gideon edged in beside him for a closer look and what he saw astonished him. Galen, keeper of Hope, leader of the Hunters, was hovering outside the fortress, white wings flapping frantically.

Usually the warrior wore a pristine white robe. To better match the angels and gods, Gideon suspected. Today, that robe was covered in soot and blood and frayed at the hem.

"You won't kill me," the keeper of Hope shouted, arms splayed, blades gleaming in both hands. His pale hair stood on end, and his sky-blue eyes were wild. There was a fanatical glint in his eyes. "I'll make sure of it."

Was this a dream? Nothing like this had ever happened before. Galen operated in the shadows, always sending humans to do his dirty work. But the warrior had never, *never* openly challenged the Lords.

"He's completely sane, right?" Gideon asked. The guy was batshit crazy.

"I don't know why he's singled you out." Torin typed furiously at his keyboard. "There aren't any Hunters on the ground that I can see. Still, I wouldn't trust him not to have backup hiding somewhere."

"Lies! Either you come out here and fight me or I burn your home to the ground."

"This has to be a trick," Torin insisted. "Or he would have already tried to burn us to the ground, rather than simply threatening to do so."

Trick or not, Gideon couldn't miss this opportunity. Capturing Galen could end the war with the Hunters. Successfully. And ultimately, that would eliminate one of the threats against Scarlet.

"I can try to shoot him down," Torin said, "and you can—"

"Yes." If Torin missed, the bastard might run away. Again. "Don't let me do it. My aim's not better."

"Lies!"

Torin nodded. "Just to be safe, I'm texting Kane and Cameo. I'm telling them to head into the forest and ensure you aren't ambushed."

"No, thanks. Now don't tell our friend I'll be out in five."

Torin nodded again and rushed to comply.

Gideon raced to his bedroom. He was already swathed in weapons since a warrior could never be too careful, but he grabbed his RPG and a grenade and grinned. He hadn't gotten to use this baby in a long, long time, Sabin having deemed it too dangerous to fire off with innocents around.

Today, there were no innocents around.

He sprinted to the side of the fortress that Galen occupied and hunkered down at the highest window, placing him above the Hunter. Galen was watching the ground, expecting him to emerge from the front door. Fool. As quietly as possible, Gideon raised the window-pane and edged the end of the barrel between the slit in the curtains.

"Lies!" the frantic immortal shouted. "Coward! Face me, damn you!"

Coward? No. He was smart. Gideon loaded the grenade in front, rested the heavy launcher on his shoulder, aimed, held steady, held, grinned again as Galen appeared in the crosshairs, and squeezed the trigger.

Boom!

Strong as Gideon was, he was propelled backward with the force of the grenade, but he straightened quickly and surveyed his handiwork through the smoke left behind.

He'd hit his target, tossing Galen several yards, spinning him through the air, and causing an explosion of fire and soot in the sky. That would have killed a mortal. Galen, however, was cut and bruised and now missing a hand—payback was a bitch—but he wasn't out for the count.

He just looked pissed.

With a roar, the now-flaming warrior propelled himself through the window in the next room over. Glass shattered, and there was a grunt, then pounding footsteps rained. Gideon palmed two daggers and darted into the hall, the portraits and freshly polished tables blurring at his sides.

He met his enemy in the middle of the walkway, flying to the ground in a punching, kicking, stabbing heap. Galen's wings were broken, and his mangled wrist was gushing blood that soaked into Gideon's clothes, warm and wet. There was a smoking hole in his shoulder where the rocket must have hit first, yet his strength was undisturbed. Determination would do that.

"You won't take my head," the keeper of Hope roared, swinging with his good hand. He'd managed to maintain a hold on his blade and now sliced the side of Gideon's face. His cheek split open, and his own blood began to gush.

With a roar of his own, Gideon slashed his knives forward. One cut at Galen's neck, slicing to spine, and the other at his uninjured shoulder. This man had been his friend for many years, yet he'd been Gideon's enemy for thousands more. No love remained. No fond memories.

They would end this. Here, now.

Galen flailed for breath, clutching at his now-open neck. Gideon disengaged and stood, panting, sweating, bleeding, staring down at the man responsible for so much of his suffering.

Had Galen not existed, he never would have thought to steal and open Pandora's box. He would have remained in the heavens, a soldier to Zeus. Perhaps he would have finally noticed Scarlet and freed her as she'd dreamed. Perhaps they would have lived happily ever after.

Or perhaps he would have been locked away when the Titans escaped Tartarus. Then again, perhaps the Titans wouldn't have escaped if he and the other warriors had been there. But that didn't matter. What was done, was done. Now, he had a chance to make things right.

In the background, Gideon could hear the thump of two pairs of boots and knew Kane and Cameo were running to help him. He laughed. So simple, so easy this seemed. This man had eluded him, caused trouble from afar, but had been taken down in a matter of minutes.

Life just didn't get any better than that.

He raised his blade. One more strike, and Galen would be out for a long, long time. Time the Lords could use to decide whether or to not kill him and free his demon. Time for Gwen, his daughter, to say goodbye.

Of course, that was when Rhea, the god queen, suddenly appeared in a flash of bright azure light. She was pale and shaky, her face tight with a scowl. Had she been watching the entire time?

"How dare you!" she cried. "He is my warrior. *Mine*. You were not to hurt him. But now...now you will pay."

In the next instant, Gideon found himself swept from the fortress and imprisoned inside a four-by-four cage, bars on every side, above and below, and looking into a palatial bedroom of velvet and marble. Ambrosia scented the air, and paintings of Titan gods decorated the walls. There was a four-poster bed with a lacy pink canopy, and a crystal chandelier that hung from the ceiling by a single vine of ivy. That ceiling, however, was clear and domed, and peered into a lovely blue sky.

Shit! Victory, gone. Defeat, his. All in a blink. He almost couldn't believe it. Hoped this was only a dream. A nightmare of Scarlet's creating. But deep down he knew she wouldn't do that to him. This was real. He had lost.

Be careful what you wish for, he thought bitterly. He'd wanted someone to take him back to the heavens so that he might search for Scarlet, and now he was there. Only, he was at the god queen's mercy.

Not that she had any.

CHAPTER TWENTY-TWO

GIDEON WAS left alone in the cage for several hours. Alone in the bedroom, too. He didn't have to wonder where Rhea was, though; he could guess. She was with Galen, seeing to his health. *He's my warrior,* she'd cried. *Mine. You were not to hurt him.*

What he did wonder about was whether or not he was trapped in something akin to the Cage of Compulsion that Lucien was in the process of hiding, where the prisoner was compelled to do whatever the owner of said cage wanted. He'd rather cut out his heart than become Rhea's slave.

He wanted her head on a platter. A platter he would then gift to Scarlet as a token of his affection.

Scarlet…

Where was she? What was she doing? He would speculate every day until he saw her. It wasn't that he was worried about her, either. The girl could take care of herself better than anyone he'd ever met. He simply missed her. She was a part of his life now. The best part.

He wanted to create new memories with her. Real memories, better than the ones she'd woven herself. He wanted to be there for her and make up for all the years he'd ignored her while she rotted in Tartarus.

First, though, he had to escape this fucking hellhole.

"Ray!" he shouted, shaking the bars. Gods, he reminded himself of Galen. Frantic, desperate. "Ray!"

Once again, a bright azure light filled his line of vision. Gideon remained on his knees, though he hated to do so. But there was no room in the cage, and standing wasn't an option.

Rhea appeared in the center of the bedroom, her pretty features tired and tight, her dark hair in tangles. No more gray, he realized. She wore a white robe that was stained with blood and soot. So yep, she'd been with Galen.

"You rang?" Hate and smugness mixed in her tone, creating a timbre that scraped at his ears. "So eager for your punishment?"

He knew no one would be swooping in to rescue him. He'd tried to remove his butterfly necklace, which blocked his whereabouts from all immortals, but somehow, some way, the metal had been fused together and now refused to part. He couldn't even lift the links over his head.

Rhea's doing, he was sure.

His guess? She didn't want Cronus finding him or even knowing what she did to him.

She waved her hand through the air and, shockingly, the bars around him disappeared. Since the bars behind him had been holding him up, he fell to his ass. Gideon was quick to recover, though, and jumped to his feet. He didn't have a weapon, as those had been magically removed.

"Smart of you," he remarked. She was as much a fool as Galen.

"Lunge at me, I dare you," she replied, remaining in place. Her teeth were bared, as if she couldn't wait to rip into him and work off a little steam.

He would have loved to accommodate her. He wanted her head on that platter, after all. But he wasn't Strider, and he didn't have to respond to every challenge. He didn't have to give the bitch what *she* wanted. Besides, he didn't know what powers she possessed, didn't know what she was capable of, but he did know what her husband could do and if she were anything like him... Gideon shuddered. He would lose before the fight even began.

"Well, coward? Just going to stand there?"

"Yes." He turned his back on her, heard her insulted gasp of breath and strode to the other side of the room as if he hadn't a care. He stopped in front of a vanity, lifted a perfume bottle to his nose and sniffed. Grimaced. Did she actually wear this shit? It was potent, like bat wings mixed with eye of newt.

"I have removed all the exits, so wipe all thoughts of escape from your puny mind. You're as trapped in this room as you were in the cage."

Truth. Lies hissed inside his head. "Sounds wonderful." He replaced the perfume and lifted a brush. Several strands of hair were intertwined in the bristles.

"What do you mean, wonderful? It's terrible, and you know it."

She knew he was possessed by the demon of Lies, she just hadn't connected the dots yet. Oh, the fun he could have with her, he thought, cutting off his grin before it could form.

"I'm not curious about why you brought me here and what you plan to do with me," he said.

"Ha! I know better. You're seething with curiosity."

He merely shrugged as he tossed the brush back onto the vanity surface, watching as it skidded and crashed into a jar of green paste. Clearly Rhea cared about her appearance. "Actually, I'm seething with worry for Galen. Please tell me he's recovered, oh, beautiful queen."

"Liar! You don't care about Galen." He never heard the woman move, but in the next instant, she was behind him, claws digging into his neck and whipping him around. "You hate him, want him dead. Well, guess what? You didn't get your wish. He's alive, and he will heal."

"Awesome."

She popped her jaw, eyes glittering. "He begged me to kill you. I told him no, that I had other plans for you."

Again, truth. Lies hissed at her. "Lucky me."

Scowling, she released him. But not for long. All too soon, she returned her hands to him, but this time, the action wasn't born of anger but of determination.

"Think yourself unflappable, do you? Well, let's see what we can do about that. Let's make you more comfortable." Her voice had become husky with sensual promise.

Hell. No. Scarlet was the only woman he wanted to bed. But he couldn't move away from Rhea. Somehow, she had pinned his feet in place. *Relax your expression, boy. Don't let her know she's getting to you.*

One of her fingers traced the center of his T-shirt and the material burned away, the cotton smoldering completely and leaving his chest bare. His skin remained cool to the touch.

Oh, yes, she was powerful.

"Wow. Thanks." Calm, smooth. No way would he let her know just how much he hated this. "This does feel better."

Bewildered, she stepped back, widening the distance between them. "I thought you liked my daughter."

"Wrong."

Her eyes narrowed with suspicion. "What game do you play?"

"No game." A grin lifted the corners of his lips.

For a long while, she simply stared at him, gauging. Then she squared her shoulders. "You're lying. You love her. I can tell. But let's see how long that lasts, shall we?" Gaze never leaving him, she reached for the scooped bodice of her robe and tugged. The material split down the center, drooped from her arms and fell to the floor, leaving her utterly naked.

Gideon's molars ground together. He could just imagine his confession to Scarlet, because no way would he try and keep something like this a secret. He wanted no secrets between them. Ever. And besides, better she hear this from him than her bitch of a mother who would skew the facts. *Hey, devil, your mom—you know, the woman you love so much—didn't disrobe in front of me and I didn't see her wax preference.*

He'd deserve another fork to the chest.

"Gorgeous, aren't I?" Rhea smoothed her palms over the jagged butterfly tattoo gracing her breasts and shoulders, then down her sides, over her perfectly curved hips and then inched around to the apex of her thighs, where her fingers dabbled at the fine tuft of dark hair.

Every bit the coward she'd accused him of being, he peered up at the domed ceiling, watching as fluffy white clouds drifted by. Dread bloomed in his veins and spread through his entire body. He could guess where this was heading.

"Well?" she demanded.

"Yeah. Gorgeous."

"*Tsk, tsk*. Your tone suggests you're lying again, but we both know you desire me. And soon Scarlet will know it, too."

Motherfucker! His guess had been right, then. She planned to rape him. And it *would* be rape, because there was no way he'd consent. Then she would tattle to her daughter. Mother of the Year Award, meet Rhea. Or not.

Once again, Rhea reached out and touched him. Her fingers danced over the waist of his pants and those, too, burned away, smoldering as they fell, yet leaving his skin cool, unaffected.

"Isn't that so much bett…er." A growl of frustration escaped her.

No doubt she'd just seen his flaccid cock. Little Gid would not be responding to her in any way. He almost laughed. Almost. "I hope you feel really good about this," he said. "About what you're planning. After all, you haven't hurt Scarlet nearly enough over the years. And I'm sure she's deserved everything you've done to her. 'Cause she never loved you, did she? Yeah, you should be real proud of yourself, sweetheart."

With every word he uttered, the queen stiffened a little more. "Finished?" She scraped a nail down his chest, drawing blood this time. Red sparks lit her eyes, revealing the demon she tried so hard to hide.

"Yeah." Only a few weeks ago, Gideon had learned that Rhea was keeper of the demon of Strife, that she fed off conflict. She couldn't blame her demon, though.

She'd been this much of a bitch before her possession. Look how she'd treated his beautiful Scarlet in prison. What's more, she could have controlled her darker impulses, but had simply chosen not to. He and his friends were proof of that.

Reyes's demon, Pain, had once wanted to hurt everyone it encountered. Reyes had learned to turn that desire inward, cutting himself to save others.

Maddox's demon, Violence, had once wanted to erupt at every cross word, every accidental touch. But Maddox had learned to hold the rage inside himself.

Lucien's demon, Death, had once wanted to steal the soul of every human it encountered. Lucien had learned to wait until those humans died before acting on the impulse.

Gideon could go on and on. Every demon-keeper had trials and struggles, but they'd done whatever was necessary to tame their beasts, to corral those darker urges. Rhea could've done the same, but she hadn't. She preferred to create discord, even among those she was supposed to love and protect.

"I've figured it out," Rhea suddenly said with a half smile. "You say the opposite of what you mean. You think Scarlet is innocent. You think I should coddle her. What you don't know is that she has plotted and planned to destroy me and take my crown. From the very beginning! She even slept with my husband. Your leader."

Lies. All lies. His demon purred with pleasure, even as Gideon fought a rage like he'd never known before. Not with Scarlet, never Scarlet, but with Rhea. How dare she utter such things about his woman. And yeah, Gideon totally got the irony.

He was tempted, so tempted, to yell at this woman, to tell her his true feelings about her and about his precious Scarlet. He wanted her to know and was more frustrated than ever that he couldn't say his thoughts outright. Had he not needed to keep his strength around her... But he did. For Scarlet.

Rhea's head slanted pensively as she reached up and dragged one of her nails along the curve of his jaw. He jerked away from her touch, but not before it burned him, searing his skin and leaving a raw, open wound.

"Well, well. Look who's willing to believe the best of such a disappointing brat. Stupid of you, but admirable. Perhaps one day you'll realize your mistake and give *me* that loyalty."

Never. "Totally possible."

She laced her arms around him and pressed her nakedness into his. His cock, of course, remained flaccid. That didn't deter her, though. She nipped at his bottom lip and rubbed against him, knee sliding up and down his thigh. "My daughter thinks to ruin me in my dreams, you know. I can feel her outside my mind, waiting. But she'll learn better than to challenge me. Do you want to know how, my darling boy?"

Gods help him.

"Every time she invades my dreams, you will make love to me." A slow, eager smile lifted her lips. "And believe me, you will."

He stiffened, though not the way she clearly wanted. "I wouldn't rather die." *You raging psycho.*

"Too bad. I'm not allowed to kill you, just as my husband isn't allowed to kill my Hunters. But there are other ways to ensure your cooperation."

He. Would. Fucking. Strangle. Her. With his feet still

planted on the ground, he leaned into her, allowing his weight to hit her full force. Because she hadn't thought to pin his hands, he reached for her, intending to close his fingers around her fragile neck. His hands met some type of invisible block.

A tinkling laugh escaped her. "Silly demon. No harm can befall me inside this room. Why else would I stay here? Now, let me show you why you'll be making love to me whenever I wish.…" One step, two, she backed away from him, forcing him to straighten.

Grinning, she spun in a quick circle. He would have laughed at her cluelessness—grinning? really?—but when she faced him again, she was no longer Rhea. She was Scarlet, and the shock was like a punch in the gut. Suddenly he was looking at Scarlet's lovely face. Scarlet's black eyes. Scarlet's bloodred lips. Scarlet's flawless skin. Scarlet's taller and stronger frame. And his body responded!

His horrified study intensified as he desperately searched for an imperfection. Shit, shit, shit. They were the same. Fuck, they were— No. Wait. Rhea lacked Scarlet's tattoos. Those amazing, lick-right-here tattoos. So, okay. All right. Fine. He could deal with this. They weren't the same. *Down, boy.*

"What? You don't like?" She even spoke in Scarlet's raspy voice.

"No." He liked. Fuck, he liked. He'd been so hungry for Scarlet, so damn hungry. And now, here she was, his for the taking. *No tattoos, no Scarlet. Don't forget.*

"Not even when I do this?" Watching him as she moved, Rhea slid her fingers up the flat plane of her belly, cupped her breasts and pinched her nipples, hardening them to little pearls.

No tattoos, no Scarlet. No fucking tattoos, no fucking Scarlet. Still. His body continued to react, unable to help itself. To his cock, this was his woman, soon to be his wife. He hoped. And his cock hungered for her desperately, had been without her for too long.

Not Scarlet, not Scarlet, not Scarlet, he told the traitor frantically, willing the blood to leave his growing erection.

Lies loved it, though. Loved knowing Rhea was *living* a lie. The demon had never been so excited, in fact.

You begged me to force Scarlet to stay. Now you're willing to betray her?

Scarlet. Love Scarlet.

A lie. But...but... *You said she was yours.*

She is. Isn't.

What the hell? *Damn you. We're on Team Scarlet. Do you understand?*

Sure, sure, was the reply.

Which meant, Lies was *not* on Team Scarlet.

What the hell? he wondered again. Was *everyone* conspiring against him?

"Told you." Rhea treated him to another grin, but there was an evil twinkle in those dark eyes, something Scarlet had never directed at him. "Let's stop playing games, and start on the pleasure."

She regally waved her hand through the air, a prelude he was coming to dread, and Gideon suddenly found himself lying on the bed, stretched out, again pinned in place and unable to move. He was like a rag doll, being tossed wherever the queen desired him, and he was sick of it.

"Listen, sweetheart, you—umph."

Rhea had whisked herself on top of him, her knees

straddling his waist. Once again, she looked like herself and his body, as well as his demon, deflated. Thank the gods.

So you're on Team Scarlet again? he asked Lies.

Yes. No.

I don't understand you.

"Oh, Gideon. This is going to be fun." Rhea's smile didn't fade. In fact, she grinned all the wider. "Look," she said, and motioned to the right.

Dread thrummed through him as he turned his head. He saw…nothing and frowned. Why had she— No, wait. Tiny white lights were flashing just in front of the mattress, growing, linking together, and then Scarlet was there. The *real* Scarlet.

She was dressed completely in black. Black T-shirt, black leather pants, black boots. Even black leather bracelets. Her hair was anchored in a low ponytail, revealing the graceful length of her neck. A neck that didn't sport a butterfly necklace.

She spotted Gideon with a grinning Rhea on top of him and gasped in shock, in horror.

"Devil," he shouted, but she disappeared in the next instant, gone as if she'd never been there. "Bitch," he then shouted at Rhea, and Lies roared inside his head. Pain exploded through him, followed quickly by that hated weakness. He grimaced, shook, hated, hated… hurt.

Not again.

But he couldn't help himself. He was filled with so much hate, so much regret, so much rage, he couldn't stop the words from flowing from him. "I will kill you. I planned to anyway, but now you'll suffer at my hand.

You'll regret all the ways you've harmed your daughter."
More pain, more weakness.

Finally, Rhea's smile fell away. Her skin even leached
of color. She inched down his body until she hit the end
of the mattress and had to stand. Her knees must have
been shaking because she swayed.

"Y-you are lying again. I know you are."

Before Gideon could reply, another voice rang out.
"We have much to discuss, woman."

As the still-naked Rhea whipped around in dismay,
Gideon's gaze—which was narrowing and darkening
with every second that passed—moved to the center of
the room. Cronus had appeared, and he had brought a…
female? Yes, definitely a female. Her skin was charred
to black and her hair had been burned away, but the
delicacy of her bones was evident. A little *too* evident.

Perhaps Gideon moaned. Perhaps the god king merely
sensed him. Either way, Cronus's focus swung to him,
and the king sucked in an astonished breath. His eyes
narrowed to tiny slits of fury.

"So. We have more to discuss than I realized. You
think to use one of my warriors." Hard, yet devoid of
any emotion. "*After* we agreed not to travel that road."

Rhea raised her chin, a white cloak appearing out
of nowhere and wrapping around her. "He loved every
minute of it, I assure you."

"That's why he looks ready to vomit." Cronus, too,
raised his chin.

"You have no right to admonish me for my actions
when my sister, *your mistress*, stands beside you." Her
gaze brushed over the trembling female. "Why did you
burn her?" She sounded surprisingly upset at the sight,

despite the fact that her sister was sleeping with her husband. "Did she fall out of favor?"

Her sister. That soot-covered skeleton was the goddess of Memory, Scarlet's aunt, then. The shit-infested day was suddenly looking up.

Gideon threw himself from the bed. He didn't have the strength to stand, could only scoot his way toward the woman, planning to grab her and hold on until he could find a way home.

"I didn't burn her," Cronus snapped. "Your daughter did. But this should be a private conversation. Gideon, I trust you'll guard Mnemosyne until such time as I can retrieve her. After all," he added with a pointed glance at Rhea, "I doubt she's in any condition to follow in her sister's footsteps and seduce you."

Rhea screeched an unholy sound, and as Gideon reached up to cover his already hurting ears, he found himself lying on his bed in his bedroom. NeeMah was on his floor, his to do with as he pleased, apparently, since a slave collar now circled her neck.

"Thank you," he shouted, praying Cronus would hear and that the king would stab his queen through her rotted, black heart.

With this latest truth, his demon roared and his pain tripled, burning through him like fire. Darkness winked over his vision, but he threw himself to the ground and crawled to NeeMah.

She whimpered and tried to scramble away.

"No reason to want to escape, darling. You're in for a treat." Maintaining a grip under her arms, he stood to shaky legs and began dragging her to the dungeon.

CHAPTER TWENTY-THREE

THAT BITCH! was the first thought to hit Scarlet as she awoke. Fuming, she bolted upright. Rhea had finally whisked her out of Budapest and into the heavens. Where she'd seen her naked mother straddling her naked boyfriend. *Then* Rhea had tossed her somewhere sunny. Where, Scarlet didn't know. All she'd known was that the abrupt switch from dark to light had utterly confused her demon. Unlike the ambrosia field, time did exist between the two locations.

She'd gotten the barest glimpse of speeding cars and towering buildings before her eyes had shut of their own accord and her mind had sunk into a deep, undisturbed sleep.

Now she was in a freaking hospital, she realized as her gaze circled her surroundings. She must have passed out on a busy sidewalk, no one had been able to revive her, and so they'd taken her in for medical care. Shit!

A heart monitor beeped beside her. Electrodes were attached to her chest, and an IV protruded from her arm. The medical staff had replaced her clothes with a paper-thin gown and removed her weapons. Local police would most likely come around to talk to her about that, too, and damn it, she didn't need that right now.

Damn it, she thought again. Motions clipped, she jerked out the needle, blood seeping from inside her elbow, and ripped away the cords. The monitor went crazy, shouting loud and long as she threw her legs over the side of the gurney.

Footsteps pounded, and then a short, plump female was rounding the corner and flying into Scarlet's room. When she spotted Scarlet sitting up, about to stand, the tension left her features, but she extended her arms to push Scarlet back down.

"Ma'am, ma'am, you need to be careful." She spoke in English, no hint of an accent. *I'm in the States,* Scarlet realized. "We don't yet know what was wrong with you and—"

"I'm fine, and I'm leaving." Determined, she brushed the woman aside and stood. Her knees were weak and almost buckled, but she pressed her weight into her heels and steadied herself, even as a wave of dizziness hit her.

What the hell had they been pumping into her vein?

Strong hands settled on her shoulders and applied pressure. Having none of that, Scarlet again knocked the woman's arms aside. "Where are my clothes?" Her butterfly necklace was in the pocket of her pants, and she wanted it back.

The human clearly wasn't used to being challenged; she paled as she backed away, palms raised and out. "Your clothes are with your arsenal."

Yep. Those weapons had gotten her into trouble. "And where's my arsenal?"

Eyes of light brown narrowed. "With the police." Hard, firm tone. "There's an officer here who's been waiting to talk with you, so I suggest you lie back down.

You shouldn't be up and around. We're still running tests, trying to figure out what's wrong with you."

Shit, she thought again. If her clothes were locked away in some police station, getting them back would take a lot of time and effort. Time and effort she didn't have. "Look, nothing's wrong with me except my clothes and belongings have been stolen. Now where the hell am I?"

"Northwestern Memorial."

"No. What city?"

The nurse blinked at her. "Chicago."

Why the hell had her mother sent her here?

"I'm just going to get your doctor and let her know you're ready to be discharged," the nurse said. Of course, Scarlet knew she was lying. Thanks to Gideon, she considered herself a living lie detector now. The nurse was going to summon the officer.

Scarlet allowed the woman to leave the room without protest. The moment she was alone, she kicked the shadows out of her head. They wrapped around her, cuddling her close, enveloping her with impenetrable darkness. Well, impenetrable for everyone else. No one would be able to see her, but she could absolutely see everyone and everything.

Rather than leave, however, she pressed against the wall, right by the doorway. Just in time, too. The officer, who was in his early twenties, physically fit and determined, came barreling down the hall, coffee in hand. He haphazardly slapped that coffee on the counter of the nurses' station without slowing his step, his other hand remaining on his gun handle.

Scarlet gasped in horrified realization. He was a Hunter. The tattoo on his wrist, a symbol of infinity, wasn't just for decoration. It was his mark, his vow to kill those who were demon-possessed.

That's why her mother had flashed her here. There was probably a contingent of Hunters based here.

Her stomach twisted. At least Rhea hadn't flashed her into the middle of that contingent. Which had to mean, on some level, that Rhea held her in *some* affection.

Wishful thinking, and you know it. Most likely, Rhea had just misjudged the distance.

When the man reached Scarlet's room, he flew past the door, just as Nurse Tattletale had, his expression resolved. He stopped and growled when he realized he was alone.

"Where'd she go?" he demanded.

None of the nurses were willing to approach and respond.

Had Rhea had time to tell him who Scarlet was? *What* Scarlet was? Probably not. Otherwise, there would have been more than one Hunter waiting for her to awaken, and this one wouldn't have left her. Even for a second. So why was he here?

There had probably been a report about her appearing out of nowhere, she realized, and he probably wanted to know how she'd done it.

Renewed anger sparked in her chest, easing the sting in her stomach. She'd fallen asleep in front of humans who could have done anything they wanted to her, and she wouldn't have been able to defend herself. Yet another sin to punish her heartless mother for.

As the officer radioed for assistance, then shouted orders to the hospital staff to lock all the building's doors, Scarlet slipped into the hallway, doing her best to remain in the shadows so that *her* shadows blended in.

Making her way outside proved uneventful. There was simply no way to lock the E.R. exits, since wreck victims were being wheeled in. Sunlight waned, creating a purple sky, the evening fragrant with summer blooms. Crickets chirped, and cars zoomed on the nearby road. An ambulance was blaring its sirens as it pulled into the parking lot.

Scarlet headed toward that lot with every intention of stealing a car. But where should she go? Her aunt was too weak to find her now. She couldn't get to the heavens to slap her mother around, couldn't block her location from the gods, so she could be found by any of them at any time and tossed into another Hunters' den.

Gideon wasn't home, so he couldn't—

Gideon. Her hands fisted. Did his friends know where he was? And *who* he'd been doing? Her nail sharpened, cutting into her palms. *Slow down. Are you sure he was having sex with your mother? He didn't look like a man lost in pleasure.*

Scarlet thought back and frowned. Sure, both Gideon and her mother had been naked. And sure, her mother had been straddling his waist. And okay, yeah, there'd been no promises between her and Gideon. She'd told him things were over, finished. In his mind, he'd been free to do whatever or whoever he wanted. But there'd been panic in his eyes. Panic and pain and fury.

What if he hadn't been there of his own free will?

She gulped, afraid to hope. And she hated herself for even wanting to. He could be in serious trouble.

But his reaction would explain why her mother had flashed Scarlet there to witness the deed and then shooed her away before Gideon could say anything. What better way to hurt her than to "steal" her man?

The very hope she feared suddenly grew wings and fluttered through her. If she was wrong about what had happened and he truly did want Rhea, she would...what? Kill them both? Try and remind him how good it had been between *them?*

No. That still wasn't an option. Was still too dangerous. Besides, after everything that had happened, Gideon deserved a long and happy life.

Finally, Scarlet knew what she had to do to save him, to give him that long and happy life. And she would have rather chewed off her leg. Because now an eternity of suffering awaited her.

GIDEON SAT in front of the dungeon's cell, peering inside at NeeMah, who was still mostly charred. However, pale hair had sprouted from her scalp, and new skin was forming on her face and limbs. She should have regenerated completely by now, but the slave collar, which prevented her from using her godly powers, had slowed her healing process considerably.

He wasn't wearing a collar, but his healing process seemed slowed, as well. After two days, he was still weak himself, and had barely made it through the fortress and down the steps to get here—where he had remained—but his determination had spurred him onward.

He *would* get answers for Scarlet.

"You will—not—" he dropped the volume of his voice for the word *not,* hopefully making NeeMah hear only what he wanted her to hear "—answer everything I ask. If you do—not—I will torch your healing skin." And that wasn't a boast. He would do it. With a smile.

"Y-yes," NeeMah said. She lay on a cot, her hands

resting under her cheek. Her lids opened, revealing the whites of her eyes, a startling contrast to the black smudges circling them. "I will."

He was used to torturing Hunters for every scrap of information, so her easy compliance threw him a little. He'd thought he would have to burn her at least once to prompt her into her first reply. That he hadn't... His suspicious nature peeked past his determination—and disappointment. Charbroiling her might have been fun.

"Why have you—not—tormented Scarlet all these years?" he asked.

"Why do you care?" Her voice was ragged, raspy from smoke. "You aren't her husband."

I want to be. One day, I will be. "Don't—" uttered quietly "—answer the question—" yelled viciously. He held up a lighter.

She flinched, even whimpered. "Boredom," she rushed out. "Favors for my sister the queen. Why else?"

Truth. He hated himself just then, because, in a way, he was just as much at fault for Scarlet's treatment as her aunt. How many times had he entered Tartarus? Countless. Why hadn't he noticed Scarlet? The woman, not the child. If he had, there were a thousand things he could have done to protect her.

Namely, he could have moved her to a private cell. He could have killed both Rhea and NeeMah, or, at the very least, warned them what would happen if they didn't stop tormenting her. Yet he hadn't noticed the lovely woman she'd become and so he'd done nothing.

How could he not have noticed her? Just how stupid

and blind had he been? She was the most important person in his life.

He truly didn't deserve her, but that wasn't going to stop him from trying to win her.

"Is there a way to undo the damage you—" he lowered his voice to whisper softly "—didn't—" then let his voice return to normal "—cause?"

"Yes. I can remove all her memories."

Which was what Scarlet wanted. Not Gideon, though. He wanted Scarlet as she was. But he also placed her wants above his own and would do whatever was necessary to make her happy. Even that, he realized now.

That wouldn't stop him from trying to romance her all over again.

"Will I erase her memories, though?" NeeMah continued, somehow stronger now. "No. Believe me, it's better to have Scarlet as an enemy than Rhea."

And yet she had become Cronus's mistress. Perhaps, though, that had been at her sister's request, a way to keep tabs on the man. Interesting. Amun would be able to discern the truth, which was why Cronus had wanted the warrior's aid in the first place.

"And to be honest," NeeMah added, almost as an afterthought, though she couldn't conceal the clenching of her teeth, "after what Scarlet just did to me, I would rather die than aid her."

As that was NeeMah's only other option, she might just get her wish. She would change her mind, though, the moment he approached her with the lighter and a can of gasoline. He was sure of it. But he didn't threaten her again. There was no need. Scarlet wasn't here, so why force the issue just yet?

"Why—doesn't—her mother hate her?" he asked, raising and lowering his voice as needed.

NeeMah rolled to her back, hissed in a pained breath. "My sister can't help herself. She thought she loved Scarlet's father, and yet he was only using her. He had a wife of his own and cast Rhea aside as soon as he learned of her pregnancy. Then the Greeks captured the Titans and threw us in prison, preventing her from gaining revenge against the foolish mortal."

"So she—didn't—blame Scarlet?" *Bitch.* He flicked the lighter on, off, as he waited for her reply, daring her to refuse him.

"Not at first. At first, she loved the infant. Or rather, loved the infant as much as she was able. But as Scarlet grew, looking so much like her father, Rhea's love died. And it didn't help that Scarlet was growing into such a lovely woman. Rhea had already had so much taken from her. Her throne, her power, her freedom. To no longer be considered the fairest in the realm was a blow her ego could not tolerate."

Because of vanity, she'd practically gift wrapped her daughter for the monsters trapped inside their cell. Calling the woman a bitch, he realized, had been an insult to bitches.

"Don't." Gideon longed to return to Rhea, a knife in hand. He would slit her throat without any hesitation— then spit on her lifeless body. *On. Off.* Flames sparked, died. "Continue."

"Then, when Strife was paired with her," NeeMah continued shakily, "all of her feelings intensified. Her hate, her jealousy, her need to prove herself. She was *compelled* to cause trouble. As you know."

"You were given a demon." A statement, not a question. Not once had her eyes flickered with red. Not once had he seen a flash of undiluted evil behind her face. Oh, there was evil, all right, just not the demonic kind.

She replied anyway. "No. I was spared."

"Why? Not," he finished in a whisper. *On. Off.*

"Zeus chose who was paired with what demon, and each pairing was determined out of spite. A punishment of sorts. I had done nothing to harm him. Nothing he recalled, that is."

Truth mixed with smug superiority.

Lies hissed.

Zeus had told some of the Lords why they'd been given their demon. Lucien received Death because he'd opened Pandora's box, nearly leading to the demise of the world. Maddox received Violence because he'd killed the most soldiers in his quest to reach the box. Paris had seduced Pandora to distract her, therefore he'd received Promiscuity.

Why, though, had Gideon been given Lies? He'd been a good warrior for the king. He'd helped steal Pandora's box, yes, but his part had been minimal because he'd felt so damn guilty for betraying his creator.

With that line of thinking, another question arose. Why had Scarlet been given Nightmares?

Lies began to purr.

Gideon frowned. Why purr? That spoke of affection. *I thought you were over Scarlet, you fickle bastard.*

Not mine, Lies said. Which really meant, *All mine.*

You can't do that, you little shit. You can't keep changing your mind like that, wanting her one minute, discarding her the next.

Not mine.

I should ask her demon to—

NOT MINE.

Wait. What? *Her...demon?*

NOT MINE.

His eyes widened as everything finally slid into place. Had the two demons been...lovers while inside that box? Or maybe inside hell?

The purring increased in volume, and he could only shake his head in wonder. All this time with his demon, and he hadn't realized such creatures could form connections like that. But Lies and Nightmares must have done so.

That explained so much. Why Lies had wanted to stay with Scarlet, but hadn't cared about Scarlet herself. Why Lies had been willing to do something abhorrent to him, like tell the truth, just to keep Scarlet nearby. Why Lies had responded to Rhea when she'd looked like Scarlet. The demon had only seen the packaging and had assumed Nightmares was inside.

Perhaps Zeus had known of the connection. Perhaps Zeus had also known of Scarlet's desire for Gideon. Perhaps he'd given Gideon the demon of Lies as a... gift.

And you were trying to find a way to kill him. He might just owe the deposed king a big fat thank-you. He would rather kiss Scarlet, though. Damn it, where was she? What was she doing?

Would she go for his throat the next time she saw him? She thought he was screwing her bitch of a mother, after all. Or would she try to avoid him for the rest of eternity?

Even if she wanted to, she wouldn't be able to do so. She was tracking NeeMah and would eventually discover that the woman's trail led here. So they *would* meet again. He would just have to make sure he was prepared. Fingers crossed she didn't kill him while he slept or remove his head before he'd had a chance to explain.

Fingers crossed she even wanted to hear his explanation.

"Speaking of memory loss...I think it's funny that you and Scarlet met again."

NeeMah's voice drew him from his thoughts, and he arched a brow at her. "Not—" whispered "—again?" Loudly.

"You probably don't remember—" she smiled at that, fleeting, but there all the same "—but you came looking for her once. Well, a little boy you discovered was actually a girl. She was grown by then and you clearly liked what you saw."

Fire ignited in his chest, then spread to his limbs. At first, Gideon didn't know why. Then he realized Lies was storming through him, so agitated the turmoil seeped into Gideon. Why?

"*Do* you remember?" the goddess asked him.

He remembered that little boy, and now knew that had been Scarlet. Yet he didn't remember ever encountering an adult version Scarlet. *Had* his memory been screwed with?

"Anyway, for some reason, you never returned. You left her there." She offered him another false grin. "Such a pity."

He hopped up, panting with the force of his sudden rage. *On. Off. On. Off.* She *had* screwed with him.

"Oh, do you wish to remember? Give me your hand, and it's done. Even with my collar, I can get inside your head."

"One day," he snarled, gripping the bars, shaking, the lighter clinking against the metal.

"Yes?" she asked, clearly thinking there was nothing he could do. She sat up, gaze never leaving him. "One day? What will you do?"

"I will—I will—" Nothing sounded violent enough.

"Will you kill me? Will you torture me? What can you truly do to harm me? Tell me I'm ugly? Tell me I'm powerless? Do it, then. And see how I punish Scarlet in turn. We both know she'll return for me. I'll convince her to hate you. I'll convince her to kill you. I'll convince her to sleep with man after man. I'll convince her to kill herself. And there's nothing—"

A roar, loud and long, echoed between them. Throughout the entire tirade, Lies had prowled and paced, a caged predator filled with rage. At the mention of Scarlet's death, the demon had erupted.

Before Gideon knew what was happening, the demon exploded from his body, a dark vision of scales and horns and bones. Of evil.

NeeMah yelped with horrified panic as the fiend chomped at her—before disappearing inside her. She jerked, hunched over. Whimpered. Soon, tears began streaming down her face.

"I'm so ugly," she cried. "So powerless. I'm unworthy of life. Oh, gods, I'm so unworthy."

All the things she'd taunted Gideon with, things she hadn't ever believed of herself. But now, with the demon convincing her that the lies were the truth, she believed, and it was tearing her up inside.

He could only watch, his own rage easing in the shadow of his combined shock and fascination. Lies had actually left him. *Left him*. And was now obviously prowling through NeeMah's head, making her believe the lies about her beauty, her strength. How the demon had done it, he didn't know. Why the demon hadn't ever left him before, he didn't know.

How the demon remained sane and Gideon alive, he didn't know, either.

Minutes later, when NeeMah was a sobbing puddle on her cot, her entire body shuddering, the demon returned to him and settled inside his head, purring with more of that satisfaction.

How did you do that? he asked, dazed.

I know.

The demon had no idea, then. *Why did you come back?*

Aren't tethered to you.

Holy hell. *Can you do it again?*

I know.

Let's find out. "You might want to buckle up," he told the goddess as he grinned. "You're about to have a *lot* of fun."

CHAPTER TWENTY-FOUR

DRY, BRITTLE foliage reached out from the plethora of trees, slapping at Strider's cheeks, scratching his skin and darkening his already black mood. He had Hadiee, aka Haidee, aka Ex, roped to him and leading the way, taking the brunt of the branch-slaps as she grumbled and complained and called him all manner of names. "Bastard" was the kindest.

Back at the hotel, he'd lain on top of her, vowing to hurt her worse than she'd ever been hurt, but in the end, he hadn't cut her into small pieces, hadn't even scratched her, and he was pissed as hell about it.

He'd raised his blade to do so. To take a finger at the very least. She deserved it for killing Baden. But she'd gazed up at him with such courage, such challenge, *wanting* him to end her it seemed. So he'd stayed his hand. No way would he give her what she wanted.

As if she sensed the direction of his thoughts—and hell, maybe she did. She was immortal now, but he didn't know how she was or what she was—she shouted over her shoulder, "You should have killed me, you stupid moron!" Her gray eyes gleamed. Her skin was flushed and dewy with sweat—that actually resembled tiny beads of ice—and her pink hair was plastered to her temples.

Even worn-out, she was a lovely sight. Thank the

gods "beautiful bitch" wasn't his type. "And end your suffering? Ha! Keep moving."

"You're the one who's going to suffer. If you think I'll keep my fury to myself, you're stupider than you look. And you look endlessly stupid! I plan to tell you about every damn thing that bothers me. Starting with the insects. They're eating me alive!"

For half an hour, she complained about the damn bugs. Only took five minutes, though, for his ears to start bleeding from the shrillness of her voice.

"Time-out," she snapped. "We've been walking for hours, and I need to rest."

"Time in. We're close to where I want to be. No resting yet."

"Time-*out*. Or are you too scared to rest for a few minutes?"

Scared? It was a challenge to prove himself, and one his demon accepted.

Scowling, Strider stopped abruptly. Ex didn't realize this and kept moving until the rope around her ankle—a rope that was tied to his wrist—ran out of slack and jerked. She tumbled to her face, quickly rolled over and glared up at him.

His scowl became a grin as he dropped his backpack at the base of a tree and flopped beside it. "Fine. Time-out."

Ex remained on the ground, though she sat up and pulled her knees to her chest. "Bastard," she muttered.

"Touch your ankle and I'll cut off your hands." An empty boast—maybe—but she didn't know that. "And here's another bitch-slap of truth, little girl. From now on, every time you challenge me, I will view it as an invitation to have sex with you." Nothing would disgust her more, he was sure.

The rosy flush abandoned her cheeks. "Warning received."

Good. Now. Since they were resting "for a few minutes," he might as well make the best of it. "Hungry?"

"Yes."

He unzipped his pack and withdrew a box of Red Hots.

Ex spotted them, and her eyes nearly bugged out of her head. "That's what you brought for field rations? You idiot! *Stupid* is too generous a word for you. Candy won't sustain us."

"Speak for yourself." He tossed a mouthful past his lips, chewed and closed his eyes at the delicious taste. Maybe even moaned.

When he next looked at her, she was frowning and holding out her hand.

"You sure you want some? These are only for idiots too stupid to bring proper field rations."

"Just give me."

He dumped a few of the precious candies into her shockingly chilled palm before he could change his mind about feeding her, then shook as many as he could fit into his mouth. Again, his eyes closed in ecstasy. Cinnamon. There was no better taste. Even females couldn't compare. Unless they tasted like cinnamon, but he'd never met one who did. Not naturally, at least.

"Where we going, anyway?" Ex grumbled.

He swallowed. "None of your damn business." He said it pleasantly, yet left no room for argument.

Truth was, he was taking her to Budapest. Only, he was taking her the long way. Through forest and desert and anything else that struck his fancy. Anything that would break her down, weaken her and force her to rely on him. Not to mention, get her boyfriend off his trail.

Right now they were on the newly risen island of the Unspoken Ones, making their way to the temple, but staying away from civilization.

After all, he'd been on his way to visit the Unspoken Ones when Ex and her friends had interrupted him, and he saw no reason to change his plans on her account. Besides, this way he had the added benefit of showing Ex what a *true* monster was.

They'd frighten her, she'd realize Strider wasn't as bad as she'd thought and be grateful he'd kept her safe. Soon she would trust him to *always* see to her protection. She would open up and tell him everything he wanted to know about her and her Hunter pals. Since he obviously didn't have the stomach to kill her—now, at least, and that *still* dropped him right into a shame spiral—he might as well use her. And then betray her. Just as she'd betrayed Baden.

When Strider finished with her, when she trusted him completely, he might just send her back to her people. After they knew how disloyal she had been to them, that is. Then *they* could kill her.

To gain her trust, though, he couldn't be too nice to her. Not in the beginning at least. She would become suspicious. Besides, he wasn't that good an actor. He hated this woman, and the thought of being nice to her grated his every nerve.

"Got any water?" she asked in that whining, complaining voice.

Gra-ted. "Yeah." He grabbed one of the bottles of water he'd brought, twisted off the cap and drained most of the contents while she watched. A whimper escaped her, and he squeezed the bottle a little too hard, crackling the plastic.

"Well? Are you going to share or not?"

With a forced shrug, he tossed her what was left. "That has my cooties," he informed her.

"Good news is, I'm up-to-date on all my shots." She drained the contents in seconds, then peered over at him, clearly irritated with what little he'd given her.

"Be grateful I gave you any at all," he said with feeling.

"Evil bastard."

"Murderous bitch." *Stop. This isn't the way to win her over. Who cares if she becomes suspicious thanks to sweet behavior?*

Win her over, Defeat commanded. *Win. Win. Win.*

Great. His demon saw winning her as a challenge. It was a challenge he hadn't needed, but there was no way around it now. He had to convince her to—he almost growled—like him.

Motions clipped, Strider dug through the backpack until he found the dehydrated meat he'd brought. He pulled out a bag of it, as well as another bottle of water, and tossed both to the girl.

She caught them easily, realized what they were and grumbled, "Thanks."

"You're...welcome." Ugh. That hadn't been fun to say. Actually tasted like ash on his tongue.

Silent, he watched her as she ate. Dirt smudged her face, and there were tiny scratches along her jaw. Bugs had bitten her neck, leaving swollen, pink circles. Her clothes were wet with perspiration and just as dirty as her face.

Why didn't any of that detract from her loveliness?

She probably made a deal with the devil. Like Legion. Unlike Aeron, he wasn't willing to die to save her. "How long have you been dating your man?"

Dark lashes lifted, and then gunmetal eyes were peering into his soul. "Why do you want to know?"

"Simple curiosity."

"Fine. I'll tell you. But answer a question for me first."

"Sure." That didn't mean he'd answer honestly.

"Do you have a girlfriend?"

"No." Truth. No reason to lie about that.

"Didn't think so," she said with a smugness that irritated him.

Strider popped his jaw. What? She didn't think he was good-looking enough to catch a female? She didn't think anyone could tolerate him for long periods of time? Well, she was mistaken. He didn't have a girlfriend because he didn't want one. His demon fed off the challenge of winning their hearts, but once that was accomplished, the demon's attraction was gone.

And then, of course, the females would try and challenge him in other ways. Ways he *hated. Bet you can't spend the entire day with me and enjoy yourself. Bet you won't call me every night for the next week.* It was just better for everyone involved if he kept things temporary.

"So," he said. "How long have you been dating your man?"

"Seven months."

Seven months? In human years—something akin to dog years—that was a very long time. "So why haven't you guys gotten married?"

She shrugged as she stuffed the last piece of jerky into her mouth.

"Let me guess. You wanted to, but he didn't?"

"Actually," she said stiffly, "he wanted to, but I didn't."

Interesting, and unexpected. "Why didn't you? Just using him for sex?"

The flush returned to her cheeks, softening her features, making her more than beautiful. Making her appear vulnerable...sweet. "Something like that," she muttered.

There was a tightening in his chest. One he didn't understand and didn't want to contemplate. *You aren't attracted to this woman.*

"Not to change the subject—and by that I mean I'm ready to change the subject. Do you remember killing me?" she asked.

"Yes." All those centuries ago, he'd slammed his blade into her stomach, raging over what she'd done to Baden. Then, when she'd doubled over, he'd taken her head. "Mind telling me how you're alive?"

She ignored him. "No guilt for your actions?"

"Hell, no. Do you feel guilty for what you did to my best friend?"

"Hell, no."

He hadn't thought so. And that...bothered him. It shouldn't have bothered him. He knew who and what she was—for the most part. Snuffing out evil was her ultimate goal, and she'd considered Baden evil. Would it have killed her to *pretend* remorse, though?

Frowning, he zipped up his bag and stood. "Time in. Again," he barked. Then cringed. He hadn't meant to sound so harsh.

Ex didn't rush to obey. In fact, she stared up at him for a long while, hands rubbing up and down her calves.

"Up," he said more gently, tugging at the rope. But there was too much give in that rope. Somehow she had managed to cut it, even though he'd never seen her fingers near it. And she certainly hadn't been gripping a knife. Not one that he'd been able to see, at least.

"Time out." Grinning, she kicked out her leg with more force than someone her size should have been capable of, swiping his ankles together and knocking him to the ground. Like a bolt of lightning, she streaked off.

Catch, catch. Win, win, Defeat shouted as Strider leaped to his feet and darted after her. *You're losing. You must win.*

As he sprinted, he reached for the Cloak he'd strapped to his chest, hiding it there because he'd known the last thing Ex would want to do was feel him up. Only, it wasn't there.

That…bitch! Somehow, she'd stolen it. Just like with the rope, he had no idea how she'd done it. He only knew he had to catch her. *Before* she reached her boyfriend.

So LOUD…so terrible. Amun was somehow on his feet, gripping a blade. William and Aeron were on each of his sides, pinning him in to protect him. A new horde of demons surrounded them—they'd already fought the first and second lines of defense—some small, some big, but all of them determined. Their thoughts…totally focused on blood and pain and death.

Taste, they thought. *Hurt. Kill.* They swiped at the warriors with their claws, biting at them with poisoned fangs, kicking and hitting, laughing and taunting.

The battle itself had been raging for hours. Maybe days. Perhaps years. Each man was exhausted, cut, bleeding, shaking, at the edge, probably in agonizing pain, and every time they killed a demon, three more took its place. But they refused to give up.

Amun tried to help them, but every time he moved, every time he reached out to slash one of the creatures, a new voice entered his mind and grew in volume, new images flashing inside his head—rapes, more tortures, more killings—nearly driving him to his knees.

Through it all, Lucifer sat upon his throne, watching, grinning, Legion at his feet. Every so often, he would pet her head as if she were a favored dog. And when she would try and rise, desperate to help Aeron, the prince of darkness would dig his claws into her scalp and hold her down until she whimpered her surrender, blood trekking down her temples.

"I don't know how much more I can take," Aeron gritted out.

"Arm...hanging...by...thread," William replied. He wasn't exaggerating, either.

Must help them, Amun thought. The air was hot, draining what little remained of his strength. And the smoke...gods, all he wanted to do was cough. Cough until he finally hacked up enough intestine to die.

Although, that might not be necessary. The scent of death clung to every inhalation, stinging his nostrils, promising a reckoning. Very, very soon.

Push through. Ignore the voice, the images. Only reason the two warriors were still standing, despite the poison probably working through them from those demon bites, was that they'd drunk the rest of the Water of Life.

If this didn't end soon, the water would lose its potency and nothing would save them.

Can't let them die. Him, yeah. He welcomed an end. But not his friends. Never his friends. With a roar, Amun raised his arm, blade at the ready. And yes, the voices and images grew in intensity, but he didn't let either stop him this time. He plowed forward, out of the protective embrace of his friends, and slashed. Slashed and slashed and slashed. Demon after demon fell, grunting, groaning, bleeding at his feet.

By the time he reached the center of them, he was dripping with their fluids, his eyes burning, his mouth filled with the taste of rot, but still he didn't stop. And soon, he didn't want to stop. The images…yes, he wanted to kill. He wanted to maim.

He cut off a demon's arm and grinned. He snapped a demon's leg in two and laughed. He removed eyeballs, tongues, even private parts, and laughed all the harder. This. Was. Fun.

Fear sparked in their crimson eyes, and they were soon backing away from him. But he was having none of that. Needed more. Was excited. Was imagining all the things he could do to them. They'd scream, they'd beg, they'd bleed.

Yes. *Fun.*

"Stop him!" Lucifer shouted, no longer relaxed. "Take his head."

"How about we take your head instead?" a new voice proclaimed. "It will look very nice in my trophy case."

Amun recognized that voice, knew it belonged to someone he admired, but didn't take time to look at the speaker. So many targets, just waiting for his blade. He sliced a throat, stabbed a heart, felt a warm splatter on his face and licked it away. *Delicious.*

"Lysander," Lucifer hissed.

"Oh, Aeron," a female shouted. "My poor darling. You're falling apart."

"Olivia! Get out of here. Go! You shouldn't see this."

"Not without you. And if you had any idea what I had to do to convince the Heavenly High Council to send an army down here, you would be begging my forgiveness for leaving me behind and then thanking me profusely for coming to your aid."

The angels had arrived, Amun thought distantly. He probably should have been happy about that, but the demons around him flew from the chamber, screaming, leaving him with no one else to kill. Or take. That was *not* fun.

Scowling, he whipped around. Saw the army of white-robed angels forming a half circle around Lucifer. Saw the prince of darkness hissing at them as he, too, tried to flee. One of those angels held a sobbing Legion, one a nearly unconscious William, and Olivia had her arms wrapped around a trembling Aeron.

If Amun couldn't kill demons, he supposed he could kill angels. Yes. Yes, he thought, he could. He smiled. They might even be better targets. They would scream louder, fall harder, hurt easier.

Grinning now, he launched forward, blade raised... swiping down...about to nail one of the winged bastards in the back. Fun, fun, fun. But a hard hand locked around his wrist, stopping him.

Amun roared out his fury. He hadn't spoken in a

while, and his vocal cords were raw, the sound they created raspy.

"What are you doing, Secrets?" Lysander demanded, shaking him. "These are my people, come to help you. You do not attack them. Ever."

Again, Amun roared. From the corner of his eye, he watched as the weakened Aeron tried to pull from Olivia's grip. "Let him go, Lysander. He isn't himself."

"Aeron, stop," Olivia said, wings wrapped around him to bind him closer to her. "Look at Amun's eyes. He's fully demon now. Stay away from him or he might infect you, too."

Infect? Amun had never felt better. Had never enjoyed himself more. His friends would be lucky to experience this.

"Just let me talk to him," Aeron pleaded. "He's like this because of me."

"Talk alone won't suffice," Lysander said, dark eyes swirling, practically peering into Amun's dark soul. His voice was calm, hypnotic. "Will it, demon?"

Amun wrenched himself free and swiped at the angel, startled to find a demon's arm cradled within his grasp. When had he ripped it off? Lysander expected the blow, however, and blocked it with one hand; with the other he created a fiery sword out of thin air.

"No!" Aeron and William shouted in unison.

But it was too late. The momentum of the angel's block had spun Amun around, and the ensuing dizziness had sent him to his knees. It was the perfect position for a beheading.

Only, Lysander didn't take his head.

The sword of fire descended, struck him in the

chest, burned through clothing and flesh and left a gaping hole.

At first, Amun was too stunned to do more than gaze down at that smoking wound. Then the pain set in, sweeping through him, eating him alive, shooting the voices and images inside his head into a tailspin of their own. He fell forward, onto his face, every muscle in his body spasming with agony.

Lysander knelt beside him. "If you're lucky," the angel said, "you'll die from this. If not, you'll survive but wish you hadn't. Either way, you'll spend your remaining days imprisoned."

CHAPTER TWENTY-FIVE

SCARLET LOCKED herself in a crypt. That lasted six hours.

She stole a boat, intending to spend her days drifting at sea. She made it two miles.

She flew to Siberia. For three minutes.

Every time, she'd been flashed back to Budapest. Inside the fortress—down the hall from Gideon's room. Every time, she'd had to sneak out without being noticed. She was tired of sneaking out, though, because she knew she would only be brought back. By whom? She didn't know. Didn't care anymore.

Obviously, someone thought she had unfinished business here. So she would finish that business and return to her self-imposed, eternal exile. No revenge. No battles. No love.

No Gideon.

It was safest that way. For him. For herself.

This way, she couldn't be used against him. If she were to hurt him because her aunt screwed with her head again...if she were to see him with her mother again, naked, and *liking* it...

Her hands fisted. She pressed against the hallway wall that led to Gideon's bedroom, her demon's shadows thickly cloaking her. No one would be able to see her, but they would certainly be able to hear her.

Nightmares's screams were as thick as the shadows. Hopefully, though, they would think the wind was merely whistling against the windows.

Knowing the Lords as she did, she doubted that would be the case. They were cautious, suspicious, and prone to act first and ask questions later. Some of the many reasons she admired them. But she was taking no chances. She would find Gideon, talk to him and leave. Hopefully for good this time.

His door was around the corner and to the right. Just a little farther...

Everything inside her urged her to rush to him, to throw herself into his arms—this was Gideon, her sweet Gideon, who had given her more pleasure than anyone else ever had—but she had to maintain the slow pace or anyone who stumbled upon her would realize something was off. Wrong. They'd never have a chance to talk. She'd be tossed back into the dungeon.

"Yeah, uh, hey," a male voice suddenly said, though there was no one around her. "I know you're there, Scarlet. Don't blame yourself for failing to hide from me, I happen to be made of awesome. Anyway, I just texted Gideon to let *him* know, so you should be seeing him any—"

"Scar!" she heard Gideon shout next. Her heart tried to crack through her ribs as he raced around the corner, quickly saying, "Torin didn't spot you inside the fortress, so I don't know you're—" He stopped a few feet away from her, and expelled a shallow pant of breath. "Here." His shoulders sagged. "No thanks to the gods."

Nightmares sighed, content for the first time in days.

And shit, Gideon was so beautiful. His blue hair was

in spikes around his head, his blue eyes bright, his skin tanned and perfect. Her hands itched to touch him. Her tongue longed to trace his tattoos. The one and only time they'd made love, she hadn't explored him nearly enough; she'd been too eager to get him inside her. Next time, she thought.

Next time? There couldn't be a next time.

"Don't let me explain what you saw," he said, still rushing to get the words out. "Your mother didn't flash me into the heavens, and she didn't burn away my clothes, somehow pin me down and climb on top of me. I didn't want her, I swear to you." The moment the last confession left him, his features contorted in pain and his knees collapsed.

Damn it. Truth. He'd told the truth. *I didn't want her.* Melting inside, Scarlet willed the shadows and the screams to subside. She bent down, arms winding around his waist to heft him back to his feet.

"Idiot," she said without heat. "I'd already figured that out." For the most part. Kind of. "You should have lied to me. You shouldn't have weakened yourself in my presence. *Idiot!*" she said again. Now she could take advantage of him....

"But...I...love...you."

"What!" Scarlet dropped him, shock pounding through her. He thumped on the floor with a grunt. "Sorry," she muttered, bending down and hefting him back up. Dear gods. He couldn't have just said... It wasn't possible....

Gideon couldn't love her; she wasn't lovable. She was too hard, too stubborn, too violent. He deserved sweet and soothing, tender and uplifting.

"I—I—" she said, then gulped.

"Don't have to say it back." He was panting now, the words falling from his lips faster, as if he knew he would soon pass out. "Just know I have your aunt. Cronus gave her to me."

She nearly dropped him again, but managed to continue marching him onward. Finally they snaked the corner and entered his bedroom. Her aunt was here. Her fucking aunt was fucking here. Her aunt could do what Scarlet now feared most.

"Where is she?" she demanded.

"Dungeon." He moaned.

"Damn it, Gideon. Start lying to me!"

"Sorry." He grunted.

More truth. "Don't be sorry. Just shut up before you hurt yourself permanently."

"Too…important…" He hissed.

"Shut. Up!" Scarlet helped him into bed, her motions stiff. As muscular as he was, he proved to be extremely heavy. But eventually, he was stretched out on the mattress, his eyelids closing, his head thrashing.

"Don't…leave," he said, the pain once again so intense it halted his speech. Blindly he reached for her, grasping for her. "Just…Scarlet?"

She knew what he was asking. Had she paired herself with another actor in her mind? "Yes, I'm just Scarlet," she whispered. "Now be quiet like I told you. Please." Eyes suddenly burning, she twined their fingers and sat beside him, unable to resist him even though she was desperate to stomp downstairs and end her aunt, once and for all. If she had the courage to even approach the woman.

Gideon calmed instantly, and her eyes burned a little more.

Moonlight seeped in from the room's window, caressing him, making his sweat-glistened skin look as if it had been sprinkled with glitter. How she'd missed him. Craved him.

Damn him. He'd ruined everything. *I love you,* he'd said, and he'd meant it. She couldn't give him up now, not even to save him from herself. *Would you ever have been able to do so?* Scarlet traced shaky fingers over his brow. He released another of those relieved sighs, much like Nightmares had, body turning toward hers, seeking. He. Loved. Her.

Seriously. How could he love her?

He couldn't, she decided. He was confused, that was all. Perhaps feeling grateful because she'd finally given him the sex he'd been craving. Well, when the newness of that wore off, he'd realize she was wrong for him. He'd realize someone else would be better for him. He'd cast Scarlet aside.

She would be *forced* to give him up.

Her fingernails were lengthening, sharpening into claws as she imagined this magnificent warrior kissing and touching another woman. But Gideon must have sensed her upset, because he started thrashing again. As soon as she gentled her touch, he calmed anew.

A long while passed, Scarlet caressing his face, and eventually he slipped into a deep slumber. Her relief was as palpable as his had been earlier. She didn't like to see him suffer. If anyone deserved peace, it was this man.

"Galen came after him, you know," that voice from the hallway suddenly said.

Her gaze lifted, moved around the room. Again, no one loomed nearby. Which meant speakers were everywhere. And clearly the guy was watching her, which meant cameras were also everywhere, showcasing her every move.

"So you've got Galen locked away, too, huh?" She'd deal with him *and* her aunt when she went down to the dungeon. If she dared, she added again. Would she be able to pull a victory out of her hat-o-tricks this time?

"No. Galen was about to fall, finally, and was babbling about not allowing Gideon to kill him, when the god queen appeared. She flashed both men away."

Galen, babbling about not allowing Gideon to kill him. Every bit of warmth abandoned Scarlet's body, leaving her a hollow shell of herself. Galen had come after Gideon specifically. *Gideon*. Because of her, she realized with horror. Because she'd screwed with Galen's dreams.

She'd meant to torment him, to make him back away. Instead, she'd drawn him deeper into the war, made him more determined to win. This was yet another thing she'd done to destroy Gideon's life. Yet another reason someone else would be better for him. She had hurt him, time and time again. Sickness churned in her stomach.

Scarlet pushed to her feet, careful not to disturb Gideon, and tiptoed from the room. Her last visit here, she'd memorized the layout of the place and knew exactly where to go.

Yes. She dared.

"I won't let you kill her," the voice said.

"Who *are* you?" she demanded as she strode down the steps. Some of the windows were stained glass, and as golden beams of moonlight hit them, rainbow shards spilled across the walls.

"Torin, keeper of Disease and protector of the universe." No matter where she stepped, his voice remained the same volume. "Well, of the fortress, at least," he amended.

"Never heard of you."

"Not even when you were locked inside Tartarus? My exploits were legendary."

"Sorry."

A sigh of disappointment. "Anyway, Gideon isn't done questioning the female, so I'm going to make sure she stays alive so that he can."

A loyal friend. She could find no fault with that and was actually happy Gideon had such a strong support system. It was something she'd always wanted but had never found. "Guess what? He was saving her for me." She thought she knew Gideon well enough to utter the words with confidence. He was a *giver*. "So I'm sure he won't care when I rip out her throat. He'll even thank me."

"He'll have to tell me that himself." Torin's firm tone left no room for argument.

She snaked a corner, strode down another hallway and hit another staircase. This one was wider, cruder, dirtier. Even the air she breathed was becoming thicker, dust coating her lungs.

"If you hadn't noticed," she said, "Gideon's a little incapacitated right now."

"Which means, what? I'll have to make sure she stays alive until he's no longer incapacitated. Trust me, I'll knock you out if I even *think* you're going for a kill shot. And I have a feeling you spend enough time unconscious."

"And how do you plan to knock me out, huh?"

He laughed with genuine humor, and it was a nice sound. "Like I'd really spill my secrets."

"Fine. I'll just talk to her," she said on a sigh. Truth or lie, she wasn't sure. She'd find out when she reached her aunt, she supposed.

Finally, she hit the bottom of the steps and entered the dungeon. She knew it well, having occupied a cell herself for several weeks. And she almost giggled like a schoolgirl when she saw her aunt trapped in the very same one Scarlet had occupied. What a nice bit of justice. Gold star for Gideon.

Wearing a soiled white robe, Mnemosyne slept atop a cot, large patches of her skin pink and healthy, while other areas were still black and charred. Some of her hair had grown back, though it was thin and short. Her chest rose and fell too quickly, shallowly.

Grinning, Scarlet gripped the bars. "Well, well, well. How far the mighty have fallen. From mistress to the god king, to immortal soup, to prisoner of the Underlords. Poor baby."

Mnemosyne's eyelids cracked open, and she focused on Scarlet. Then her aunt was whipping to a stand, backing up and pressing herself against the far wall. "What are you doing here?"

That fear delighted her even more than it delighted her demon. "I've come to say hello to my favorite aunt, that's all."

The pink tip of her tongue swiped over her blackened lips. "And beg me to erase your memories, I'm sure."

"Beg?" Scarlet chuckled. "No."

Her aunt raised her chin, anger obviously giving her courage. "It would do no good, anyway. You owe me thanks, little bastard child, not condemnation."

"Do I?" She arched a brow in taunting salute as she razed her knuckles over the bars. "For what?"

"You wouldn't have had the audacity to seek out your Gideon had you not thought he'd already wed you. You had watched him from afar for years, too afraid to draw his attention, too afraid he would spurn you."

"For thousands of years, I also labored under the belief that I'd witnessed my son's murder. So, thank you?" She gripped and rattled the bars with so much force the entire structure shook, dust falling from the ceiling. "No again. That won't be what you receive from me."

"Kill me, then." Her aunt's chin lifted another inch. "Do it."

Scarlet allowed every dastardly deed she'd ever committed to shine in her expression. "I already told you. That's not how I'm going to handle you." So she wouldn't be killing her aunt today, she realized, even though the desire *was* there and she *was* tempted. Not for Gideon, but because the woman didn't deserve to drift off into nothingness, no pain, no suffering.

Really?

Fine, she thought, scowling. She wasn't going to act now because Gideon hadn't yet given the order for the woman's death. Scarlet wanted to be as loyal to him as his friend was. Perhaps then she would be worthy enough to be his woman.

Did she want to have to prove herself worthy of him, though?

Yes. Yes, she did. More than anything else in the world, even vengeance against her aunt. She loved him. She loved him so much she ached. He wasn't her husband, but still she loved him as if he were. Maybe it was because of the memories she'd created, maybe not. Either way, he owned her heart. Had *always* owned her heart. If there was a chance they could be together, even a small chance…

"Your man came to me, you know," Mnemosyne said with relish, drawing Scarlet from her sanguine thoughts. "He wanted to know why I hate you so much, but I refused to tell him." Smugness joined the relish.

Scarlet shrugged. "I honestly don't care why you did what you did to me, only that you did it at all."

Mnemosyne blinked, composure slipping before she shook her head and schooled her features. "You care. I know you do."

"Once, I might have. But you know what? You aren't important. Besides, what you did drew me to Gideon, as you said." With that, Scarlet turned, ready to go back up and be with her man. To comfort him. To give him everything he needed.

"Where are you going? Get back here, Scarlet."

One step, two, she climbed.

"Scarlet! You can't leave. Your mother couldn't kill you while we were prisoners, you know that. To even try meant she would begin to age. But to succeed meant she would become aged for all eternity, no hope for the return of her once-great beauty. Therefore, she tasked me with your torment, and I accepted because… because…"

Scarlet paused. Her aunt's cell was blocked from view by the wall, but her voice, oh, her voice…shrill, but truthful. "Go on."

"If you wish to know, you'll come back here and face me."

A moment passed. Another. Could be a waste of time, but… Curiosity got the better of her, and she backtracked until she once again stood in front of the cell.

Mnemosyne nodded, troubled expression smoothing

out. "One day a seer was thrown into the cell with us. That seer took one look at you and laughed, claiming you would kill your mother and assume the heavenly throne. I removed the memory from everyone except Rhea and Cronus. They deserved to know the truth about you."

"So? What does that have to do with anything?"

"They are linked in a way you cannot possibly understand, though I will tell you that when one dies, the other will automatically follow. The fact that you would kill Rhea meant that you would also kill Cronus."

All the moisture left her mouth.

"The seer," her aunt continued, "we killed. You, we kept busy with romance and tragedy, hoping you would end your life yourself. You never even tried, though, did you?"

But how many times had she been *tempted* to do so? Countless.

"So now do you comprehend the real reason Cronus gave me to Gideon?"

"No."

Mnemosyne was the one to grin now. "It was so that I could prove my loyalty to the crown...and eliminate you once and for all."

Before Scarlet had time to move, Mnemosyne had withdrawn and thrown three small silver stars. Sharp, they cut through Scarlet's throat, each of them slicing veins and arteries, even her voice box. Of their own accord, the shadows and the screams shot from her head, enveloping her, crying for her.

And then, like Gideon, she knew nothing more.

CHAPTER TWENTY-SIX

"GIDEON. GIDEON!"

Torin's frantic voice tugged Gideon from his slumber and straight into a river of pain. Burning, clawing, bones breaking apart and shooting jagged shards through his bloodstream, cutting everything they encountered, pain.

"Gideon, man. Can you hear me? You have to wake up."

Why was he—oh, yeah. He'd told Scarlet the truth. Worth it, he thought next, almost grinning. Scarlet was here, his beautiful Scarlet, and she now knew he loved her. Finally.

She knew he hadn't slept with her mother. She'd called herself Scarlet. Not Scarlet Pattinson. Not Scarlet Reynolds. Just Scarlet.

His Scarlet.

She had to want him, too.

When his strength returned, he was going to romance the hell out of her, as planned. He was going to prove they were meant to be together.

Even Lies purred with the rightness of that plan.

Don't want to find her.

"Gideon!"

Though his mind and body yearned to sink back into unconsciousness, Gideon forced his eyelids to open.

Moonlight was waning, sunlight fighting for its place in the sky. His woman would be falling asleep soon. He could hold her. He could simply breathe her in.

"Scarlet was injured. Kane's carrying her to your room now. Should be there in less than a minute. He's tripped a few times and twisted his ankle. That bitch goddess did something to his mind and he let her out of her cell. She's working her way out of the fortress, and there's no one here to stop her."

Gideon's thoughts locked on the first sentence, every protective instinct he possessed falling into a tailspin. *Scarlet was injured.* Fuck no. He bolted upright, panting, sweating, gaze savagely scanning. How bad were the wounds? Where was she?

His door flew open and Kane hobbled inside, a motionless Scarlet cradled in his arms. Blood soaked her neck, shoulders and T-shirt and matted her hair. Gideon moaned. No. *No!*

He scrambled from the bed, knees collapsing on impact. As he hit the ground, Kane gently laid Scarlet atop the mattress. Not a sound did she make. Gideon fought his way into a crouch, vision swimming as he peered down at his woman to survey the damage.

There were three deep grooves in her neck. One rode the length of her carotid, one her trachea and one the curve of her shoulder. Two were kill shots, even for immortals, and one was simply meant to prolong her agony. Inside, he wailed.

"What—"

"Don't know," Kane said, silencing him. "She—"

"The goddess screwed with his memory," Torin said, silencing *Kane*. "While he was busy gathering Scarlet in his arms, Mnemosyne reached between the bars and latched onto his ankle. She told him Scarlet was inside the cell and he needed to open it to get to her. So he did. She also told him there was no one else in the cell, so he paid no attention to the goddess as she darted out of the dungeon. I recorded everything. Oh, and good going, everyone." He clapped, and somehow the action itself exuded sarcasm. "You did a great job of searching the bitch for weapons."

Gideon should have killed her while he'd had the chance. He hadn't, and now Scarlet...his Scarlet... Tears ruined what remained of his vision. He flattened a shaking palm over her heart. The beat was shallow, erratic and dangerously slow.

The cuts were still seeping, and if they weren't closed soon, she would bleed out. Torin was a no-go as far as doctoring went. No way would Gideon allow his woman to be infected with the warrior's disease, even though he'd once thought keeping her to himself would be nice. Yes, Torin could wear gloves to prevent skin-to-skin contact, but that was risky. And Gideon was unwilling to take the slightest chance. Weak as Scarlet was, the disease might actually kill her. If the slices didn't.

Kane was a no-go, as well. The man could barely keep *himself* alive. Plaster loved to fall on him, and floors loved to collapse while he stood upon them. No way would Gideon allow the man to operate on Scarlet.

That left Gideon, weak and shaky as he was. There just wasn't time to get her to a hospital.

"I don't need a field kit," he said. He'd stitched himself and his friends up a thousand times.

"You can't—" Kane began.

"Not *now!*" he growled, every ounce of his impatience and worry ringing out.

Kane nodded and limped into action.

Gideon could hear Lies whimpering inside his head, chanting, *Sweet dreams, sweet dreams, sweet dreams.*

Gideon translated: Nightmares, Nightmares, Nightmares. He had to bite back a roar.

"You're going to be okay, Scarlet," he said. There wasn't a renewed shock of pain, nor an increase in his lethargy. His mind and his demon viewed his words as a lie. "You're going to be okay," he repeated, tears falling freely now.

His hands trembled as he smoothed the hair and blood from her face. The action caused the muscles in his shoulders to knot, but he didn't care. Pain was nothing in the face of *this.*

"You're not in any shape to do this," Torin said, grave.

Like there was another choice. To do nothing was to watch her die. And he would *not* watch her die. She was going to pull through, no matter what any of them believed.

Kane raced back inside the room, white streaked over his cheeks. Plaster must have fallen on him along the way, as Gideon had known it would.

"All yours." Kane dropped the black leather pouch on the bed. "I just hope you know what you're doing."

Shaking more intently, Gideon unrolled the material. He lifted the thread and the needle and the tiny scissors, then got to work. Took him forever to stitch a single slice, his eyes constantly fogging over, his grip weak, but he did it. Then he moved to the next one, and then the next one, until Scarlet was no longer bleeding.

But the fact was, she'd lost a lot of blood already and he didn't have the equipment to do a transfusion. Which she needed. Desperately. And would have. So he'd just have to do it the old-fashioned way, he supposed.

Immortals had the same blood type, and didn't have to worry about a negative reaction the way humans did. Scarlet was half-human, however, and he'd never transfused a half-human before. Only himself and the other Lords. Still, that wasn't going to stop him. He grabbed the syringe from the pouch, jabbed himself in the crease of his elbow and withdrew as much life-giving fluid as the vial would hold. Then he stuck the needle into Scarlet's arm, slowly pushing that fluid inside her.

If she later complained about sharing a needle, he'd spank her. After he hugged her. And made love to her. And hugged her again. They were immortal, as well as lovers. It'd be okay.

He repeated the process so many times he lost count. Repeated it until Kane grabbed hold of his wrist and said, "That's enough. You're draining yourself."

True. He was weak. Weaker than he'd ever been. But if Scarlet needed more, he would give her more. Would give her every drop.

"There's nothing else you can do, man," Kane said, as grave as Torin. "Except wait. And pray."

Sweet dreams, sweet dreams, sweet dreams.

Like hell there was nothing else he could do, Gideon thought darkly. There *was* something. He could summon Cronus.

SHADOWS and screams enveloped Scarlet, dragging her into a sea of darkness and screeching noise, and holding her captive. They were stronger than she was and trapped inside her, so they had no other outlet, no other way to feed. And they needed fear to feed. Lots and lots of fear.

Fear they would get from her.

Horrific image after horrific image played through her mind and nearly all of them involved Gideon. Gideon with another woman and loving every moment of it. Gideon being beheaded by Galen. Gideon going after Mnemosyne to avenge Scarlet's death and dying himself.

Scarlet attempted to insert herself into every scene and change the outcome, but that only made things worse. Gideon would laugh at her or go for her throat. And gods, did her throat *hurt*. She was having trouble breathing, and her limbs were heavy and cold. And she knew what she was imagining was wrong, things Gideon would never do, which added guilt into her riotous mix of emotions. She—

Blinked in surprise. A warm fire had ignited in her blood, and was traveling through her, leaving tiny pockets of energy. That energy grew and interlocked, until she was consumed by it. The darkness and the screams at last settled, and she slipped into a peaceful sleep.

How much time passed until she next became aware, she didn't know.

"Devil! Can't you hear me?" A rumbling male voice called to her from a long, dark tunnel. "Can't you see me?"

Gideon. Gideon was near. She blinked open her stinging eyes, excitement pounding through her as his face came into blurry focus. Blurry, because screaming shadows were seeping from her and dancing around him.

A surge of disappointment and rage destroyed her excitement. This was another trick, she thought.

Gideon was nothing more than a mirage, a way to torment her.

"Devil. Don't talk to me. Please."

Can't be real. "Go away," she rasped, and gods, her throat still hurt. She tried to roll away. "Leave me alone."

"Always." Strong fingers cupped her jaw, a blanket of warmth in the middle of a winter storm, and angled her head, forcing her to maintain eye contact. Slowly, he grinned. "You're not going to be okay. I wasn't so afraid... Didn't pray to Cronus, didn't beg him to help you. Didn't inform him he owed me for ignoring me about Aeron. He didn't tell me he'd brought you here. Didn't give you a vial of *his* blood."

He was babbling, and even knowing this was another nightmare, she drank him in, her gaze cutting through the darkness. Shaggy blue hair, electric eyes. Pierced eyebrow, muscled body. Her heartbeat sped up, was suddenly stronger, steadier.

"I'm not sorry you were injured. I'm not sorry I didn't take care of your aunt while I had the chance."

She frowned. Why would this dream Gideon apologize to her? That was a pleasure, not a frightening terror. Not that he had any reason to apologize; he'd done nothing wrong. But still, this wasn't something her demon would do. Joy wasn't his favorite thing.

That could only mean...Gideon really was here. He was close to her, talking to her. Touching her.

She could only stare up at him in wonder. "I'm awake. I'm *alive*. I don't understand."

"Didn't give you my blood, Cronus's blood." Those callused hands slid up and he traced his fingers along her temples. "You're not going to survive, right? *Right?*"

He'd given her his blood? That must have been the shot of strength she'd experienced, of peace. And that he'd approached Cronus on her behalf, the very being who'd asked her aunt to strike at her... Why Cronus had agreed, she didn't know. She only knew there was no better man than Gideon.

This warrior really did love her, she thought, awed. He'd been hurting from telling the truth, yet he'd somehow found the strength to give her what she needed.

You're melting again. He'll get hurt if you stay with him.

I was already melting. In fact, there was no ice left around her swelling heart.

"Yes. Yes, I'll survive," she told him. And would kill Mnemosyne at last. "Because of you, I feel stronger already." Especially now that he was here with her.

"Bad, so bad. My demon wanted—" His words halted as the shadows and the screams swirled around him more intently.

They now had another target. And for once Nightmares didn't seem to notice or care that the new target was Gideon. The hunger was simply too great, she supposed.

In the next instant, thousands of tiny spiders appeared on his body, crawling all over him.

"Not a lie, not a lie, not a lie," he chanted, unable to hide his alarm. He was trying to remind himself that the images were an illusion, she knew.

"What about your demon?" she asked to distract him. She wound her arms around him, elbows catching under his arms, and cupped the back of his neck. He was so hard, so hot. "Tell me. Please."

"Didn't want...a go...at yours." He was tense, clearly

fighting the urge to slap at the little creatures. But to slap at them would have been to believe they were there. He would have lost the battle against his mind.

"Then let him have a go at mine," she said. Hopefully, a tangle with Lies would distract Nightmares.

"Sure. It's not dangerous at all."

"Do it and I'll let you kiss me." If he still wanted to do so, that is. After everything she'd—

"How?"

He still wanted to kiss her; her relief was palpable. "How will I kiss you? By pressing my lips to yours, thrusting my tongue into your mouth and savoring your delicious flavor."

His mouth twitched at the corners. "You don't know what I mean."

Good. He was properly distracted. And he wanted to know how he could let his demon have a go at hers. "I honestly don't know. I thought you did. My best suggestion is maybe…give up control? When I lose control of myself, Nightmares leaves me, like now, even though he remains tied to me."

Gideon ran his tongue over his teeth. "Lies didn't take over earlier today or yesterday, or whenever. He wasn't overcome with anger and didn't force himself out of me. So maybe you're wrong. Maybe I can't make it easier for him. But if he caresses you…"

If he hurt her. "He won't." Maybe. "It's worth a shot." *Please work, please work, please work.* "Please."

A nod. Gideon closed his eyes, expression tightening with concentration. Several moments passed, but nothing happened. He was a warrior, and relinquishing control would be difficult, so Scarlet planted little kisses along his jaw, reminding him of what awaited him should he succeed.

"It's…it's…not working." Slowly, so slowly, a dark mist began to seep from his skin. An eternity seemed to eke by before that mist finally pulled free of him entirely, taking the shape of a tall, scaled creature with horns that protruded from its head, its shoulders. Hell, from every inch of it.

At last Nightmares stilled, the screams quieting, leaving only a deafening silence. Then, with a groan, her demon took shape, as well, growing into an even taller scaled creature, with fangs that cut a path to its chin and muscles that put every Lord of the Underworld to shame.

The two creatures rushed forward, meeting in the middle and throwing their gnarled arms around each other. Their lips were the next to meet, and then those scaled bodies were falling to the ground, writhing together, Nightmares grinding a huge erection against the smaller Lies, whose legs were open.

"My demon's a *girl?*" Gideon said, astonished.

Truth. He'd just spoken the truth, but he wasn't suffering. Did he realize? "You didn't know? I've always known mine was male."

"Clearly you're the smarter of us."

Their eyes met, and they shared a husky laugh.

Gideon's expression softened, and he gifted her with the sweetest little nip to her chin. "Gods, I adore your laugh."

Her eyes misted, and she quickly returned their conversation to the demons. Before she cried like a baby in front of him. "I think they like each other."

"I think they *love* each other." He sobered, frowned.

"I'm speaking the truth," he said, "yet I'm not in any pain."

No, he wasn't. "Are you…happy about that? That you can speak truthfully, I mean."

"Hell, yes."

Thank the gods. She would've hated herself if she'd beseeched him to do this and he ended up regretting it.

Grinning, Gideon peered down at her with adoration in his eyes. "I have so much I want to tell you, and I was so afraid I'd lose you before I had the chance. I love you. You're so beautiful."

Hearing him speak his mind was odd, and at first, she found herself trying to decipher his meaning.

"I admire your strength and courage and want to spend my life with you. I want you to marry me for real this time. I want to have babies with you."

"Like Steel," she couldn't help but whisper.

"Like our darling Steel," he said, and they shared a tender look. And yet, his grin faded and his expression tensed. "How do you feel about me, Scarlet? I have to know."

And she could deny him nothing. "I shouldn't tell you. I just… You're my weakness. You can be used against me, and have, time and time again, and you've been hurt for it."

"I'm your weakness?" His grin returned, a leisurely lifting of his lips.

Her pulsed fluttered as she nodded. She was treading on thin ice—with cleats. "Yes, and as long as we're together, you're in danger. Which makes me a selfish bitch for wanting to be with you anyway, but…"

"You can't help yourself."

Another nod. "I want you to know that I—I like…I—"

He pressed a finger against her mouth, silencing her. "All that matters right now is that we want each other. We'll figure everything else out later. Right now, my darling girl, I'm going to romance the hell out of you like I've been craving."

CHAPTER TWENTY-SEVEN

GIDEON PRESSED his lips against Scarlet's and savored her sudden intake of breath, as if she was breathing him in, savoring him as he was doing to her. Some part of him—his cock—wanted to rush, to get inside her as quickly as he could so that they would be joined, one being. And damn, it felt like forever had passed since he'd last enjoyed her. But he was determined to take his time. To make this sensual assault last. To do everything he hadn't done last time.

Like lick every single one of her tattoos. Like watch her lick every single one of his. Besides, he needed to prove he had *some* skills in this arena. Last time, he'd come from a single thrust; his manhood was at stake now. He could last, damn it, and he would.

After their tongues rolled and thrust for minutes, hours, after he had no more air in his lungs, he lifted his head and peered down at this woman he so loved. "Can you not— Sorry." He had to get used to telling the truth. "I mean, can you take us somewhere else? A daydream?" Away from the moaning, writhing demons beside them.

"Yes," she replied softly.

"Do it. Please."

Her gaze pulled from him and circled their surroundings. A moment later, the bed they lay upon seemed to be whisked out of the bedroom where the two demons were locked in a live porno, and to a tranquil beach with glistening white sand. Crystalline water washed onto the shore, and birds soared overhead, singing softly.

"I've always wanted to lounge on a beach and watch the sun set with you," Scarlet said with a blush. "Movies don't compare, do they?"

Such a simple desire, but so telling. She'd been born in a prison, with walls always closing her in. Then, after her possession, she'd lost her ability to walk during daylight hours. And even though the times she slept varied, she was never really free to do what she wanted, at any time she wanted. Now, she craved what everyone else took for granted. What *he* took for granted.

"It's lovely," he replied, then rasped straight into her ear, "Though not as lovely as you."

"Hey," she snapped, pushing at his chest. "You just called me...lovely." She shook her head, frown vanishing. "Sorry. I'm not used to you telling the truth. I'd almost rather you called me ugly."

"Ugly, ugly, ugly," he whispered now, cupping her jaw and forcing her to look up at him. "There's no woman uglier, no woman I crave less...."

She licked her lips, and it was a full-on invitation.

"Now you're asking for it, angel." He dipped his head and once again claimed her mouth, their tongues playing together, her decadent flavor consuming all his senses. Driving him wild. *Don't rush...*

Her arms began to wrap around his waist, but he stopped her.

"Wait." He gripped the hem of her T-shirt and pulled the material over her head. That soft fall of hair tumbled to her bare shoulders. Gorgeous pale skin, a lacy black bra. "Now you can hold me."

Their lips met yet again, and she wrapped those strong arms around him, fingers dabbling at the waist of his pants before gliding up his back, massaging his muscles. Her hands were callused from holding blade hilts, and created the most erotic friction.

Heat sparked through his bloodstream, warming him up, urging him on. *Slow.* But maybe he could speed this up *a little.* He unhooked her bra and cast the garment aside, exposing her dazzling breasts.

With a moan, Gideon tore his own shirt off. He moaned again when his flesh met Scarlet's. Fanfreaking-tastic. Her nipples were hard little pearls of pleasure. Oh, yes, she was asking for it.

More. He worked at her pants. Lucky fabric, having been so close to her. Soon he had the leather off, along with her panties, leaving her completely bare, and his gaze ate her up. She didn't try to cover herself and didn't blush. She bit her lower lip and undulated her hips, letting him know how much his scrutiny aroused her. Hell, it aroused him. She was magnificent. All that creamy skin, lean legs, flat stomach, small, firm breasts with the rose-tinted nipples and elegantly curved shoulders.

"Wet for me?" he asked roughly.

"Yes."

"Let me see."

She blinked up at him, suddenly unsure. "But I...I thought I was in charge in this area, so shouldn't I—"

"We'll take turns. Right now, I'm in charge. Let me see."

Without hesitation, she parted her thighs, giving him a peek into heaven. Her pink folds were damp, hiding the sweetest spot he'd ever had the privilege to see. His gaze moved, latching onto the colorful butterfly tattooed nearby, and his mouth watered.

Lucky tattoo.

Lucky me. Gideon bent down and traced his tongue along the wings, riding the length of her inner thigh. Goose bumps broke out over Scarlet's limbs. Her fingers tangled in his hair, her nails digging into his scalp. He licked and sucked and nibbled that brand, paying it proper homage, as it was one of the reasons they were together right now.

"Yes," she groaned. "Yes."

Though he wanted to fall into her and eat her up, consuming every drop of her, he palmed her hips and flipped her over. She gasped, looked at him over her shoulder, expression confused.

"The others need a little attention, too," he explained. Then, starting at the top, he worked his way down her back, kissing every single tattoo she possessed. *TO PART IS TO DIE* he laved until he was panting. Sweating. Hurting.

He didn't stop there. Couldn't. He paid her ass equal attention, nibbling on those sweet cheeks and tonguing the crease between bottom and leg, all the while teasing that moist, waiting sex by blowing and humming but never actually touching.

When she was writhing, begging him to penetrate her, even reaching between her legs to assuage the ache herself, forcing him to grab her wrists and pin them behind her back, he finally stilled. Took stock. His cock was straining against the fly of his jeans, and every breath he dragged into his lungs was like fire.

"Gideon," she gasped. "Please."

Pain was mingled with arousal in her voice, and he frowned. He wanted her out of her mind, yes, but not pained.

"Need the edge taken off, angel?"

"Gods, yes."

Releasing her wrists, he flipped her back over and finally allowed himself to do what he'd wanted to do all along. Taste her fully, deep and thrusting, as if his tongue was possessing her. Instantly she screamed, hips bucking up, meeting him, sending him even deeper.

"Yes, yes, yesssss!"

Her orgasm rocked her, her skin like fire, her knees clamped against his temples, her fingers fisting the sheets. He swallowed every drop of pleasure she gave him, her sweetness better than ambrosia as it flowed through his veins, branding him, delighting him.

Only when she stilled did he raise his head, licking at his mouth as he sought her gaze. Every drop belonged to him, even those. Her eyes were at half-mast, her chest quickly rising and falling in shallow succession, and her arms and legs draped at her sides as if they were too heavy to lift. Never had a woman looked more sated. And never had he experienced more pride. He had done this. He had given this to her.

The sunlight she'd created caressed every inch of her, adding a golden tint to her skin. At the base of her neck, her pulse hammered wildly. Her nipples were darker now, as if blushing under his scrutiny.

"Thank you," she rasped. "Thank you."

"My pleasure."

Perhaps she heard the pain in *his* voice, because she eased up on her elbows, gaze roving to his straining erection. "Want me to take care of that?" she asked huskily. "'Cause, darling, it looks *so* good."

He almost choked on his own saliva. "Not yet." Barely audible. Not until she was out of control again, desperate for him.

"A lie, I hope."

"Truth. Kind of. I just need a little more of you." Gideon lowered his head and flicked the tip of his tongue over one of those beautiful nipples. He plucked at the other, not wanting it to feel left out.

This was his woman. His darling. Every moment with her was precious. And torturous. Gods, he hurt. *Will be a man. Will act like a man. Will last for her.*

When she was once again arching against him, and shit, rubbing that sweet, wet spot against his shaft, causing it to pulse and lengthen as never before, he slid his fingers down her stomach, past that tiny tuft of dark, silky hair and into her sheath. Wet again, dripping.

Ready.

Sweet heaven.

Gideon pulled from her, severing all contact. He ripped at his clothes, gentleness not even a concern. Soon the material lay in tatters around him, and he was back on top of his woman, her legs opening for him, her black gaze glistening like polished onyx.

"Ready?" A croak.

"Beyond."

"I'm gonna hit you so deep." He positioned her legs on his shoulders, so that her calves were pressing into his back, and then fed his cock into her opening. He didn't press inside, though. *Not yet, not yet, not yet.* He already wanted to explode. *You gotta calm down.*

"What are you waiting for? I *need* it!"

If he had to do fucking math equations in his head, he was going to last. "Just…need…to…breathe."

"But I'm already starting… Gideon! I'm coming."

Just the thought of him being inside her sent her over the edge? Fuck, yeah! He thrust to the hilt, slamming forward with a single rocking of his hips. Those warm, wet walls closed around him, tight as a fist, squeezing him just right. Shit, the pleasure. Once again, it was almost too much. Especially since her second orgasm was causing her to pump against him. But he chewed the inside of his mouth, drawing blood, and began to move.

Once, twice, yes, yes. So good. So damn good. He kissed her, tongue mimicking cock, thrusting, retreating, thrusting. Her hands found their way to his ass, her nails cutting past skin as they urged him forward, deeper. This was it, what he'd craved his entire life.

"You are…everything," he told her.

"Gideon! I love…I love…this."

Was that what she'd meant to say? He wasn't sure, and even the thought that she might love him excited him so much that he went caveman. *Claim her. Fully.*

"Scarlet!" Hard, deep, so hard, pistoning in and out, feeding his cock to her over and over again, riding the waves of her climax so very hard that he sent her body spiraling into a third.

She clutched at him, practically jerking the seed out of him in the next instant.

The release was so intense, so mind-numbing, he actually saw stars winking behind his eyes as his every muscle petrified to stone. He couldn't move, couldn't breathe, could only feel. And then he collapsed on top of her.

"Now that's stamina," he panted however long later.

A laugh escaped her. A true, honest-to-the-gods laugh, and it delighted him to his soul. Was more satisfying than even the sex, causing his chest to constrict. She didn't laugh enough, but by the gods, she would laugh in the future. He would make sure of it. A vow he would see through with his dying breath and every one in between.

Gideon rolled to his side, pulling Scarlet into the curve of his body. "I want to marry you. For real." It was a *need*. "But I already told you that."

She stiffened, tried to pull away, but he wouldn't let her. "Yes, but…"

"No buts," he said with a shake of his head.

"*But* you're overlooking the fact that I'm a liability to you. I think I had decided to stay with you. Right now I can't even remember my name. But what if you're hurt because of me? I would rather die—"

"Actually, I've overlooked nothing. I just don't care." His arms tightened around her, this precious treasure he wouldn't give up. "I want you in my life, and that's all there is to it. I want to pledge my life to yours like the warriors of old pledged their lives to their kings. And there's no better time, either. I can proclaim the truth right now."

The thick, oppressive silence that followed razored him.

Still, he gave Scarlet the time she needed to digest his admission and come to grips with what he wanted. No way would he pressure her. That would make him a little too much like that bitch NeeMah. But gods, he wanted to. He wanted to force the issue with every possessive instinct raging inside him.

"I don't understand this, Gideon." A tortured whisper.

"What's to understand? I love you." So easily admitted, after he'd fought it so long. How foolish he'd once been.

"But you could do better," she said, agonized.

But, but, but. He was sick of that stupid word. "Do better than you?" He rolled back on top of her, smashing her and holding her in place. "There's *no one* better than you. You are ugly and weak and I *never* get aroused just by thinking of you."

Her lips twitched, but she fought her amusement and never gave him a full-on grin. "What if you later regret this decision?"

"I won't." He'd never been more certain of anything in his life.

"Are you sure? Because there's no undoing it once it's done."

"That's the best thing you've said all day. Even better than 'yes, yes, more.'"

Still no full-on grin, but there was now a twinkle in her dark eyes. "Yes, but how can you *know* you won't regret it? I mean, what if my aunt screws with my memory again and—"

"Every couple has problems, angel." He cupped her cheeks, forcing her gaze to remain locked with his, to probe deeply, to perhaps catch a glimpse of just how much he meant to her. "We'll deal with it."

Tears muted the twinkle, and each droplet cut at him. "Yeah, but it would hurt you and I've hurt you so many times already."

What could he say to make her understand? "If you hadn't noticed, I considered all those times foreplay."

Her lips twitched again, and she couldn't cut off her amused snort. Damn, he was getting good at this. At making her find the humor in any situation.

See? They were perfect for each other.

"Fine," she said on a sigh, the tears gradually drying. "We can get married for real, but I swear to the gods, Gideon, if my aunt screws with my memory again, if my mother abducts you, I'm leaving you."

Thank the gods. "Rhea, I'm not worried about," he replied, heart beating so hard, he knew the organ would be forever bruised. "NeeMah, though? We'll track her down and kill her. I mean, what better honeymoon for us?" No way would he let Scarlet get away, not for any reason, but he wouldn't tell her that and spook her. Wouldn't tell her that he'd follow her wherever she went, for as long as necessary. "I don't want to wait. And like I said, I *do* want to do this old school. But if you want a big wedding, too, we can do that later."

She rolled him to *his* back and straddled his waist. "I don't need a big wedding. But if you're going to do this old school, so am I. I'm a warrior, too, you know."

"Believe me, I know." That was one of the things he loved about her. All that strength...shit, he was getting hard again and his body should have been unresponsive for weeks considering the pleasure it had just experienced.

Blended with that arousal was straight-up excitement. He was about to marry the woman he loved.

Scarlet leaned over and down, nipples brushing him. He licked and sucked and she gasped and moaned. When her head cleared just a little, she remembered to palm one of the blades hidden under his pillow. As she straightened, she sliced the tip between her breasts. Skin ripped open and blood beaded before trickling and running down her stomach.

"Are you sure about this?" she asked shakily. "Last chance to—"

He took the knife and slashed himself in the center of his chest, exactly as she had done. No hesitation. Blood ran in both directions, raining down his ribs, up to his neck. "I've never been so sure of anything in my too-long life. Now come here."

Scarlet eased down until she was lying on top of him, their blood mingling. She was trembling.

He stared into her eyes, those perfect dark eyes. "I am yours, and you are mine."

"I—I am yours and you...you are mine," she repeated.

He claimed her free hand and flattened it over his pounding heart. "From this moment, until the end of time."

Her fingers jerked against him, but she didn't pull away. "From this moment..."

Come on. Say it. Ancient power swirled around them, as thick as the silence had been. Waiting...

"From this moment...until the end of time."

Yes. *Yes!* Finally.

A stream of fire slammed into him, and he cried out. The same must have happened to Scarlet, because her shout blended with his. That fire blazed along his soul, tearing it in two. But then, a sweet, cool ice crystallized, filling the wounded void. Making him whole again. Making him more than Gideon. Making him Scarlet's man.

"And so it's done," he said, voice rumbling with his

satisfaction. So simple, so easy. And yet, she was his. She was his wife. Now…always. Every bone in his body, every cell, vibrated with the knowledge. "To part is to die," he added, sure now that he'd come across the phrase when she had entered his dreams all those centuries ago. They'd been connected, even then.

"I hope you never regret this," she whispered.

"Never." He urged her closer for a soft, quick kiss, then smiled. "Now don't you have something else to say to me?"

"To part is to die," she repeated. "And I want you to know…I was never with another man. After I came down here and saw you. I lied to you."

He hadn't expected the confession, and his eyes closed for a moment, exhaling a warm breath. "I'm glad. I understood why you'd done so, but I'm glad you lied. So damn glad. You're mine."

"Yours," she said brokenly, as if the word was impossible to believe.

One day she would. Completely. Two of his fingers stroked the ridges of her spine. "So, who are you today?"

"Scarlet…Lord."

Sweet mercy, but he liked the sound of that. That was as close to a declaration as he was going to get. Because, knowing her as he did, and he liked to think he knew her pretty well, she wasn't going to cop to her feelings. And yes, she had them, he knew it, otherwise she wouldn't have married him. But until her aunt was dead and her mother dealt with, she'd try to maintain some kind of distance.

Which he would see to, all of it. At least Cronus was no longer a threat. Otherwise, the king wouldn't have helped him heal Scarlet. Still, Gideon knew he would receive no more aid. He'd be on his own. But battling two beings that were stronger and more powerful than he was didn't scare him. Not when the prize was Scarlet's heart.

CHAPTER TWENTY-EIGHT

ARMS SPLAYED, Strider turned in a circle while standing in the center of the Temple of the Unspoken Ones. This was his last resort, his *only* resort. Otherwise the female Hunter, Ex, would escape him. *With* the Cloak of Invisibility in her possession. He would be a failure, a loser, and she would have won the challenge between them.

That, he wouldn't allow.

"I need your help," he called. "I've come to bargain."

Last visit, they'd made him wait. This time, their reaction was immediate. A huge beast materialized between two of the pillars, exactly as before. He was totally nude, but then, he didn't need clothing. His skin was furred as if he were a horse. And rather than hair, thin snakes hissed from his head. Like the creature, those snakes possessed fangs.

Muscle was stacked upon muscle, his nipples pierced by two large silver rings. Metal chains circled his neck, wrists and ankles, and while he had human hands, his feet were hooves.

Beside him, between two other pillars, another beast appeared. A male whose lower half was covered by dark red fur and whose upper half boasted human skin. Skin that was a mass of scars. He, too, was bound by chains.

Those chains didn't detract from the menace radiating from either of them.

A third beast appeared, this one female. Unlike her friends, she wore a leather skirt. Her breasts were bare, wonderfully large, and her nipples pierced, as well. Only, she wore diamonds rather than silver hoops.

She stood in profile, and Strider could see the small horns protruding from her spine. The horns he actually liked, almost as much as her breasts. Her face, however, was beaked like a bird's. That wasn't something a man could get over easily. She, too, was furred and chained.

A fourth and fifth appeared in quick succession, both so tall and wide they were like living mountains. They didn't have snakes for hair, though. What they had was worse. One was bald, yet shadows seemed to seep from his skull. Thick and black and putrid. And hungry. Yeah, they looked hungry.

The other creature had blades. Small but sharp, they spiked from his scalp, each glistening with something clear and wet. Poison? Probably, though nobody had been able to gather tangible data about the creatures' powers.

There was a reason these fiends were known as the Unspoken Ones, after all.

As before, the female stepped forward, her chains rattling. "And so a Lord of the Underworld returns to our midst. There can be only one reason for that. We requested Cronus's head. Where is it?" Her voice brought to mind a thousand souls bound together, desperately trying to escape. They screamed from her, echoing through the temple, their tears practically soaking him.

"Uh, I don't actually have it," he said, and the

Unspoken Ones immediately began hissing and growling at him, tugging at their chains to reach him and, he was sure, claw him into pieces. "Not yet," he added in a rush.

Yes, they were willing to give him the fourth artifact—the Paring Rod—in return for Cronus's head, and yes, they'd offered the same bargain to the Hunters. But Rhea was leading the Hunters, and if her life truly was bound to Cronus's, as Torin had told him last time they'd spoken on the phone, then Rhea wouldn't allow her men to take her husband's life.

Humans would have a hard time destroying a god, anyway. So Strider wasn't worried about the Hunters winning the Rod anymore. And if there was no competition, the Unspoken Ones had no bargaining room. It was all about supply and demand, baby. They had the supplies, but he had the demands.

Win. Defeat snarled, making *its* demands known.

I will.

"Then why are you here?" the female demanded.

"I want to give you another artifact."

That silenced them. They stared at him intently, confused, probably trying to figure out his angle. Why would a Lord of the Underworld, a warrior who had been valiantly searching for the very things that would lead him to Pandora's box, thereby preventing his enemy from ending his life, give up something he needed to win the war?

"Why?" the female finally asked. "And what would you expect in return?"

"There's a human female on this island. I want her. Flash her here, and I'll give you the Cloak of Invisibility." He would have to be careful with Ex, though. She could thieve without his notice and hide things so that he couldn't see or sense them. How she did it, he didn't know, but he was determined to find out.

The female grinned, revealing teeth sharper than daggers. "She is here, yes, though she will not be so for much longer. And once she leaves this island, we will no longer be able to locate her or flash her anywhere. This is our only place of power." *For the moment,* her words clearly implied. "Why do you want her?"

Shit. Ex was about to leave the island? That quickly? What a fucking time crunch, he thought, urgency rushing through him. "She killed my best friend. I *must* punish her." Surely these creatures would understand the need for revenge. They wanted Cronus's head because he'd enslaved them, after all.

The female's horns seemed to grow, wrapping from her spine to her arms. "The girl has the Cloak, however. Not you."

Shit, he thought again. He'd hoped they wouldn't realize that.

One of the males, the one with snakes atop his head, stepped forward. "We cannot take from a human. That is forbidden." He sneered the last. "Therefore, if we bring her here, you must take it from her."

Forbidden, huh. One of Cronus's rules, most likely, and as the god king's slaves, they had to obey him. They shouldn't have admitted to that. It was like giving him the ace he needed for a four of a kind. "Agreed." Besides, that's what he'd planned to do, anyway.

"As do we," the female said with a nod. "The girl is yours in exchange for the Cloak."

Perfection.

Strider had to cut off his grin. This had worked out

for him in so many ways. These creatures already had one artifact, and were keeping it safe. Now they would have two to guard, and the Hunters would never be able to take them.

"Then let's get this done before it's too late." Ultimately, Strider would have to return and retrieve both artifacts. Somehow, some way. Perhaps even bargain with them, finally giving them what they wanted. Or perhaps Cronus would find a way to retrieve the artifacts. He wouldn't want these creatures to have them, and he didn't want the Lords to die. They were the only ones who could keep his wife in line. Win-win.

The creatures reached out and joined hands. Once they formed a complete circle, a hum of power rent the air, dust motes thickening to jelly. Jelly that wavered and glistened. A muted buzz filled Strider's ears, and that buzz quickly grew in volume. Grew so much, he dropped to his knees, hands covering his ears, temples throbbing sharply.

Then, suddenly, the buzzing ceased. He removed his hands, saw that blood was smeared over his palms, and pushed to shaky legs. His heart was pounding in his chest at the thought of seeing—

Ex materialized just in front of him.

Win, win, win.

His blood instantly heated. Pink hair was plastered to her head and cheeks, dirt smudged every inch of her and her clothing was ripped. She was panting, sweating, spinning around with wild eyes, clearly trying to figure out where she was and what had happened.

She screamed when she spotted the Unspoken Ones.

The Cloak lay at her feet, as if she'd had it draped

around her but the flash from one location to another had forced it from her shoulders.

Win! Strider lunged for the small square of material, swiping it up before Ex even realized he had moved. She latched onto his arm, not to snatch the Cloak but to jerk him in front of her and use his body as a shield. *Won. We won!*

"What are they?" she croaked.

Pleasure shot through him, filling him up, giving him strength and hell, making him hard as a rock. "They're your downfall, sweetheart." He raised the Cloak high in the air. "This is now yours." None of the creatures reached for it, but the material disappeared. "Thank you."

"We will be speaking with you again, Defeat," the female Unspoken One said. "Of that, I have no doubt."

With that, all of the creatures disappeared.

"I—I don't understand," Ex said on a trembling breath. "What's going on?"

Strider spun, facing her, and gripped her upper arms. Arms that were still so shockingly chilled. He couldn't help it, he was grinning. "I traded them for you, sugar. Which means you. Are. Mine."

MARRIED. She was married. It was the first thought to fill Scarlet's mind as she opened her eyes from the deep, healing sleep she'd just enjoyed. After making love with Gideon. After *marrying* him. There was that word again.

Moonlight streamed through the bedroom window, muted and pretty. The air was clean and smelled of freshly washed linen. Their demons were back inside their bodies, resting after hours of fornicating. As if they, too, were married.

Married.

She'd actually done it. She'd actually said the vows that bound her to Gideon for all eternity. One part of her wanted to luxuriate in joy. The other part of her wanted to run before something bad happened to this man she so loved. A man sleeping beside her, turned toward her, his arm thrown over her belly and his leg bent over hers. Possessing her, even in slumber.

She tried to sit up, but the scabs riding the length of her throat pulled, threatening to split open, so she remained prone. Funny. She hadn't noticed the injuries while making love with Gideon. Or *marrying* him.

"Take it easy," a male voice said.

Intruder! Breath froze in her throat as she searched the chamber and stealthily reached under Gideon's pillow. After the wedding ceremony, she'd returned his blade there. Now she gripped the hilt, inching the weapon from hiding. Protect!

A man leaned against the far wall, his arms crossed over his chest. He had white hair, dazzling green eyes, black brows and a face more beautiful than, well, hell, anyone she'd ever seen before. He was innocence mixed with wicked and sprinkled with heroin.

How many women had fallen under his spell?

She pressed the cool metal of the blade against her forearm, preventing the man from seeing it as she turned toward him, all the while inching over Gideon to be his shield. If the intruder approached, she would slice his heart in half before he realized she'd left the bed.

"Plotting my death, I see. Well, you can stop. I'm Torin," he said, raising a hand covered by a black glove and waving. "Keeper of Disease. Gideon's friend. We've chatted before."

Ah, yes. Disease, self-proclaimed protector of the universe and the guy who hadn't wanted her to kill her aunt because Gideon hadn't yet issued permission. Scarlet liked him already. With an apologetic grin, she slipped the blade back under the pillow.

"I've been waiting for you and Gideon to wake up," he said.

Waiting? "How long?"

"Few days."

Days? Damn. While she'd been sleeping, her aunt was out there, healing. Probably fully healed by now, in fact.

Beside her, Gideon stretched. His eyelids flickered open, and then he was peering over at her, lips edging into a grin. "Good—" He blinked, frowned. "Bad morning," he said.

His demon wasn't going to let him tell the truth, she realized. She didn't mind. She actually liked his lies. "Yes. Bad morning."

He reached up and gently cupped her nape, drawing her closer for a kiss. The action hurt her neck, but she didn't allow herself to grimace. She would endure much, much worse for a kiss from Gideon. Her husband.

"Okay," she breathed against his lips. "*Now* it's a good morning."

He chuckled huskily. "It's about to get much worse."

Torin cleared his throat. "Much as I'd like to watch you guys make out, I have to talk to you about something."

Frowning again, Gideon looked over at his friend. "Stay. Want you here."

Meaning, *Get lost, you're a pest.* Of course, Torin didn't take the hint.

Grinning, the bad boy held up both hands in a display of blamelessness. "Yesterday I summoned Cronus and showed him the video of Mnemosyne trying to kill Scarlet. He was pissed that the goddess blamed him for the attempt. Said he had no need to hire out for such a thing, that he was well able to take care of Scarlet on his own. If that's what he so chose. I suspect that's why he helped you, Gideon."

All those years ago, Cronus, too, had tried to kill her. That's why he'd aged the way he had. So, why would he have changed his mind about her? Even to prove himself innocent of her aunt's claims?

"Cron means to on her now?" Gideon lashed out.

On her? Took Scarlet a moment to translate, and when she did, her gaze sharpened on Torin. Did Cronus mean to *off* her?

"He didn't say. Anyway," Torin continued, "I'm supposed to—"

"No need," a new voice interjected. "I'm here."

Cronus.

Suddenly the king stood beside Torin, his white robe as pristine as always, his dark hair pulled back in a ponytail and without a single strand of gray. His skin was smooth, his eyes bright. He'd never looked so young.

Gideon whipped upright, palming the dagger Scarlet had returned to him. The mattress bounced, making her cringe, and he kissed her bare shoulder in apology, though his attention never left the god.

Bare?

She glanced down at herself and saw that she was topless. Hurriedly she dragged the sheet up, covering her breasts as her cheeks heated. Normally, she didn't care about such things. Having been trapped in the same cell with men for most of her life, she *couldn't* care about such things. But she was married now, no longer out to punish Gideon, and knew he didn't like for other men to see her. He wanted her all to himself, and that delighted her.

"As Torin said, I didn't command Mnemosyne to kill Scarlet," the god said, his displeasure clear. "But I'm not here to kill her myself, either."

A moment passed, then Gideon looked at Scarlet, confused. "He's lying."

So. Truth. "Then how did my aunt hide those stars from the Lords?" Scarlet demanded. "She was wearing a slave collar. A collar that's supposed to glow when its owner is in possession of a weapon. It wasn't glowing."

"Her sister, my darling wife, visited her, exchanged her collar for a fake, and they planned your murder together," Cronus replied evenly. "And no, Torin, you wouldn't have seen her on your cameras. Like me, she can tamper with such things. She meant to kill you, escape, and for Gideon to hunt her, either keeping him busy or allowing Mnemosyne to convince him to join the Hunters. Against me."

Proof that Scarlet's reservations about marrying Gideon, about being with him, hadn't been in vain. Had her aunt succeeded in killing her, Gideon would have gone after the goddess. Her aunt would have manipulated him, and he would have willingly become that which he despised most.

She should have felt betrayed by her family, but she didn't. Maybe she'd come to expect this. Maybe she'd gotten used to it. Either way, they had to die. It was the only way she could stay with Gideon and not destroy him. And she desperately wanted to stay with him.

"I know of your bargain with Rhea," Cronus said to her. "You are to stop Gideon from giving me what I asked of him. Finding Amun so that I might deduce Mnemosyne's intentions."

She pressed her lips together, refusing to respond. She didn't want to get Gideon in trouble for not yet keeping his end of the bargain.

"However," Cronus continued, "I no longer have need of such a service. I *know* Mnemosyne has betrayed me." His gaze swung to Gideon, flickers of relish lighting his irises. "Therefore, I'm changing the terms of our bargain. I ask now that you live in misery. Which means you," he said, gaze returning to Scarlet, "are to stop him from doing so."

Shock overwhelmed her, and her jaw dropped. He… what? Surely she had misheard him.

Gideon chuckled, warm and rich, her only anchor in the sudden tempest of her uncertainty.

Cronus frowned, clearly irritated with their reactions. "Do not think me soft. My motives are hardly selfless. I know the fury my wife will face when she realizes that her daughter is happy because of *her* bargain. But you will leave the queen alone. Do you understand? Or I *will* finally strike at you."

"No," Gideon said with an easy nod.

That, too, she should have expected. Her aunt had

told her that Rhea and Cronus were somehow connected, and that when one died, the other would follow. But she hadn't let that stop her from planning her mother's murder.

"Do you. Understand?" Cronus gritted out.

"Yes," Scarlet barely worked past her now raw throat. She did a good job of keeping her horror from her voice. Did a good job of hiding the tears now burning her eyes. She'd already realized that there were two things she needed to do to be able to stay with Gideon, to keep him safe. Only two damn things. Kill her aunt. And kill her mother.

That's why she'd allowed herself to marry him. Because she'd believed there was hope. A chance. Now… with Cronus trying to stop her…she would fail. Should she even approach her mother with death on her mind, Cronus could very well hurt Gideon in punishment.

"And no, thank you," Gideon added, so happy he looked ready to burst. "But why are you not helping us?"

"You mean, why am I helping you when Scarlet is supposed to kill me?"

Every bit of warmth drained from her. Why pursue that line of thought further unless he meant to act?

"Touch her and live." Rage had clearly replaced Gideon's happiness as his mind clearly went in the same directions as Scarlet's. He shoved her behind him, causing her to flop to her back. She quickly righted herself, inserting herself beside him again.

Cronus rolled his eyes. "As you'll recall, Lies, she isn't the only one foreseen to end me. That monumental task has also been bestowed upon Galen. So which vision is correct? One? Both? Impossible. And that means visions can be changed, the future altered. I will alter mine, even as I alter yours. And Mnemosyne's."

Gideon relaxed.

"And now," Cronus continued, "I have a wedding present for you." He clapped his hands and Scarlet suddenly found herself caught up in the clouds. Again. Only this time, she wasn't in the Titans' heavenly palace, but in a vast expanse of…nothingness. Of white. Scentless, endless.

Gideon stood beside her, and both of them were dressed in the clothes of a warrior. Flexible shirts, leather pants. Mnemosyne stood in front of them, out of striking distance but without her slave collar. Fake or otherwise. She was completely healed, as Scarlet had feared.

Cronus bridged the gap between them, arms extended to prevent anyone from attacking.

"What's going on?" the goddess demanded. When she spotted the king, she softened her expression. "Cronus, darling, I'm so glad you found me. I—"

"Enough." He peered at her, devoid of emotion. "Mnemosyne, your sister was only too happy to betray you and admit what the two of you planned. She does like to boast, doesn't she?"

Mnemosyne's cheeks leached of color. "No, I— Rhea lied. I swear to you, she lied. I would never act against you. I love you. We're meant to be together. Don't you remember? We're—"

"Finished. I enjoyed our time together, but you betrayed me and that I will never forgive." Cronus smiled with genuine humor. "However, I will not destroy you myself. Rather, I will give you a chance to redeem yourself. All you must do is defeat…one of them."

Her wide-eyed gaze flew to Scarlet before darting to Gideon. "Wh-what? I don't understand."

"I have removed all of your weapons, as well as theirs, so this will be hand-to-hand. You may choose whom you desire to battle, Mnemosyne. Gideon or Scarlet. But doubt me not. There will be a fight this day. This petty feud *will* end, for I need my soldiers' undivided attention."

The goddess studied Gideon, who looked stronger than ever, rested as he was from his truth-curse. She then studied Scarlet, who was still pale and whose neck was still scabbed.

"As you wish, my king." Slowly Mnemosyne grinned. "I choose Scarlet."

CHAPTER TWENTY-NINE

MISTAKE, Gideon thought. He might have killed her quickly. Even weak as Scarlet was, she was going to make her aunt suffer. He'd never been more confident about anything. Except, perhaps, how much he loved his woman.

He gripped her wrist with one hand and her jaw with the other, pulling her close while forcing her to face him. Her gaze remained on his mouth. "I hate you," he said. "And I know you're going to fail." Even injured, she wouldn't lose. Too much was at stake. Too much rage was directed at that bitch of a goddess.

Silent, she nodded, still refusing to look up at him.

He frowned. What was this? "Hey. Don't look at me."

"Gideon," Cronus said, impatient, and Gideon scowled at him.

"Don't need a moment," he snapped, returning his attention to Scarlet. The fight could wait. "Devil. Don't look at me. Now."

Slowly her gaze rose. Tears swam in those beloved eyes and dripped down her cheeks.

"Devil," he said, chest constricting. "What's right?" Wrong.

"I will kill my aunt. You're right about that. But afterward, I can't stay with you. When I thought I could find and kill my mother, too, there was a chance that I could make you happy. But now…with her alive…she'll use me to get to you, and I can't allow that. Which means I *must* leave you."

"Yes, yes, yes." No, no, no. "You didn't hear Cronus. You are to keep me miserable, and I can't be miserable without you in my life."

"For now, yes. But what happens after she sends her soldiers to attack you for the tenth time? The twentieth? The hundredth? What happens when she tries to abduct and seduce you again? She'll never stop. You make me happy, so she'll never stop. You'll get tired of it, and in turn, become tired of me. And you really *will* be miserable then."

He shook her violently. "Always. I'll always be tired of you." Never. For eternity.

The tears streamed down, one after the other, and she sniffled. "I can't be with you and lose you again. I just can't."

"You're going to lose me." He was desperate to make her understand. "I can be happy without you. Your mother matters, she really does. What do I have to do to dissuade you of that? Keep her alive?" Kill her. He would do it. He would betray Cronus in a heartbeat. Anything to keep Scarlet with him.

"No, I've hurt you enough. I—"

Okay. Time for tough love. He hadn't reached her any other way. "I thought I had married a weak woman, but look at you. Strong. Look how confident you are. Look how confident you are in *me*." He forced the words to emerge on a sneer. "This isn't disappointing at all. Here I am, unwilling to give you everything that I am. My heart, my life, my support, and here you are, willing to stand beside me, unflinching. You are absolutely the warrior I thought you were."

Gods, had that hurt to say. A far different pain than when he lied, mental rather than physical, and yet, so much worse.

Shocked, she blinked up at him. "You thought I was strong but now you think I'm weak? You think I'm not confident? You're *disappointed* in me?"

He forced himself to nod.

Eyes narrowing, she popped her jaw. "I'll show you. Just for that, you're stuck with me. I don't care how many times my mother approaches you. You'll have to deal with it, you cruel bastard."

He knees almost buckled, so great was his relief. "And it won't be my pleasure. Now. Don't go. Don't fight your aunt. And when you're done, we won't go on a real honeymoon. One with lots of violence."

"Bastard," she said again, but there was no heat in her tone. For the sweetest moment, she rested her forehead against his sternum. "You used reverse psychology on me, without the reverse. Right?"

Rather than admit it, he simply said, "I hate you, Scar. So much."

"Gods, but I hate you, too." And with that, she severed contact and stepped forward, ready to begin.

She hated him, he thought, a grin bursting forth. She really hated him! She'd never said the words before, and now that she had, he just kind of collapsed on the ground, laughing and crying and happier than he'd ever been. Yeah, that other happiness, when he'd married her, *paled* in comparison.

Soon as the fight was over, he was going to hold his

woman and smother her with his love. And he didn't care how chicky that made him.

"Finally," Cronus said on an exasperated sigh. "I give a gift, and I'm ignored. And for the oddest conversation I have ever heard."

Everyone just looked at him.

"What? You recall my presence now? You desire what I offered?"

What a baby.

After a little more huffing, Cronus said, "Ladies. You may begin." In the next instant, he appeared at Gideon's side with a bowl of popcorn. "This is what humans enjoy during spectator sports, is it not?"

"Certainly isn't." Gideon grabbed a fistful of the kernels and popped them in his mouth. Without weapons, this wouldn't be too bloody of a fight, but it *would* be violent. That, Gideon would stake his life on.

Scarlet was finally going to get her pound of flesh.

He couldn't wait.

There was no trash talk, no circling each other. Scarlet simply lunged at NeeMah, ready. *Contact.* The two women were propelled to the ground in a tangle of arms and legs. Amid screeches, punches were thrown, nails were bared and used (by NeeMah), and elbows and knees were slammed (by Scarlet).

When they pulled apart, a wheezing NeeMah got lucky, grabbing Scarlet by the shirt, swinging her around and tossing her. Cronus must have erected some sort of air shield because Scarlet crashed into nothing before sliding to the floor. She didn't stay down long. A split second later, she was on her feet, blowing the hair out of her face and stomping forward.

Bitch goddess was gonna be sorry now.

"Got hot sauce for this disgusting snack?" he asked Cronus as he reached into the bowl for another helping.

"No." The king shuddered. "Why would you want hot sauce? Who puts hot sauce on popcorn?"

Just before Scarlet reached her aunt, she whipped out her arm as if she were throwing a blade. Only, her *demon* flew from her fingers, black and writhing, arcing a swift path to NeeMah. That black cloud hit, and she screamed, dropping to her knees and slapping at her skin.

Spiders? he mused hopefully.

Scarlet closed the rest of the distance, balled her hands and struck, flinging the goddess to the ground, on her side and still slapping at herself.

"My turn." When Scarlet held out her hand, the darkness raced back to her as if she'd switched on a vacuum.

"No. It's *mine*." With an unholy screech, NeeMah kicked out her leg, connecting with Scarlet's ankles. Scarlet toppled beside her, air abandoning her in a whoosh.

"You deserve everything I'm going to do to you," Scarlet growled as she stood.

NeeMah jumped up, attention never wavering. "Bitch!"

"Whore."

"Nuisance."

"Whore."

Good girl, Gideon thought when his Scar repeated herself. Why deviate from the truth?

"While I'm killing you," NeeMah said, circling her as she hadn't gotten to in the beginning, "I'll make you thank me. I can make you do anything I desire. Remember how you cried for Gideon? Remember how you ached for Steel?"

Without a sound, Scarlet kicked out her legs and sent the whore to her ass. A second later, Scarlet had again closed the distance between them. She fisted the goddess's robe, momentum giving her strength as she flung the goddess around and around before releasing her and sending her soaring.

Like Scarlet had done, NeeMah slammed into nothing. She wasn't as quick to get up, though, and Scarlet used that to her advantage, rushing forward and elbow-diving for all she was worth. *Smack.* Bone cracked.

Gideon couldn't help himself. He whooped, slinging popcorn in every direction.

Cronus leveled him with a glare.

What? he silently mouthed, then turned back to the massacre.

Blood dripped from NeeMah's nose and mouth, her bottom lip was split and her jaw sporting a swollen knot, all courtesy of Scarlet's elbow. An elbow that wasn't done. *Boom, boom, boom.* As the goddess flailed to sit up, pushing at her, Scarlet nailed her three times in a row, knocking teeth right out of NeeMah's mouth.

Sweet heaven. Sexiest sight *ever.*

NeeMah's pain must have given her strength, an adrenaline rush, something, because she finally managed to land a punch in Scarlet's throat. Scarlet fell backward, gasping for air, probably seeing stars.

"Ouch," Cronus said.

"Heaven's about to reign," Gideon replied confidently. The fires of hell were going to rage.

NeeMah lumbered to her feet, and Scarlet did the

same. The goddess obviously expected to circle her prey again, stealing a few minutes to recuperate, because she stepped to the side. Scarlet simply lunged and popped the goddess in the chin, causing her head to whip to the side, her feet to stumble.

Scarlet jumped on top of her, straddling her and sending her skull cracking into the ground. Her aunt clawed blindly, and actually managed to rake a hand down Scarlet's stitches, ripping every single one open.

"My former mistress is such a...girl," Cronus said, disappointed. "Where are the pounding fists?"

"Well, my man ain't got no skills," Gideon replied proudly. He wanted to stand up and point to himself and shout that Scarlet was his. That she belonged to him. "Don't you just wait and see."

A moment passed in silence, then Cronus shook his head and said, "How do the others stand you?"

Gideon ignored him. "You can't do it, devil," he called.

Maybe his "praise" gave her strength, because she shook her head as if clearing her mind. Blood trickled down her neck, and savage brutality pulsed from her. "You're gonna pay for that."

"You don't have the strength to—"

Panting, expression dark, she tackled the rising NeeMah even as she bit into the woman's throat and ripped. The goddess screamed so vehemently, even Gideon cringed. But as she lay there, gasping for breath, Scarlet straddled her waist a second time and grabbed her head, slamming it over and over against the ground.

NeeMah dug her fingers into Scarlet's neck wounds and tore them further. "Give up," she gritted out. "You want to give up. You deserve to die by my hand. You want to die by my hand. Remember how I—"

"No." Scarlet punched again, seemingly unaware of her own injuries. Blood sprayed, and the ground actually trembled. "I...don't. I don't think I want to give up."

While the goddess tried to shield her face with one hand, she again reached out blindly with the other... until flattening her palm over Scarlet's heart. "You don't want to hurt me." Gritted, barely audible. "You want to save my life, don't you? Remember? Just as I once saved yours."

Scarlet stilled, panting.

"You deserve to die. You've always thought so. You *want* to die. Remember?"

Fuck. "Not a foul. Not a damn foul!" Gideon tried to stand, but Cronus latched onto him and held him in place. Popcorn scattered. If Scarlet's memories were tampered with, she'd—

"Scarlet used her demon," Cronus said. "The goddess is allowed to use her powers."

"But—"

Gideon watched in horror as Scarlet's head canted to the side and her eyes glazed over. As she nodded. "Yes. I deserve. I want."

"I hate you, devil," he shouted. "Please, forget how much I hate you. Please."

"You want to save me, because I saved you," NeeMah said, voice stronger now as she continued to weave her tale. "I saved you from Gideon. He's the reason you're cut and bleeding. He's the reason—"

"No." Scarlet suddenly hissed. "No. These are my memories, and I love them. I do *not* want to save your life. I want to end it. I do not want to die. Gideon loves me. *Me*."

"How can you be sure? You are—"

Scowling, Scarlet grabbed her aunt by the neck and twisted with one brutal slash. The woman's spine was instantly broken, her body flopping lifeless to the ground. But she could recover from that, and Scarlet had to know.

Gideon opened his mouth to tell her she would have to find a way to remove the head from the body, but she beat him to it. She found a way. With her bare hands.

That's my girl.

"That won't kill her for good, will it?" he asked Cronus, just wanting assurance. Worked for immortals, but he'd never delivered the deathblow to a straight-up god or goddess.

"Time will tell," Cronus replied cryptically.

Gideon would just go ahead and take that as "bitch was wasted forever."

Panting all the harder by the time she finished, Scarlet straightened. He jumped to his feet and ran to her, the air shield gone, but just before he reached her, Cronus swept the two of them back to Gideon's bedroom. So when he collided with her, they tumbled backward into his bed. A bed he never wanted to leave again.

"I did it," she said, peering up at him through swollen eyes, split lips curled into a grin. "I really killed her."

Gideon planted little kisses all over her face, careful of her injuries. "Not proud of you."

"Thank you." Shaky arms wound around him. "When she tried to get inside my head, I felt her this time. I knew it was her, and knew that what she was trying to convince me of was false. Because my real memories were so strong. And cherished."

"Not glad, not glad." He hugged her tight. "Gods, I hate you so much."

Finally, she kissed him back. "I love you, too."

This was even better than hearing her repeat his lie. *She loved him.* He seriously couldn't ask for more than that. Oh, wait. He could. "And you'll leave me, right?"

"I'll stay," she said without hesitation. "After all, it'll piss off Mommy Dearest and as much as I hate to admit I have something in common with Cronus, I'm starting to enjoy messing with her. Or at least I'm not scared to cross her anymore. Look what I did to her sister. I'll do the same to her if she comes near you. And who knows. Maybe I can help you find Pandora's box and we can lock my mother inside. Now wouldn't that be fun?"

Now this was the confident, vengeful Scarlet he so adored. They were going to be *so* happy together.

There was a bang at his door, and Torin called, "Stop playing around, you two. Amun, Aeron and William just returned home with Legion. And you'll never believe who came with them."

"How doesn't he always know where we are and what we're in the middle of doing?" Reluctantly Gideon disengaged from his woman. If he'd hadn't missed his friends so much, if he hadn't needed to see for himself that they were all right, he would have ignored Torin's summons.

Scarlet stood beside him, a little wobbly on her feet, and linked their fingers. "Come on. Let's check on them. Plus, you need to officially introduce me so they'll stop trying to capture and kill me."

Such a darling girl, and so understanding. "No deal."

They strode out of the bedroom, down the hall, down the stairs and into the foyer, only to stop short at the sight that awaited them. A contingent of angels stood in a circle, murmuring to each other. Bright lights glowed around each of them, and they were so physically perfect it actually hurt to gaze upon them. Most were males, but there were a few females. No matter their gender, they all possessed white wings threaded with gold, stretching and invading every inch of space.

Determined, Gideon pushed his way through them. Where were— He spotted his friends in the center of that circle. They were lying on their backs, barely breathing. They were more ragged and injured than he'd ever seen them before. And shit, he'd seen Amun fucked up pretty badly. They were covered in soot and countless bruises and abrasions and reeked of sulfur.

Olivia, Aeron's female, had the warrior's head in her lap and she was smoothing the hair from his brow. William was moaning, calling for Gilly, one of his arms nearly detached from his body. Legion wasn't moving at all, just lying in a pool of her own blood.

Amun, though...Amun was the worst. He was clutching his ears and biting his lower lip, clearly lost in an agony even Gideon couldn't comprehend.

"Do not look him in the eyes," Lysander, leader of all the warrior angels, said. "His mind is infected."

"With what?" Scarlet asked, suddenly beside Gideon and wrapping a comforting arm around his waist. She squeezed him, offering support.

"Demon," Lysander replied.

Gideon just blinked over at him.

"We know that," Scarlet said for him. "We're all infected by a demon."

"No," Lysander insisted. "He is *fully* demon. You are merely bonded with one, but his mind is evil, no goodness is left inside it. If he looks at you, he will see into your soul and poison it with darkness."

Oh, shit, Gideon thought. He drew Scarlet deeper into his side. He loved Amun, but he wouldn't risk his woman. "What can't we do to help him?"

"He means, what *can* we do to help him?" Scarlet interpreted.

He squeezed *her* this time.

"Kill him," Lysander said matter-of-factly.

"Yes!" Gideon shouted. *No!*

"No, that's not gonna work for us," Scarlet said.

The angel sighed. "We wanted to imprison him in the heavens, but Olivia convinced us to bring him here."

"We'll take care of him," Scarlet assured him, as well as the other angels. "We'll help him. Without killing him," she added.

"Bianka wouldn't want you to give us time," Gideon said.

"Meaning she would," Scarlet clarified.

A muscle ticked below Lysander's eye. Bianka was his mate, or wife, or whatever the angels called their significant other, and Lysander lived to please her. And as Bianka was sort of related to Amun, in a roundabout way, she truly wouldn't be happy if Amun was killed.

"Very well. You can try to save him," the angel said stiffly.

"Thank you," Scarlet said for Gideon.

"But I cannot give you long. A week, perhaps two. And do not think to run with him." Every word hardened

into iron. "We would only find you. And we would be...
angry."

"So noted," Scarlet said.

After that, the angels began disappearing, one by one.
Gideon helped cart the three men and Legion to their
beds. Amun, he noticed, never tried to look at them,
but kept his eyes closed. As if some part of him knew
what had happened to him, and still thought to protect
them.

When everyone was situated, Gideon and Scarlet
stood at the side of Amun's bed. Olivia was caring for
Aeron and Legion, and Gilly for William.

"He needs a doctor trained to tend immortals," Scarlet said. "I know you guys don't have one, but don't
worry. We'll find one. Your friend will heal."

Truth or lie, Gideon didn't know. He faced her, took
her hands. "I hate you," he told her again. He'd tell her
a thousand times a day.

"I'm glad. And just so you know, if I ever hear you
tell me you love me, I will kill you."

His lips twitched. He had learned how to ease her
from her dark moods, and she had clearly done the same
for him. "So I'm not stuck with you?"

"Oh, you're stuck with me. Forever."

"Shit," he said, and she laughed. They shared a soft
kiss. "I'm not sorry the honeymoon doesn't have to
wait."

"I know. But just being with you is a honeymoon."

He kissed the back of her hand now. He owed her
more than this, and he would one day give her more, but
her support meant so much to him. Especially since she
couldn't be fond of his friends. But because she loved
him, she was willing to forget how they'd treated her.

More than ever, he knew he didn't deserve her. But would he give her up? No. She'd chosen him, and his Scarlet got what she wanted. Or else.

Of all the tasks he'd ever undertaken, ensuring she was happy was the most important to him.

"We're going to get through this," she said. "Successfully. And so is he." She motioned to Amun with a wave of her chin. "I promise. He's infected by hundreds of demons, but so what. We'll find a way. We always do."

Yes. They would find a way. Before the angels returned. Nothing was impossible; he knew that now. Otherwise, he never would have won Scarlet—goddess slayer, warrior tamer…future queen of the gods, if the vision Cronus had spoken of was to be believed.

"Gideon? Do you believe me?"

"No. You're wrong, devil. We'll fail." No pain, no weakness. Lies.

She rested her head on his shoulder, snuggling close. "Good. Because it's time Team Gidlet kicked some ass."

Team Gidlet? Despite the direness of the situation, he found himself once again fighting a grin. "I'll love you for a single day, devil," he said, as close to a declaration of eternal devotion as he could get.

"I'll love you for a single day, too. And then all the ones that follow."

For them, to part really was to die. And he wouldn't have it any other way.

* * * * *

LORDS OF THE UNDERWORLD
Glossary of Characters and Terms

GLOSSARY OF CHARACTERS AND TERMS

Aeron—Former keeper of Wrath

Alastor the Avenger—Greek god of Vengeance

All-Seeing Eye—Godly artifact with the power to see into heaven and hell

Amun—Keeper of Secrets

Anya—(Minor) Goddess of Anarchy

Ashlyn Darrow—Human female with supernatural ability

Atlas—Titan god of Strength

Baden—Keeper of Distrust (deceased)

Bait—Human females, Hunters' accomplices

Bianka Skyhawk—Harpy; sister of Gwen and consort of Lysander

Cage of Compulsion—Godly artifact with the power to enslave anyone trapped inside

Cameo—Keeper of Misery

Charon—Gatekeeper to hell; guardian of the River Styx

Cloak of Invisibility—Godly artifact with the power to shield its wearer from prying eyes

GLOSSARY OF CHARACTERS AND TERMS

Cronus—King of the Titans, keeper of Greed

Danika Ford—Human female, target of the Titans

Dean Stefano—Hunter; right-hand man of Galen

dimOuniak—Pandora's box

Galen—Keeper of Hope

Gideon—Keeper of Lies

Gilly—Human female, friend of Danika

Greeks—Former rulers of Olympus, now imprisoned in Tartarus

Gwen Skyhawk—Half-Harpy, half-angel

Haidee, aka "Ex"—immortal Hunter; formerly Bait

Heavenly High Council—Angelic governing body

Hera—Queen of the Greeks

Hunters—Mortal enemies of the Lords of the Underworld

Kaia Skyhawk—Harpy; sister of Gwen

Kane—Keeper of Disaster

Legion—Demon minion, friend of Aeron

GLOSSARY OF CHARACTERS AND TERMS

Lords of the Underworld—Exiled warriors to the Greek gods who now house demons inside them

Lucien—Keeper of Death; leader of the Budapest warriors

Lucifer—Prince of darkness; ruler of hell

Lysander—Elite warrior angel and consort of Bianka Skyhawk

Maddox—Keeper of Violence

Mnemosyne—Titan goddess of Memory; sister of Rhea and mistress of Cronus

Olivia—An angel

One True Deity—Ruler of the angels and head of the Heavenly High Council

Pandora—Immortal warrior, once guardian of *dimOuniak* (deceased)

Paring Rod—Godly artifact, power unknown

Paris—Keeper of Promiscuity

Reyes—Keeper of Pain

Rhea—Queen of the Titans; estranged wife of Cronus; keeper of Strife

GLOSSARY OF CHARACTERS AND TERMS

Sabin—Keeper of Doubt; leader of the Greek warriors

Scarlet—Keeper of Nightmares

Sienna Blackstone—Deceased female Hunter; new keeper of Wrath

Strider—Keeper of Defeat

Tartarus—Greek god of Confinement; also the immortal prison on Mount Olympus

Titans—Current rulers of Olympus

Torin—Keeper of Disease

Unspoken Ones—Reviled gods; prisoners of Cronus

Warrior Angels—Heavenly demon assassins

William—Immortal warrior, friend of Anya

Zeus—King of the Greeks

HIS POWERS – INHUMAN. HIS PASSION – BEYOND IMMORTAL...

Ashlyn Darrow has come to Budapest seeking help from men rumoured to have supernatural abilities and is swept into the arms of Maddox.

Neither can resist the instant hunger that calms their torments and ignites an irresistible passion. But every heated touch and burning kiss will edge them closer to destruction – and a soul-shattering test of love.

www.mirabooks.co.uk

SHE HAS TEMPTED MANY MEN…BUT NEVER FOUND HER EQUAL. UNTIL NOW.

Anya, goddess of anarchy, has never known pleasure.
Until Lucien, the incarnation of death, draws
her like no other.

But when the Lord of the Underworld is ordered
to claim Anya, they must defeat the unconquerable
forces that control them, before their thirst for
one another demands a sacrifice of love
beyond imagining.

www.mirabooks.co.uk

HE CAN BEAR ANY PAIN
BUT THE THOUGHT OF
LOSING HER...

Although forbidden to know pleasure, Reyes craves
mortal Danika Ford and will do anything to
claim her – even defy the gods.

Danika is on the run from the Lords of the
Underworld who want her and her family
destroyed. But she can't forget the searing touch of
the warrior Reyes. Yet a future together could
mean death to all they both hold dear...

www.mirabooks.co.uk

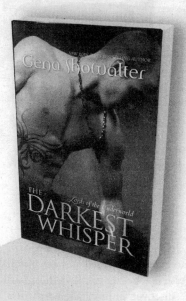